Dead South

Nina DeGraff

First paperback edition March 2026

Book design by Nina C. DeGraff
Front cover, Big Island sunset photo: Nina C. DeGraff
Back cover, morning surf photo: Nina C. DeGraff

*Poem excerpt, acknowledgments page:
"Who Makes These Changes" Copyright 1997,
THE ESSENTIAL RUMI, Coleman Barks, with John Moyne,
HarperCollins Publishers, New York, NY

ISBN 979-8-9937-6980-6 (paperback)
ISBN 979-8-9937-6981-3 (ebook)

Round Pond Publishing, LLC
54 State Street, Suite 804 #9162
Albany, NY 12207

www.roundpondpublishing.com

Who makes these changes?

I shoot an arrow right.
It lands left.
I ride after a deer
and find myself chased by a hog.
I plot to get what I want
and end up in prison.
I dig pits to trap others
and fall in.

I should be suspicious
of what I want.

Rumi
(1207-1273)*

1

Amid the tropical warmth and Hawaiian vibe of Maui's Kahului Airport, I joined the stream of passengers heading toward the jetways, hoping to find a quiet spot, but across the echoing departure area, different versions of a familiar, painful news story blared from every television in sight. Chip Henderson competing in the Ironman Triathlon. High-fiving his friends at the prestigious arts academy he'd attended on the Big Island. Grinning. Flexing for the camera. Saving entangled humpback whales.

"You'll want to duck when a humpback comes up for air," Chip said over the growl of an outboard engine as he bobbed in an inflatable boat surrounded by the blue waters of the Pacific. "You've got krill doo-doo and stomach juices firing at you in an aerosolized spray, but you'll come away smiling. Their eyes are incredible—intelligent and thoughtful—and they have hair follicles, just like us. Tons of fishing gear gets left behind every year, and every inch of it can last for five centuries. When a whale is entangled, we use specialized tools to cut it free."

Next, archival footage from two years earlier showed Chip in one of two inflatable crafts conducting a cagy dance with an entangled whale as it surfaced for air and smacked the water with a huge flipper that was dark above and white below, nearly a third of its body length. Wrapped around its tail was a line of abandoned rope, a hazard known as "ghost gear." As the distressed animal felt Chip's effort to cut the rope with a saw at the end of a long pole, it lashed out with its entangled tail, creating a churning wake that nearly capsized his inflatable craft.

The newscast turned somber, showing police boats surging toward the marina with Chip's unresponsive body. At the time of that clip, I was a silhouette among the onlookers, hanging back in a blue hoodie with sunglasses shielding my face to avoid being recognized as the photographer who'd joined in the whale rescue the previous day. Overnight, the jubilation of untangling a magnificent leviathan had turned on end.

Suddenly, the footage cut to Chip's tearful mother, Carol Henderson, shouting that her son would never have gone on a solo mission at night. There I was, with my sunglasses off and my hoodie pushed back, criticizing insensitive reporters and barking orders at a police detective who was spouting theories before technicians examined the evidence.

Unable to find a quiet sanctuary within the departure gates, where the voices of travelers created a restless, inescapable cadence of noise, I gave up searching for a spot to check my whale rescue photos and focused on my next steps. First, I planned to spend a few days on Kauai, on the northern end of the island chain, then I would conclude my getaway with a stay on the Big Island, where I would snorkel in my favorite coral reefs and hike to the fiery summit of Kilauea Volcano to reflect on life's mysteries. With my camera's memory cards filled with videos and photos, I could handle the snow and ice storms back home in Maine by updating my website and enriching my stock photography collection.

A burger café beckoned ahead, but first I stopped at a shop to buy essentials for achieving the proper Hawaiian vibe, from reef-safe sunscreen and a floppy straw hat to a T-shirt decorated with tropical flowers. Extra sunglasses were a must. In front of the mirror on the carousel, I held up different styles, liking how my tight ponytail made me look businesslike. Joining me in the reflection, ten feet away, was a middle-aged black man in pressed slacks and a business jacket. I'd bumped into him during my stops and starts in the terminal, beginning at the TSA checkpoint. Now, with a magazine open in his hands, he was watching me closely, unaware that I was watching him in return through the mirror.

After months of being followed by the kind of dirt-mucking private investigators that unscrupulous defense attorneys hired in hopes of sparing their guilty clients from prison, I didn't waste time questioning my first impression. As I headed away with my purchases and the man fell into place behind me, I stopped in my tracks and confronted him.

"Explain yourself," I said. "Make it fast."

"Easy does it," he said, motioning for calm. "I noticed how you paused to frown at every news story about Chip Henderson's death. Are you a current cop? A former cop working as a private investigator? You're reacting, so that's a maybe. Did Chip's family hire you?"

"I'm a photographer here on vacation, but I understand his mother's concern," I said. "It strikes me as odd that Chip would head out at night to find the ghost gear alone, but back to this moment. I thought *you* were a private investigator. Somebody from Maine."

"Not even close," he said. "I'm in law enforcement."

A glaring match ensued, during which we caught onto the mistaken impressions in play. As a law enforcement professional, he possessed the seriousness and resolve that kept him steady in that moment. As a tourist whose life had fallen apart 5,000 miles away in Maine, I wanted nothing more than to reverse away as quickly as possible.

"All of a sudden, you're visibly nervous," he said.

"Being followed is a trigger for me," I explained. "I'm recovering from a shock in my personal life. Plus, there are other complexities."

"Let me guess," he said. "Somebody convinced you to swallow a bunch of condoms filled with cocaine. They're eating a hole in your gut."

I gaped. "That's your first assumption?"

"It happens all day, every day," he said.

"So do epiphanies, like the one I'm having about my rights," I said. "Show your identification. Prove who you are."

Looking left and right to maintain privacy, he slipped his hand into his chest pocket and used his lapel for cover as he flashed his identification. I hadn't just landed in front of an officer of the law. I'd landed in front of Ted Telford, unsmiling agent of the FBI.

"I'm *not* a drug mule," I said. "If you must know, I caught my boyfriend kissing another woman. There's a list of compelling reasons why we aren't a good match, so I've ended things for good."

"You pictured him hiring a PI?" Agent Telford asked.

"Of course not. Maybe for a minute." I closed my eyes and regrouped. "I'm a witness in several court cases in Maine. The defense attorneys are trying to dig up dirt instead of playing by the rules."

When asked to show my driver's license, I felt compelled to hint that my name might trigger further flags in the police database.

"Suddenly, the drug mule angle is the least of my concerns," he said with a twist of eyebrows. "Might there be a nutshell version?"

"I'm touching on the history because my ex is a state trooper," I said, rallying under pressure. "If your inquiry reaches his ears, he might take it as a signal to dive in and rescue me. It's the opposite of what's needed. I stepped away to help both of us move on."

"I'll be careful," Agent Telford said. "He won't get wind of it."

I smiled hopefully. "So, can I be on my way?"

"Not quite yet," he said. "At the very least, I want a clear picture of your relationship with Chip before you leave town."

I paused. "Do you suspect foul play in his death?"

Prompted to follow Agent Telford without further context, I cast a longing glance at the list of destinations to consider if my luck continued to implode. New Zealand? Japan? A wind-swept island off the coast of Argentina, where I would only encounter seals and seabirds?

I brightened as Agent Telford led me to the café, where the delicious aromas of hamburgers and French fries felt like welcoming hands drawing me onward. I rolled my suitcase to the side and settled into a booth. Before stepping out to make calls, Agent Telford chatted with a pretty waitress in her forties, wearing a tropical-print blouse, with every hair in place despite her hectic job, and a light touch of makeup.

With a nod, she crossed straight to my table, as if under instructions to make sure I didn't escape, but instead of eyeing me with a wary look as she arrived, her face lit up with a friendly smile.

"I'm Mary," she said. "Ted and I go way back. Some police types are scoundrels, but Ted is as solid gold as his badge."

"I think most badges are made of brass," I said carefully. "But I get what you mean. I'm looking for a hearty, but quick meal."

"It's Ted's habit to order a cheeseburger and fries, even for breakfast," Mary said. "To spare him an extra stop for lunch."

"In that case, make it two," I said. "And coffee, please."

Once Mary filled my cup and stepped away, I decided my photos from the whale rescue were the fastest way to explain my connection with Chip. Opening my daypack on the seat beside me, I unzipped the main compartment and pulled out my camera. After pressing the "on" button and waiting for the sensor cleaning to finish, I went through the steps to access the images, then stared at the words "no card in camera."

I paused, nearly certain that I'd left the SD card in place, but the empty compartment said otherwise. I was meticulous about uploading images to my cloud account directly from my camera. It was a routine, a lifelong habit to make sure I didn't lose any photos. I couldn't recall removing the SD card the night before, after dinner, or before bed.

Paranoia flared for a second, the worry that someone had slipped into my hotel room and *stolen* the data card, then I rubbed my brow, grasping that if a burglar had broken in while I was in the shower, they would have taken the entire camera bag. From a clear-headed, unstoppable strategist who'd confronted my father's murderer face-to-face three months earlier, I'd fallen into a state of tripping over rugs, forgetting my phone's passcode, and dropping nearly everything I touched. Lest I damage my camera from that kind of fumble, I carefully tucked the body and attached lens into the center compartment and closed the bag.

Across the restaurant, parents were shepherding their children into seats, business travelers were frowning at emails and texts on their phones, and a newlywed couple was tipping their heads together and smiling at the selfies they'd taken on their whirlwind honeymoon.

Suddenly feeling homesick, I pulled out my phone and opened the app linked to the trail camera perched along the driveway of my strawberry and sheep farm in Maine. First, I scrolled to an earlier photo of my neighbors tossing hay to Dodge, my Belgian draft horse, during a moment when his whinny emerged in plumes of steam from the cold. Behind him, the silky ringlets of my flock of sheep shimmered in the winter dawn.

Later images were streaked by a light snowfall, and then sudden shifts of wind and increasing precipitation painted a picture of a Maine storm, with snow slanting sharply left, then right, then swirling in circles. Now the sky was clear, and the fence was rimmed with a blanket of fluffy white.

The crystalline beauty of the scene tugged at me, but on the upside, I had escaped days of chapped skin from the sub-freezing wind and the bother of bundling up in a hat, gloves, and a parka.

"Here we are," Mary said, smelling of floral perfume as she leaned in to deliver my cheeseburger plate. "Forgive me for being nosy, but I'm shivering from the video you're watching on your phone. Who's the guy applying his muscles to the fresh load of snow?"

"It's my ex-boyfriend," I said tiredly.

"Looks like he's trying to make amends," Mary said.

Briefly, I explained the underlying problem of an artist dating a police officer. I wasn't sensible enough or careful enough. Apparently, I wasn't sexy enough. When that week's kissing incident hit the fan, I'd learned that a shower scene had taken place with his ex-girlfriend-colleague back in November, the day after I'd saved his mother's life.

"Granted," I said, "Dan and I had only been dating for seven weeks. He described the shower scene as a closure moment."

Mary sighed. "It's the lying that's the most hurtful."

"That's the dealbreaker," I agreed. "I'll pay now if you have the bill. I need to check in for my flight to Kauai."

With a look of pity, Mary took a second cheeseburger from the tray she was carrying and placed it on the other side of the table.

Until Agent Telford got back, I wasn't going anywhere.

2

Tucking his tie to one side to keep it from landing in the ketchup on his plate, Agent Telford dug into his meal and invited me to recount my history from a year earlier, when I inherited a strawberry and sheep farm in rural Maine from my biological father, Raymond French.

"It felt like we shared a lot of traits," I said. "I wanted to know more, so I moved to his farm. Along with income from my strawberry field, I make ends meet through freelance photo shoots, including for *Coast & Candle* magazine. For now, an article about humpback populations in the Pacific versus the Atlantic is in the concept stage, but the editors think it might work. Hence, why I joined the whale rescue."

"All that appears to add up," Agent Telford said. "My eyebrows got a workout as I checked into the flagged entries that surfaced in the crime database. You've put in a startling arc of field time."

"I'm an artist, so there's a natural curiosity about the world," I said. "And fate seems bent on landing me in harm's way."

"Explain that part," Agent Telford said. "Fill in the blanks."

Countless times in recent months, I had been called upon to explain why I seemed off base, dull in the head, perplexing, prone to risk-taking, clueless, and other indications that my own life was out of my depth. This time, the story came out in a leaden tone. I made a rolling motion to stay focused. Skeleton hand. Gunshot victim on the road. Armed burglars in my boyfriend's house. Kidnappings. Explosions. Elite cops. Elite criminals. In every instance, my grim sense of a job well done was snatched away by searing lectures on how I'd tossed caution to the wind.

"When it comes to civilian involvement, there's a fine balance," Agent Telford said. "Policing is a rule-oriented endeavor, but there's no denying the mantra. If you see something, say something."

"Exactly," I said. "It feels like a double-standard."

As a black, middle-aged FBI agent, Ted Telford must have handled complex cases across the board, but judging from his keen assessing gaze, he'd never come across the likes of me. I noticed the same could be said of the barrel-chested man with a crewcut sitting at a nearby table, listening in with a fascinated gaze in between times when he wasn't smiling at Mary as she refilled his coffee cup. Despite his best efforts to coax her into dinner plans, she informed him that he'd blown his chance.

"Back to the whale rescue the other day," I said. "I'm not certified for hands-on involvement, so I shadowed the operation and took photos from the second boat. I'm distraught when I think of high-fiving Chip after we docked. It's a vivid memory, in broad daylight, with both of us smiling. It's impossible for me to accept that he took drugs."

"You had no other contact?" Agent Telford asked.

"Well, I went to the party," I said.

"Which party?" he prompted.

"Everyone gathered to celebrate the successful rescue," I said. "To be honest, I could barely keep my eyes open after diving into action before I recovered from jet lag, but on my way out of the bar, I heard Chip placating someone on the phone. It wasn't about ghost gear left in the water. His exact words were, 'I'm getting answers. I'm on it.'"

Agent Telford studied me, massaging his chin.

"Notice the setting," I said. "With flight announcements in the air and my luggage nearby. If you have a related question to ask, a thought to share, or a point to make, do get on with it."

With a wry smile, Agent Telford opened his briefcase and pulled out an electronic tablet, casting the scent of his starched shirt across the table as he switched chairs to show casework photos.

"A while ago, a double-homicide occurred here in Maui," he said. "At a networking event for the affluent and famous. The teenager in these two photos, with big eyes and pink highlights, bussed tables to earn extra cash. Smart and talented. Korean American. Instead of disclosing the extent of what she saw and heard leading up to the knife fight, Jasmine has been elusive and wary. A cocky detective bullied her."

"Imagine being tough on a young girl," Mary said, tucking sugar packs into the caddy on our table. "Jasmine is nineteen. A bit stalled in buckling down to her college path. If she's afraid of stepping forward, it's because she's mistrustful of harsh authority figures."

"That's her defensive instinct kicking in," I said. "In my mind, it's a good sign, so instead of using pressure tactics—"

Suddenly aware that Mary's admirer at the next table was even more tuned in, I folded my arms and glared at Agent Telford.

"I bet if I check the news coverage of Chip Henderson's body being brought in, you'll be in the background," I said. "Instead of hiding behind a magazine while I was trying on sunglasses, you knew I would see you in the mirror. You wanted to catch my attention."

Smiling, Ted said, "What do you make of it?"

"Mary knows Jasmine personally," I said. "Some element of quid pro quo is going on, where you both benefit from helping her. Jasmine is either traumatized or foolish to the point where she's trusting the wrong people. It's going to take a specialized kind of help."

"I'm getting goosebumps," Mary murmured.

"You're an FBI agent," I continued. "Hence, whatever went wrong at the networking event involved white-collar crimes sprinkled in with drug trafficking. I'm worried about Jasmine, but it sounds like you want me to wade into a high-level case. The answer is no."

"The homicide case was open-and-shut, so you wouldn't face threats based on our current understanding of it," Agent Telford said. "If Jasmine is lying low out of rebellion against strict parents, that's the simple answer, but I want to make sure she didn't see or hear anything concerning. Enlisting your help would amount to a delicate approach. Easy does it. At the first sign of trouble, you would bring it directly to me."

"I'm used to being told to butt out," I said.

"You've fought that mindset for a good reason," Agent Telford said. "We need smart people in the field who can collaborate with professionals. In this case, there's no salary, but you get to stay in paradise in exchange for … darn it, you threw me off track. First things first."

"Let's start with your take on Chip Henderson's death," I said. "It's the main reason I followed you without complaint."

"You're right, let's cover that first," he said. "Chip's stay on Maui was about the whale rescue. He's from the Kona area on the Big Island. It will take weeks to evaluate all the factors that led to Chip's death. You're adept at unearthing hidden elements. That's all well and good, but out of respect for his family, I would urge you to tread lightly."

"I'm always careful with grieving families," I said.

"I'm emphasizing the point because Jasmine isn't on Maui these days," Agent Telford said. "She's sheltering on the Big Island in Kona, the town where Chip grew up. As it happens, a commercial pilot who resides in that area let a rock band stage an event at his vacation house. Fans and party crashers lost their reason and judgment, so now the pilot has a mess to sort out. He doesn't dare tell his insurance company."

"Did Jasmine attend that party?" I asked.

"Not to my knowledge, but let's save our questions until after I've conveyed the basics," Agent Telford said, opening a folder that showed four rockers in their mid-fifties during a concert. "As you can see, the band is called 'Force Eject.' The intense guitarist is Axe, the bassist is Shredder. The drummer goes by Riff, and Chill is the vocalist."

"It's crossing my mind to ask if they 'faced the music' after the damage they caused," I said. "I assume there was backlash."

"They're celebrated alumni of a local arts academy," Ted said. "It's one of those situations where the rich get away with murder."

I paused. "Not literally, right?"

"Everyone has been accounted for," he said. "They tossed some cash at the pilot, but it's hard to find the right repair crew."

Handed his tablet, I scrolled through photos of the wrecked house: rooms with head-sized holes punched into the walls, wine stains on teak flooring, rips in the woven palm wall treatment, broken crockery, bedding that needed to be thrown out or sent to the nearest crime lab, a deck railing marred with machete marks, a hot tub filled with dirty water and crushed beer cans, and other signs of human behavior gone wild.

"Check out the view from the deck overlooking the garden," Ted said. "The Pacific is a mile or two away. That shot captures the sunset. Notice how the light dances across the water."

"I feel rested just looking at it," I said.

"I added photos of the local snorkeling site and the 1871 Trail," Ted said. "A fascinating landmark. Historically significant."

"I've hiked the 1871 Trail on past trips to the Big Island," I said. "And I am fully aware that I've landed in another sales pitch."

"It's an addendum to the original pitch," Agent Telford said. "Face it, the bulk of what went awry in your recent history was being told to stay in your own lane, despite your major wins. I'm from the opposite camp, eager to enlist the help of a motivated citizen with an impressive track record. In this case, there's no salary, but you get to stay in paradise in exchange for repair work. Essentially, you'll be replacing Mary in that role. She's been flying to the Big Island once a week, pecking away at the fixes as she pecks away at counseling Jasmine. You tell part of the truth. Mary is busy and can't visit. Get to work and make yourself known."

"Anything else?" I said dryly.

"This guy is a friend of Jasmine's," Ted said, flashing a photo of a dark-haired, mid-twenties man performing what looked like a cha-cha routine. "A ballroom dance pro who rides motorcycles. I know the ink is still drying on your license, but imagine touring Hawaii on a bike."

"It's a long story how my motorcycle classes came about," I said. "But you're right. The ink is still drying on my license."

"There's a car you can use, free of charge," Ted said. "Naturally, you'll want to meet the commercial pilot who owns the house. To seal the deal, you can describe how you helped Dan, your ex-boyfriend, get an inherited house ready for sale, including lots of repair work."

"Hang on," Mary said. "Sonny, make sure to search your heart. Would the work trigger bad memories of helping your ex?"

Seeing kindness in Mary's gaze, I experienced an inner thaw as Ted's proposal felt like a viable option, especially given his hints of agreement about Chip's death. In Kona, I could quietly ask around.

"Mary is right?" Ted asked. "It's a snagging point?"

"My memories are linked to the young guy who left his house to Dan," I said. "Who he was and why he took his own life. On a very dark night, his ghost came through for me. That's what I've learned about doing a good deed. One way or another, it pays off."

"Harve, it's time to introduce yourself," Agent Telford said.

Smiling and already rising from his chair, Mary's admirer approached our table and shook my hand with a bear-like grip, introducing himself as a former Honolulu police detective turned private investigator who owned a small four-seater plane ready for takeoff.

"As in, we can head to Kona right now," Harve said.

"I'm scheduled to fly to Kauai in an hour," I said.

"With island travel," Agent Telford said, "it's easy to exchange the ticket for a later flight, and I *might* have already alerted the airline. Stop looking stunned. It's a sweet deal. You can't say no."

Glancing from Agent Telford's shrewd gaze to Mary's hopeful smile, I reassured myself that backing out was always an option. If Harve's plane looked sketchy, I would bail. If the engine died, I would bail, hopefully with a parachute at a safe altitude. If the rental house's owner, Jasmine, or anyone else looked like a murderer, I would bail.

"I was planning to visit the Big Island," I said.

"I know," Ted said. "Let me help with your bags."

* * *

At nine a.m., I stood on the airport tarmac near a general aviation hangar, fanned by the propellers of a passing twin-engine plane. Even with sunglasses on, I squinted against the angled morning sunlight, with the sleeves of Mary's windbreaker tied around my waist in case I needed an extra layer of warmth for the flight from Maui to the Big Island. Once the departing aircraft bumped its way over the asphalt past my position, the gusts from its propellers intensified into a gale, whipping my hair around my face in chaotic circles that promised to become tangles.

During our walk to the hangar, I'd learned that Mary had gotten to know Jasmine and her parents over a span of years during their trips from the mainland. When the teen suddenly went into hiding, Mary turned to Harve, who reached out to Ted. Harve freely admitted that he stood to earn a fee if he steered Jasmine back to her college path. With no apparent memory of being rebellious at an early age, he'd adopted a strict approach, which, unsurprisingly, had the opposite effect.

"Hey, Littlefield," Harve said, in aviator sunglasses with a flight plan tucked under one arm. "Are you with me?"

"Only if you're asking about a plane ride," I said. "In parting, Mary warned me that you're a flirt and bad news."

"That's a stab in my heart," Harve said. "I've assured her that my wild days are over. I'm ready and willing to commit."

I met his assurance with a skeptical eyebrow raise.

With my luggage and camera pack stowed in the back seat of his Cessna, I climbed into the cockpit, where the leather seats faced a dashboard of controls Harve pointed out and loosely explained: altimeter, directional gyro, speed indicator, airspeed indicator, and other gizmos essential for operating a gravity-defying vehicle. Unlike a car, the passenger seat was meant for a copilot, with a yoke that controlled the plane's pitch and roll through flaps on the wings and tail.

"In case I clutch my chest and pass out," Harve said.

"Maybe I should take the ferry," I said.

"Relax, I'm in the prime of my life," Harve said, grinning. "Brave as you are, you get a little wide-eyed now and then. I assume that's normal for you, some kind of glitch in your operating system."

"Like a phone," I agreed.

"You're gonna be all right," Harve said, fist-bumping my shoulder for the third time. "Especially with a dance studio a short drive from the rental house. Ted mentioned you have a background in ballroom."

Startled to learn the extent of Agent Telford's deep dive into my life, I couldn't help but smile as I recalled my three-year secret struggle against my mother's wishes in my early teens, swapping ballet classes for salsa, cha-cha, and tango lessons with my best friend, Arlene.

"Mary tried her luck with ballroom lessons," Harve said. "She ends up with sore feet and an aching back, but she's determined to stick with it.

Midlife crisis stuff. You'll need to complete the class application with your experience in mind. Styles of interest, fitness level, and so on."

"I know how to fill out a form," I said. "I heard you on the phone with the house's owner. He's on board with my help?"

"Yeah, Barry agreed to meet us at the marina to seal it up," Harve said. "Commercial pilot. Ribs me for flying a toy airplane. He's worried that Mary is taking her time with the repairs, only able to dive in for a half day here and there. You're the solution. Tell Barry you've got experience and know-how. A little of your sob story might help. He's a charitable guy. Don't mention the Jasmine angle, of course."

Harve checked the propeller on his way around the front of the plane, then he smiled as he climbed in and left his door open.

"On a sunny morning like this," he said, "I keep the doors open for the breeze as long as possible, or we'll bake alive."

As I turned to study the bags and suitcases piled next to mine on the back seats, Harve explained that to succeed in Hawaii, a person needed to be resourceful in making ends meet. His side hustles included reconnecting passengers with their lost luggage, ferrying gear from island-to-island, organizing sightseeing tours, outing cheating spouses, and other jobs that came his way as a private investigator.

"Before it gets noisy in here," Harve said, opening the photo library on his phone. "Ted told you about the double-homicide Jasmine possibly witnessed some months ago. Another kid who bussed tables at that same event didn't fare well in the aftermath. Take a look."

Handed Harve's phone, I winced as I confronted the reality of a young body beside a dumpster with a needle in his arm.

"See the bruising on his fingers?" Harve asked. "It's unclear if the injury was from a skateboarding fall or punishment."

"If Jasmine heard about this, it's no wonder she's elusive and wary," I said. "I'm glad to be in a position to lend support."

"With that in mind," Harve said carefully, "be aware that Mary has let a certain dynamic run amok. She's buying Jasmine's favorite foods, doing her laundry, and leaving sweet notes. The stray-cat approach. It's fine for you to start that way, but then the messaging needs to take on a serious tone," Harve added, twisting his hands to indicate tightening screws. "Ted and I think you'll have success with a big-sister approach. Gentle, but firm, with your brushes with death as cautionary tales."

"More and more, it feels like Ted left out major pieces of the picture," I said. "Is there a particular focus to keep in mind?"

"Ted is leery of throwing you off with a biased narrative," Harve said. "What's behind Jasmine's behavior? That's the question."

With a nod and my sunglasses on, I decided not to let Harve or Agent Telford dictate how I earned Jasmine's trust, nor would I necessarily steer the teenager toward any particular goal they had in mind. Were they seeing her as a witness to wrongdoing? A suspect? Either way, my main ambition was to give Jasmine a voice in deciding her future path.

"You buckled up and ready to roll?" Harve asked.

"Yes," I said. "I'm ready."

After some fits and mysterious chugging sounds, the engine cranked over, sending the propeller into a spinning blur and filling the cockpit with a vibrating roar. Harve handed me a headset so we could talk. Still holding the door slightly open against the propeller's fierce wind, I expressed concern that, unlike a car door, the barrier keeping me from plummeting to my death was thin. Harve laughed and fist-bumped my arm.

The plane taxied past aircraft, fuel trucks and luggage carts, with its wheels thumping over cracks in the asphalt, and then we swung into position near a runway behind another small plane waiting for takeoff, with Harve alternately speaking to the control tower and to me.

"Online," Harve said, "there's no mention of Antoine, the Canadian cop who helped nab your father's murderer. I take it to mean he's an elite agent. You're turning pink. He snagged a kiss?"

"After an explosion," I said. "He wasn't right in the head."

"An explosion?" Harve asked. "You're joking, right?"

"It seems like we're wasting a lot of gas," I said.

"We're cleared for takeoff," Harve said. "No, don't shut the door just yet. This is the best air conditioning on the planet."

Once the plane swung into position on the runway, Harve brought it to a stop with the engine roaring and the propeller spinning in a blur. With the brake applied, the aircraft shuddered and rocked, like a furious dog held back on a chain, revving and howling as if it wanted to press forward and raise hell. Seconds passed, with wind blustering into the cockpit and my hand struggling to keep the door open, as instructed.

Suddenly, Harve released the brake.

We surged forward down the runway, gaining speed with a loud roar and vibrations that shook me in my leather seat. On and on we sped, with no sign that we would eventually be airborne. And then it happened. We lifted off the ground, sharply tilting as a tropical gust toyed with the wings, and then the plane steadied as Maui fell away below us on all sides, surrounded by the bluest water on the planet.

Pressed into the seat, yet lifted from the pull of Earth's gravity, I felt a rush of elation, a sense of lightness and freedom that felt foreign and unique. A commercial aircraft was different in every respect, with seats and walls that imparted a sense of sitting in a cylindrical living room. The growling, four-seater plane felt like a living thing that had scooped up my weight on a fierce mission that involved the clouds.

"Yeah, go ahead and shut the door," Harve said, though I'd already decided that cooling the air was the less crucial element.

As Harve banked away from the Maui airport in a smooth arc, my window mostly faced downward toward the Pacific, and then we leveled off and climbed steadily upward. Beyond the horizon was my former boyfriend, the golden paths of my strawberry field under a layer of snow, Dodge and my sheep, plus my friends, old and new, who had yet to learn that I'd abandoned my plan to visit Kauai. I would address that once I met Barry, the last hurdle before finalizing the plan.

"New land as far as the eye can see, courtesy of the ring of fire 16,000 feet below sea-level," Harve said, pointing to the breathtaking view of distant islands. "New land for shaping your new life."

"Not everything needs to be new," I said.

"I read between the lines regarding your efforts to become a PI," Harve said. "Maybe Dan, your ex, stopped it short?"

"It didn't feel like a healthy path," I said. "My only prospective clients were people who wanted to out a cheating spouse."

"It's not for everyone," Harve said. "Next, you'll ask for my opinion on Chip's death. To free an entangled whale, buoys are used to limit its diving ability. It's fast-paced work, and it's easy to lose track of a buoy or a section of the ghost gear. Chip was a dedicated guy. I could see him tossing in bed, worried about loose gear entangling another whale."

"His mother is arguing the opposite," I said.

"By and large, I agree with her," Harve said. "Chip was a devotee of rules and regulations, and it's tough to picture drug abuse, given his clean-living mindset. It's likely you'll cross paths with Carol Henderson on the Big Island, since they live in the Kona area. It's similar to Maine. A lot of places in Hawaii have a small-town feel."

"How well did you know Chip?" I asked.

"He sat in your seat half a dozen times," Harve said. "Took up more space, of course. A fit, easygoing guy. He's one of many successful alumni of the Ellika Arts Academy on the Big Island."

"Is it a performing arts academy?" I asked.

"Every kind of art under the sun," Harve said. "Including fabric design, Jasmine's specialty. It's unclear how close she was to Chip. It's been weeks since I last spoke with Jasmine, but my sense is that any time they spent together came about through mutual friends."

"Like Jason, the dance pro?" I asked.

"Exactly," Harve said. "It was a big deal for Jasmine's family to let her attend school in Hawaii. If she didn't show serious income potential after graduating, she was to buckle down and earn a college degree in science or business. That was the deal. I don't want to sway your opinion, but Jasmine doesn't strike me as scared. She's defiant and rebellious."

"I'll keep it in mind," I said.

"Back to Barry, the pilot we're meeting," Harve said. "His wife is the VP of Enrollment at Ellika Arts Academy. From what I understand, we're meeting Barry at the marina because he and Pauline are taking some high-end prospective parents out for lunch on the bay."

"Hopefully not the rock band?" I asked.

"No, Force Eject is performing in Japan," Harve said. "A short stint, so brace yourself if they hear a new knockout is in town."

"I hate that word," I said tiredly.

"Even in the sense that you can clock a guy?" Harve asked. "It might come in handy with Axe and Chill. Riff is pretending to be a family man, and Shredder is an introvert, the opposite of his name. Back to Axe, it's to his credit that he stepped up as a single father."

"I suppose that's a mitigating factor," I said.

"Hey, sleepyhead," Harve said, pointing toward the window. "There's a pod of humpback whales at two o'clock."

Smiling, I pulled off my sunglasses and cupped my hands against the window, spellbound by the sight of five sleek giants and two youngsters, with rainbow glints shimmering within the mist that discharged from their blowholes. The window was streaked and slightly dinged, so I settled for shots that showed the cockpit, with the sky and blue water roughly visible to share with my friends when I returned home.

"Try your hand at the controls," Harve said, gently demonstrating how the yoke controlled the plane's pitch and roll. "Easy does it, understand? It's like what the police tell criminals. No sudden moves."

I nodded. "Got it."

With a flutter of nerves, I secured the yoke with both hands and soon realized the aircraft needed flexibility, buffeted by gusts that called for a slightly looser grip. Giddy from seeing the shadows of cotton-ball clouds and the plane's distinctive shape skimming across the Pacific below us, I marveled that just a few days earlier I had traveled to the islands on a commercial airline. Now I was flying a plane myself.

Startled by a slight plunging sensation, I said, "Some of these gusts are strong, but I'm getting the hang of it."

"You're an ace, Sonny," Harve said. "No question about it."

Harve had his faults, but his tireless tips and commentary helped dim my vivid memory of Chip Henderson being carried out of a police boat, dripping wet and ashen-faced, destroying any hope that he would save whales or gaze across the sea that he loved ever again.

3

While Harve gassed up his plane and arranged to deliver his cargo of lost luggage to the correct destinations, I set up my laptop on a table in an air-conditioned room that Harve had escorted me to with a look of pride. Only trusted, connected airport insiders could "make it happen" when a person needed to conduct a private video chat.

With my heart and stomach in knots, I told myself to stay strong as Dan appeared on the screen, covered in sawdust from construction projects in his house as he sat along his kitchen countertop.

"Your farm is fine," Dan said. "Your plow guy alerted me to some icy spots. He doesn't know that we're in a pause."

"Dan, you know it's not fair to call it a pause," I said, determined to reflect steadiness, despite the depth of my sorrow. "After our misguided holiday trip, our bond was fragile. Now you're experimenting with other women. I made myself clear. It's the last straw."

"Sonny, I know I've screwed up," Dan said. "However it looked, the kiss that you witnessed was a five-second stroll down memory lane. There's a history from high school. The bigger lapse, the night with Nicole back in November … I've been told not to claim that it was meaningless. It was a stressful, tumultuous week. Highly charged."

"Which loops us back to the flash point that has surfaced many times," I said. "You can have a dangerous job, take risks, and bend the rules. I'm not allowed, not allowed, not allowed. I'm short on time, so let's get to your texts alluding to a hidden element that might hit the fan."

"It's one of those things I'd hoped would solve itself," Dan said, sending a rain of sawdust onto his shirt as he tiredly rubbed his neck. "Back to the holiday trip, I wasn't honest when you pitched it as a chance to transition our relationship to platonic footing. I figured you would change your mind once we got to Florida, but I was wrong."

I frowned. "That's why you blew a gasket?"

"Kind of yes, and no," Dan said. "If you recall, there was a discussion about your father's last journal. I'd hung onto it when we suspected his death wasn't an accident. Often, diaries offer leads."

My biological father had recorded his thoughts and activities for 18 years: over 6,000 entries about places I'd never visited and people I'd never met. The pace of dire events had forced me to tackle the reading with a scattershot approach. Every volume was irreplaceable.

Eyeing Dan warily, I said, "If you're wincing because you lost the journal, spit it out. You're making my heart implode."

"It's safe and sound," Dan said. "But there was a short time when I did think it got tossed out accidentally. You know how my mother stops by to cook and clean. When I asked her if she'd moved it, she burst into tears. Your father wrote about family friends, so she brought the journal home to read. She's saying she forgot about it, and I believe her, but with the defense attorneys trying to dig up dirt, it could turn into a shitstorm. It was eating a hole in my gut. Hence, why I wanted to talk."

Blinking in confusion, I said, "We're talking about journal entries from the last year of my father's life. Are there red flags that would have spared us a rocky investigation and a painful takedown?"

"Nothing obvious," Dan insisted. "Names appear, but it's Raymond's usual style. Philosophical tangents, and so on."

As the shock faded, I focused on the endgame.

"Tell your mother not to worry," I said. "Put the journal in an envelope and leave it with my neighbors across the road."

"This is worse than having you blow up," Dan said. "You're letting it drop because you want out. No more contact. No more anything."

"Dan, it feels like you don't remember what happened in Florida," I said. "Instead of clearing the air so we can coexist in the same small town, you spelled out your low opinion of me in a way that—" I closed my eyes. "I need to go. I've got a meeting in the wings."

"Sonny, please hear me out," Dan said. "I attributed a wrong motivation to your push to get Raymond's journal. Scratch that, I believe you *will* delve into any crimes that he wrote about, but my intensity level was from panic on behalf of my mother. The next thing I knew, I was off the rails. I didn't mean half of what came out. *Most* of it."

"You apologized," I said. "But you're a big guy with a police vibe, so maybe think twice next time. Or not, since we've reached this point for a reason, and it feels inevitable. The other day, I was on hand when a crew was untangling a whale from fishing gear. Ghost gear," I added. "When I heard the name, I realized it's what I've become this past year. Ghost gear cut loose from its purpose and drifting in the ocean."

"That's from the nonstop arc of crimes and chaos," Dan said. "Taking risks and straying off the beaten path. Yes, I hear myself implying that you need to change. It's a rut. I'll try to do better."

"It might be surprising for you to know that my worst nightmares are about the killers getting away," I said softly. "I have faith that you'll land in a good place, but it's not going to happen with me in the picture. We can talk all day without any change in the basic argument. I hope I've helped you heal more than I've hurt you."

"You're tightening down," Dan said. "You're making it final."

"I wish the best for you," I said tearfully. "I truly do."

"Please don't hang up," Dan said.

"Be strong," I whispered. "Be well."

As I ended the call, Dan's look of distress disappeared from my laptop screen, but not from the air in the room, and not from my mind, and not from my soul. With Harve waiting for me in the doorway, I had no choice but to stow my laptop and forge on with the rest of my life.

"I'm impressed that you were kind about it," Harve said. "As a former cop, I can conjecture that Dan might be torn between the rush of undercover work and his rule-oriented factory setting."

"That's a good way to see it," I said.

"At this sort of juncture, there's a tendency for women to bail on men entirely," Harve said sagely. "I think you would have a different experience with an older guy. We're grounded and more reliable."

"Putting aside Mary's dim assessment of your worthiness," I said, "how would Ted view this moment of pressing your luck?"

"I'm talking in general terms," Harve protested. "But, if need be, I'm a safe shoulder to cry on regarding your breakup."

"Leave it alone," I said. "I'll be fine."

"I've caught on that you're missing your dog and your farm critters," Harve said, helping with my luggage as he led the way out of the airport to the parking lot. "There's a pet peacock that comes and goes at the house, and geckos that will eat jelly out of your hand."

"I'll keep an eye out for them," I said.

During the drive through Kona, Harve pointed out stores where I could buy groceries and supplies, and stopped at a station to fill the gas tank, since the cluttered but serviceable car would be my borrowed ride during my stay on the Big Island. The real test awaited us once we reached Honokohau Harbor. From the air, the white pleasure boats and docks had looked like the toothed open mouth of a barracuda. On the walk from the parking lot to the wharf, Harve knew exactly where he was going, having joined Barry on fishing trips and other excursions.

"There he is," Harve said, waving to signal our arrival.

Looking damp, as if fresh from a swim, the attractive fifty-something pilot peeled away from a group of people who looked like they had stepped off the pages of a catalog advertising casual wear for the wealthy. As we shook hands, Barry seemed impressed by my firm grip.

"So far so good, Harve is on the money in terms of your capable vibe," Barry said. "Though it feels like I'm in a version of the old tale where a bird, a cat, and so forth are sent in to catch a fly."

"Along with Mary's efforts," Harve explained, "Barry hired two guys who live at the end of the lane. There's a growing sense that stuff is getting moved aside and all around instead of fixed."

"Big projects can be overwhelming for people," I said. "It's important to be systematic. I helped a friend prepare his house for sale, and I thrive on fixing broken stuff. There's a corresponding effect in my mind, but I won't dive in for just anybody. What are your feelings regarding the rock band who trashed the house? Are they friends?"

After a moment of surprise, Barry tilted his head to look at Harve over the top rim of his sunglasses. "She's interviewing *me?*"

"I told you Sonny is a straight-shooter," Harve said.

"Well," the pilot said, putting on a smile. "For the record, I was 35,000 feet in the sky when the bright idea of hosting the band came about. The main culprit is over there, standing next to my freshly cleaned boat. Let's cover that base." Barry motioned toward the group. "Gavin, peel yourself away. This nice young lady needs a quick word."

"Who is it?" Gavin asked.

"She's a Littlefield from the Boston area," Harve called out.

"Gavin knows my family?" I whispered.

"Of course not," Harve whispered. "Just roll with it."

Plump and self-important, like some of my Boston relatives, down to wearing shoes unsuited for a marine setting, Gavin extended a damp hand that wasn't holding up well in the morning heat and conveyed that he was Dean of Admissions at Ellika Arts Academy.

"How is your father?" Gavin asked.

"I'm not sure which one you mean," I said.

"Donald Littlefield died when Sonny was ten," Harve said. "Her biological father, Raymond French, met a sudden end last year."

"Good Lord, I'm so sorry," Gavin said. "It feels like we're surrounded by tragedy lately. You heard about Chip Henderson's shocking death on the news, of course. Psychologists say the male brain doesn't mature until the mid-twenties, so he was barely over the wire."

"Often, the upgrade never takes," Barry said. "Friends with names like Axe and Chill, for instance. What could go wrong?"

"Don't mind Barry's dry ribbing, he's on board with any venture that benefits the Ellika Arts Academy," Gavin said. "Given the national trend of declining enrollment, we strive to stir excitement through our successful alumni, and you can't top the fandom around Force Eject. As a side note, think twice if anyone dares you to test your mettle against Hawaiian moonshine. Two sips led to two hours of vomiting."

Barry frowned. "Hopefully, outside …?"

"One doesn't always get to choose," Gavin said. Turning his wry smile toward his group, he signaled invitingly and hollered, "Pauline, come and meet your husband's lovely new friend!"

"*Don't* put it that way," Barry hissed.

All along, I'd noticed the piercing glances of an attractive woman in her mid-forties mingling with the wealthy elite at the far end of the dock. Crossing briskly toward us in burgundy lipstick and spotless resort wear, she looked me over and then raised an eyebrow at Barry.

"Don't start in front of company," he murmured.

"I'm Sonny Littlefield," I said, shaking Pauline's hand. "I've heard good things about the Ellika Arts Academy. I'm sorry to interrupt on a busy day. You're the Vice President of Enrollment?"

"That's me in a nutshell," Pauline said. "And you?"

"Sonny is an acquaintance of Mary's," Harve said, offering a recap of my anticipated role. "I can confirm that she's known for delivering wins. A true go-getter. On top of owning a strawberry and sheep farm, she's a freelance photographer for an East-Coast magazine."

"Which magazine?" Pauline asked, studying me with interest.

"*Coast & Candle,*" I said. "Based in Maine."

"Nice to meet you. I'm sorry for being in a rush." With her polite smile delivered, Pauline snagged Barry's arm and led him down the walkway, but not quite out of hearing range. "You know I don't like to handle the boat alone. Why are you dressed like a bum?"

"I can't hose off the boat in my tuxedo, darling," Barry said. "I've done my part for the greater good. My priority is sleep, lest I spark panic during my next flight. *That's* where I can't look like a bum."

"Surely you can spare a few hours," Pauline said. "What if the boat's motor malfunctions and we end up stranded?"

"Resist the temptation to drink seawater, since it'll make you thirstier," Barry said. "And try not to become cannibals."

"You can be *such* an ass," Pauline hissed.

After receiving a cursory acknowledgement that he'd earned points by cleaning the boat, Barry watched his wife and Gavin return to their group of wealthy potential donors, then he raised his eyebrows at me.

"Get the picture?" he asked.

"Not really," I said.

"Then let's spell it out," Barry said. "Pauline and I stay together to make sure our son doesn't drop out of college. The rental property is where I will lay my weary head in two years or so, if a divorce becomes a reality. If you didn't catch on, the damage occurred thanks to her colleague, who summarized his ineptitude as 'my bad.'"

"You really are an ass," Harve said tiredly.

"Miss Littlefield needed details," Barry said. "Despite some ambiguity in her proposed involvement, she now has the unvarnished scoop. What do you think? Am I worthy of help or not?"

I'd learned to take bursts of temper seriously, but I saw Barry as a jaded pilot who longed to retire from the grind of hauling passengers around the world sooner rather than later, and he regretted venting at the wrong person. With a sigh, he waved off the last five minutes.

"I'm sorry," Barry said. "It's not the best day."

"I'm going through a rough patch myself," I said. "I'm the opposite of a slacker. Busy and engaged from dawn to dusk. While I'm addressing the fixes, it's not your house. It's my house. I'll work like hell, but I don't want drunken visits from lonely men. That goes for you as well, Harve. Now you have my side of the unvarnished scoop."

Sweating in the heat, with a sunburned brow, Barry grasped that I was a stronger, fiercer package than I looked. Without further argument, we shook hands. Harve asked Barry for a ride to the airport, and that was that. I was a match for Ted Telford's citizen-action plan after all.

4

After a quick stop to buy groceries, I left the burning rays of the Hawaiian sun behind and felt relief in the shade as I found the half-hidden lane leading to Barry's rental house. On both sides, coconut palms and tropical vegetation crowded close to Harve's sedan, with ruts along the dirt road reminiscent of my driveway in Maine. My luggage was in the back seat with a bag Mary had planned to bring on her next visit, including work overalls, plus a few "slutty numbers" I could borrow if I felt up to a night on the town. Paper coffee cups and other debris confirmed my sense that Harve would never be accused of being exacting and fastidious, but the paperwork I'd found in the glove compartment was up-to-date.

In the dried-up yard of a bungalow with a carport, a man looked up from scrubbing a barbecue grill. Lanky in build, with dark, tousled hair, he shot a raised eyebrow at a second man sunning himself in a deck chair with a beer, despite the early hour. Receiving a shrug indicating I didn't look familiar, the grill scrubber brushed off his hands and crossed over to greet me. Harve had described the neighbors, both in their late twenties, as an unusual mix of shiftless and full of themselves, and added that I should feel free to give them an attitude adjustment.

For all I knew, they were Jasmine's closest confidants, so I decided to start on a friendly note as the taller man squinted at me.

"You look puzzled to see a stranger driving Harve's loaner car," I said. "I'm Sonny, eager to pitch in while Mary is busy."

"I'm Moritz," he said. "That's my roommate, Raja, in the lounge chair getting a sunburn. In what capacity will you be pitching in?"

My explanation inspired exasperated pacing and eyerolls.

"Barry has the mistaken impression that our progress is slow," Moritz said furiously. "Mary is a nice lady, but she lacks the proper coordination and skills. If you're similarly non-adept—"

"I'm highly experienced," I assured him.

"How do you know Barry?" Moritz prompted. "Because if you're his latest secret crush, let's get it out in the open."

"I just met Barry for the first time," I said. "I'm working in exchange for a roof over my head, so don't worry that I'll cut into your paychecks. If I heard right that you work most nights at a bar, that's perfect because I'll be living at the house. I'll need downtime."

"I guess on the bright side, it's a fix for the drama of Mary screaming at spiders and hammering her thumb," Moritz said, waving off his initial reaction. "We're heading out for supplies, then our shift at the bar, so you'll have the slice of busted-up paradise to yourself."

"Sounds great," I said. "Nice meeting you."

"You as well," Moritz said. "Sorry for blowing up."

"No worries," I said. "It's the theme for the day."

Driving onward past his yard, I followed the gentle uphill slope. Looking to my right, I saw two slender white pipes half-hidden by tall grass, a reminder that beneath the dirt road, solid volcanic rock extended straight down over 16,000 feet to the ocean floor, leaving residents to use rainwater, scattered aquifers, and reservoirs wisely and sparingly. A hand-painted sign on a connecting dirt lane pointed toward a coffee grove and bean mill, showing that farming was possible, and both Mary and Harve had told me the rental property was home to a small papaya tree grove.

Fifty feet further up the lane, I passed a peacock preening itself by the roadside and caught a glimpse of Barry's house between the trees on my right. With only one other property further along, signaling felt pointless, but I fell into the habit anyway as I swung into the driveway and eased to a stop beneath a giant eucalyptus tree. In front of me, the doors of the two-bay garage were marred by a paintball spree, leaving a man-shaped void amid the vivid splashes of blue, orange, and red. Imagining a dare involving a drunken volunteer, covered in plastic, goggles, and, hopefully, a helmet, I reluctantly saw it as a form of art.

As I climbed out, the neighborhood's pet peacock strutted closer, eyeing me hopefully. I promised to check online for his favorite treats and focused on getting my groceries inside. A wooden walkway led me past a connected one-story addition that housed the office and massage room, where the table was askew from a missing leg. Looking to my right, I paused to take in the stunning view of low-level foliage descending for a mile or two down to a black lava shoreline that sharply contrasted with the shimmering Pacific Ocean. Providing shade on either side of the yard, coconut palms swayed in the breeze, and a small patio built of stone pavers was bordered by a garden of ferns and tropical flowers.

I opened the door and paused on the threshold, struck by the extent of damage that Ted's photos hadn't shown: possibly a hundred holes, torn drapes, stuffing popping out of the couch cushions, and other numbing chaos, including a box of glass shards indicating that one or more windows had been broken and replaced. To my left a shelf had been violently ripped from its anchor bolts, leaving a row of holes in the drywall. With goosebumps on my arms, I touched the jagged, chalky edges of the damage, just as Barry and Pauline must have done when they entered their sanctuary after the party, unable to understand how a crowd of people could cause such destruction and then post about it online.

The interior featured an airy, open-concept design with sliding glass doors on my right that led to a deck accessible from both the living room and the bedroom. Above, teak ceiling beams and a light fixture with an attached fan displayed a collection of dangling socks and dish towels—an easy fix if I could find a tall stepladder. A teak half-demolished shelving unit ran along the left far wall, with an efficient kitchen area occupying a half-wall at the midway point. Beyond, I could see the bedroom on the left and a stylish natural tile bathroom on the right. Every room was cluttered with tools, power cords, sanders, paint cans, drop cloths, and dust-covered boxes with replacement blinds and other components.

Thankfully, Mary had prioritized transforming the bedroom from a crime scene into a refuge. The gauzy fabric on the canopy bed suggested the likelihood of mosquitoes at night. As I sat on the edge of the new mattress and bounced a few times, I noticed that the Pacific-facing side of the room was protected from the elements by rice paper doors that could be rolled open on warm nights, revealing the shimmering water a mile or two beyond the black lava shoreline. A new label on the doors suggested the party crowd had been unable to resist the temptation to punch through the fragile barrier and create a human shape.

The refrigerator was filled with fruit, cheese, muffins, and other foods that Mary had left behind. After I put my groceries away, I opened the sliding glass doors and stepped onto the deck, which served as a shelter for the entrance of a studio apartment on the house's first floor.

A walkway led from the end of the deck down a gentle hill to the paved patio, where a wooden table was caked with pools of wax from melted candles. A musty smell caught my attention as I looked past a screen of ferns and tropical flowers to a hot tub filled with stagnant water, its bottom littered with cans and bottles. I imagined the party animals practicing their aim as they tossed litter into the tub and across the property, and the beautiful ferns showed signs of being hacked at with a machete that had been left stuck into the tabletop after a drunken spree.

Finally alone, released from the need to appear strong, I felt drunk myself as I staggered toward the Pacific, dropped to my knees, and sobbed, clutching the brittle grass in my hands. Against all odds, torn to pieces by heartbreak, an eleven-hour flight to Hawaii and the fleeting elation I'd felt after saving an entangled whale, only to be slammed by the lead rescuer's death, I had made it. As the peacock pecked at the grass and watched me, I mourned the loss of my murdered father, the painful end with Dan, the criticism I'd endured, and the victories I hadn't been allowed to process. For months on end, it had seemed as if fate was working against me, but thanks to my resilience and strength, I'd pushed past the numbness and found a sanctuary where I could begin to heal. Trash and broken walls were nothing compared to what I'd faced in the past year.

As my tears subsided, I honored the moment by snapping a photo of the uniquely beautiful peacock with my phone, and he was happy to oblige, expanding his magnificent tail feathers and strutting past me with clucking sounds. As if an iridescent blue head and chest weren't enough of a fashion statement, his crown was topped with spikes ending in neon blue tufts. It was impossible not to marvel at the mysterious genetic workings that had created the peacock's train of glorious five-foot-long tail feathers, which he unfurled into a mesmerizing, vibrating fan.

"I'm sorry," I said. "I'm not your type."

While eating a snack of cheese, I pulled out my camera to document the damage within and without the house, intending to complete the repairs professionally and verifiably. With a new SD card in hand, I paused, shocked to find one already in the designated slot.

With narrowed eyes, I remembered the moment a TSA agent pulled me aside that morning for a "random" check. Zippers were opened and items inspected as I responded to texts from friends. Hours later, I left my luggage with Agent Telford for safekeeping while I went into the restroom before flying to the Big Island with Harve.

Fuming, I dialed Ted's phone number.

"Sonny," he said. "Are you all settled in?"

"The SD data card that went missing from my camera is mysteriously back in its slot," I said. "You figured I wouldn't notice?"

"A part of the vetting process was to check your photos against your story," Ted said. "Hooray, you passed a major test."

"Darn, you flunked one," I said. "Not to mention, unless another party unfolded here, you downplayed the extent of the damage. In essence, the house is a victim of foul play, and a law enforcement professional is asking me to erase the evidence. It strikes me as odd."

Chuckling, Ted said, "I love how your mind works, but the house isn't a crime scene. It's a private residence, owned by people who've decided to be understanding about the bad behavior involved."

"I would be furious about it," I said.

"Allow me to put it this way," Ted said. "A few weeks from now, if you come home to find Brumby's barn clothes smelling terrible in a corner, dirty dishes in the sink, crushed soda cans littering the floor, and signs that he's entertained women in your bedroom—"

"How do you know about my blacksmith?" I demanded. "Never mind, you've made your point. If my animals are safe and the damage doesn't involve the fire department, I would move on."

"I'll call in a few days to check on your progress," Ted said. "And I've volunteered you to ride a motorcycle to Hilo."

I paused. "When? Why? *What?*"

"I did say your license would come in handy," Ted said. "Riding in the open air in Hawaii is fun. Prepare to thank me for it."

"The house is on a hilly, pitted dirt lane," I said. "I'm not experienced enough to balance a motorcycle on such a … hello?"

"Apologies, I'm back," Ted said after three seconds of silence. "I muted you to confirm that Jasmine secured a part-time job in Hilo, but she travels to your location now and then. Hopefully, you can narrow it down and begin the mentoring sooner rather than later."

"I've already got a list of questions for you," I said. "Might there be a time when you'll be on the Big Island so we can meet?"

"I feel it's better not to lead you by the nose," Ted said. "Use your best judgment. Happy hunting, and keep me posted."

As he hung up, I said, "Well, that's just dandy."

With my camera in hand, I scrolled through my photos, looking for gaps in the file names, but didn't find any signs of deleted shots that would suggest a shady reason for "borrowing" my data card. Admittedly, it made sense for Agent Telford to corroborate my account, but at some point, I needed to verify his intentions in return.

Once I documented the "before" condition of the house and yard, I changed into the overalls from Mary's bag of clothes and got to work. My plan was simple: to blaze through the list of chores and projects at top speed, leaving only the detail work for later. That way, I could relax with minimal guilt and enjoy the place for a day or two.

With an empty garbage bag in each hand, I made swift progress across the yard and garden, putting beer and soda cans in one bag and trash in the other, creating a lively tune. Clank-crunch-clank-crunch-ding-ding-crunch-crunch-clank-clank-clank.

From the small kitchen waste basket, I pulled out several crumpled notes Jasmine had written for Mary in bold letters.

Need cash, plus some $50 prepaid cards.
Tell Mom to chill. I'm fine.
Stop sending Harve! He's an oaf!
No smelly soap on my clothes! It blows my cover.
Need individually wrapped granola bars.

Given the bossy tone, I tended to agree with Harve's assessment that Jasmine was rebellious rather than wary and afraid.

My search for the washer led me to the garage, where I found laundry that the teen had left for Mary to handle, with a note stipulating that she didn't want to smell like a grape popsicle. Frowning, I wondered if Jasmine's concern, "It blows my cover," might be an indication of covert activities—an alarming thought made even more urgent as I noted her petite, youthful clothing. Even in a smiling photo, there was a fierceness about her, but she was nineteen and possibly in over her head.

"At least she draws hearts on her directives," I murmured.

At the top of each note was a logo with "Kukuna Mahina," surrounded by waves, which also appeared on matchbooks and on one of Mary's sweatshirts. I wondered if it was from the bar where Moritz and Raja worked. Finding good restaurants was always a priority.

Seeing patched holes that needed sanding, I drew on yoga and tai chi moves to systematically scour the walls, windmill style, and then I followed up with a damp cloth so the surfaces were ready for painting in the coming days. Finding drywall sections already cut to size to fill holes, I nailed each piece into place and used tape and spackle to smooth the seams.

I drained the unpleasant water from the hot tub, removed the bottles and cans, sprayed the icky residue with a non-toxic cleaner, and assessed the components for damage. During my childhood, my mother had been appalled by my habit of chatting with the inground pool experts. A hot tub was a similar vessel, with inflow and outflow. I was certain I could get the unit running if I found the instruction manual.

As a gecko darted onto the walkway, shimmering in the sunlight with green, yellow, and red markings, I zoomed in on its dark eyes and turquoise lids with my phone, and texted the shot to my friends, along with the news that Dan and I were parting on good terms.

So began a flurry of check-in calls, during which I expressed brave assurances that I was coping well and moving on. To calm my worries in return, my closest neighbors in Maine sent photos of my sheep and draft horse looking picturesque in their winter coats. Luke, my King Shepherd, was in high spirits with snow on his whiskers after playing with his lobster toy. My house sitter, Brumby, was noisily eating from a snack bag during our call, just as Ted had predicted, including a woman in the background telling the notoriously "busy" blacksmith to hurry up.

As always, one friend or another served as the designated driver for the job of condensing the twists and turns of my life into an accurate version to share with friends, acquaintances, and the town at large. Tall and dark-eyed, with features reflecting her Passamaquoddy ancestry, Sue Black had gained an almost spooky insight into my inner workings through hypnosis and Reiki, so I wasn't surprised when she texted her intention to catch up through a video chat to talk face-to-face.

While I waited for Sue to join my chat invitation, I brought my laptop to the patio and looked up the rock band, all the more curious now that I'd waded through their chaos. One shot of the middle-aged group showed them performing with their shirts unbuttoned to reveal ripped chests and abs, their tight jeans adding to their rock-star vibe. The drummer, Riff, wielded his sticks with fierce intensity, while the singer, Chill, growled out a tune near Axe and Shredder at the front of the stage.

Pressing play to hear one of the songs that had put them in the local spotlight twenty years earlier, I had to admit, I might enjoy a non-violent version of their concert. Next, I looked up the dance studio's website. Intrigued by lesson options like hula and Polynesian fire dancing, I didn't see a way to explain that my formal ballroom lessons ended when I was fourteen, though I'd kept in shape for Latin parties ever since. A notification asked if I wanted to join a ballroom practice session open to all skill levels. Pushing myself to the max was my preferred means of getting a good night's sleep, so I clicked the "confirm" button.

Finally, Sue Black appeared on my screen.

Glimpsing the view behind me, Sue said, "Sitting under swaying palm trees with the Pacific in view is cruel. We've woken up to snow every day, even when the sky was supposed to be clear."

Briefly, I told her about my arrangement at the house so that at least one friend would know to alert the FBI if I needed to be rescued *from* the FBI. With looks of sympathy as I described my call with Dan, Sue agreed that giving his mother the benefit of the doubt was the best move, but advised me to delay reading my father's last journal.

"That way," Sue said carefully, "if you do come across a red flag that might have outed Raymond's murderer without the horror and turmoil, you'll have gained enough perspective to remain calm."

"I'm already there," I said. "Ready to move on."

On my laptop, Sue folded her arms with a twist of eyebrows asking if I was finished pretending to be strong and impervious.

"If you knew how many withering critiques that I'm trying to unhear, you would be impressed by my imperviousness," I said. "If that's not a word it should be a word because I'm nailing it. *Why* did I agree to the trip to Florida? Instead of relaxing, Dan blew a gasket."

"His secrets were like rocket fuel," Sue said. "He convinced himself that you were the one who needed fixing. How bad was it, Sonny?"

"If you insist on knowing the details, I'll write an account in tiny letters once I'm home," I said. "As always, the slams that hurt the most reflect my own worst fears. Normal guys aren't built to handle my quirks, so I need to think creatively. Maybe give Brumby a shot."

"Dear God, you can't be serious," Sue said.

"He's capable and good with animals," I said. "A guy who's upfront about his philandering seems like an upgrade."

"If you truly want an upgrade," Sue said, "it's time to give your feelings for Antoine a chance to breathe. Unlike the other men who've tossed their hat at you, he embraced your mindset, deputized you into an active role, and stayed by your side to keep you safe."

Faced with a recurring theme in Sue's counseling, I opened my camera bag, where I'd tucked the flip phone the enigmatic Canadian supercop had left after helping me capture my father's killer, though as always, the screen didn't show the slightest flicker of activity. Technology played a role in Antoine's methods, but I had to admit, finding the lifeline dead when I'd faced my father's murderer had ignited an adrenaline rush that had carried me through the interaction with a clear head.

"There's always a problematic fine print clause," I said. "Antoine's past includes Nicole, the same woman who lured Dan."

"I've never accepted that story as the truth," Sue insisted. "Believe in Antoine's sincerity when he declared his feelings."

"Maybe I only dreamed those moments," I said. "He left town without saying goodbye. Plus, he's a colleague of Dan's."

"You need to let go of the guilt," Sue said. "Even without the cheating episodes, there were signs that Dan couldn't live up to his promise to accept your creative side. Your heart sought refuge in a fantasy about another man. You know, Antoine's retreat can be seen as chivalrous. He left it up to you to reach out if your loyalties changed."

"I'll give it some thought," I said, though as I returned the flip phone to my camera bag, it was with the intention of finding an electronics store with a bin for recycling parts. "Back to Brumby, you know I'm not serious. He gets on my nerves after five minutes."

"Any more trip highlights you want to share?" Sue asked.

"Now that you mention it …"

Smiling, I texted her a snapshot Harve had taken of me while I was piloting his plane from Maui to the Big Island.

"My version of having friends in high places," I said.

"This is perfect," Sue said. "I'm going to relish showing it to the critics who see your sudden trip as a sign that you're crushed."

After we blew kisses and waved goodbye, I ate cookies to refuel my energy and returned to my list of chores and repairs, with a reminder set on my phone for an hour before the dance class.

Throughout, I kept thinking, *Look at me cope.*

5

With colorful posters in the windows, the Petrel Martineau Dance Studio looked like a welcoming space, sparking memories of swapping my ballet classes for ballroom and Latin dance lessons with my childhood friend, Arlene, when we were eleven. For three years, my secret pursuit depended on my mother's dislike of attending classes and recitals.

Then came a shocking day when she followed up on a rumor. Instead of finding me in a tutu and ballet flats, she turned a corner and saw me in a sequined dress, lipstick, eyeliner, rouge, and tons of hairspray. Nearby, practicing spins and spicy footwork for our cha-cha routine was Arlene's cousin, Frederico, who, even at fourteen, was a Puerto Rican heartthrob in a ruffled black shirt. As my friends froze in place, my mother shot me a look that made me feel like I was turning to ash, then she headed back to our house to remove every secretly hidden dress and stash of makeup. To her, styles "of that sort" were a slippery slope, a belief she liked to repeat now that I'd taken up pole dancing as a sport.

Inside, I stepped into a spacious room with gleaming hardwood floors, a wall of mirrors reflecting my entrance, and chairs along the back for family and friends who came to watch. Photos showed the owner, Petrel Martineau, looking thinner years earlier. Even with extra weight around his waist, he looked lively as he moved from person to person, offering smiles and greetings in dark, loose-fitting pants and a matching shirt, with the flair of a man who was proudly and openly gay.

If toddlers started assembling, signaling a mistake in my online registration, I would slip away and try again later, but adults of a wide range of ages were arriving through the front door or from the locker area. Their vibes were diverse as well, from friendly to haughty.

After stopping here and there to give hugs, a handsome guy in his mid-twenties crossed toward me with tousled dark curls and a smile that gave him an instantly likable vibe. With a long torso, sculpted waist and hips, and chest muscles trained to lift a dancer with ease and land her lightly on her feet, he moved with the relaxed air of an athlete confident in his ability to point his toes without losing any masculinity.

Up close, his light brown skin hinted at native Hawaiian heritage. I recognized him as the fire dancer in the website's video, and from the lineup of photos Ted had shown me as a part of his pitch.

"I'm Jason," he said. "Are you Alison?"

"Yes, call me Sonny," I said.

"You're fully licensed and up to speed?" Jason asked.

I paused. "A license is required in Hawaii?"

"I imagine every state requires a license," Jason said, looking surprised by my question. "What kind of bikes have you ridden?"

"You're talking about a motorcycle license," I said, silently thanking Ted for the heads-up, however vague. "I was supposed to tour the Florida Keys with my boyfriend, but—*yes*, I am fully licensed."

"Long story short," Jason said, "the bike in question is a rental from my uncle's shop in Hilo, a two-hour ride from here with the coast in view most of the way. If you've got time for sightseeing, there's an access road to the southernmost point of the United States."

"I've visited the cliffs on past trips," I said. "To clarify how the proposed ride came about, who mentioned my name?"

"My uncle didn't text that level of detail," Jason said. "On my end, I'm thrilled to trade private dance lessons for delivering the bike. We can figure out the logistics after the class. Speaking of that, your online application hinted at experience, but it's been a while?"

"My formal lessons ended when I was fourteen," I said. "But I practice yoga and tai chi, so hopefully, I'll be able to keep up."

"Did an injury end your classes?" Jason asked.

"No," I said. "My priorities changed."

"You're in the right place," Jason said. "This is an informal session with a mix of different skill levels. Don't push yourself too hard, and be aware that Petrel likes to tag dancers to join me in demonstrating steps from time to time. If that happens—" Jason paused and frowned at my feet. "If I'm not mistaken, those are Katrina's shoes."

"I found them in a closet where I'm staying," I said, delving into a brief explanation of my arrangement. "It's not the usual path for a vacation, but the tradeoff feels ideal. I get to live in paradise."

"You won't hear any arguments from me," Jason said. "Katrina and I stayed there a few times, which explains the shoes. We've been together since we met in grade school," Jason added, motioning toward a poster of a bubbly, dark-haired dancer. "It's her rental bike that you'll be bringing to Hilo. At the moment, we're experiencing a pause."

"A *pause?*" I said sharply.

Jason hesitated. "Yeah, umm …"

Abruptly self-aware, I said, "I'm sorry for how forcefully that came out. This morning, the guy I was dating … never mind the context. Pauses are healthy, as long as both people see them that way."

"I take it he totally messed up?" Jason asked with a sideways grimace. "In our case, Katrina's new job is sort of to blame."

"Good communication is key," I said, striving to sound neutral. "Are you sure Katrina supports returning the bike?"

"She's conveyed that outings are not a priority," Jason said. "In essence, I'm paying for a rental that's not being used."

"I'm sorry to pry," I said. "It's just …"

"No need to explain," Jason said. "You're here to dance and we're about to start. Signal me if you have any questions or issues."

With a smile, Jason continued saying hello to the dancers, drawing the gazes of several young women but seeming unaffected by their flirting. So far, I was impressed by his businesslike approach.

"Okay, let's warm up," Petrel said, clapping his hands. "We'll begin with last week's steps. I hope everyone practiced."

Thankfully, Petrel demonstrated the opening steps before playing a song over the ceiling speakers. By watching the nearest dancers, I fast-tracked learning the footwork, with my hips, torso, shoulders, and arms falling into the rhythm of steps I'd perfected in my youth. Still, I signaled for a late arriver to join the row in front of me, preferring to stay in the back to avoid confusing anyone if I lagged behind the beat. As the music blared from the speakers and the dancers became a shifting tide of legs, hips, and arms moving mostly in unison, Jason strolled along the edges of the class, pausing to offer praise or remind dancers to maintain proper posture, with their torsos relaxed and open rather than tense.

"Remember the goal," Petrel called out, wiping his face with a cloth as he paused the music. "There's room in the Spring Spectacular for those who put in the effort. All right, let's start again."

Doubling down on grit and determination, I caught glimpses of myself in the mirrored front wall, striving to correct my mistakes and push myself to execute cha-cha steps with speed, precision, and grace. My ankles ached in the slightly loose shoes, but my strength from yoga and pole dancing practice kept me in the game long after some of my classmates stepped away to rest on the sidelines. I enjoyed the sexy, flirty feel of some of the steps Petrel had built into the dance. It might take a dozen more failed romances, but one day I would find true love, and Dan would too: a woman who didn't throw him into constant turmoil.

"Stop!" Petrel hollered.

Using a remote control to turn off the music, Petrel motioned for the first few rows of dancers to step aside as he marched toward me. Breathing fast from exertion, I hesitated when he stopped in front of me and lifted his chin to make up for his slightly shorter height.

"What did I just witness?" he asked with a look of concern.

"Umm, I tried to sign up for a beginner class," I said.

"Nonsense, you're not a beginner," Petrel said. "I saw you catching on at warp speed, but *this*—" Petrel indicated my face. "It was like watching an animated corpse. It's going to haunt me in my dreams."

Across the room, dancers shifted to get a better look at my apparent deadness, and Jason arrived with an apologetic grimace.

"I told you Petrel singles people out for 'special guidance,'" he said with air quotes. "If I'm not mistaken, your intense focus had to do with the shoes. They're a borrowed pair. A little loose."

"That's a part of it," I agreed.

"Now she looks ready to flee," Petrel said, assessing me like a doctor striving to nail a tricky diagnosis. "The solution for stage fright is to take the stage. Shake off the hesitation. You'll thank me for it."

"I'm years out of practice," I said.

"Give it a try," Jason said. "You're up to it."

Gently taking my hand, Jason guided me through cha-cha half-steps, reminding me to keep my weight on the balls of my feet, with my hips in motion and my knees close together to create a lively cadence.

"Put on a smile, even if it's fake," Petrel chided.

If for no other reason than to contrive a fast exit, I forced a smile and fell into rhythm with Jason's chest and shoulder motions, with his face so close at times that I could hear him breathing.

"Excellent," Jason said, smiling as he completed the final beat. "Your mind-to-muscle memory kicked in thanks to the hard work and discipline you put in years ago. It's crucial in sports."

"Clearly, you keep in shape," Petrel said, closing in to study me with sharp gray eyes. "Swimming? Gymnastics?"

"All that, and … it's from pole dancing."

Abruptly excited, Petrel turned to Jason. "Try the rollover lift you used to perform with a certain other person."

"This is Sonny's first lesson in years," Jason said.

"Nonsense," Petrel said. "She's strong and fit."

"Let's demonstrate first," Jason said.

Beaming with pride at being chosen, an experienced dancer used the momentum of a solo spin to clasp Jason's hands and launch upward to his right shoulder in a swift motion, then, facing backward, roll behind his neck in a split. Almost too fast to see, Jason let go with his left hand to free his arm, secure her torso, and guide her down to her feet.

"Our right hands were in contact throughout," Jason told me. "There's a pause as you reach my shoulder, then keep hold through the roll, and trust that I'll guide you down with my left arm."

"Yes, I remember the sequence," I said.

As if to capitalize on my stunned state, Jason guided me to the ideal spot to start my spin and prompted me to begin. Keenly aware of his muscles flexing, I entrusted myself to his guiding hands and the power of my momentum as I launched upward to his right shoulder. His right hand and subtle cues guided me through a split across his shoulders and the back of his neck, then his left arm smoothly locked around my waist, supporting my downward-forward twist and slightly flustered landing.

"Back on your feet?" he asked.

"Yes," I said, steadying myself. "You're very brave."

"I've got solutions for wobbles and mistakes," Jason assured me. "You might have focused a bit too much on not going limp. Somewhere between super tight and a noodle next time, okay?"

"I doubt there will be a next time," I said.

"The landing was a mess," Petrel said, assessing me anew. "But there's potential. How long will you be in town?"

"A week," I said. "Maybe two."

"You're traveling alone?" he asked.

Wincing, I said, "Yes, I'm kind of …"

"Recovering from a breakup," Petrel said, nodding sagely now that all the factors were revealed. "No wonder you look empty inside. Jason, take Sonny out for drinks. It's what you both need."

With a look of apology, Jason signaled for me to ignore the comment as he and Petrel stepped away to resume the class.

"Don't feel singled out," a fit older woman whispered with a cheering shoulder squeeze. "Petrel is a pain in the butt sometimes, but he brings out the best in us. I joined the class after a divorce."

"Exercise is a magical remedy," I agreed.

"All right, places everyone," Petrel said. "With five minutes left, it's time to give it your all. And for heaven's sake, smile!"

As I resumed my position, I indulged a moment of celebration as my mind caught up with the fact that I had performed a lift for the first time since I was fourteen. Whereas dancing with Arlene's cousin had involved moments of insecurity when he'd steered with his hands too much, Jason followed the classic, polished approach of signaling steps and initiating changes of direction through his shoulders and chest.

Once the music launched and the class was in motion, I committed myself to the steps, though every spin offered glimpses of an elderly man who had taken command of a chair along the back wall. With his hands gripping his cane, he glared at me, and then he scowled at me, and then he appeared to be baring his teeth in a fierce display of animal menace. As I missed a step, thinking my imagination was playing tricks, Jason noticed and crossed to the man with a patient gaze, as if addressing a known problem. When the class stopped and the music ended, I could hear Jason's patient tone as he strived to reason with the man.

"Who is the older gentleman?" I asked the nearest dancer.

"That's Reginald White, known to friends and family as Pop-Pop," she said. "He's Katrina's grandfather. A bit of a flirt. At least, he was back in the day. He's a little worse for wear lately."

On my way to the door, and catching on that my presence might have caused the trouble, I hesitated as I neared Jason.

"For the last time," Jason was saying, "Katrina dumped me, so I'm not the one to ask about her busy schedule." Signaling for me to step closer, Jason added, "Sonny, this is Pop-Pop, Katrina's grandfather. He gets confused when he sees me partnering with other dancers."

"I'm a tourist," I said. "From the East Coast."

"That means you're the hottie staying at the rental house, the opposite of a get-out-of-jail card on the 'partnering' front," Pop-Pop said. "If there's one thing we know about Barry, he doesn't learn."

"I'm not involved with Barry," I said. "Or with Jason, or any other man in Hawaii. I'm a tourist who arrived this morning."

"Katrina is too busy with her important new job to pick up the phone," Pop-Pop said, as if to explain his bad mood. "And it's a steam bath in here. What happened to the air conditioning?"

"It's actually very cool," Jason said.

"There's more than one woman who'd love the fact that I'm having hot flashes," Pop-Pop said, mopping his brow as he eyed me suspiciously. "You're hot the other way. What's your story?"

This time, as I described my arrangement, I decided it was a chance to mention that I hoped to connect with a friend of Mary's.

"Perhaps you know Jasmine," I said.

Suddenly, Pop-Pop went from fractious to boiling mad.

"If you're in league with that schemer, it's all we need to know," he growled. "Jasmine is at the bottom of a pack of lies."

"What are you talking about?" Jason asked.

"She sees me as a bad influence," Pop-Pop said. "It's the opposite. I'm the reason Katrina has smarts and business sense."

"We're forgetting our indoor voice," Petrel said, sweeping toward us with a look of worry. "Jason, what's the trouble?"

"Pop-Pop is having a bad spell," Jason whispered. "It's not just his memory. Look at him. He's sweaty and pale."

"I know what all the whispering is about," Pop-Pop growled, shaking his cane at us. "Putting me in a care facility like I'm a broken-down mule. Meanwhile, look where the loan money went, bells and whistles and new flooring. You think I'm too dim to notice."

"Reginald, I think you've come down with a flu," Petrel said, resting a hand on his forehead. "You're quite feverish."

"This seems like a good time to slip away," I said to Jason. "Should I leave Katrina's shoes with her grandfather?"

"No, I'm belatedly remembering that Mary was using that pair," Jason said. "They fit her pretty well, but on you, they're a twisted ankle waiting to happen. I'll see if I can find a better fit."

"That's kind of you," I said. "Regarding the bike …"

"Yes, let's firm that up," Jason said. "When you're ready, we'll meet in the parking lot to make sure you're comfortable on Katrina's bike. To sweeten the deal, I'll pay for a rideshare for the trip back. I can connect you with a trustworthy guy. Let's exchange numbers."

Once our phones were tucked away, I felt it was time to admit that Mary had urged me to spend time with Jasmine.

"In that case, I'll fill in some of the background," Jason said. "Basically, Jasmine and I are in the same boat, out of favor with Katrina for reasons that might have to do with Reginald's past. His nickname is a hint," Jason added, mimicking shooting a gun with his right hand. "Pop-Pop spent time in prison for some kind of white-collar crime, but his conviction was overturned. He's loaded from the resulting lawsuits."

"Forgive me," I said, silently fuming at Agent Telford. "No one mentioned an ex-convict with a weapon-related nickname."

"See it as a lighthearted touch," Jason said. "Reginald's way of turning lemons into lemonade. Picture his eyes twinkling as he drops hints during poker games. That's the Pop-Pop I've come to know, but I'm shocked by his rapid decline. He's in his early sixties at most. Today, Reginald looks ten years older, and his use of a cane is new."

"Maybe he should be discouraged from driving," I said.

"You've got a wry tone, just like Katrina," Jason said. "A mix of fun and sensible. I think Jasmine might respond to you."

"I've heard she might be in Hilo," I said.

"As you saw just now, Jasmine's strong opinions were causing friction, so I encouraged her to lie low," Jason said. "She's doing odd jobs for my uncle in Hilo, but it's only a matter of time before she wears out her welcome. Don't get me wrong, Jasmine is a super person."

"Mary seems fond of her," I said.

"Your arrival is starting to feel like kismet," Jason said. "Hawaii is like that. There's magic in volcanic ground."

"It's why I keep coming back," I said. "On a previous trip, I counted ten rainbows in one day. I'm told it has to do with mist."

Smiling, Jason said, "That sounds better than attributing it to Kilauea's sulfuric emissions. Halema'uma'u is spectacular these days."

"I've got my eye on you, pretty boy," Pop-Pop growled, despite Petrel's efforts to calm him. "You too, girlie girl. I know your type."

"I'm sorry," Jason whispered.

Seeing that Katrina was well-loved, I had no complaints.

* * *

With Jasmine's clothes fluffing in the dryer in the garage, I changed into my work overalls and decided it was time to try one of the avocados Mary had left to ripen on the countertop. The knife glided easily through the dark outer rind, revealing a buttery green interior that I topped with fresh lemon juice and coarse black pepper. With eye rolls befitting the delicious treat, I savored the combined flavors of avocado and Camembert cheese, tucked into a sandwich of fresh, sweet bread I'd bought at the store.

"Yeah, this counts as paradise," I said.

Using water sparingly, I finished cleaning the hot tub and confirmed that the jets and filtration system were functional. Under a sky of pink and gold clouds set afire by the setting sun, I turned on the jets and adjusted the temperature to the perfect setting. Getting the chemistry right would have to wait until the next morning. Halfway through lifting the insulated lid to keep bugs and leaves at bay, I turned toward the house, hearing a faint chirp, like a smoke detector's dying battery. It was an intermittent sound, impossible to pinpoint without a careful search.

I prioritized checking the bedroom, thinking it was the most likely place for fate to gleefully nudge a battery toward a slow death, but the next beep came from the kitchen or living room. Moving from one spot to the next, I paused and listened for more signals, ending up next to the couch, where everything was quiet except for my footsteps. Maybe luck was with me for once. The failing battery had let out its final gasp.

Dressed in a T-shirt and my tropical flower pajama pants, I climbed into bed, vibrating from fatigue at 6:30 p.m., the hour of sunset in Hawaii in February. Splayed on my stomach, I kept the rice paper doors closed to keep mosquitoes from bothering me while I was unconscious. Hard work had done the trick. I was out in less than a minute.

6

The forest was awash with echoes, from a light *tap, tap, tap,* to the whispers of pine trees reaching their fragrant needles toward the night sky. With every step, my footfalls were softened by leaves that had piled up over the course of eons. Up ahead, Antoine turned to me.

"What are you not telling me?" he asked.

"You lit a flame that refuses to extinguish," I said. "It's maddening and distracting. Why would you do that and then leave?"

Suddenly alone, I cast about in the darkness, tripped over my loose sneakers, and fell into the fallen leaves. With a wry smile, Antoine tightened my laces and rested his fingers under my chin.

"What's troubling you, Berrichon?" he asked.

"It feels like I must have let you down in some way," I whispered. "If I fell short, I need to know. Silence is confusing."

"One time," Antoine said, "when my vehicle was encased with ice, I used my Glock as a scraper. It got the job done, but it's not useful as a weapon anymore. At one point or another, we all end up being the Glock. Used in a way that's wrong."

"I think I hear you clearing the ice away," I murmured.

"No, that's the judge," Antoine said. "He likes to use his gavel."

"I don't want to be grilled on the witness stand," I said, covering my eyes. "I'm here to forget the horror of what's to come."

"Rest your mind," Antoine said. "I will fix it."

"No, stay and talk to me," I said, alarmed to feel his sheltering hug fading, as if he'd turned to vapor. "Please don't leave …"

Reaching out with both hands, I clutched at the warm, tropical air, still hearing the *tap-tap-tap* of the gavel. Shocked awake by a hard landing on the floor, I spun in confusion and slowly realized that I'd tumbled out of bed for the umpteenth time. "An overactive life can translate to overactive dreams," Sue Black had once theorized.

With a groan, I used the bed to climb upward, parched from mouth-breathing while I slept. With my eyes half-closed, I drank a full glass of water and staggered back into the bedroom.

Tap-tap-tap. Tap-tap-tap-tap.

Shocked to realize the sound was very real, I squinted at the ceiling in the darkness, horrified as the taps merged with a drawn-out scraping noise, as if someone was weakly dragging their feet or hauling a load of trash from one side of the roof to the other.

"Mary?" I said hopefully.

Shocked even more by a sudden silence, I stepped wrong and felt my shin hit the bedframe, where gauzy fabric was draped from the canopy like a shroud. Breathing in gulps, with my heart racing, I froze as the light footsteps and scraping sounds started again.

Tap-tap. Tap-tap-tap.

With goosebumps crawling over my skin, I used my phone's flashlight to find Mary's rubber ankle boots. Ready to lock myself inside if needed, I eased open the deck door, stepped into the cool night air, and scanned the yard to see if the intruder was casting a shadow from the moon's bright light. No such luck. Carefully, slowly, I descended the path leading to the patio, pausing to look up at the roof expecting to see a crouched figure, but the tapping continued without an obvious source.

"Maybe an empty can was tossed up there," I said. "Courtesy of the rock band. It's shifting and sliding in the breeze."

A plausible explanation fueled my courage as I crossed around the first-floor rooms to fetch the aluminum ladder lying next to the outside wall. Aiming my phone in all directions to look for signs of sudden activity, I hoisted the ladder upright, pulled the rope that extended the rungs to the roofline, took a calming breath, and started to climb. With each upward step, the metal rattled from my trembling hands.

Grimacing in anticipation of an attack as I crested the roofline, I froze as a fierce red eye and a flash of iridescent blue glowed in the spooky light of my phone, then I saw it was the peacock.

"Good God," I managed. "What are you *doing* up here?"

The bird clucked and preened its feathers.

Trembling and exhausted, I crawled to a spot that was hopefully free of peacock guano, and winced from the sharp stab of debris on my palms and knees. Scanning the roof with my phone, I saw that the bird had been pecking at a swath of corn kernels and sunflower seeds.

"I *hate* the rock band," I growled.

Quickly, I descended the ladder to fetch a broom. As I climbed back up with the awkward load under one arm, the bird objected to the noise and took flight, landing in a hidden spot in the darkness. With minor aches from a day of work and being tossed across Jason's shoulders, I swept the kernels toward the forested area behind the house.

Pushing stray curls from my forehead, I squinted as a bright light cut through the papaya trees that flanked the lane and confirmed that a sedan was approaching. Kicking myself for leaving a lamp on in the living room, I relied on silence to bring the intrusion to a swift end.

Crouching, I watched two shadows emerge from the car. Once they neared the walkway lights, I recognized Barry's wife, Pauline, and her colleague, Gavin, heading past the office and massage room.

"Miss Littlefield?" Pauline said, lightly tapping on the door. "I would have called, but I don't have your phone number."

"I'm not seeing or hearing any signs of movement," Gavin said. "It's eight o'clock, too early for anyone to turn in."

"If you have a piece of paper, I'll leave a note," Pauline said.

"Nobody carries paper anymore," Gavin said. "Instead of fretting that Barry is cheating again, you owe it to yourself to learn the truth. Maybe there's a clue in the house. Do you have a key?"

"Of course I have a key," Pauline said.

"Wait here," Gavin said. "I'll handle it."

As the door below me opened with a whine of hinges, light from the living room spilled down the lawn and across the patio, with the moonlit Pacific in the background. I thought about announcing my presence, but another sedan was slowly coming up the hill.

"Hello?" Gavin called out.

"Why are you looking under the couch cushions?" Pauline asked.

"If I don't, you'll chide me for not being thorough," Gavin said. "And it's possible I left something during the party."

"Dear God, Barry's car is approaching through the trees," Pauline said. "Either he's bringing Sonny back from a date, or Petrel has outed my suspicions. This is humiliating beyond words."

"I'll say we're here about the article Sonny is writing for *Coast & Candle* magazine," Gavin said. "We're curious, and so on."

With a sigh, I stretched out on my back and gazed at the fringed leaves of the coconut palms swaying in the breeze, with the moon shining like a colossal pearl. Damp from dew, I chose to see the moment as a chance to learn about the local populace rather than a grim reality.

"Barry, you have a history with female guests at the house," Gavin said after his fibs fell short. "Your past is to blame."

"As always, you're overinflating a lone incident," Barry said. "It's rich for you to accuse me of infidelity when you're always in the background during your arts academy trips with my wife."

"You can't imagine I would break up a friend's marriage," Gavin said. "Nor will Sonny, apparently. She's out on the town."

"Most likely, she's with Jason," Petrel said. "Midway through today's class, I was convinced that my rival on Oahu had sent another spy to steal my choreography. Once I confronted Sonny and saw that her despair was genuine, I felt terrible, so I encouraged Jason to take her out for drinks. I've rounded the corner with a resounding win."

"I'm not sure Katrina will see it that way," Pauline said. "Sam, is that you standing in the shadows? Which one of you decided it was a good idea to expose Axe's son to the party aftermath?"

"My father caused all this damage?" Sam asked.

"You know how focused he is when playing his guitar," Gavin said. "I tried to maintain order, but outsiders got wind of the party. Here's the good news. A small fire was put out. It didn't spread."

"What's your plan for reimbursing me?" Barry asked in a wry, heated tone. "Maybe we could sell your portrait on the garage doors."

"Chill alluded to a donation if I participated in his aspiration to create a paintball masterpiece," Gavin said. "Even with goggles and a plastic cape, it hurt like hell. I think he was aiming for my face."

"The garage doors might sell quite well," Petrel mused. "Why hasn't the academy hosted a memorial service for Chip?"

"Drugs were found in his system," Pauline said quietly. "The trustees are leery of revealing that another alumnus was an addict."

"There've been others?" Sam asked.

"Technically, no," Gavin said. "The teen who died on Maui dropped out, but it's a connection we can't deny. We'll hold memorial services once the dust settles. Their families will understand."

In the wake of a series of dings, Petrel said, "Sam, I believe that's your phone. You're quite popular tonight."

"If only," Sam said. "Dad is texting from Japan."

A silence unfolded, except for Sam's retreating footsteps.

"I've always hoped that his long-lost mother would reach out," Petrel said. "Ask Axe about her, and you'll be put in your place. I suppose there's sense in leaving an old wound untouched."

"Where you see wounds, I see success," Gavin said. "Sam is a high-achieving kid on his way to earning a master's degree."

"Holy shit, look at the progress Sonny made," Barry said, sending his voice across the yard. "Even from outside, I can see evidence of sanding and patching. Moritz declared the hot tub a lost cause. He priced out a new unit at ten grand. Sonny cleaned the trash. The water is hot, the jets flowing. I'm tempted to jump in and splash around."

"It's the power of manic energy," Petrel said. "Some people retreat to bed and give up. Sonny copes through activity."

"Mary is a genuine sort," Pauline said. "Repairs in exchange for a stay in paradise made sense, but what do we know about Sonny?"

"Her family in Boston is quite well off," Gavin said. "She's young and striking, able to afford a high-end resort, yet here she is patching drywall. We should make sure she isn't a schemer."

"Because that would be *crazy*," Barry said. "Somebody other than the present company being obsessed with cash flow."

"She's a suffering soul who needs protection from the local prowling dogs," Petrel said. "It's time to go. Get moving."

The lights spilling across the yard went dark, and footsteps retreated to the lane. Logic dictated the rides home: Barry and Pauline would leave together; Gavin and Axe's son would ride with Petrel.

As the sedans departed, I enjoyed the hillside's peace and quiet, with coconut palms swaying in front of the moonlit clouds above me and the cheeps of frogs far below in the garden. With a tired sigh, I climbed down, returned the ladder to its spot beside the house, and headed up the walkway to change out of my damp T-shirt and pajamas, which were covered with asphalt gravel and sticky corn kernels.

Exhausted, but overly alert, I flopped onto the couch with a slice of cheese, deciding it made sense to work another day to make sure Barry and Pauline saw quick progress and to avoid the risk of Jasmine arriving the moment I left the house. The following day, I would meet Jason and ride Katrina's motorcycle to Hilo. After befriending Jasmine, I would find new quilts, drapes, and pillows based on Mary's specifications and visit the artisan who could create new woven palm panels for the bedroom. By then, I would have earned a day or two of downtime, so I planned to visit Kilauea Volcano before heading back to the rental house.

In parting, Jason had promised to spend time with me in the parking lot until I felt comfortable riding an unfamiliar bike. My training had covered the challenge of being on a small-profile vehicle that often went unnoticed by other drivers. What if engine failure or another problem caused me to be stranded on the road after dark? Was it legal to ride a motorcycle at night? The instructor never addressed that question.

As I pulled out my phone and typed "is it legal to" in the search field, the automatic results that started loading prompted a frown.

Is it legal to dumpster dive?

Is it legal to marry your cousin?

Is it legal to shoot down a drone?
Is it legal to own a tank?
Is it legal to own a capybara?

"What in the heck are people doing?" I murmured.

Hopefully, Jason could fill in the blanks.

On my way to the light switch, I stopped, hearing the iffy smoke alarm battery again. Pausing every few seconds, I repeated the pattern of heading in a direction, then stopping to listen, until I traced the faint beeps to my camera bag on a chair. Hesitating, I pulled Antoine's flip phone out of the side pocket, opened the lid, and heard a static hiss.

"Hello?" I said.

The device crackled with sputtering, echoing noise, as if I'd reached the bottom of a trash can in a busy train station.

"You're going to need to speak up," I said.

Hurrying through the living room and then outside to the deck to see if the signal cleared, I faced the silence that had greeted me every time I'd dared to hope the phone might work. The plastic felt so chilly and blank that I wondered if I'd imagined the faint beeps. Then again, batteries were batteries, no matter the device. They quit without notice.

"This is perfect," I said. "Super timing."

Too agitated to sleep, I crossed to the liquor shelf and grabbed a bottle of tequila by the neck, similar to how I wanted to grip a tiny version of Antoine, and upended it without fetching a glass.

Choking as liquid fire hit my tongue, I blew it across the room in a fine mist. A hand-drawn skull on the label confirmed that I'd found the Hawaiian moonshine. Furious, I slammed the bottle onto the shelf and sniffed a bottle of whiskey. It was definitely whiskey.

I gulped a burning swig and started pacing.

"It's a cruel twist to be drinking because of a man's *support*," I said. "A lone warrior on the Sonny front. Thoughtful and warm. That's why, when you served up your plans and stings, I didn't ask questions. I dove in. Nose to the grindstone. Nearly got killed. Once the shock wore off, I was desperate to talk to you," I managed, blinking rapidly as I gulped down another shot of whiskey. "But no, it was a job to you. Instead of allowing a second chance and confessions of shared feelings, you left a bogus phone that connects to the bottom of a garbage can."

As always, after a tumultuous moment of self-awareness, the room's silence was palpable and overwhelming, except for my stifled crying and pounding heart. I put the whiskey on the shelf and threw the phone into my bag, vowing to find a place to recycle its parts.

With the lights off, I slipped into bed and hugged a pillow, praying that dawn would bring some semblance of a normal life. Engulfed in a swirling whiskey haze, I realized how lucky I was to be alive, unlike Chip Henderson and the youth who'd indulged his last high next to a dumpster, one of the saddest places on Earth to die. Dumpsters were for getting rid of things that were troublesome or no longer useful.

A year ago, I was a version of a vibrant, modern woman. Now, more often than not, I spent the last moments of wakefulness with ghosts hovering over me in the darkness, asking, "Who is going to make sure I'm remembered for who I am, if you don't step in and help?"

"Kind of busy right now," I murmured.

7

Up ahead along the coastal road, at one with his gleaming motorcycle, Jason signaled right or left to warn me of upcoming turns and pointed to speed limit signs. After giving a thumbs up, he resumed resting his hand on his thigh as he glided along the road in a jacket similar to the one that he'd loaned me for the ride, featuring a dramatic Milky Way fabric on the front panels and back—a bright, visual marker that helped me keep track of him when we were briefly separated by other vehicles.

When I'd met Jason in the dance studio's parking lot at seven o'clock that morning, I was surprised to learn that he'd decided to join me for part of the ride to make sure I felt comfortable on the bike and also because he wanted to reclaim his favorite pastime. He'd looked sad when he talked about his past adventures with Katrina, like stopping to watch dolphins in the distance or having picnic lunches on the water's edge.

With my hands carefully positioned on the handlebars to apply the brakes, increase or decrease the throttle, or navigate a bend in the road, I enjoyed gliding along at a steady 45 mph during straight stretches, engulfed by wind and the engine's steady growl, but keenly aware of the unforgiving asphalt racing by under the fast-spinning wheels.

As always, it was a unique experience to see the world through the curved visor of a motorcycle helmet, with my breathing audible, along with my chirps of surprise whenever a crack in the road jostled me slightly.

Through wireless speakers in our helmets, my back-and-forth with Jason focused on upcoming turns. His suffering mindset was reflected in his playlist, which included songs like "Jealous" by Labrinth, a heartfelt, intense song about lost love that was also on my playlist.

As I chirped again, Jason said, "Are you okay?"

"Sorry, the bumps catch me off-guard," I said.

"You're doing great, Sonny," Jason said. "Up ahead, I'm stopping to gas up my bike. There's a restroom in the store."

"Thanks, I'm all set for now," I said.

Glimpsing my reflection in the store's windows as I slowed to a stop and balanced the bike's weight with my sneakers on the pavement, I felt that I'd taken a step forward in developing my inner badass. A nervous, handlebar-clutching badass, but in terms of facing critics when I got back to Maine, it was a move in the right direction.

Without the wind buffeting my torso and legs, I felt the sun's heat through my clothing, but I kept the helmet on lest I devolve into another round of putting it on and wrenching it off to extract a hair from my right eye, then my mouth, then my left eye. On the downside, I experienced imposter syndrome when we passed another biker or a group of pedestrians who recognized Katrina's jacket and motorcycle. Afraid to take my hands off the handlebars while we sped along at 45-50 mph, even for a split-second wave, I resorted to delivering a queenly nod.

Now, waiting for Jason to finish at the gas pump, I watched a pickup truck come to a rough stop on the road. With his helmet off, Jason would be able to clearly see the truck and its occupants, but he remained stone-faced as he tucked the hose back into its compartment.

Alerted to potential trouble, I opened my visor and stared at the truck driver and his passenger, both heavily weathered and older, possibly in their fifties. There was a third man in the extended cab, less visible, but as he leaned forward, I saw he had a beard. All three men wore hats with a familiar logo, but I was distracted by the realization that Jason and I were vulnerable targets, exposed on our motorcycles.

"How's it hanging, dance king?" the driver hollered.

"Enough, all right?" Jason snapped. "*Enough.*"

The flare-up ended as a car approached, prompting the truck to surge away down the road. Looking irritated, Jason jammed on his helmet and signaled for me to walk my bike back with my right foot, then my left, alerting me to the need to park sideways next time.

"What was that about?" I said into my helmet microphone.

"Nothing," Jason said. "Don't worry about it."

Fifteen minutes later, as we reached Ka Lae, the southernmost point of the United States, Jason swung into the parking lot, rumbled to a stop, and balanced his bike with a sneaker on each side in a smooth sequence of steps. Once he engaged the stand and climbed off, he offered a helping hand as I cut the engine and carefully dismounted.

"Easy does it, take your time," Jason said, steadying me until I found my footing. "I can cancel my obligations at the studio."

"Because of those guys?" I asked.

"They're long gone by now," Jason said. "You were yelping over cracks and looking tense, even on straight stretches."

"I've got the hang of it," I assured him.

"Let's rest before you decide," Jason said. "I'm curious to know what you think of your workmates, Moritz and Raja."

"So far so good," I said.

In truth, I pictured them pecking away at the repairs in the downstairs apartment instead of making real progress. Throughout our first full day of work, they took breaks to fetch tools from their bungalow and returned with a six-pack of beer. Instead of appreciating my efforts, they seemed determined to slow me down, asking me to prove my skills before letting me pick up a power tool. Harve's opinion that they were a mix of shiftless and full of themselves had proven accurate.

Before crossing to the stunning cliffside view of thunderous Pacific breakers beyond the parking lot and coastline walkway, I wrenched off my helmet and shook out my waves and curls to give them a break before finishing the last stretch of the ride to Hilo.

"My heart skipped a beat, seeing you do that," Jason said, pulling out his phone. "Check out this slow-motion clip."

Turning the screen to avoid glare from the sun, I watched a video of Katrina riding toward me on her motorcycle. Smooth and relaxed, she stopped with both sneakers on the pavement, pulled off her helmet, and shook out her hair with a mesmerizing slow-motion effect. The light was perfect, highlighting her radiant smile and dark curls.

"Wow," I said.

"Yeah, wow is the right word," Jason said, looking resigned to misery as he tucked his phone away. "If you want to torture your ex-boyfriend, I can create a similar video of you with your phone."

"No, I want him to move on," I said.

"Technically," Jason said, indicating the stunning view as we crossed to the ocean overlook, "Ka Lae is the southernmost point of the 'incorporated' United States. I'm told the one in Samoa is farther south, but this is the spot people consider the real deal. It feels that way."

"I've been here on previous trips," I said.

With tourists taking selfies nearby, I leaned my hips against the wall of lava boulders with the Hawaiian sun blazing down from above, an ocean breeze on my face, and my eyes squinting against the glare of the whitecaps stretching to the distant horizon. Below me was a forty-foot drop, where waves roared in from the moon's force, spraying explosive water in all directions, then pulling back against the churning surf.

Beside me, with his elbows on the ledge, Jason asked above the noise, "What's Maine's coast like compared to this?"

"The water is a darker blue," I said. "And the scent of seaweed is often in the air. Unlike this black lava, Maine's coast is made of granite, quartz, and other rocks. It's a place of seabirds and barnacles, with buoys clanging in the distance and the chug of lobster boats. I love the coast of Maine, but it's cold this time of year. To stand on the brink like this, we would need to bundle up in hats, scarves, and coats."

"You revere the land," Jason said. "It's good to see."

"Why were those guys picking on you?" I asked.

"You heard what they called me," Jason said. "The dance king, like it's a liability. Same with my Hawaiian ancestry."

"Lowlifes are intimidated by people who are successful and well liked," I said. "All the same, I know it's tough to be bullied."

"There's a connection to Katrina's grandfather, Reginald, so maybe it's good to put them on your radar," Jason said. "Some years ago, they served time for money laundering. If I got the story straight, they heard about Reginald's wrongful conviction. Specifically, they heard about his reputation for helping ex-cons who show signs of contrition."

"In principle, it's a noble philosophy," I said.

"Katrina and I were there when the two of them showed up with their hands out," Jason said. "They agreed to whatever jobs Reginald sent their way, no matter how tough and menial. You glimpsed the real deal in terms of their attitude, but they had a serious side and landed jobs. Within maybe a year or two, Reginald chided himself for being soft."

"He felt they were bending the rules again?" I asked.

"Reginald summed it up as some people being a lost cause," Jason said. "Based on the third guy I saw in the cab, they're spreading the poison, but it seemed like he was wincing rather than smiling. A rough sort, like they'd plucked him off the street to do menial chores."

With a troubled look, Jason fell into silence, staring out to sea with an air of debating whether to share more. He'd taken time out of his busy schedule for a reason, so I waited out his hesitation by capturing still shots and short videos of the explosive surf with my phone.

"Can I bend your ear about Katrina?" Jason asked. "Be aware it's with a goal in mind. First, what's your impression of me?"

"For starters, I would have postponed the ride if you hadn't taken the time to familiarize me with the bike," I said. "It's consistent with my initial experience at the studio. Despite the inviting smiles of pretty women, you remained professional. Unlike less skilled partners from my past, you led with your chest and shoulders rather than your hands, and you only proceeded with a step when you felt I was in sync."

"I'm impressed that you noticed," Jason said, studying me with relief. "The phrase 'it's a dance' applies to all human endeavors for a reason. Even though it looks like a pro dancer is pulling his partner from here to there with his hands, it's a matter of subtle cues. My role is to athletically support and poetically lead a partner through the steps."

"It comes through," I assured him.

"Katrina tossed other dance partners to the wayside, so it felt special when we clicked," Jason said. "We had a dream of starting our own dance studio. Reginald was willing and able to make it happen, but his prison past bothered me, so that turned into a conflict. Strike two was my assumption that having lots of kids was a given. Pregnancy adds complexity to a dancer's life, so I came across as blind."

"You argued over it?" I asked.

"In hindsight, I'm open to adopting," Jason said. "But my original stance came back to bite me. I apologized and told Katrina I would lay the world at her feet. The next thing I knew, she was crying, pushing me away, and calling me naïve. That was that. No more us."

"Did you try again after she cooled off?" I asked.

"To no avail," Jason said. "The favor I'm hoping you'll grant is to share whatever you learn from Jasmine. Even though she and I are equally out of favor with Katrina, she knows more than she's telling me. I don't want to speak ill of the other person possibly involved."

I hesitated. "Is it someone who passed away?"

"You won't have been in Hawaii long enough to have gotten to know Chip Henderson," Jason said. "A super guy, with a molten core unparalleled on the planet. He dove in and saved whales with his bare hands. A lot of people are messed up over his death, but I've got a particular pain in my gut because I've been robbed of reclaiming our friendship. From our time at Ellika Arts Academy, we were a tight bunch of friends, ambitious and focused. Chip and Katrina were close growing up."

"Did they ever date?" I asked.

"No, Chip supported me as a match for Katrina," Jason said. "To the point where he got in my face when she cut ties with me, saying only an awful slip-up would make her throw in the towel."

"There's nothing to that notion?" I asked.

"Nothing beyond what I thought were minor arguments," Jason said. "Chip let up. He believed me, mostly, and confronted other guys, like Axe, the lead guitarist in the band behind Barry's house getting trashed. Axe is one of the notorious dogs in the area."

"How did it go when Chip confronted Axe?" I asked.

"You're opening a can of worms, and I'm due back at the studio," Jason said, looking frustrated as he checked the time. "To answer your question, Chip and Axe nearly came to blows for a second time. The first time, it was about the band endangering wildlife with 'godawful' noise during a shipboard concert. Chip threw Axe's guitar into the bay."

"Yikes," I said. "Was Chip charged for destruction of property?"

"No, it was all smoothed over," Jason said. "Back then, Reginald wasn't fading like he is now. He got everyone to calm down."

"I hope you understand that I might not be able to share what I learn from Jasmine," I said. "Let's call it a maybe."

"Sounds good," Jason said. "Are you okay continuing alone?"

"Yes, I'm rested and focused," I said.

In truth, my heart fluttered at the prospect of riding on my own, but as he'd done in the dance class, Jason offered straightforward feedback on my strengths, with a hint that my tension wasn't helpful.

"It's good to be mindful on a bike," Jason stressed. "But remember to breathe because nerves can cut down your reaction time."

"I'll practice deep yoga breathing," I said.

"You'll do great," Jason said, squeezing my shoulder. "I'm shutting off the wireless speakers, so you'll lose that distraction factor."

As before, Jason took the lead, but when we neared the main road, he signaled for me to pull up beside him. It was too late to realize I should have agreed to the restroom visit, but seeing his smile through his visor, I gripped the handlebars, gave an assuring nod, and looked both ways before making a smooth right turn onto the main road. Trembling slightly, I increased the throttle as Jason's presence faded in my rearview mirror, and I focused on finding another station with a restroom.

* * *

"Praise the Lord," I said, seeing a restroom sign on a marquee up ahead, then to my bladder, I added, "Hold tight. Almost there."

Like an automaton, I completed the steps for leaving the bike and headed inside to find the stall surprisingly clean. Minutes later, feeling relaxed and ready to roll, I washed my hands at the sink, estimating I was ten minutes from Hilo when a truck halted outside with a chirp of tires. Peering through a crack in the window, I froze, seeing that the dirtbags who'd hassled Jason recognized Katrina's bike.

As the driver neared the door, I ducked into the stall and wrenched my phone out of my pocket. Jason was miles away, so I opened my camera app and pressed the record button in case the police needed to reconstruct the last moments of my downward plummeting life.

Backing up to make space for a defensive kick, I steadied my phone as the outside door banged open, spilling light into the cramped room. Then I heard the thug's coarse sniff and loud breathing, and the tip of his half-laced work boot appeared on my side of the barrier. His fingers gripped the top of the stall door, shaking it to test the lock, then he pounded the metal so hard that its hinges rattled and threatened to give way.

"Tell the old man we're not afraid of his threats," he growled above his banging. "A deal is a deal. Make sure he gets it."

With patrons emerging from cars in the parking lot, he left as quickly as he'd arrived, reassured by my rapid breathing that his message had been heard. Once his shadow receded, I stepped out of the stall and nudged the outside door open with my toe enough to aim my camera at the thug as he crossed in front of his truck. With my phone raised, I filmed the vehicle pulling away, and its tires chirping sharply.

Replaying the clip, I confirmed there was a passenger in the front and another in the extended cab. The license plate was too blurry to read, but the video was evidence of a troubling pattern of behavior.

Thanks to a contrary quirk of my personality, my resilient side took charge after a shocking confrontation, especially when I realized I wasn't the only one facing a threat. Unlike the nervous woman who'd rushed into the bathroom, I stepped out with a sense of control over the motorcycle as I released the stand, turned the key, and revved the throttle. Gliding forward and then purring to a stop at the edge of the parking lot, I checked that the lanes were clear, swung out, and headed for Hilo.

A traffic light near the motorcycle shop offered a view of the interior. Seeing a teenager with Asian features pushing a broom in an open two-bay garage, and recognizing her chin-length hair and a vibrant pink side braid, I smiled at the good luck of finding Jasmine without an extended search. As I arced into the parking lot toward the garage, my arrival caught the attention of a mutt sitting near Jasmine.

Streaking toward me with a mad look in its eyes, the dog celebrated my arrival with bouncing, barking, and cavorting that threatened to topple me as I climbed from the bike and engaged the stand. Seeing a female rider in Katrina's jacket, Jasmine smiled and rushed toward me.

"You're finally *here,*" she said. "I can't believe it!"

Unable to wrench off my helmet fast enough, I absorbed the impact of Jasmine's hug and endeavored to break free.

"I know I've rattled cages across the island," Jasmine said. "What was I supposed to do? You scared the crap out of me."

"I'm sorry for the wrong impression," I said, finally yanking off the helmet. "I'm Sonny, a friend of Mary's."

Gaping, Jasmine hollered, "Wrong impression, my ass! Who gave you permission to ride Katrina's bike and wear her jacket?"

"Hey, enough," a fiftyish man said, stepping from the garage to join us. "We talked about a proper work attitude."

"Was it your idea to take Katrina's bike?" she demanded.

"What of it?" he asked. "By all accounts, Katrina is focused on work. It's called reaching adulthood. You should try it."

"Like, hacking up a lung from smoking cigars and getting blackout drunk?" Jasmine asked. "That kind of adulthood?"

"You're lucky you remind me of my little girl," he growled. "And by the way, instead of training a true watchdog, you've got a mutt that makes people holler, 'Watch out, here it comes!'"

"You're giving him treats against the rules," Jasmine said.

"My shop, my rules," he said. "Capiche?"

"Hang on," I said, motioning for calm and asking for a minute alone with Jasmine. "Meanwhile, you can process the bike."

"As long as she keeps a civilized tone," he said.

A slim, pint-sized force of nature at five feet tall, Jasmine scorched his back for a second, then aimed her glare at me.

"You have five seconds to explain yourself," she said.

"Again, my name is Sonny—"

"*Four,*" Jasmine said.

"Three, two, one," I said. "Now what?"

"Mary told me an East Coast busybody was joining the effort to bring me 'back into the fold,'" Jasmine said, using air quotes. "Once I vet you properly, I will be in touch if you're not too wet behind the ears. Until then, keep your yap shut," she added, poking my sternum to drum in her points. "My business is none of your business. You never saw me. We didn't talk. See the sights. Be a tourist. *Period.*"

"Jasmine, my experience outstrips anything you've ever—"

"Blah blah," she said. "Why are you wincing? Mary sent a crybaby?"

"Insults are a sad tell," I said. "As for poking people …"

With a quick motion, I snagged her hand in a self-defense finger lock for three seconds, careful not to cause damage.

"It's not smart to poke a stranger, especially under a security camera," I said as I released her hand. "It can be seen as assault."

"What do you call grabbing my fingers?" she asked.

"You're cocky instead of confident," I said. "A loose cannon instead of informed. Once I vet you properly, I will consider weighing your concerns. In the meantime, let your parents know you're okay, thank Mary for doing your laundry, and stop acting like a toddler. *Period.*"

With the helmet in hand, I crossed to the garage to finish my business with Jason's uncle. I'd never resorted to insults, but the teenager's loyalty to a friend brought a single, rattling thought to mind.

Dear God, Jasmine is a version of me.

8

Through Jason's uncle, I hired a rideshare driver who had enough time available to take me to multiple locations in Hilo instead of just one. Likely in his fifties, with a relaxed vibe and a willingness to share tips about where to stay and what to do across all the Hawaiian Islands, he lifted my spirits within minutes of getting me into his car.

"Call me RG, short for rideshare guy," he said, casting red-cheeked smiles at me when our gazes connected in the rearview mirror. "It's a solution for sparing travelers the need to remember my name. Truth be told, I was providing rides on the Big Island long before it became a newfangled craze. I missed out on being a mogul."

"It's great if you enjoy driving," I said.

First on my list of visits was the upholstery store to drop off fabric samples for replacing cushions and drapes in the house, followed by the artisan who'd made the woven palm panels. After the dimensions for new panels were conveyed, I ordered woven palm fish, bunnies, sunhats, and placemats to send to my friends in Maine and Boston, along with some panels to add a touch of the tropics to my farmhouse.

"Where to next?" RG asked as I got back to his car.

"A bookstore, then the botanical garden," I said.

During the drive from one side of Hilo to the other, RG gave me a moment of privacy as I answered texts from friends and sent snapshots of the woven fish heading their way, with hearts and kisses.

Once I finished, RG said, "Jason's uncle told me Mary asked for your help with Jasmine. Are you a friend of the family?"

"No, I stumbled into the situation," I said.

"Mary's a fine person," RG said. "Anybody in her good graces is an ace in my book. Make sure to tell her I said hello."

"I will, though I'm not sure how often I'll see her," I said. "There's the bookstore. Thank you for making multiple stops."

While RG idled next to the curb, I hurried inside to buy a copy of *The Hawaiian Archipelago*, a storytelling-style collection of letters written in 1873 by Isabella Bird, an explorer I'd learned about during my crime-solving week in November. In my rush to leave Maine, I'd forgotten to toss my dog-eared copy of the book into my luggage.

Flipping through the pages, I found a passage describing her journey from New Zealand to Hawaii on a dilapidated steamer.

"In this deck-house," Isabella wrote when a hurricane struck the vessel two days out of Auckland, "the strainings, sunderings, and groanings were hardly audible, or rather were overpowered by a sound which, in thirteen months' experience of the sea in all weathers, I have never heard, and hope never to hear again, unless in a staunch ship, one loud, awful, undying shriek, mingled with a prolonged relentless hiss." Of the peril, Isabella wrote, "we understood by intuition that if our crazy engines failed at any moment to keep the ship's head to the sea, her destruction would not occupy half-an-hour. It was all palpable. There was nothing which the most experienced seaman could explain to the merest novice."

For three months, I'd dreamed of having the book in hand to compare Isabella's descriptions against present-day Hawaii. I preferred not to experience a hurricane or the earthquakes that shook the islands in the 1800s, but after immersing myself in my biological father's writing for a year, it felt good to lean on a woman's voice and courage.

When I returned, RG was outside his car.

"My God, I've never heard the likes of it," he was saying to a caller on his phone, pacing with a hand clamped to his brow. "*How* many dead? That's nuts. I'm with you. Let's pitch in all we can."

I hesitated. "Is the volcano blowing up?"

"No, that was Jason's uncle," RG said. "He got curious and read about your recent history online. He called me right away."

I sighed. "If you're worried about giving me a ride—"

"Are you kidding?" RG said. "We're thrilled that the Jasmine situation is in the hands of a seasoned professional."

"That's not entirely true," I said. "I'm not a psychologist."

"You're a photographer, we got the whole scoop," RG said. "Including your arrangement at Barry's trashed rental house. Kona is a couple of hours away on the other side of the island, but you've stumbled into an enclave of folks who've known each other for years."

Suddenly, I decided to tap into RG's deep knowledge.

"In that case, can you take a look at a video?" I asked. "I need help identifying some guys I encountered earlier."

"I'd be excited to join the action," RG said.

With my phone in hand, RG shook his head as he watched the events unfold, especially when the thug growled, "Tell the old man we're not afraid of his threats. A deal is a deal. Make sure he gets it."

"I think he mistook me for Katrina," I said.

"I'm afraid you're right," RG said. "Even all these years later, Reginald feels fallout from the wrongful conviction. Katrina is his greatest joy, so I can picture wrong-minded people with ulterior motives using her to pressure him. That's the criminal way. Twisted, made-up rules."

"It would help to know their names," I said.

"At the moment, I can't recall specifics," RG said. "But this comes on the heels of Jasmine poking her nose into Reginald's past. That's why she's in Hilo. She even upset Katrina with her meddling."

"Maybe I should try talking to Jasmine again," I said.

"Give me five minutes," RG said, calling Jason's uncle for a strategy session that ended with a smile as he pressed the hold button. "You tapped into Jasmine's sensible side after all. She's agreed to meet you at the Kilauea Iki lava lake, which you mentioned wanting to visit. It's a great spot, remote and mystical. What do you think?"

"If Jasmine is willing, it's a good sign," I said.

In short order, RG finalized my change of focus and took charge of my overnight accommodations at a lodge in Volcano Village.

"It's a rustic place," RG said, ushering me into the front seat as a show of friendship. "Started out as a school camp years ago. My wife and I spent a night of terror in a downstairs room, thinking a poltergeist was making itself known above us. A staccato sound, like a drum roll from the beyond. All of a sudden, we heard someone descending the stairs. We crept to the window, and a *nun* stepped out of the lodge."

Smiling, I said, "You're making this up."

"It's the absolute truth," RG said, heading southwest toward Kilauea. "Come to find out, every room has a ribbed foot roller. It's a miracle cure after a long hike. I'll never forget the sound of that thing rattling and clattering back and forth on the floor above."

"If necessary, I can use earplugs," I said.

Waving off my resolve, RG called the lodge and booked one of the cabins located in the rainforest behind the main building.

"You're going to want to give Sonny the royal treatment," RG told the front desk. "Mum's the word, but she's a bit of a celebrity."

"Please don't tell them why," I whispered.

"It sounds like they already know," RG whispered back.

From struggling and feeling my way along, I'd catapulted onto the fast track, so I decided to let go of the minor issues.

"Hang on, your landlord is checking in," RG said, snugging earbuds into place, then answering his phone. "What's the trouble, Barry? Well, our first stops were about replacing the torn cushions and palm panels, so I'm not sure why you're upset about Sonny being in Hilo. According to rumor, she saved you ten grand in repair bills for the hot tub alone. Yes, I will pass along your effusive thanks. Catch you later."

"Did I overhear some mention of Moritz?" I asked.

"Yup, it's Moritz who painted your visit in a wrong light," RG said. "I bet it's out of concern that you'll outshine his efforts. I expect you might not know that Barry's friend, Gavin, was married to Moritz's mother for a stretch of time. As often happens, financial upheaval led to a divorce, which caused further difficulties. Moritz's mom had a bad turn with pills," RG quietly confided. "An overdose situation. She died."

"Was Moritz close to his mother?" I asked.

"I'm sure they shared good moments over time," RG said diplomatically. "The blame game lasted for a while, with Moritz and Gavin arguing over who dropped the ball to the point of ruin, but people see Moritz's work in Barry's house as a sign of progress in his character. He's self-involved and a bit of a chauvinist, but hopefully, you can extend the same patience to him as you're doing with Jasmine."

"I'll keep it in mind," I said.

"Chew on the following as well," RG said pensively. "Before his health took a sad downturn, Reginald was known for shellacking people at poker games. The way the world works, I bet it's not just cash that exchanged hands when people won or lost. It's coming to mind from hearing the thug growling that last part, 'A deal is a deal.'"

"RG, your tip is tripling by the minute," I said.

"Nonsense, this is the most fun I've had in years," he said. "You can return the favor by revealing your secret to solving crimes."

"Given how things are panning out," I said, casting silent barbs at Agent Telford. "It's possible you're in the thick of it."

* * *

In Kilauea Volcano National Park, the Kilauea Iki lava lake was a steep-sided remnant of a past eruption, accessible from several points along its three-mile circumference. Although its name added a wry touch in keeping with my recent history, I ruled out the Devastation Trail in favor of the Kilauea Iki Overlook access point. With smoke rising from the active summit a half-mile away, I enjoyed the serenity of the zigzag path that descended through a forest of huge tree ferns, offering a glimpse of a primordial time on planet Earth. From previous visits, I knew that if I listened carefully, I would hear the call of a reclusive o'mau thrush and might see a pheasant slipping through the undergrowth.

Above me, the trills of nectar-seeking ʻapapane birds floated in the air as they dipped their curved bills into the crimson blossoms of ʻōhiʻa trees. Underfoot, the soft ground silenced my footsteps, except when I looked up instead of keeping an eye out for roots. Heading steadily downward, I passed misty, dripping vegetation along the next stretch of the zigzagging trail, where the voices of other hikers echoed toward me.

Past the belt of tree ferns at the bottom of the trail, I started crossing the lava lake formed by an eruption in 1959. Guided by scattered cairns across the wide moonscape, I marveled at how the cooled lava still showed the swirling patterns of its liquid state, with cracks and vents that told the story of the lake's violent origins. At 2,140 degrees Fahrenheit, the churning, thudding display had shot upward to a height of 1,900 feet, just beyond the parking lot where RG had dropped me off. Separated by decades from its deafening beginning, the crater was eerily quiet except for the soft crunch of my sneakers on the black volcanic sand.

Seeing Jasmine hiking toward me from the far side of the crater, I crossed to a ledge marking the halfway point, sat on a flat spot, and peeled off my sweatshirt as the sun came out. Flipping through *The Hawaiian Archipelago*, I found the passage in which Isabella Bird described her grueling 30-mile horseback ride from Hilo to Kilauea's summit. Amid a hard rain, "dead from fatigue," Isabella was startled to see a glaring red light up ahead in the night sky. "A sound as of the sea broke on our ears," she added, "rising and falling as if breaking on the shore." In lodgings near the fiery caldera, Isabella spent a bitterly cold night watching the turbulent light play across the sky, "accompanied by a dull throbbing sound."

"Did you clean off your boots?" Jasmine asked without preamble as she arrived. "A fungus is threatening the ʻōhiʻa trees."

"Yes, I cleaned my boots," I assured her.

As I started to tuck the book into my bag, Jasmine asked about the title, as if eager to have a neutral topic to talk about as she sat nearby on the ledge with her sunglasses shielding her eyes.

For starters, I thought she might appreciate Isabella's decision to toss propriety to the wind and ride astride like a man.

"Not that her borrowed Mexican saddle was a breeze," I said. "When her group took off at a gallop and her feet were jerked out of the stirrups,

Isabella says, 'every corner was a new terror, for at each I was nearly pitched off on one side, and when at last Upa stopped, and my beast stopped without consulting my wishes, only a desperate grasp of mane and tethering rope saved me from going over his head.'"

"Are you sure it's not a fake story?" Jasmine asked.

"Isabella Bird was a real person," I said. "Her unflinching zest is a good fit at this point in my life. By the way, it wasn't until after we met that I noticed your label on the collar of Katrina's jacket. Dance styles are a part of the design. Did you create it for Katrina?"

"For her birthday," Jasmine said. "I could cover this crater with fabric. It's the one area where I slip into addictive habits."

"With photos, I'm a slave to test printing," I said.

"That makes sense," Jasmine said. "Every surface reacts to ink with different intensities. Paper, canvas, linen, cotton."

In a shirt patterned after rainforest ferns, Jasmine used her sunglasses to keep stray wisps of her black, chin-length hair and pink highlights at bay. With a cell phone outline visible in the front pocket of her jeans, she stood in stark contrast to the ancient, dramatic landscape of neutral grays. I sensed that she'd come to bargain rather than confess, but as a group of tourists crunched past us, Jasmine joined me in shaking her head as a child picked up a lava stone and hurled it into the distance.

"I guess it's easy to mistake this landscape as dead," she said.

"I feel the opposite," I said. "It's primordial and timeless."

"So far so good," Jasmine said. "Let's hear your mentor speech."

"Let's see, in random order," I said, "I've been trapped in an 1800s tomb, punched in the face, held at gunpoint …" I counted on my fingers. "Only four times? It felt like more. I've been tased, gassed, drugged, kidnapped, and thrown into the trunk of a car. Two times each. I've been catapulted into a ditch after a car chase, duped into believing in true love, and told that I'm a reckless idiot by my best friend."

Jasmine hesitated. "End of speech?"

"There's more, but I don't want to brag," I said.

"You're the gentle follow-up to Harve's heavy-handed effort to 'instill the right perspective,'" Jasmine said with air quotes. "I love my parents.

They've worked hard to ensure a solid future for me. I want to go to college. My delay in heading home is about helping a friend who might be in trouble. That's supposed to be admirable."

"It is admirable," I said. "Without a doubt."

Fiddling with the cap of her water bottle, Jasmine looked conflicted and mistrustful, and then she heaved a sigh.

"Katrina, Jason, and I met at Ellika Arts Academy," she said. "They'd graduated, and I was a freshman, so I was thrilled that they loved my fabric designs. We worked together on their dance costumes and became best friends. It felt like having two older siblings."

"I can tell Jason cares about you," I said.

"That's good to hear," Jasmine said. "He was leery of Katrina taking the job at the arts academy, but I encouraged her. She's got a business-oriented mind to balance out her passion for dance. They discussed saving enough money to start their own dance studio. Petrel can be controlling," Jasmine added. "Very supportive in some ways, but Katrina and Jason wanted to move on sooner rather than later."

"That's natural," I said. "A fact of life."

"Except, life is freaking expensive," Jasmine said. "If you saw the before pictures of the Petrel Martineau Dance studio, you would appreciate the transformation. Petrel had to overhaul a bargain store because building from the ground up was an impossible reach."

"Does Katrina find her new job satisfying?" I asked.

"It's a great salary with benefits, but it involves a lot of travel," Jasmine said. "She's a magnet for men. Out of caution, we agreed on a tornado text symbol to send each other if trouble arose. Months went by, then she sent a tornado text at midnight. A flaw in the system was that I didn't know the details of her travel plans in advance. I sent messages to find out where she was and how I could help, and got silence."

I said, "Waiting had to be agonizing."

"I pictured her struggling to get away from someone," Jasmine said. "I hesitated to call Jason because … you never know."

"Uh-oh," I said. "Had you ever seen them fighting?"

"No, it's always been the opposite," Jasmine assured me. "But you hear about calm people snapping. Jason's worst fear was that Katrina would fall for a wealthy arts patron with dazzling good looks. He's oblivious to the flip side, namely how women lust after him."

"If so, that's a sweet quality," I said.

"Finally, Katrina responded to my texts," Jasmine said. "The tornado symbol was about a waitress named Sally. Young and pretty, sought after by lots of men in the area. She fell overboard."

I hesitated. "Like, from a ship?"

"Not to question your sharpness," Jasmine said, wryly nodding toward the sweatshirt I'd set aside. "But you've been wearing an article of clothing with a logo that's significant to this part of my story."

"It's Mary's sweatshirt," I said.

"I know, it's got familiar paint speckles," Jasmine said. "For future reference, it's the logo for the *Kukuna Mahina*, a small cruise ship that offers trips around the island chain. Most of the locals you've met own shares in the vessel. I'm told it was refurbished after previous ownership. A pricey upgrade, but it can be scrapped if the venture folds."

"I'm grateful to be informed," I said.

"Back to the night things went sideways," Jasmine said. "Technically, Katrina used the tornado text in context with a woman in distress, but it was meant to alert me to *her* imminent peril."

"I've learned the hard way that texts can add to the chaos during fast-moving events," I said. "Hopefully, Sally was rescued."

"No, it happened at night, so her absence went unnoticed for a while," Jasmine said. "There's footage of Sally acting high. Katrina brushed off my offers to meet for a hug, saying she'd caught a cold. I was busy with fabric projects. If she was fine, I was happy to focus on my work."

"All that makes sense," I said.

"Katrina's claims of feeling sick went on for weeks, and started feeling off," Jasmine said, "What kind of flu makes a person change her hairstyle and tighten down? Her other excuse was about money being a problem, so I wondered if a debt had hit the fan, maybe from her grandfather's business deals. His history of being wrongly imprisoned skewed his thinking when a couple of ex-convicts showed up with their hands out."

I hesitated. "Have you brushed paths with them?"

"Harve will have told you about the ill-fated Maui event," Jasmine said. "Citing their knowledge of how criminals operate, the ex-convicts set up shop as a two-man security detail. Bear in mind, the Maui event preceded Sally's death on the *Kukuna Mahina*."

"I'm with you so far," I said.

"Me and a few friends flew to Maui to bus tables and earn some extra cash," Jasmine said. "Long story short, a couple of drug dealers sliced each other to pieces. I was subjected to hours of repeating that I'm not involved with drugs, nor did I witness the conflict."

"Did the security guys get grilled?" I asked.

"Of course, but as you can imagine, they were desperate to pass the buck," Jasmine said. "I pointed out that while it's noble to give ex-convicts a chance, perhaps the organizers got it wrong."

"Mary has the sense that you were traumatized from being bullied," I said carefully. "It sounds like you held your ground."

"It *was* traumatizing," Jasmine said. "But it's in my nature to emerge from injustice with an attitude. In the end, the incident was cut-and-dried, caught on security cameras. When rebuked for their lax methods, the ex-cons promised to do better. In parting, I *might* have given the impression that I would be watching them closely."

"Yeah, why not make it worse?" I said dryly.

"The worst part came after Sally's death," Jasmine said, wincing as she recalled the memory. "I confronted Reginald, having heard the ex-cons filled security slots on the *Kukuna Mahina* during special events. I belatedly learned that they were not on board that night."

With Jasmine glancing at the time, I showed her my video from the gas station in hopes of establishing the men's identities.

"I *knew* they were capable of this kind of threatening, dirtbag behavior," Jasmine said, vibrating with excitement to have her dim sense of them verified. "They thought you were Katrina."

"It seemed so," I said. "What are their names?"

"Good luck figuring it out," Jasmine said. "To market their services, they used the line 'put a Korker in it.' They claim to be brothers with that last name, but I think it's a fake identity to avoid the stigma of their past.

It worked on the police detective. In his eyes, a nineteen-year-old with pink highlights was more suspicious than ex-convicts."

Nodding, I said, "You've had months to reflect on the circumstances. Are there any further details you can share?"

"You're giving me goosebumps," Jasmine said, rubbing her arms with a torn look. "Chip asked me the same question."

Suddenly, my arms were covered in goosebumps as well.

"Did he convey the nature of his inquiry?" I asked.

"I've been spelling it out for half an hour," Jasmine said, looking at me like I was dense. "Katrina sent a tornado text, then switched personalities overnight. Chip was upending the world to get answers. Now he's gone." Abruptly, Jasmine stood. "It's a long walk to my car, and I'm due back at the shop. How long will you be in Volcano Village?"

"Overnight," I said. "Longer if you need to talk more."

"With Katrina shutting me out, I'm left to worry and spin my wheels, so maybe it's best to let it go," Jasmine said, pausing before turning away. "But thank you for caring. I can tell you mean it."

"Stay safe," I said. "That's all the thanks I need."

As Jasmine walked away with her hands in her pockets, I knew that pressing her for further details might derail my fragile progress.

With a sigh, I put on my sunglasses and headed across the moonscape with a renewed sense of purpose. For starters, I needed to find unbiased sources who could shed light on Katrina's mindset, since even my closest friends didn't know the full extent of my secret turmoil.

* * *

Since my cabin still needed cleaning, RG suggested a quick drive down the Chain of Craters Road before taking me to the lodge. Past a series of turnouts where the destruction from past eruptions showed a variety of lava types, from heaps of brittle, cakelike spatter to sinuous coils and hardened, car-sized bubbles, RG stepped out to join me in the gusting wind at an overlook with a breathtaking view of the blue Pacific, fronted by a half-mile of coiled, lustrous dark gray pahoehoe lava.

"Listen to this letter dated January 31, 1873," I said, reading a passage from Isabella Bird's *The Hawaiian Archipelago*. "The pahoehoe 'lies in hummocks, in coils, in rippled waves, in rivers, in huge convolutions, in pools smooth and still, and in caverns which are really bubbles … a very frequent aspect of pahoehoe is the likeness on a magnificent scale of a thick coat of cream drawn in wrinkling folds to the side of a milk-pan.'" Pointing, I added, "It's right here in front of us."

"Super, but listen." Striving to look nonchalant, RG nudged me and whispered, "Last week, I saw that same guy at a diner in Hilo with a brief-case overflowing with official FBI dossiers."

Looking past him, I groaned when I saw Agent Ted Telford checking his phone next to a sedan twenty feet away.

"I can neither confirm nor deny the man's identity," I said.

With a knowing nod, RG said, "Got it."

Congratulating myself for wearing Mary's *Kukuna Mahina* sweatshirt, I crossed to Agent Telford, and invited him to speak first.

"For starters," Ted said. "Thank you for meeting Jasmine in a moonscape with zero cover for anyone to eavesdrop. Hopefully, you smoothed things over after the rocky encounter at the bike shop?"

Maintaining my poker face, I zipped up the sweatshirt to reveal the ship logo that symbolized the many elements Ted hadn't mentioned. For further emphasis, I added an adhesive note on which I'd written "Sonny Littlefield, Victim Advocate" within a badge shape.

"You have excellent penmanship," Ted said. "Feminine, yet impactful, with a matching pointed stare. My main interest in stopping by is to make sure you're not experiencing buyer's remorse."

As if to further convince me, Ted tucked his sunglasses into his pocket. Maybe his sincerity could be trusted, or maybe not.

"A peacock is disturbing the peace in Kona," I said. "Pecking on the roof at night. Whose department handles that?"

"Typically, birds rest at night," Ted said, studying me with a frown. "But I imagine they can be motivated by a treat. Peanuts? Grapes? Corn? You're alerting on corn. Popped or whole?"

"It was kernels," I said. "Kind of …"

"Wet, like from a can?" Ted asked.

I paused, recalling the need to change out of my pajamas because of the squishy corn, as if it had been freshly poured.

"Your dance class took you away from the house for a few hours," Ted said. "It's known that Moritz and Raja aren't keen on your help with the project. What's your take on their mindset?"

"Why do you want to know?" I asked.

"It's normal to seek clarity in the wake of a surprise," Ted said. "However low-level, tossing corn onto the roof indicates aggression."

"I made it up," I said. "For laughs and fun."

"I'm not trying to trap anyone without reason," Ted said. "If they step up their harassment, let me know. Got it?"

I sighed. "If you're done being annoying …?"

"Yeah, I think I've hit all the highlights along those lines," Ted said wryly. "Thank you for the sharp tone, a taste of life at home."

Once Ted climbed into his sedan and swung onto the road, I rejoined RG, ready to call it a somewhat successful day.

"With concerning elements piling up," I said. "It's best not to broadcast my inquiries. Mum's the word, okay?"

"I'm thrilled to be your covert eyes and ears," RG said, watching Ted's car speed away. "Does he know this is a dead-end road?"

I shook my head. "Apparently not."

9

Whether from the misty rainforest air or the lodge's floral shampoo, my waves and curls tumbled into an agreeable frame for my face rather than rebelling against an unfamiliar blow-dryer. Wrapped in a towel, I stepped into the cozy living space of Cabin #3. Wooden shutters on the windows complemented the soft yellow walls, and a quilted bedspread and matching chairs added a sumptuous tropical touch to the interior.

Beyond the windows, mist drifted through the rainforest, and a small porch overlooked a garden of lilies, orchids, and ferns. Even amid tropical lushness on a Pacific island, with a churning volcanic caldera open to the sky within ten minutes' drive, the scent of wood smoke coming from the restaurant's stone fireplace stirred thoughts of home. Instead of Hawaiian mesquite, smoke from oak and maple logs would be drifting from the stone chimney of my snow-covered farmhouse five thousand miles away.

I closed my eyes and pictured Luke, my King Shepherd, sleeping on his green plaid pillow in the warm glow of the wood stove, with my house sitter, Brumby, on the couch, surrounded by crumpled soda cans and snack bags. If I had my time zones right, it would be two o'clock in the morning at my hilltop farm, and with me not there, a silent night.

Aiming for a polished look as I prepared to eat among fellow travelers, I slipped into my peach clamdigger pants, a knit shirt, and a sheer wrap from Mary's bag. Holding it out to admire the fabric, I noticed Jasmine's name printed along the edge amid a design of trailing vines and fuchsia flowers that promised to complement bare skin.

"Jasmine, this is where your energy belongs," I murmured.

Finally, Mary called at our scheduled time.

With my phone in hand during our exchange of news, I tried the foot roller RG had mentioned. Sure enough, the ribbed wood had a relaxing effect on my soles and made a frightful din against the floor.

"Jasmine still misses Katrina," Mary said. "But talking with you seems to have helped put her in a positive frame of mind."

"Jasmine explained the moon logo on the sweatshirt that I borrowed," I said. "The *Kukuna Mahina* is a small cruise ship?"

"It's one of Reginald's dream projects," Mary said. "Spared from the scrap heap after the old girl was retired from regular service. If his annual birthday celebration comes to pass, it'll amount to a three-day excursion around the islands. I'd like to go, but I'm torn."

"Mary, do you have a sense of Agent Telford's inquiries?" I asked. "I heard his briefcase is overflowing with case files."

"I'm getting goosebumps from Ted's prediction that you would ask me that question," Mary said. "I have been instructed to urge a tight focus on counseling Jasmine. All other matters, including Chip's death, are in the discovery phase and are strictly need-to-know."

"Are you done quoting him?" I asked.

"And ready to explain why I'm debating the annual birthday cruise," Mary said. "Thanks to Reginald's desire to give guys a second chance, two ex-convicts set up shop as a freelance security duo."

"Jasmine mentioned the name Korker," I said.

"They're either brothers with the same name, or they set themselves up for business that way," Mary said. "Lots of ex-convicts turn their lives around, but it didn't look good when drug dealers duked it out under their noses at an event in Maui. They quit to avoid the stigma of being fired. So began a spiral that ended with a waitress named Sally falling overboard during a high-roller island cruise event to benefit the Ellika Arts Academy. It's hard to fill security slots at the last minute."

"I'm afraid the Korkers are reverting to the habits that landed them in prison," I said. "If you see them, head the other way."

"Duly noted," Mary said. "As sensible people, you and I would have postponed the cruise until proper staff were hired, but attendees had been signed up for months, with flights arranged. It's human nature to assume the best. Harve jumped in to fill the void, despite misgivings. He left police work because of its terrible aspects, only to end up hitting the panic siren when reports of a missing passenger reached his ears. It haunts Harve to this day. There's no hope in the dark of night on the open Pacific. With drugs in her system, I think Sally went down very fast."

"It's terrifying to contemplate," I said. "It sounds like you don't trust the ship's shareholders to have learned their lesson."

"Reginald is the one who made it a world-class operation," Mary said. "He instituted the standard of excellence that worked for years, but you've met him in recent days. He's not his old sharp self."

"By most accounts, Katrina isn't herself lately, either," I said. "But she's bound to be shaken up after the ill-fated cruise."

"Exactly," Mary said softly. "Now that you've met Jasmine, I can share my private view that Katrina might have emerged from the shock with the old adage in mind. Life is too short for nonsense."

"Sally's family must be devastated," I said.

"Sadly, I believe she was alone in life," Mary said. "A beautiful girl with a troubled past. Fate can be very unkind."

"Now it's me having goosebumps," I said. "So much for my healing journey. I'm up to my eyebrows in complexities."

"Now, honey," Mary said. "You're an example of how hard knocks can build strength and character. Harve told me how kind you were to your ex, despite how broken you felt after his cheating episodes. I've always had the same mindset. Instead of tearing your ex down with pointless anger, think of it as releasing him back into the wild."

"Mary," I said. "That's the perfect way to see it."

* * *

It was impossible not to love the rustic charm of the lodge, with a two-story hotel flanked by tropical gardens. The tiny cabin I rented felt even more private, surrounded by ʻōhiʻa trees that attracted ʻapapane birds.

Every morning at dawn, year after year, they gathered outside the windows to sip nectar from the crimson flowers sparkling with dew. Few birds I'd ever seen matched their cheerful trilling as they moved from branch to branch, endlessly engaging with each other.

The restaurant served standard fare topped with pineapple and mango slices. The staff was friendly, occasionally stopping to chat with longtime lodge guests. Seated at a table for two near the grand stone fireplace that released a subtle hint of delicious mesquite smoke into the cozy room of Hawaiian artwork and decor, I ordered teriyaki chicken with extra sweet rolls, rice, and pineapple slices, starving after my long day.

With the fire softly crackling less than fifteen feet away, I felt warm enough to untie Mary's sheer tropical design wrap. Perched at 3,750 feet above sea level, the tiny town of Volcano, Hawaii, had a temperature range from the 50s to the 60s, similar to springtime weather in Maine. If I was lucky, my homecoming would align with a mild spell that would ease me back into the rigors of winter in the Northeast. The latest feed from my trail camera was consistently wince-worthy: frame after frame of chaotic streaks of snow and sleet swirling in all directions.

Sipping white wine in between bites of sweetly accented chicken and red peppers, I was encouraged to see that no one at the other tables was glued to their phones. Visits to the volcano always put me in a state of wonder and reflection. It seemed that way for everyone.

As a whisper of fresh air and activity signaled someone behind me, I braced for a tourist's daypack or a child to bump into me, but the person— most likely the waiter—caught hold of my sheer wrap as it slid toward the floor and gently tucked it around my shoulders.

I turned to smile in thanks, but the waiter had either vanished or was never there to begin with. The space felt oddly empty.

"May I join you?" a man asked.

Turning to face forward with a confused frown, I froze in shock to see Antoine Chamaillard, elite Canadian cop and possible ex-spy, taking the liberty of sitting across from me at the table in a white tropical-weight shirt and tan cargo pants that were a departure from the threadbare jeans and dark shirts that he'd worn in Maine. Looking relaxed, in no hurry to explain himself, Antoine rested his elbows on the table in a way that high-lighted his muscles as he searched my face for a reaction. Instead of a ponytail, his hair was cropped into a mostly tame pile of sun-streaked waves on top, with trimmed sides. I wasn't aware that I was smiling until his lips curved into a matching indication of warmth.

"How are you, Berrichon?" Antoine said softly.

"You can imagine I'm stunned," I said, then I fell into confusion. "Dan enlisted your help in 'talking sense' into me? Is that it?"

"I haven't spoken with Dan in months," Antoine said, looking puzzled as he added, "I called you before I left, then during a layover, and when I landed. You haven't been checking your messages?"

"No," I said. "I've favored being unplugged."

"Sue Black reached out," Antoine said. "Thinking I might not know aspects of what went on, and … she was right."

Flushed and mortified, I said, "My friends mean well, but they don't always have an accurate sense of my mindset."

As the waiter arrived, Antoine ordered an iced tea and discussed dessert options, giving me a chance to stare at him without restraint. Even if Sue Black had told him I was in Hawaii, tracking me to a specific table on the chain of islands seemed a mystifying feat. Then, as awareness blazed through my mind, I pulled the flip phone out of my bag, placed it on the table, and raised my eyebrows to ask if I was right.

"It hasn't been charged in months, so the signal was thready," Antoine said. "I tried calling that number a few times, then I focused on keeping the battery alive as long as possible. I'm sorry this moment is months overdue. I think we'll find that signals were crossed."

I frowned. "What signals?"

"Here we are," the waiter said, gliding in to deliver Antoine's iced tea and a slice of pie, then asking me, "You're in Cabin #3?"

"Yes," I said. "Please put our food on my tab."

Before walking away, the waiter paused to convey that the weather was expected to be clear, Kilauea's fiery summit was a must-see spectacle, and the restaurant appreciated advance dinner reservations.

Antoine listened attentively, as if giving me a moment to calm my racing heart. In November, my moral code had helped dampen the sparks that ignited whenever he flirted, or simply stood there looking thoughtful and intriguing in the sunlight. While Jason had the "pretty boy" looks that inspired women to compete for his attention, Antoine's face was quietly handsome and captivating, a mix of chiseled features and softness, as if Nature intended him to be a poet instead of a cop.

"Shall I remove this?" the waiter asked about my neglected plate.

I focused on him. "No, I'm not finished."

The waiter could take that however he wanted. Not finished with my meal. Not finished aching over Antoine's thoughtless departure after his official tasks were done. I took a quick, unladylike gulp of wine, then set the glass down with a loud clank against my plate.

"Sonny, help me know where to start," Antoine said. "Where we left off, if that's helpful. I'm sure you have questions."

"Yes, I've got questions," I said. "Forgive me for starting at the end. The other night, after a very long day, I had a dream about a guy who talked about using his Glock to scrape ice from his car. Seeing that he'd ruined the weapon, he had an epiphany. At one point or another, we all end up being the Glock. Used in a way that's wrong."

"Sonny, I'm desperately sorry for the confusion," Antoine said, looking pained as I jerked my hand away. "If we can talk in private—"

"*Now* you want to talk?" I said, furious to see my sharp tone drawing gazes across the room. "Excuse me for a moment."

"Sonny, please hang on—"

Dimly aware of Antoine catching my tipped chair, I hurried past the families who were there to hug, share inside jokes, and all other joyful activities of a normal life. Not for the first time, my sudden entrance into a lady's room caused a woman at the sink to flinch, leaving a streak of pink lipstick across her face. With a rush of apologies, I grabbed paper towels from the dispenser and wetted them, one at a time, to help her blot away the mark until her lipstick was neat and flawless.

With a tight smile, I slipped into the stall and fanned my face, for all the good it did, since my reflection in the mirror told me I looked as if I'd been hung by the heels for a couple of hours. A minute later, I found the woman lingering at the sink with an air of wanting to help.

"Forgive me for prying," she said, "but I saw your shock when that guy joined you at the table. I'm sensing a cheating episode?"

"Our history is complicated," I said. "I helped him and he helped me, then all of a sudden … it's hard to explain."

"I've landed one of the good ones," she said, wiggling her fingers so I could admire her ring. "After *forever*. Miracles can happen."

"Of course," I said. "Congratulations."

"Aloha," she said.

"Yes, Mele Kalikimaka." With a wince, I added, "Sorry, that's Merry Christmas in Hawaiian. It's well past the holidays."

"Honey, if there's this much turmoil in the early stages, with signs of the love only flowing in one direction, end things now, even if it's painful," she said in parting. "On behalf of your future self."

"Thank you," I said. "You're very kind."

Peering out to ensure Antoine was facing away, I slipped out the back door and headed to my cabin to change clothes. Wearing jeans, sneakers, and a sweater, I was ready to sprint across Kilauea's barren landscape and toss my belongings into a steam vent. That's what a desperate woman had to do when dealing with an elite cop who'd used a special phone to track her down. My plan of action was simple. Find shelter. Eat scraps if I could. Nap if I dared. Leave my fractured life behind.

Then sanity returned. With my pulse slowing, I practiced some yoga breathing and took the honeymooner's advice to heart. Whatever had fueled Antoine's resolve to meet face-to-face, probably out of concern that my breakup with Dan would disrupt the solid cases, I wasn't the one who needed to leave Volcano Village on short notice.

10

My anticipation of sparking a look of surprise by returning to the table in different clothing was short-lived once I saw the direction of Antoine's gaze. From the moment I'd lurched up and walked away, he'd been able to keep track of my reflection in the front window.

"You've arrived when I'm about to visit the Halema'uma'u caldera," I explained. "If you're not too tired, we can catch up there."

"Of course," Antoine said. "If that works for you."

As always, Antoine showed his gallant side by stepping forward to open doors and settle me into his car, looking handsome as he slipped into his seat. Over ninety days had passed since we'd explored Maine in search of clues in a similar dark sedan. It felt like ninety years ago.

"It's a relief to return this," I said, dropping his special flip phone into the cup holder. "It was destined for a recycling bin."

"Sonny, while we're paused here—"

"As you can imagine, recent events took a toll," I said. "It's part of my recovery to call the shots. Are you able to dial back?"

"Absolutely," Antoine said. "Lead on."

"Take a right at the exit, then another right a mile down the road," I said, filling the air with chatter during the drive to the Kilauea Volcano National Park. "My best friend's family invited me to join their trip to the Big Island during our high school days. Hawaii has always been a special place for me. It's been a hectic week. A hectic day. This morning, I rode a motorcycle to Hilo for a friend. It's a long story."

"You're licensed to operate a motorcycle?" Antoine asked.

"No, I figured it's a laid-back kind of island," I said. "Once I learned how to shift and keep the thing from tipping over, I raced cars and trucks along the coast. Talk about an adrenaline rush."

"I'm striving to learn more about your travels," Antoine said softly. "I know it's caught you off guard to see me in a different context from our time together in Maine. I'm that guy, but I'm not that guy. The more complex the case, the more I tend to …"

Antoine's voice faded as we emerged from a belt of trees and neared the Halemaʻumaʻu caldera, where the churning, thudding inferno of the Earth's core was close enough to the surface to be seen and heard, wreathed in crimson vapor and low-hanging clouds.

"Je suis rarement sans voix," he murmured.

"At last, you're dropping into French," I said, pointing to a parking space. "You've been sounding like an American."

"I've been refining my Maine accent," Antoine said.

As always, the breathtaking drama of the fiery caldera pushed all other thoughts from my mind. Smiling at Antoine's amazement as he beheld Kilauea's active summit for the first time, I let him rest his hand on my shoulder as we navigated the dark trail leading to the overlook, where dozens of people were silhouettes against the crimson light. Above them, vapor formed otherworldly shapes, drifting upward into the sky. Our sneakers crunched on the coarse black gravel that rimmed the outer crater, and the sharp air irritated my nasal passages, smelling of sulfur and molten rock. Leaning close to each other in the night, the onlookers pointed out fountains of fire dancing above the smoldering lava lake.

As Antoine and I stood side by side in silent awe, with cool air against our backs and the warmth of the fiery pit against our faces and chests, I embraced the notion of standing on newly formed land. The intense glow of the fire made the surrounding night seem even darker. Sudden pops, hisses, and explosive underground thuds vibrated through my bones, and sprays of molten lava shot into the shadows, cascading onto the ground in broad swaths and fan shapes, fiercely glowing and then quickly fading. It was like watching a painter at work, flicking her vivid palette to the left, and then to the right, ephemeral in form yet deeply imprinted on my mind. Beyond the fire fountains, a pool of expelled lava responded to the cool air by fracturing into ribbons of searing red light with black edges. Amid murmurs of awe among the onlookers, I indulged the fantasy that I'd joined Isabella Bird on horseback, riding across the trackless stretches of ancient lava flows. Earlier in the day, I'd memorized Isabella's description of her first grueling hike to Kilauea volcano's explosive summit.

"As we ascended," Isabella wrote using an inkwell and pen on January 31, 1873, "the flow became hotter under our feet, as well as more porous and glistening. It was so hot that a shower of rain hissed as it fell upon it. The crust became increasingly insecure, and necessitated our walking in single file … I fell through several times, and always into holes full of sulphureous steam, so malignantly acid that my strong dog-skin gloves were burned through as I raised myself onto my hands."

"You've got an air of secret knowledge," Antoine said.

As I opened my phone to my snapshot of the continuing passage from *The Hawaiian Archipelago*, Antoine leaned in close.

"Suddenly," Isabella wrote, "we stood on the brink of Hale-mau-mau, which was about 35 feet below us. I think we all screamed. I know we all wept, but we were speechless, for a new glory and terror had been added to the earth … there were groanings, rumblings, and detonations, rushings, hissings, and splashings, and the crashing sound of breakers on the coast, but it was the surging of fiery waves upon a fiery shore … and what we saw had no existence a month ago, and probably will be changed in every essential feature a month hence."

"Je suis étonné," Antoine said, recognizing Isabella Bird's name. "She was mentioned in the letter that you and I discovered."

"It's been nice to add a woman's perspective to my father's journal entries," I said. "With Hawaiian guides leading the way, Isabella rode astride like a man. She plunged into raging torrents and rode up nearly vertical cliffs on tracks no wider than her horse. She fought altitude sickness and camped on the icy summit of Mauna Loa. Imagine if her acquaintances had criticized her for being brave and different."

"Your point is duly noted," Antoine said. "And your arched eyebrow is demanding further notice. Isabella tangled with criminals?"

"In Colorado on a later trip," I said. "Mountain Jim. Thief. Drunk. Anger issues. He admired her pluck. They became friends."

"If you recall, I enabled your endeavors to the point where I feel I need to apologize," Antoine said. "If I pushed you too far—"

"You didn't push," I said. "Not in that regard."

With new arrivals behind us, jockeying for a better view of the crater, I led Antoine to a spot where we could talk privately.

"I see every one of us out there," I said, indicating the park. "All across the volcano, you'll find different stages of the cooling process. I'm creative and geared to thrive amid unknowns. Most of Dan's life reminds me of the cooled, structured lava—slow to accept change. If he'd been lucky, he could have stayed in that stabilized state his whole life, but his friend's death was like this eruption happening in front of us. That's what I saw in Dan when we first met. The pain of upheaval and loss. I got the wild idea that we had enough in common to make it work."

"I've seen the aftermath of a breakup or two," Antoine said, looking maddeningly handsome in the otherworldly light, and succeeding in holding my hand now that I received the gesture as a fleeting last touch. "A certain amount of dish-throwing is to be expected. You're using words like 'stabilized,' as if we're talking about engine parts."

"Technically, you witnessed our breakup," I said. "You blew up at the murderer so much that I had to hold you back. Dan blew up at me." Tears welled in my eyes as I waved away Antoine's anguished gaze and his urge to hug me. "Dan and I forged on through Thanksgiving, but then over the holidays, things fell apart during a trip to Florida."

"What happened, Sonny?" Antoine asked.

"I'm sensing that Sue shared her worries about that," I said. "I'm tired, and it's chilly. Let's head back to your car."

"Yes, of course," Antoine said.

I lagged behind as we navigated the dark path, railing at my hands for shaking as I secured a ride to the lodge through an app. I had ten minutes to find the right words to make our goodbye permanent.

Antoine studied me. "Is everything okay?"

"Let's pause here," I said near the parking area.

In the face of my calm tone and folded arms, Antoine listened attentively as I expressed heartfelt gratitude for his admirable qualities during our crime-solving week in November. His confidence in me was a rare instance where a man embraced aspects of my personality that others considered flaws. My curiosity. My thirst for justice. My ability to pivot and strategize. Antoine not only supported my need to find my father's killer but also crafted a targeted plan that let me achieve my goal without landing me in the grave. My friends worried it would cause nightmares for years to come. Instead, I walked away feeling victorious.

The aftermath was a different matter entirely.

"The statement stage was a shining moment," I said, unable to keep sarcasm at bay. "In response to the lead detective's blistering questions, I delivered answers like, 'Huh? No way! *What?* I don't have a clue!' Apparently, it's not normal for a woman to put faith in an undercover sting without knowing the details beforehand."

"Sonny," Antoine said, "In that sort of situation—"

"No need to explain," I said. "Any hint of prearranged answers would have upended the wins. Quite persistently, I was asked if our tight teamwork included having sex behind Dan's back. Tightness in *that* area was his forte, but nobody bothered to enlighten me."

"By the time I found out—" Antoine closed his eyes. "There's no excuse. I am deeply, sincerely sorry for each and every—"

"Water under the bridge," I said. "If you recall, my friends were away that week. When they got back, Dan told them I'd gone off the rails. I had two options: either reveal all the private, upsetting details about his poor judgment on the work front, which led to the threat in the first place, or stay silent. You can guess which way I went."

As an unfamiliar rideshare driver pulled up in a hatchback and flicked his lights, I signaled to him that I needed another minute.

"Dan's own life was a mess," I said. "He needed to fix something, so he endeavored to 'fix' me. None of that is your fault, but you left me to handle the aftermath alone. You went on your merry way, so allow me to do the same. Thank you for the tour of crimes. If I ever see a flip phone, I will smash it to bits so there's no chance of a surprise visit that ranges from baffling to wrong. That covers it. Goodbye."

The rideshare car's heater was on, letting me slide into warmth as I opened the door and settled into the back seat.

"Umm, is everything all right?" the driver asked.

"Yes, you can proceed," I said. "We're ready to roll."

Just then, Antoine arrived outside the driver's door and motioned with his right hand for the window to be opened.

"This happens all the time," the driver said. "Loved ones wanting to check my credentials to make sure I'm legit."

With a cheerful hello, he handed his information to Antoine, showing that his ID matched the photo sent to me through the app.

"Thank you for being candid," Antoine said.

"Anything else?" the driver asked.

"Can you please convey to your esteemed passenger that I did reach out to her in the days after we arrested her father's murderer?" Antoine said. "I left three voicemail messages."

"Hang on," the driver said. "If you're talking about murder, it needs to be sorted out. How about you show *your* credentials?"

"Certainly," Antoine said.

Awash in the glow of the interior lights, I leaned forward to glimpse Antoine's billfold-style ID, complete with a badge.

"Canadian Border Intelligence and Enforcement," the driver murmured. "That sounds like some high-level stuff."

"We call ourselves cabbies," Antoine said, tucking his ID back into his pocket. "It takes the edge off the elite cop implication."

The driver pointed at me. "Is she a fugitive?"

"No, she's a friend who is striving to heal from awful events," Antoine said. "I'm here to help. Whatever it takes."

"Canada is a long way off," the driver pointed out.

"Over five thousand miles," Antoine agreed.

The driver turned to look at me. "That's impressive."

"It might be if he *had* left messages," I said. "Perhaps his skill as an elite cop didn't include training on how to use a keypad."

"Allow me to demonstrate," Antoine said.

His phone glowed in the night as he launched a voice recording. First came an official-sounding statement with the date and time, along with the news that the call was possible in the wake of giving our statements to the Maine state police. His attorney added that they were documenting the call out of an abundance of caution. After a pause, Antoine's voice softened, and I imagined him leaning in close to his phone.

"Berrichon … Sonny," Antoine said. "I'm told you're having second thoughts about the sting. I need to hear it in your own words. You've handled flak in the past, but there's more than expected this time. You need to emerge from this moment on a strong note. That's my main concern, and I need to set the record straight on what you were told about Nicole. I want to reintroduce myself, I guess, free of my worries around keeping a tight lid on … a tight lid in all regards. Today or tomorrow, whenever you're ready, let's bring each other up to speed."

"That's a lot to unpack," the driver said, peering at me between the seats. "Does somebody besides you have your passcode?"

I hesitated, picturing Dan opening my phone when my hands were sticky from pizza dough and other trust-based moments.

"I'm sensing a maybe," the driver said. "It's got to do with a woman named Nicole. She's trouble and bad news?"

As the question hung in the air, I focused on Antoine's sorrowful gaze, asking for a chance to explain his intense version of the aftermath. In that moment, I remembered that Antoine had never described Nicole as his girlfriend. That story, from start to finish, had come from Dan—a quick way to stem my suspicions and keep his old-fashioned parents from hearing unseemly stories. Thinking about it, I wondered if Dan had gone further and blocked Antoine's number on my phone.

"I take it the ride is over?" the driver asked.

"Yes, my ex and I have parted for good," I said. "You're talking about *this* ride. That's over, too. I'll pay the full fare."

I finished the transaction with a five-star review and a tip that Antoine doubled with cash. As the hatchback drove away, Antoine led me to a spot where we wouldn't get run over by incoming cars. As he paused to collect his thoughts, I could see that he'd shaved in advance of seeing me, which would have involved getting pitched to-and-fro in a cramped airplane bathroom with other passengers banging on the door.

"When you told me Dan's claim that Nicole was my girlfriend, it came as a shock," Antoine said. "Be aware, it's possible he believed it based on whatever she'd told him to get what she wanted."

"I can picture that," I said.

"Cases were exploding in all directions, so instead of setting the record straight, I changed the subject," Antoine said. "Fast forward. My feelings for you intensified. I didn't want to put you in an emotional bind, so I held back. Mostly. Dan was bound to notice, but the main friction between us stemmed from my agency being authorized to take the lead in the case. If I'd known that Dan had gone so far as to block my number and delete my voicemails—" Antoine closed his eyes. "I am deeply, sincerely sorry for my role in a painful arc that extended for months."

"There's no need for you to apologize," I said. "I'm sure you've heard that the defense attorneys have been playing dirty tricks, but if they think they can inspire me to undermine Dan on the witness stand, they're wrong. I'm sorry you came all this way for nothing."

Antoine studied me sideways, with a puzzled frown.

"So, you didn't hear the part about my emotional bind," he said. "You don't recall that I lost control and kissed you, seeing it as landing in heaven in the wake of an explosion. On the last night that we saw each other, I clarified how I felt. I poured my heart out."

"I do recall all that," I said. "It wasn't until you left that I felt the depth of our bond. I regretted turning you down."

"What about now?" Antoine asked. "Your arms are tightly folded."

"I'm giving you a chance to come to your senses," I said. "The Canadian whatever agency sounds like a big deal."

"Berrichon," Antoine said softly. "Can I call you that?"

With a nod, not trusting fate enough to express how much I'd longed to hear his nickname for me, I watched in confusion as Antoine unbuttoned his shirt cuffs and rolled up his sleeves. When I saw the goosebumps on his forearms, he cupped my face in his hands.

"Even after three months," he said, "this is how my body reacts when I think of how brave and clear-eyed you were in the face of threats. I've never seen anyone step up so powerfully, much less a civilian woman. The second I understood the reality you were facing, six hundred miles per hour felt slow and tedious. I wanted to get out and push the jet with my bare hands. I wish you could see yourself through my eyes."

Choking and tearful, I let him pull me into a tight embrace, too over-whelmed to say or do anything except savor the instant comfort of being wrapped in Antoine's strong arms and warmth. Every time we touched, it felt like my cells were tiny tablets dissolving into fizz, blending with his living essence. I'd fought my feelings for Antoine during our week of fighting crime. I'd let misguided loyalty steer my choices.

We leaned away to see each other with the barriers tossed aside, this time in the flickering glow of an active volcano. Studying me in the night, Antoine brushed his fingers over my face and kissed me, a soft brush of lips, followed by a melting interlude befitting the fire fountains playing against the dramatic sky. Why did Antoine smell so delicious up close? Chemistry. Pheromones. Signals that ignited my brain.

With eye contact and a heat level that felt like an electric charge, we agreed that we needed to continue our update in private.

And *fast*.

* * *

At the lodge, we peeled away from the friendly staff who asked if we'd enjoyed the Halemaʻumaʻu overlook, and picked up a brisk pace on our way toward my cabin tucked into the forest, where the cheeping of frogs added a touch of wildness to the night air.

"Sonny, wait up!" a man called out behind us.

"Ignore it," I whispered.

"He seems very insistent," Antoine said.

With a groan, I stopped and waited for RG to puff toward us from the parking lot, where I'd seen him dropping off a family of four.

"Sonny," RG said. "Sorry, I was on the road from Hilo when you called for a ride. To make it up to you, I asked a friend on the staff to turn on the gas fireplace in your cabin so it's nice and toasty."

"You didn't need to make a fuss," I said. "Antoine is a friend who just arrived. He's bogged down with jet lag, so …"

"My rideshare friend shared the basics," RG said, shaking Antoine's hand. "I'm bummed to be swapped out of the action, but I get the need to call in reinforcements. We had fun with it, didn't we, Sonny? Intrigue and clandestine meetings. Any more run-ins with the thugs?"

"It's old news," I said. "All in the past."

"I guess this morning is in the past," RG said. "Well, your ace friend looks puzzled, so let's get his accommodations sorted out."

"Antoine feels it best to stay close at hand," I said. "To be extra careful, though complexities are *highly* doubtful."

"I'll keep my ear to the ground," RG said. "Let's stay in touch."

"You've been very kind," I said. "Thank you again."

After seeing him off, we fumbled with the key, and started kissing as soon as we crossed the threshold into the flickering glow of the gas stove, with Hawaiian music drifting from ceiling speakers.

As Antoine peeled away my sweater, I unbuttoned his shirt, all but climbing him in my heated-up state, and then I stepped on the foot roller with a startled yelp. Catching me mid-fall, Antoine swung us onto the couch for a partial landing, and then we slid off and tumbled to the floor. Unfazed, and not slowed down, we dissolved together in delicious heat, caught up in the dreamy interplay of our lips brushing, then melding with stirring warmth, then brushing again, all with dizzying speed.

With our legs entwined, we rolled into different positions, reaching for each other, and holding each other. As Antoine drifted onto his back, I pushed forward with soft moans, wanting to embrace him and wear him and drink in every sensation, from his intense warmth to the delicious scent of his neck and jaw, and then as my fingers brushed over a thin scar on his chest, I fixated on the spot, awash with goosebumps as I remembered seeing the scar in similar light, but not from a cozy fireplace. Amid a perilous time, a near-death moment, he'd had to shed his shirt in favor of his tactical gear, and shortly afterward, he'd nearly died.

Feeling Antoine's fingers touching my chin, I focused on him looking at me with absolute awareness of where I'd gone in time. With an assuring gaze and a soft kiss, he returned me to the present.

"I want to reverse time and be there for you," I said.

"There are a thousand ways we might have been knocked off course, Berrichon," Antoine said. "All that matters is now."

With a squeeze of his hand, he pulled me with him as he climbed to his feet, followed by a kiss that turned our journey across the room into a drifting, slowly revolving orbit. Near the bed, we shed his cargo pants, my shirt, my jeans, my bra, and finally, my black undies.

Soon his warm skin was pressed against mine, his shoulders and face defined by the firelight. I smoothed my hands over his chest, aware of his heartbeats, his muscles moving as he picked me up and delivered me to the bed, where the Hawaiian quilt and blankets had been turned down, exposing a king-sized expanse of sheets and pillows.

With his eyes closed, he brushed his lips over my face, savoring my softness, and then his lips moved to my ear, igniting ripples of pleasure across my skin, his hands roaming all over the place. I shivered, unable to recall a time when I'd felt so pliable and heated up with lust. His soft caress was asking things, saying things, stirring pleasure.

As he rolled onto his back, draping me across him and drawing my thighs down to his sides, I tipped forward, at one with him at last. We communicated through kisses and caresses, fast breathing and moans, claiming each other and liberating each other. With pleasure building, a fierce glow, I was aware of his hands holding me in place, ecstasy contained, with a soulful, loving gaze that conveyed his wish to remember every detail, every second of our first time, intensifying the rockets all the more. At last, he released me into a world of rippling pleasure.

As the room dissolved, I clutched his chest, undone from wavelets of ecstasy, and then I sank into a warm haze, wrapped in his arms and nearly senseless as he kissed me, as if savoring what I'd felt, and then he rolled me onto my back and slipped his arm under my knee, locked in and unleashed. Hawaiian music floated around us, enhancing the dreamlike atmosphere, and the fierce internal glow was rising again. With his moans in my ear, I succumbed to ecstasy slowly, in swirling degrees, aware of his helpless, flexed connection to the cosmos, then we lay there together with our pulses racing and our minds drifting in space.

"Hello," he murmured. "My name is Antoine."

"I'm Sonny," I said. "Mistress of Chaos."

Smiling, we settled side by side, admiring each other's nakedness for a dreamy stretch of time. In between his kisses, I ran my fingers through his hair, enjoying the feel of his unruly curls and waves as my own hair spilled over the pillows in wild disorder.

"There's a *slight* wrinkle," I said. "In that I publicly ruled out dating another police officer, ever, ever, e-v-e-r."

"Thank God I'm a cabbie," Antoine said.

"About the thugs RG mentioned …"

"The Sonny effect has crossed the Pacific?" Antoine asked.

"A minor matter mostly resolved," I said. "Now that I know about your role, I'm worried that you left amid a pressing case."

"I'm owed a thousand days of PTO," Antoine said, drifting his fingers over my curves and contours. "Say hello to the new me."

"I hardly know the old you," I said.

In a captivating display of muscles in motion, Antoine reached into the pocket of his pants on the floor, pulled out a pink-and-green crystal about three inches wide, and placed it in my palm.

"This is my father's watermelon tourmaline," I said.

"It symbolizes the bond we forged in a matter of days," Antoine said. "I wouldn't have survived without you, and you wouldn't have survived without me. We resisted temptation of a certain kind, but we were deeply connected, Sonny. In ways that truly matter."

For an hour or more, we revisited our fast-paced arc of solving crimes, sharing how we'd handled the harsh realities and smiling at how we'd exasperated each other. With my face resting on Antoine's chest, I savored the way the rumble of his voice lent depth and clarity to his assurance that we'd secured wins that would withstand the rigors of the legal system. Amid the flickering light, with our legs entwined, caressing each other, we fell asleep roughly at the same time. At least, I assumed so.

11

Unlike other men in the restaurant who wore golf attire or Hawaiian shirts, Antoine preferred to blend into the background with a plain white shirt and tan cargo pants, day after day. I'd counted five of each in his carry-on bag. Watching how the light defined his quarterback frame and admiring the back view of his cargo pants during our entrances and exits, I decided that "practical" suited him well, with the side benefit of dispelling the awkwardness I'd felt after past instances of letting lust take over. Whether he was shaving, dressing, or discussing the weather, Antoine settled into a relaxed rhythm, unafraid to deliver a kiss as we crossed paths in a doorway, as if we'd been sharing quarters for decades. Now, as I watched him across the table in the morning light, his return glances were just as warm, creating a bubble of intimacy around us as we ate breakfast.

As always, I cautioned my inner optimist to "settle down." A vacation high was a magical realm all its own, easily vaporized by the pressures and rules of normal life. Having agreed that exploring was a better use of our time than stopping for lunch, we demolished a basket of sweet rolls, asked for a second serving of papaya and lime juice, finished an extra serving of bacon, and cut down our "hungry man" omelets so thoroughly that forensic experts would struggle to gather evidence from our plates.

"Tell me more about Zach," I said.

"It's similar to your story," Antoine said. "I didn't know I had a son until he was six. His mother was … not a fling, exactly, but we weren't a good match. It's why she kept me in the dark. Then she married a decent guy who wanted Zach to be raised with the right picture in place. They don't need financial support, but I've set aside money for his future. All in secret. The enemy who died in November never found out."

"Thank heaven for that," I said.

"Zach and I had a rough start," Antoine said. "He was bound to think the stories about the pressures and end-to-end threats were a cooked-up excuse for dropping the ball as a father."

"How old is he now?" I asked.

"He just turned eight," Antoine said, showing a photo on his phone.

Leaning in closer, I felt a rush of emotions as I saw a young version of Antoine's features with a touching, mistrustful glare: a window into what Antoine might have looked like during his tough early years in the crime family he'd landed in after his parents were murdered. In November, I'd thought our difficult childhoods made us too similar to be a good match. Instead, it was a way for us to understand each other.

As an alert appeared on Antoine's phone, I handed it back.

"I asked my colleagues to take the reins as much as possible," he said. "This text is marked urgent. If you don't mind …?"

"Go ahead," I said. "See if it's important."

With a kiss on my cheek, Antoine pushed his chair back and headed toward the door, already checking voicemails.

Sitting at the next table, the honeymooner I'd met in the restroom the previous night cast me a look of sympathy.

"His work is very intense," I confided.

"What does he do for a living?" she asked.

"He's, umm, he's a cabbie," I said. "It's more than just driving people around. He's a hands-on kind of guy."

"Did I hear him mention a son?" she asked.

"Yes, Zach is eight," I said. "A wonderful age."

"From a previous marriage?" she asked.

"No, from a dalliance," I said. "A fling, no big deal."

"Goodness, look at the time," she said, signaling to her husband that her rescue effort was a lost cause. "Best of luck."

"You too," I said. "Enjoy Hawaii."

As she crossed paths with Antoine, he hesitated at her piercing look, then he resumed his seat with an air of intrigue.

"The Sonny effect took an unexpected turn," he said. "Agent Telford is about to step in, and he's not alone. At some point I'll toss a smooth exit your way. Use the moment to learn what you can."

"Specifics would be helpful," I said.

"You'll do fine," Antoine said. "Trust your instincts."

Hearing voices beyond the windows, I looked past Antoine's shoulder as three people stepped into the restaurant, reduced to silhouettes by the morning light. Along with Agent Telford heading toward our table, Harve emerged from the glare, followed by a woman dressed in black pants and a revealing shirt. With flowing, shoulder-length hair that curtained her face, she kept her head bowed until she arrived above me.

"*Darling* Sonny," Nicole said, bestowing kisses on my cheeks, despite my horrified grimace. "At last, we meet again."

Plucking a sweet roll from the basket, Dan's ex-girlfriend stood behind me, raining crumbs onto my shoulders while Ted introduced himself and Harve, who'd arrived with a toothpick in his mouth.

"Chicago cop before I got a clue and cut loose," Harve said, gripping Antoine's hand. "Now I'm a PI in paradise. Sonny will have told you about my four-seater plane, which she flew like an ace."

"There's no need for extended introductions," Antoine said. "I'm here to dial back and take PTO. It's about visiting Sonny."

"All that washes with what I've heard," Ted said. "Harve, wait outside while Nicole and I catch up with these two."

"Is it permissible to stand in the shade?" Harve asked, then when Ted looked irritated, he added, "On my way. Sorry, boss."

Motioning for Nicole to sit across from me, Ted joined us at the table and signaled for coffee. With his shirt sleeves rolled up, he reflected the tired air of a seasoned agent who was fed up with the nonsense side of his job but determined to make a difference for the greater good. Briefly, he praised me for my understanding approach to my breakup with Dan, and reported that Nicole was in the same mental space: no hard feelings about our rocky history with the same state trooper.

While Ted droned on, Nicole sat across from me, eating a sweet roll the way a jaguar would demolish a rabbit, complete with flashing eyes. On autopilot, my inner photographer assessed the light, the waitstaff in the background, and the Hawaiian décor in case I wanted to capture the conflicting message of Nicole's pretty face and her aura of menace.

For three months, I'd been wrestling with a phantom version of Dan's ex-girlfriend in my mind. Now that my relationship with him was over, I understood why Nicole fit his undercover role and why he, in turn, might have appealed to her as a plaything. What had gone wrong in Nicole's life to turn her into a thrill-seeker with a mean streak?

"Sonny," Antoine said. "It's clear that Ted came for a specific reason, but it's not fair to saddle you with shop talk."

"Sonny's input might be needed," Ted said.

"Fortunately," I said, poised to step away. "You and I covered every conceivable angle yesterday. I'll wait outside."

Awash in morning light on the wide wooden porch, I pulled out my phone and launched a video showing a close-up of the oil gauge inside the house that Dan inherited from his best friend. While helping him prepare the house for sale in November, I'd discovered the camera Dan used to monitor the oil level when he was out of town. Every clip on the memory card showed a steady view of the gauge with background sounds, including Nicole's ambush that had left me with a shoulder bruise.

As expected, the door opened, and footfalls approached.

"Mind if I join you?" Nicole asked.

Next to the railing overlooking the driveway, I folded my arms amid the heat and glare of the sunlight at the edge of the porch. I'd dressed for the tropics. In black from head to toe, Nicole had not.

"Which version of reality did you tell Ted?" I asked.

"He knows the basic arc," Nicole said, resting her hands on the railing beside me. "You were the one to blunder into my good thing, not the other way around. Dan and I were only 'sort of' finished."

"Don't hold back," I said. "Fill in the blanks."

"We'd argued a few weeks earlier," Nicole said. "Flirting with dirtbags was part of my job. After witnessing one such moment, Dan made a comment about the unlikelihood of my being invited to meet anybody's mother and father. I slapped him and walked out."

"That's sad on every level," I said.

"Look at us talking like we don't loathe each other to pieces," Nicole said, bumping my shoulder. "You'll want to keep it up."

I raised my eyebrows. "Meaning …?"

"Unlike last time, I'm here with the feds, so my orders should not be taken lightly or ignored," Nicole said. "Bring me up to speed on Jasmine, then have your fleeting, special time with Antoine. It will end badly, of course. You're not a good match for a cop."

"Back at you," I said softly.

With the volume on low to keep her recorded hollering from disturbing the guests who were chatting on the porch nearby, I watched Nicole's face flush in response to the news that her outburst in Maine had been enshrined in digital form from start to finish.

"Sweet, isn't it," I said. "When fate favors a victim."

"Who else has heard this?" Nicole asked.

"Officials who would rather avoid a shitstorm," I said. "I'm the injured party, quite literally, so they're leaving the decision up to me. First off, it's important to realize that you're not well-suited for dealing with a troubled teenager. Oops, I think I hear Ted's voice coming closer. Should I play this clip for him, or are you done being a jerk?"

"Put it away," Nicole hissed. "I hear you."

As Antoine and Ted stepped out of the restaurant, they were finishing their conversation, with Ted seemingly on the losing side.

"I won't change my mind," Antoine said.

"Think about it," Ted said, turning to Nicole with a look of concern. "Am I right to sense tension instead of agreement?"

"Nicole shares my disgust with the detective who bullied Jasmine," I said. "Now that I've calmed the waters and established a rapport, Nicole and I agree that I should remain the sole contact."

"Nicole?" Ted prompted. "That's you're sense of it?"

With averted eyes, she said, "Yes, let's stay the course."

Nodding, as if in agreement, Agent Telford looked frustrated, but resigned to accept my take on how to handle Jasmine.

"Moving on," Ted said. "I didn't see the need to sweep the house for hidden electronics, but Antoine feels it's best to err on the safe side. I'm dispatching an agent. It'll be done by the time you're back."

"What if Moritz and Raja are there?" I asked.

"The agent will pose as a building inspector," Ted said. "Given that it's a rental property I didn't imagine any cameras would be in place, but you never know. It'll be good to rule that out."

"Are you staying locally?" I asked with trepidation.

"We'll be on Maui chasing leads," Ted said, casting about as he neared his FBI-issue vehicle. "Harve, where the hell are you?"

"Right here, boss," the PI said, emerging from the shadows with a sly look that told me he'd made a point of trying to eavesdrop.

As Nicole glared at me, I motioned for her to calm down and not think the worst. Harve wouldn't have heard the video, and I was certain that he could be bargained with. As if we were trusted colleagues, Nicole nodded and signaled that she would take it in stride.

With his arm around my shoulders, waving at the departing visitors, Antoine didn't appear to realize that complexities were exploding all over the place. I'd lied to Nicole about officials in Maine knowing about the video. Even Dan didn't know about the video.

"Ted imagined I might join his team," Antoine said, steering me down the path toward cabin #3. "I listened in the interests of shaking out his pockets, but he's a cagey guy. Given Nicole's specialty, one or more cases must involve problematic men who are easily lured."

"Like a certain mutual acquaintance," I said.

"I was picturing perpetrators," Antoine said. "But even good guys can fall under Nicole's influence, depending on what's going on in their lives. I'm curious to know how you shut her down."

Even in the shade, Antoine's shirt absorbed the warmth of daylight, nearly glowing as it framed his handsome, self-assured features. Far from the renegade undercover operative I'd thought him to be in November, Antoine was the real deal—dedicated to solving high-stakes international crimes. With a sigh, I led him to the gazebo in the garden to share the whole story of my Hawaii trip, starting with the whale rescue, and ending with the recording I'd used to contain Nicole.

"The airport is that way." I motioned. "Head south."

"There is a famous French phrase," Antoine said. "Je n'ai pas vécu sous un rocher, which translates to, I haven't lived under a rock."

"I just blackmailed a federal agent," I whispered.

"If Nicole hadn't backed down, you would have shown the recording to Ted," Antoine said, pensively narrowing his eyes. "In mentioning his plan to chase leads on Maui, he's chumming the water, thinking I'll take interest and bite. It's definitely curious that the ex-cons who mistook you for Katrina handled security at two venues connected to fatalities, though it sounds like they quit before the instance on the cruise ship. It's no wonder Ted is looking toward Jasmine for a breakthrough. She's lasered in on suspicious matters where the police have failed."

"I'm not throwing Jasmine under the bus," I said.

"Of course not," Antoine said. "I'm thinking out loud."

"Regarding the search for listening devices," I said carefully, "It feels like you've opened the door for Ted to *plant* electronics."

"Rest assured, I will find them," Antoine said. "It's possible he knows I'm striving to test his intentions. Time will tell."

"Antoine, I'm thrilled to spend time with you," I said. "But it doesn't feel right to drag you into a complicated mess."

"I'm jumping in on every level, so arguing is pointless," he said. "You and I have more in common than not. We're self-aware, creative, and open to the unknown. I was lucky to land a career that lets me seek justice with minimal flak. I have some ideas for shoring up your skills. A strategic plan with a clear goal. We can start right now."

I hesitated. "What would it involve?"

With hand gestures emphasizing his reasoning, Antoine spelled out a plan of action that sparked the need for a time-out.

"You're used to the way things unfold in Canada," I said. "This is the United States. Views and norms apply. Show some respect."

"Would I lead you down the wrong path?" Antoine asked.

"You shaved it pretty close in Maine," I reminded him.

"And voilà," he said. "Every case was solved."

"This isn't like anything you've ever faced. Someone could get hurt, and by the way," I added in a whisper, "we are less than five miles from Halemaʻumaʻu, an epicenter of swirling, godlike energy you saw with your own eyes. Your plan amounts to crazy talk."

"Let's step into the sunshine," Antoine said, guiding me to a spot outside the gazebo. "Now, with your advocacy role in mind—"

"I get it," I said. "I see your point."

Aware that he wouldn't give up until I at least tried, I scrunched my face and focused on the bright glow of tropical sunlight filtering through my eyelids. With winces and my fingers crossed—

"Don't cross your fingers," Antoine chided.

With a sigh, I said, "I am a successful woman, not a target of invisible forces that wish me harm. I am kind of allowed …"

"You are allowed, *period*, Berrichon," Antoine said softly. "To feel happy, hope for the best, and wish for a perfect life. If you want to be a champion for other victims, you need to embrace your worth and ditch the critics who've taken hold of your mind."

"I suppose I do need to be convincing," I said.

Slowly, I articulated the advice I often shared with others who landed in harm's way and, at least for now, tentatively began to apply it to my own life, including the idea that it was okay to ask for help. After I finished my affirmations, Antoine had a more challenging climb in mind.

To have a normal, fun-filled day.

"Maybe not on the volcano," I said.

Antoine nodded. "Bon. We'll head for the coast."

12

At the turnoff to my favorite snorkeling location, Antoine's sedan rumbled over black lava stones along the sandy lane, and then in the small parking area, he swung around to point the front hood toward the main road, per his instinct to allow for a fast escape. As we climbed out, Kilauea's volcanic vog formed a misty haze over the hillside to the east.

"Having met my adversary," Antoine said in response to my questions about his life in Canada. "You can imagine that my home got trashed more than once. Repairing drywall is second nature to me."

"In a house?" I asked. "An apartment?"

"I'm tucked into the top floor of an old shirt factory," Antoine said. "It solved the problem of apologizing to neighbors. The level below is a gym. A place where colleagues can practice skills."

Turning toward the sound of an approaching sedan, Antoine signaled to the driver and told me he would be right back.

"It's the specialist Ted sent to check the house for hidden electronics," Antoine said. "I asked him to meet us here."

With a smile and a kiss on my cheek, he crossed to the sedan, having assured me that, compared to the cold of a Canadian winter, helping with the project was a fair trade for his introduction to the wonders of Hawaii's Big Island. During the drive from Hilo, he insisted on visiting Punalu'u Beach to see Hawaiian green sea turtles basking on the black sand, then stepped out of the car in the Puna district to marvel at the bulldozed path through the lava flow that had cut across the road in 2018. When I mentioned the southernmost point, he headed straight for the access road to enjoy the thundering waves and sea air on his face.

For the better part of a year, my own life had felt like a drifting, tumbling leaf caught up in a gale. Somehow, Antoine had emerged from his turbulent past with an unshakable conviction that all problems could be resolved by breaking them into manageable, step-by-step pieces. I'd traced his upbeat attitude to huge success at an early age, given that he'd upended a criminal organization when he was just ten.

The incoming sedan's window slid down, revealing an agent wearing sunglasses. After a brief exchange, Antoine waved in thanks and crossed back to me with towels, two beach bags, and snorkel gear.

"Given your volunteer contributions," Antoine said. "I thought it was only fair to spare you an extra trip to the rental house."

With a flourish, Antoine unzipped his cargo pants and let them fall to the sand, revealing that he'd been wearing his royal blue mid-thigh-length bathing suit underneath during our drive.

"Voilà," he said. "I am ready for snorkeling."

In the shelter of the back seat, I slipped into my one-piece bathing suit with a flirty skirt. As I stepped out, Antoine offered flip-flops for my feet and a waterproof pouch for my phone. Fifty feet away along the water's edge, a familiar man was sunning himself in a beach chair.

"That's Gavin," I said. "Hopefully, he won't recognize me."

With beach towels and wetsuits draped over our arms, we crossed the flat stretch of hardened black lava, where cracks and fissures from ancient eruptions were filled with tidal pools reflecting the blue sky. I cautioned Antoine to step carefully in the flip-flops, having seen tourists end up with scraped knees after tripping on the gritty, porous surface.

In a skimpy suit that seemed a mismatch for his large belly, Gavin answered a call, barking responses like "I've explained the bottom line" and "make it happen," then he performed stretches with no apparent sense of their purpose. Pose one! Pose two! Soon, it was clear his efforts were meant to impress a woman floating in the water fifteen feet from the black lava shoreline. Gavin motioned for her to move aside, assumed a stance fit for a cliff dive, and dove in with a dramatic splash.

In turn, the woman emerged from the water with exaggerated tugging at her bikini, as if to make sure anyone within a mile radius would stop and admire her cosmetically enhanced butt and D-cup rack.

"She's twenty years younger than Gavin," I said.

"A little more than that," Antoine said.

By the water's edge, we zipped into shortie wetsuits, snugged flippers onto our feet, prepared our masks with anti-fog drops, and high-fived each other for looking ridiculous. In exchange, we could stay in the chilly water for an extended swim and protect our backs and upper legs from a serious sunburn. Antoine splashed in first and swam ahead to avoid a collision. With every surge of incoming water, roiling bubbles partially obscured the neon yellow tangs rushing in to feed on algae on the lava, then they rode the rebounding wave out in a repeating, daily cycle.

With my camera's wrist strap secured and my phone in its waterproof pouch, I timed my entry so a wave wouldn't knock me into the ledge, and then I plunged into the cool water, with my hair flowing in all directions, bubbles tickling my skin, and ocean salt slipping in through the sides of my mouthpiece. All around me, the crackle of snapping shrimp blended with the lively rhythm of underwater bubbles.

Surging forward with flipper kicks, I watched the tangs from my new vantage point below the surface. Aware that Isabella Bird hadn't mentioned swimming among the fish she'd admired from the decks of various vessels, I thanked heaven to be visiting during a time when I wasn't encumbered by social conventions and layers of clothes.

With tropical sunlight creating wave patterns across our faces, arms, and legs, I led Antoine across the reef with our masks pointed downward at the fish resting or feeding in sheltered sand patches that took on a dusky shade of blue from the twenty-foot depth. My shortie wetsuit kept my torso warm even as cool water slipped in at the neckline.

Conveying points of interest in American Sign Language, I led the way to my favorite spots along the reef, bringing us about a hundred feet from the shoreline. Soon, our shadows combed across a thirty-foot cavern between two coral formations where I could count on seeing unicornfish, sailfin tangs, butterflyfish, and other species sporting vibrant neon colors, with the long spikes of red sea urchins adding texture in the divots along the coral. Floating in place, I signaled for Antoine to see a gorgeous three-foot "puhi la au" black-and-white banded snake eel looping toward us and then gliding away in a sinuous, graceful motion.

As I slowly kicked forward, a shift of movement drew my gaze to a pile of submerged rocks. I stared at the spot, treading water as I pressed my camera's "on" button and adjusted the color balance to the underwater setting. Floating nearby, Antoine looked confused as I recorded a twenty-second video of the seemingly lifeless rocks. From experience, I could detect the tiny movements of an octopus camouflaged among the textured background. As always, I was captivated by the diversity of life forms and grateful to witness them with my own eyes.

"O-c-t-o-p-u-s," I signed to Antoine.

He spread his hands and shook his head.

I smiled, pleased to have better vision than an elite cop.

We paused as a turtle drifted below us, scarcely moving a flipper while it looked left and right like a landowner enjoying his garden. I switched my camera to single-image mode and captured several shots of our distorted, alien-like shadows cast on the reef floor with the turtle in the foreground. Antoine expelled bubbles, laughing when I showed him the photos, and then we headed toward the deep harbor beyond the reef. Slowing my pace, I searched the blue depths below us, enchanted by how the light created angled, downward streaks through the water. Here and there amid the seamless blue, the slowly-moving shapes of spinner dolphins appeared. Antoine touched his arm, sharing my wonder in feeling their chatter tickling our skin and ears: a mix of crackling, squeaking, vibrating calls issued in a lively rhythm. Reassured by our calm and stillness, an adult dolphin surfaced with a youngster beside it, gliding effortlessly upward to take a breath, and then sinking back into the blue depths.

At a leisurely pace, we began the journey back to the lava outcrop, pointing out different fish as we neared the coral canyon, until we reached the spot where the octopus was still familiar to me but unseen by Antoine. I captured a video of the fluidly graceful snake eel, and then I braced myself against the shifting current to take some still shots of Hawaii's state fish: a gorgeous reef triggerfish with neon blue face markings.

Relaxed but chilled after our swim, I signaled that it was time to head back to shore. Antoine treaded water and watched as I demonstrated how to use the momentum of an incoming wave to carry me onto an underwater ledge two feet below the surface. Swiveling as the current carried me upward, I grabbed a seat, let the water flow around me and recede with a loud rush, then I climbed to a higher spot to stay out of the way.

Emerging and climbing quickly to his feet, Antoine helped steady me as we removed our flippers and crossed to our bags and towels, vibrating from the rush of returning to gravity after being weightless.

"If I'm not mistaken, the masked fish was a humuhumunukunukuapua'a," Antoine said, smiling as he dried his face.

"My mind doesn't react well to repeating vowels," I said. "Maybe you saw the fish when you visited Maui however long ago?"

"That's right, you will have learned a thing or two from my colleagues in November," Antoine said. "The Maui excursion was a training exercise during the rainy season. This is my first leisurely snorkeling experience, but I've done some scuba diving to fetch things."

"Explosive type things?" I asked.

"No, to retrieve fentanyl and other drugs so our lakes don't become a toxic soup," Antoine said. "After sinkings, etcetera."

With our wetsuits drying and our towels spread on a flat spot, we took turns applying sunscreen to each other's northern skin. Antoine's fading tan confirmed my assumption that he was active outdoors during the summer months. I used the need to cover every inch of skin as a chance to study the nicks and healed-over scrapes from his history of being pitched into car chases, take-downs, and other instances of hand-to-hand combat, like the awful showdown I'd witnessed in November.

Antoine's sunglasses reflected my worried frown as he sat beside me, dropped a straw hat onto my head, and put on a cap to lessen a sunburn. Leaning in close, he shielded my camera from the glare as he joined me in reviewing my underwater photos, quietly marveling as I zoomed in on the octopus. As we pondered the snake eel's menacing look, I recounted my story of losing track of danger while capturing photos of an eyelash viper in Costa Rica. If not for my friend Arlene hollering for me to notice how the viper was glaring at me, I might not be sitting there.

"You're giving me goosebumps," Antoine said softly. "You mentioned that snake during a dire moment in Maine."

"Now you know the backstory," I said.

"Dovetailing into possible human snakes," Antoine said, "After Ted's agent ruled out the presence of eavesdropping electronics in the house, he paid a friendly visit to your neighbors at the bottom of the lane and noticed a stockpile of canned corn in their carport."

"It's concerning, but not a surprise," I said. "We shouldn't bake here for too long, and Gavin is heading in this direction."

Thankfully, the arts crusader's progress across the expanse of ancient lava was slow, giving us time to stow our gear. Pulling a blue T-shirt over his head in a display of muscles in motion, Antoine offered me a hand up in the same moment that Gavin arrived.

"I'm guessing that you stay in shape through sports," Gavin said, puffing as he shook Antoine's hand. "Soccer? Baseball?"

"I'm a cabbie," Antoine said.

"Of course," Gavin said. "All the swerving to get people from here to there through traffic would require a lot of strength."

"Are you here with your wife?" I asked.

"Heavens no, she's an acquaintance," Gavin said. "After you stepped away at the marina, I kicked myself for not urging you to keep your luggage out of sight and locked. If Moritz is on the straight and narrow, bravo, but my brief marriage to his mother opened my eyes to the souring effect of a parent who suffers from alcoholism and drug addiction. Instead of building character, Moritz is prone to iffy habits."

Frowning, Antoine said, "Is there a history of stealing?"

"Not in the sense that he's burglarized a bank or held up a liquor store," Gavin said. "But he's not averse to hacking into files. For a while, I thought I was losing my mind, then I realized Moritz was dipping into his mother's accounts on the sly. Instead of helping me curb his selfish behavior, she gave her blessing for his wrong moves. It's the awful seesaw of striving to make up for times when she'd let him down."

"It sounds very sad," I said.

"Indeed, it was," Gavin said gravely. "If Barry and Pauline are correct in seeing Moritz's work as a sign of growth, I will admit to being wrong, but it's not fair for you to live there without the full picture."

"I'll keep it in mind," I said. "Thank you for alerting me."

"Antoine, Sonny's faith in you is a strong endorsement," Gavin said. "She's a Littlefield from the Boston area."

"It was misleading for Harve to mention that," I said.

"A modest approach, very admirable," Gavin said. "If you recall, I'm Dean of Admissions at a prominent arts academy here on the Big Island. I've got a stake in keeping our female staff and donors safe when they're out and about. I'm sure it's obvious where I'm heading with this thread. We could use a driver who can handle himself."

"To curtail a specific known threat?" Antoine asked.

"This is what I'm talking about," Gavin said, clapping Antoine's arm. "Most guys with your build are hotshots, eager to dive in without knowing the details. You're the opposite. In fact …"

Signaling Antoine to follow him to the side, Gavin conducted a whispered exchange with hand gestures indicating he was talking about the buxom beauty sunning herself to a crisp on a low-profile chair near the water's edge. The woman responded with a smile and some finger wiggling that translated to, "I asked for you specifically."

"What makes you think I might be for hire?" Antoine asked.

"Sonny needed a ride from Hilo, and the fact that you've been included on some 'sightseeing' adds to the picture," Gavin said with a wink. "Given your high-end sedan, I made an intuitive leap."

"Sonny is a close personal friend," Antoine explained. "Her father died a year ago this month, so I'm here to lend support."

"A thousand apologies," Gavin said, waving his glaring blunder away, then reaching into his shirt pocket and pulling out a business card. "In case you need extra cash, let's stay in touch."

As Gavin crossed back to the woman with a shrug indicating he'd tried his best, Antoine looked at me over his sunglasses.

"First Ted's pitch, now this," he said. "Two job offers in one day."

"Gavin tried to pimp you out," I furiously hissed. "Hell will freeze over before I let him seek donations from my relatives."

"It's a given that he'll try," Antoine said, frowning toward the retreating dean of bad judgment. "He claims a part of his role is to answer the whims of high-level donors. Apparently, his bikini-clad prospect landed in the winner's lane after her elderly husband died."

"The old adage is true," I said. "Only the fittest survive."

"That's the guiding principle behind my group calling ourselves cabbies," Antoine said. "We learn more when flying under the radar, and apparently, Gavin isn't done keeping us informed."

As we responded to his hellos and waving near the water's edge, Gavin cupped his hands to deliver his message to all of Kona.

"If you're planning to visit local tourist spots, please avoid the Place of Refuge, at least for this afternoon," he hollered. "Katrina is helping Pauline with a tour of parents and distinguished alumni!"

"*Gavin,*" the woman in the chair chided.

"We're not here," Gavin added more quietly through his hands, which he formed into a funnel. "My main point is, have a care for Katrina's feelings. She's upset that you ripped her motorcycle away."

I gaped. "I was told she wasn't using it."

"Yes, all that is true, but you know how people are," Gavin said. "And breaks are fine, darling, but don't let Barry catch you goofing off for long. It's best for all of us if you resume the project."

Once again, Antoine looked at me over his sunglasses.

"Place of Refuge next?" he asked.

"Yeah," I said. "And step on it."

13

In a little over four hours, Antoine and I had descended from the misty summit of Kilauea Volcano, rounded the southernmost point, snorkeled among yellow tangs, unicorn fish, and dolphins, and now stood at another sea-level spot where the air was still, and the heat from the equatorial sun pressed down on us like a weight, turning the landscape of white pathways, green foliage, and ocean water into a shimmering mirage.

"The academy's minibus is in the parking lot," I said. "My preference is to bump into the group casually and see if Gavin is right about Katrina's attitude. I hope you don't mind hanging back."

"Not at all, I've got a project of my own," Antoine said. "I don't recall having a fascination with quests and mystical powers at Zach's age, but I'm told it's normal. I think he would love this place."

"The sky is a perfect blue," I said. "You've got about a minute before the next group of tourists steps in the way of a shot."

With the brim of his hat pushed back and his sunglasses in his shirt pocket, Antoine conducted a slow pass in front of the fearsome grimaces of two six-foot-tall, heavily weathered, hand-carved wooden statues that stood guard over Puʻuhonua O Hōnaunau, or Place of Refuge. Positioned near a sandy cove with the blue Pacific Ocean as a backdrop, the carved statues, known to Native Hawaiians as "Ki'i," symbolized an ancient tradition that offered a safe haven for warriors and lawbreakers if they reached the sacred ground before their pursuers.

Endeavoring to create captivating photos to send to his son, Antoine zoomed in on the right-hand statue to capture the long, intricately carved braids, and then he framed the other scowling, possibly hollering statue at an angle to emphasize its teeth and fierce eyes.

With Japanese tourists waiting to take selfies in front of the statues, we crossed to a sacred area surrounded by tall wooden posts lashed into a solid fence. Inside the enclosure, ten-foot carved idols soared against the sky, with coconut palms casting shadows over their grimaces and scowls. Antoine zoomed in on the faces and headdresses to show the intricate detail of the carvings, with rows of chisel marks indicating hair.

"I'll give you some privacy while you make your call," I said.

"That's kind of you, Berrichon," Antoine said, lifting my straw hat to give me a quick kiss. "But I know you've noticed familiar faces in the distance. If I'm right, the young woman among the group of hikers near the 1871 Trail matches Katrina's description."

"Let's meet here in thirty minutes," I said.

Looking relaxed, with his white shirt standing out against the Pacific, Antoine stepped away to call Zach's mother to make sure he was right about sending photos of grimacing idols. The last thing he wanted was to cause nightmares for their eight-year-old child.

With sunglasses in place and my hat pushed back, suspended by the long strap, I smoothed my curls before I drifted toward Pauline in her neat, sophisticated resort wear and tennis sneakers. Katrina was equally stylish in slacks and a modern, Hawaiian-style blouse.

Seeing the group swerve away from the trail of white sand that followed the coastline, I altered my path as well, drawing Pauline's gaze. She apologized to the group and headed toward me.

"Show some sense," Pauline quietly urged. "You can't imagine Katrina wants to see you after you ripped her bike away."

"I'm sorry if it came across that way," I protested. "According to Jason, the bike was a rental, sitting unused for months."

"Logic doesn't always rule the day," Pauline confided. "Otherwise, I'm impressed to know you're an organizational dynamo."

Squinting, I said, "In which area?"

"Somehow, you obtained the correct building permits and had an inspector visit this morning," Pauline said. "He clarified things for Moritz and Raja about dismantling your drywall repairs."

I paused. "They were *dismantling* my work?"

"Men don't see women as capable of doing anything right," Pauline said tiredly. "Barry skews in that direction as well, but your clever move of bringing in an inspector has turned the tide."

"I'm glad to have that settled," I said. "By the way, I'm here with my new boyfriend. Man friend. Person of interest." I closed my eyes and regrouped. "A close friend from the East Coast who will be joining me in the work. Willing and able. Highly experienced."

"And … he's also diving in for free?" Pauline asked.

"For a roof over his head," I said.

"I'm sorry for snapping a minute ago," Pauline said, softening all the more. "You know how people waffle after a breakup. Once Katrina's mind settles, I think you'd get along." Pausing to frown at a group of tourists arriving, Pauline said, "Where *is* that blasted man?"

"I haven't seen Barry," I said.

"I'm talking about Gavin," Pauline said, using her binoculars to scan the parking lot. "He's supposed to be lending a hand."

After a momentary hesitation, I disclosed her colleague's whereabouts, as well as the proposal he'd pitched at Antoine.

"So much for Gavin having a dental appointment," Pauline said. "Not to mention, the bikini-clad alumna claimed to have a touch of the flu. The older gentleman in my group imagines her 'attributes' equal a happy future. Instead of holding my tongue, I'm tempted to explain the benefits of not thinking with his—" Suddenly, Pauline raised her binoculars to her eyes. "Dear God, as if I don't have enough to deal with."

As I followed her gaze, I held my breath, seeing a bearded man with a green baseball cap pulled over his messy hair, using the ruse of studying a shell in his hand to conceal his fixation on Katrina's group. In an instant, I connected his beard and his hat, especially the *Kukuna Mahina* logo, to the third man I'd glimpsed in the extended cab of the truck that belonged to the surly, threat-delivering thug.

"He's the reason I cut our hike short," Pauline said. "He's got an iffy look about him, and he's staring at Katrina."

"Can I borrow your binoculars?" I asked.

"Your sunscreen will mar the eyepieces," Pauline said. "He's dressed in baggy clothes, typical for a certain type of student. Perhaps he's seeking Katrina's advice. She's a role model on campus."

"From afar, it's hard to judge his age," I said. "His beard fits the look of a guy who's been keeping company with a couple of thugs."

Pauline looked appalled. "A gang?"

"No, it was middle-aged men in a truck," I said.

Seeing her group drifting toward the stalker, Pauline yelled, "Hello, I'll be with you in a minute! I'm talking to a friend!"

As Katrina stopped and looked at us, the lurker also took note of our presence and quickly retreated down the trail.

"Crisis averted," Pauline said.

"Rejoin your group," I said. "I'll go after him."

"That's the opposite of sensible," Pauline said. "The best path is to alert the staff so they can keep an eye out for him."

"Go ahead and do that," I said. "Tell Katrina I'm sorry for any missed signals, but if she wanted the bike, she should have made it clear to Jason and paid the rental fee herself. I saw the paperwork."

"Alison, it's not smart to confront a stalker," Pauline said.

"I'll be fine," I said. "Return to your group."

Leaving Pauline behind, I tried to catch up with the bearded man at a brisk yet casual pace. Although straight and open to the sky, the 1871 Trail was a relic of 1871 conditions, with half-buried lava boulders along the path of broken shells and sand. The need for a hasty getaway caused the man to miss his footing and stumble several times.

"Excuse me," I called out. "Is this the 1871 Trail?"

As he glanced over his hunched shoulders, he halted in his tracks, possibly recognizing me in the wake of Pauline's hollering.

"Now that you've turned toward me," I called out, "I think I bumped into you near Hilo. You were with two guys in a truck."

"I was alone yesterday," he hollered. "Fishing at sea."

"Please talk to me," I said, taking a few careful steps to start narrowing the hundred or more feet between us. "Maybe I'm wrong, but those men had a bad vibe. You seem more reasoned."

"You're that meddler from the East Coast," he said. "Mind your own business, or you'll upend—stuff. People's lives."

With that, he told two hikers that I was his ex-girlfriend-stalker, and asked if they could help him escape, thereby igniting my afterburners as I sprinted along the path, determined to catch up.

Having run for my life through the deep forests of Maine in the dark of night multiple times, I scoffed at the clearly visible hazards of the 1871 Trail, from half-buried lava boulders to vines that promised to snag my ankles and send me hurtling through space if I didn't plant my sneakers on solid ground with precision. Instead of heeding my signals to clear the way, the two twentyish hikers planted themselves in my path.

"Halt, in the name of the law!" one hollered.

Puffing, I said, "If you're an off-duty officer—"

"I'm talking about the laws of sense and reason," he said. "There are plenty of fish in the sea. It's time to let go."

"Yeah, tap into your better self," the other hiker said, securing my arm, and then drawing away with a grimace. "You're a little sticky, like you've been in the ocean. Cleaned up, you would be hot."

"Uh-oh, who's the bullet train in a white shirt and cargo pants coming at us?" the first hiker asked. "He looks fierce."

Seeing Antoine vaulting the same hillocks and vines I'd navigated, I motioned for him to slow down. Once he arrived, I explained the events that had sparked my sudden dash down the path.

"You saw the stalker up close?" Antoine asked the hikers.

"According to the guy, *she's* the stalker," one of them said. "But yeah, we saw him. He's in sad shape. A homeless kid."

"No, he's old," the other hiker insisted. "Whatever age it takes to have white in his beard and signs of thinning hair."

"With sweat involved, it's hard to say," his companion said. "For sure, he was wearing a grayish hat with a football logo."

"It was a green hat," his friend said. "Are you blind?"

"I am unable to see green properly, dumbass," the hiker said. "Thanks for paying attention the billion times I told you."

"Well, I have an inability to compute stuff that's out of my own experience," the hiker said. "You can't see the bushes?"

"I see them fine," his friend said hotly. "In shades of *gray*."

Antoine was second to none when it came to getting eyewitnesses to calm down and focus. Remaining at odds with each other until the bitter end, the hikers confirmed that we were either looking for Albert Einstein or a washed-up, teenaged surfer hooked on meth. As for my input, I would know the hat anywhere if I saw it again; one of thousands.

Before sending them on their way, Antoine took their information and gave them a number to call if they remembered a further detail.

"I guess I shouldn't be surprised," I said. "I've seen news shows about studies where people are subjected to a fake mugging or some other event. The different interpretations are shocking."

"The stalker's reaction suggests it was him in the truck," Antoine said. "Perhaps his cohorts directed him to evaluate Katrina's behavior after they delivered the warning at the gas station."

"Except it was me in the bathroom stall," I said worriedly. "I'm kicking myself for not sharing the video with Ted."

"Let's set clear parameters," Antoine said. "If you send me the video, my colleagues can frame it with language about protecting your rights and privacy. We protect witnesses all the time."

After the file uploaded to his phone, Antoine made the necessary calls to the specialists who would then contact Agent Telford.

"Ted will tell Katrina to be watchful?" I asked.

"I will make sure of it," Antoine said.

As we headed toward the Place of Refuge, Antoine was happy to tell me that his gut feeling about his son's interests was correct.

"The photos were a resounding success," he said. "Which means the magic of the place works on warriors of all kinds."

"I'm thrilled," I said. "I'm sorry for the mad dash."

"From now on, let's agree to a shared goal of alerting each other in advance of a sudden sprint," Antoine said with a gentle squeeze and a wry smile. "You made mention of a hot tub at the house?"

"With a view that you won't find in Maine, Canada, or anywhere in between," I said. "I hope Moritz and Raja aren't there."

Forty minutes later, with the back seat of Antoine's sedan brimming over with grocery bags filled with pineapples, mangos, French baguettes, yellowfin tuna steaks, a half-dozen kinds of cheese, and other supplies, I was eager to drive past Moritz conducting his daily grill scrubbing in front of his bungalow, but Antoine wanted his presence known.

"The agent who checked for electronics told me they were dismantling your hard work," Antoine said, showing a rare moment of ire. "If their territoriality is about their paychecks, that's off in its own right. Gavin's warning about Moritz demands a closer look."

Climbing out with his utilitarian undercover cop smile intact, Antoine shook hands with the neighbors, squinting as he talked, as if striving to recall the specifics of our friendship back East. It seemed a typical male bonding moment with a mention of bottled beer.

"You're here for how long?" Moritz asked.

"It's up in the air," Antoine said, making a twirling motion that encompassed the next day into eternity. "I'm told you work nights?"

"Yeah, no worries if you need 'alone' time," Raja said slyly. "Hopefully, you're up to speed on Sonny's wake of chaos."

"Ignore him," Moritz said. "I think it's great that Sonny has a supportive friend. We heard you visited the snorkeling spot."

"I heard about your day, too," Antoine said.

After a fractional pause, Moritz and Raja exchanged worried glances, as if Antoine had delivered a serious threat, then he was smiling, shaking their hands, and wishing them a good night.

"What was that?" I said as he slipped into the car.

With a look of innocence, he shifted gears and continued up the lane, wincing at the paintball mess on the garage doors and other signs of destruction that Moritz and Raja had amplified by ripping into my drywall repairs. With the food stored in the refrigerator, I offered a tour that highlighted the hot tub, the stunning view, and a gecko, which struck me as a neon mini-monster to photograph and send to Zach.

"Let's hope the geckos aren't radioactive," Antoine said, fractionally sharpening his gaze. "Or we'll be in big trouble."

"I think you're joking," I said slowly. "Though all of a sudden, you're oddly silent in the wake of your eyes flaring weirdly."

"Like *I'm* radioactive?" Antoine said measuredly.

"If so, can I have a head start?" I asked.

With a sudden grin, Antoine chucked my chin.

"Now you know why Moritz and Raja exchanged a startled glance," he said. "Was it a warning? A trick of the light? Instead of pegging me, they'll waste time and energy trying to figure me out."

"Am I doing it now?" I asked, widening my eyes.

"I'm not sure I want you to perfect it, Berrichon," Antoine said. "It's not a part of police training. I learned it from bad guys."

Taking me by the hand, Antoine led me to the deck, as if wanting to study me in a new tropical setting as the sun approached the horizon and burnished the low-hanging clouds with golden light. With a worried look, he delivered a quick kiss and brushed a stray curl away.

"Even though I understand your approach to healing, I'm troubled to see where you've been resting your head in the wake of turmoil," Antoine said. "This isn't just a house, Sonny. It's a victim."

"I had that same thought," I said, turning within the circle of Antoine's arms to look into the chaotic interior with his warmth against my back. "If staying here feels off, we can spend the night in a hotel."

"Not a chance," he said. "I'm built the way you are, drawn to the beauty of the place, and determined to understand the chaos."

"Human eccentricity," I said. "A wrong idea of fun."

"Oui," Antoine said. "Let's hope it's just that."

14

Immersed in pillows, and squinting against a mote of sunlight warming my face at 6:30 a.m., I watched with interest as Antoine stepped out of the bathroom, freshly shaved and only wearing his modern boxers. With his muscles flexing, he checked his phone messages with a thoughtful frown, then slipped into his worn jeans and battered T-shirt.

"Make sure to ask about Chip at some point," I said. "When I brought him up, Moritz got quiet. He changed the subject."

"It's not unusual for people to shut down after a recent death," Antoine said. "I'll see if I can coax out some insights and details, but keep in mind that our coworkers might be late, and not at their best."

With a smile, Antoine emitted a sound I'd heard ten times the day before: a sharp hiss and click that mimicked the split-second release of pressure as a bottle cap was pried off. Either to befriend him, undercut his alpha vibe, or both, Moritz and Raja had offered Antoine beers throughout the day. Not wanting to buy into their scheme or create recycling litter, he'd mimicked the sound while pretending to open each offered beer, then he'd hidden the full bottle when he had the chance.

Moritz and Raja were the only ones experiencing hangovers.

"Show me how you're making the hiss and click," I said.

"Keep trying, you'll get it," Antoine said.

In the doorway, Antoine froze in place, hearing a subdued, forewarning rumble, then as a thunderous, undulating, heaving motion shook the house, he reached out to steady me after I lurched from the bed, where the canopy fabric swayed as if caught up in a gust of wind. Aside from dishes rattling in the kitchen and a screwdriver clattering to the floor, the house took the earthquake in stride, and then all was quiet.

Smiling, with a look of wonder, Antoine scooped me into a twirl, and then he squeezed me as he returned me to my feet.

"That was magma shifting underground," he said. "The view of the Pacific is misleading. From this spot to the ocean floor, it's about 16,000 feet of volcanic chambers and violent pressure. I've experienced seismic activity in Canada now and then. Nothing like this."

"Isabella talked to people who went through a time in 1868 when the island shook for a week," I said. "Thousands of aftershocks, with almost no pauses in the quakes. People went mad from it."

"Find that section, I want to read it," Antoine said, continuing onward to make breakfast. "Next time, let's create a video."

In my clamdigger pants and T-shirt, I opened the rice paper doors to spill dawn light through the bedroom. With my yoga mat in place on the deck, I tried to focus my whirling thoughts with a Sun Salutation pose. With my arms outstretched, I leaned forward at the waist for a deep hamstring stretch, then shifted into the dolphin pose, a tree, and then a triangle. Sitting on the floor in a twist, I appreciated the full-body benefits and calming effects of the Lord of the Fishes pose.

All the while, rustling sounds drew my gaze to Antoine's shadow playing across the newly installed drapes. First, the coffeemaker was set into motion, and then his shadow bounced a fresh cantaloupe in one hand, with a machete deftly twirling in the other. His shadow disappeared out of sight toward the kitchen cutting board.

Thwack.

"Excellent état, bien huilé," he murmured.

"If you're saying it's well oiled, that's a relief," I said. "Hopefully, it's not the machete that somebody used to dig a trench."

"Yoga is supposed to relax a person, non?" Antoine asked.

Drawn by further rustling sounds, I crossed to the doorway and saw him reshaping a paper clip with needle-nose pliers.

"I'm curious about the locked kitchen drawer," he said, signaling for me to join him. "You've experienced being trapped, so this is an essential skill. Using the looped clip as a wrench, explore the inside of the lock with the second clip. Determine which way the key would turn."

Kneeling behind me, Antoine took control of my hands to show how the looped clip created tension. Even with his guidance it took a minute for the pins to pop free with a satisfying *click*.

"Voilà," he said. "Let's see what's inside."

Stepping closer, I raised my eyebrows, seeing a set of double-edged throwing knives in the drawer. Antoine picked one up and began a series of flips that spun the blade in vertical arcs, landing the handle in his palm, then, without warning, he hurled the knife at the wall, producing a sound like a whirling lariat, followed by a *thud* as it sank deep.

"It's a reflex," Antoine said. "I will fix the hole."

"Actually," I said, "I'm used to a man throwing a knife in a kitchen. My farrier, Brumby, tried to hit a wolf spider, and it jumped at his face. It's amazing how shrill a man's scream can be."

"He's from Australia, where spiders are deadly," Antoine said, pulling the blade from the wall. "Next time you're in the garage, check out Barry's history with these things. The older target reflects poor aim and too much steam. The newer one shows scary accuracy."

"Maybe it's a local sport," I said. "Like darts."

Sitting on a countertop stool, sipping coffee, I watched Antoine crack eggs into a mason jar he found in the cupboard. With his right hand shaking the mixture into a frothy blur, he plucked a skillet from a shelf and placed it on the burner. Soon, a dollop of butter was melting over a low flame, turning the stove into a hub of sizzling sounds and inviting aromas. In no time, a richly browned goat cheese omelet was delivered to my plate with a blueberry muffin seared to perfection. If we were to be equals in terms of skills and perks, I needed to step up my game.

Smiling as he sat next to me and began to eat, Antoine said, "You look as if a man has never cooked for you before."

"Umm ... possibly never," I said.

"I find it helps me focus," Antoine said. "Just now, I was drifting along, enjoying the known tasks, when the party chaos puzzled me all over again. Strangers are handling the damage while the rock band is out there touring and living their lives. According to Moritz, Force Eject is due back from Japan today. See what you can learn at your dance class."

"I'm not leaving you here to work alone," I said.

"I am experiencing déjà vu," Antoine said.

"I left the argument alone because I didn't want to spoil our time in the hot tub," I said. "Now it's daylight. We've covered the lion's share of work. Let's clock out and spend the day hiking."

"You're up to speed on my calls with Zach and his mother," Antoine said. "I'm planning to visit them in California before heading home. That gives us two days to prove the opposite of my usual work norm. Essentially, that the project you've undertaken is threat-free."

"We're already there," I said. "The double-homicide in Maui was open and shut. Katrina outgrew her friendship with Jasmine. Moritz is full of baloney and beer, so count me out regarding his report of friction among the *Kukuna Mahina's* shareholders. Reginald was opposed to scrapping the ship for a quick gain. Others got cold feet, as people often do." I shrugged. "Normal disagreements, normal dysfunction."

"What about the thugs?" Antoine asked.

"I'll avoid them," I said. "Piece of cake."

After a moment of careful thought, Antoine said, "In November, I was shocked to learn that my enemy named me as his heir. It's possible there was a bit of remorse in his gesture, but I believe he enjoyed burdening me with the task of sorting out his ill-gotten gains."

"He punished you with paperwork?" I asked.

"And a Learjet," Antoine said.

Squinting, I said, "What …?"

"I'm a licensed pilot," Antoine said. "An aircraft would be an asset in certain regards, but again, it's an ill-gotten gain. Sorting out his estate involves government agencies and full-time accountants."

"You own a private *jet?*" I demanded.

"It's a burden that demands pity," Antoine insisted. "But others will react according to their mindset. To speed up my assessment of the players before I leave for California, I sent Harve the specs and asked if he knew anyone looking to buy a jet for a bargain price."

"What if it backfires and causes trouble?" I asked.

"We will handle it with Ted's help," Antoine said. "Leave the dishes for a moment. I believe in showing rather than telling."

Snagging the last half of my blueberry muffin to eat along the way, I followed Antoine down the walkway to his sedan, where he opened the trunk to reveal a serious-looking briefcase that could not be opened with paperclips. He used the key and lifted the lid to show two sidearms, several knives in sheaths, and electronic gizmos … on the top layer.

"The goal is to avoid needing any of these," Antoine said.

Staring, I asked, "You carry this stuff everywhere?"

"This is my simplified kit," he said.

"Gosh." I nodded. "I guess I shouldn't be surprised."

"In an ideal world, I would have been told you were being followed in Maine," Antoine said. "As you know, communication broke down. Once Sue alerted me, I came in loaded for bear."

"I reported the cars that followed me," I said. "It's the age-old problem of a woman's concerns being dismissed as paranoid."

"It's being expedited by my group," Antoine said. "At the end of the cases, we delivered irrefutable evidence. In recent days, the communication factor has clarified remarkably. In a nutshell, you won't be called upon to testify in court, Sonny. To the point that it might not make the evening news. There's a shared wish to curtail publicity."

"I've dreamed of a quiet outcome," I said. "Now there are two reasons never to forget this day. Two earthquake moments."

"On a further note," he said. "In case you haven't caught on, the Sonny effect is not entirely unique. There is an Antoine effect."

With a slow smile, I had no trouble recalling how he'd been ahead of the curve and unpredictable, allowing him to protect me, flush bad guys out of hiding, and be in the right place at the right time.

"Our inner blueprints play a role," Antoine said. "But I think it's about growing up as outsiders. Instead of feeling constrained by conventions and norms, we're able to pivot. After flying Harve's plane, you're aware of the effect of wind. Sheer is volatile. Loft is necessary."

"Let me guess," I said. "I'm mostly the 'sheer' element."

"Everyone has the potential for both," Antoine said. "The dynamic varies from person to person. I'm a creative cop. You're a creative, strategic artist. We mix yin and yang in a seamless blend. The main goal is to get what we need and live to see another day."

"Living to see another day is a good point," I said. "Given my history of not knowing my father, I'm sensitive to your situation with Zach. I've appreciated your help on the project, but there are limits. You will head to California on schedule. No ifs, ands, or buts."

"I appreciate how you support Zach," Antoine said, indulging his new habit of wryly tweaking my chin. "To be clear, the Sonny effect translates to loft, to the point that intractable iron objects begin to float. Conversely, it tends to expand outward, with sketchy impact within. Is it possible for you to pause for *one* moment and appreciate your wins?"

"My mind is slow to process good news," I said. "Especially with your unauthorized Learjet plan already in motion."

With a sigh, Antoine said, "Bon. Let's get to work."

* * *

Leaving the afternoon heat behind me, I stepped into the dance studio amid the giggles of twenty children in fanciful fairy costumes in the wake of their lesson. While Jason praised them for the benefit of their beaming parents, Mary and Jasmine popped up from the chairs along the back wall to my right, looking pleased to catch me off guard with their visit. All the more startling, Jasmine was the first to hug me.

"There's a minor favor I need to ask," she confessed. "But mostly, after talking things through with Mary, I feel awful for giving you a hard time at the motorcycle shop. I was overly intense."

"No worries," I said. "We rounded the bend."

"We don't want to impinge on your lesson," Mary said, and then with a covert look signaling a reference to Agent Telford, she added, "I heard mention of your intention to stop in and see Reginald."

"Tomorrow, if all goes well," I said.

"Then maybe you can help," Jasmine said. "I need to retrieve some clothes I left in Katrina's bedroom, but Reginald sees me as an opinionated menace. Mary thinks it's best for me to stay away."

"I'll be happy to fetch your clothes," I said.

To help narrow the search, Jasmine opened her phone to send shots of the jackets and shirts she'd left in Katrina's closet.

"I'm not asking for the presents I gave her," Jasmine specified. "I still hope that Katrina and I can work through whatever went wrong. Toward that end, tell Pop-Pop I'm sorry for any confusion."

"That's a thoughtful added touch," Mary said, catching my eye with a pleased look. "I'm sure Reginald will appreciate it."

"Here's his phone number," Jasmine said, sending it along. "He's leery of unknown callers and his voicemail is full. If you text me your ETA, I'll try to be available to answer any questions."

"Here comes Jason," Mary said. "Enjoy your class."

After hugging Mary and Jasmine on their way out, Jason grabbed a box from a chair and opened it to show the new shoes he'd promised as a replacement for the ones I wore in my first class.

"The way things are turning out, I'll owe you ten pairs of shoes," Jason said quietly. "There's lots to talk about, but let's focus on your lesson. We'll switch gears once Petrel steps out for a meeting."

"I need to warm up," I reminded him.

"Absolutely, let's get to it. According to Arlene, you were an ace at the paso doble," Jason said, clasping my right hand, with my left hand lightly on his opposing arm, with reminders on maintaining a rounded frame with space between us. "Relax your shoulders."

"Wait," I said. "I'm still stuck on, 'according to Arlene.'"

"You do realize this is the information age," Jason said, smiling. "I've fast-forwarded your progress by talking to your friends."

"You *talked* to Arlene?" I asked.

Shaking me a little to get my attention, Jason said, "We're not starting with a dance of mine. I spent most of last night learning the routine that you perfected when you were fourteen."

I paused. "You mean …?"

"Yeah, buckle up," Jason said. "Your brain is about to take over."

"Can we walk through the steps first?" I asked.

"Arch your back a bit more," Jason said, putting me at ease with his steadiness and calm as he guided me through the routine in graceful slow motion. "Perfect, let's increase our speed, forward, forward, swivel-close. Embody the paso vibe, strong through your core."

Stunned, but smiling, I followed Jason's call for an appel light stomp to close my left foot, then gliding steps forward, to the side, and finally a "whisk" step that put us in a promenade position. Watching our reflections in the mirror, I corrected my posture and footwork through the stylized steps that I likened to stirring water aside with my toes.

"Appel left," I said, taking over the narration. "Smoothly back on my right foot, wide, saucy swing left, slow-close right."

"*Very* nice," Jason said.

Twenty minutes later, we resumed our rounded, arched embrace as a timer counted down, then music thundered around us.

With swift turns and rhythmic pauses, we performed the poetic dance that symbolized a matador's stances and flourishes, separating into spins, and then closing into our rounded frame to execute fast-moving footwork: a dynamic partnership that demanded quick breathing and sharp focus. Throughout, Jason's chest and shoulders provided structure, his legs provided momentum, and his expression gave subtle cues.

With a flick of his eyebrows, he signaled a dip, then, with his left arm behind his back, he supported my arch with his right arm, allowing me to gracefully drape and point my toe at the ceiling. Lifted upright and on the move again, my memory of the steps truly kicked in through a sequence of spins and footwork that ended in a dramatic final pose.

Grinning, Jason said, "Welcome, time traveler."

"Indeed, bravo!" Petrel said, sweeping toward us in a flowered jacket and white trousers. "The choreography didn't include a wow factor, but never mind. Your potential is obvious. *Do* try a tango."

"Maybe in a later session," I said, sadly out of breath.

"We'll build up to it," Jason said.

"Listen," Petrel said confidentially. "I heard some mention of a plan to visit Reginald. Given his rapid decline, he's been forgetful about delivering our loan agreement. As far as I know, the document is signed and sealed. All that remains is the 'delivered' step. Tuck the folder under your arm, perhaps. Casually, on your way out."

"Only with Mr. White's permission," I said guardedly.

"Check if you must," Petrel said. "From what I've heard, your house-guest can handle things if Reginald is grouchy."

"Petrel, if I'm not mistaken, you've got a meeting in the wings," Jason said. "With the folks who want to rent the space upstairs."

"As always, thank you for being my conscience," Petrel said on his way to the door. "Sonny, let me know how it goes."

Motioning for me to be patient for a moment, Jason listened for the sound of Petrel's car pulling out of the lot, then he used the remote control to shut off the ceiling camera for added privacy.

"He's a bit of a snoop," Jason explained. "According to Jasmine, the ex-cons followed you after we parted on the road. According to my uncle, you were calm when you returned the bike."

Hoping to limit fallout and complexities, I lightly pressed until I was assured that Jasmine hadn't told Jason about my video.

"Thankfully," I said. "I recognized the truck pulling into the lot and hid in the bathroom stall, so don't let it worry you. While we're resting, I feel it's time to tell you that I briefly met Chip."

"Mary mentioned it," Jason said. "Along with a bit more background on why you're pitching in at the rental house. Hopefully, you'll stay on, even though you've got Jasmine back in gear."

"I'm committed to finishing the house project," I said. "And I'm still in shock over Chip's death. Even though our interactions were brief, it's impossible to picture him taking drugs."

Nodding, but frowning in deep thought, Jason draped his face towel over his shoulders and led me to the back chairs. Sitting with his elbows on his knees, he looked torn and undecided.

"A year ago, I would have denounced the rumors outright," Jason said. "Even in school, he was more of a myth than an actual guy, constantly on the move to save whales and coral reefs. You know those super-caffeinated drinks? Chip chugged those now and then, and he definitely had that vibe when he blamed me for alienating Katrina. Maybe he needed a means of balancing out the jitters at the end of the day."

"Did you have a follow-up talk?" I asked.

"Yeah, he sought me out and apologized," Jason said. "With grumbled remarks about others, like he wasn't finished rattling cages. Jasmine was convinced that Reginald's business affairs led to financial troubles, but I'm worried that somebody got fresh with Katrina."

"If so, why wouldn't she tell her best friend?" I asked.

"Hence, why I was concerned to hear Reginald's prison cronies hunted you down," Jason said. "The whole situation is like trying to see a star in the night sky. It shifts in and out of view. All of a sudden, Jasmine is upbeat and smiling. I'm the opposite. Next time the bastards cross my path, I'm inclined to step up and beat their ass. In case you don't know, I'm a fire dancer. There's an ancient fierceness involved."

"It's not helpful to lose your cool," I said. "I'm planning to see Reginald tomorrow. In the meantime, promise you'll hold back?"

"Yeah, I promise," Jason muttered.

"When is your next fire dance?" I asked.

"If I'm not mistaken," Jason said with a raised eyebrow. "You're about to ask me for tickets *and* fire dance lessons."

"Let's start with tickets," I said. "What's it like?"

With a rare display of swagger, Jason helped me to my feet to deliver double fist-bump taps and explosion hand signals.

"It's like that," Jason said. "But with fire."

15

Still overheated from my dance session and distracted by my fierce resolve not to let anything derail Antoine's visit with his son, I lingered in the cool comfort of the dairy aisle, squinting at the sell-by date on the lid of a tub of coconut yogurt. I loved the flavor, but not enough to buy a product that might have expired days or even weeks earlier.

"They do this on purpose," I said. "They use gray ink that smudges, so we're lured into buying items that should be tossed out."

Stepping aside to let a man reach around me, I put the yogurt back on the shelf and checked a second container, for all the good it did me. The possible smudged date ranged from last week to the end of the month, and judging from the exchange of murmurs behind me, I wasn't the only one who was fed up with corporate America.

"She's right, this lettering is total crap," one man said.

"Try using your glasses," another chimed in.

"Check the peach flavor to see if it's different," a third guy said.

"Same deal, they're all crap. Unbelievable."

"Help Sonny out," the first guy said. "This is getting sad."

Slowly, I turned in place and looked at the four fiftyish men who'd assembled themselves around me like stadium lights in a coliseum. As if poised to launch a golf outing, they wore slacks, short-sleeved shirts, expensive watches, and soft-soled shoes, which apparently allowed for traveling silently. As I looked at them with raised eyebrows, they smiled in response and, one by one, reached out to shake my hand.

"I'm Axe," the man in the red shirt said. "The dude in green is Riff. Chill favors blue, and the guy in yellow is Shredder."

"You're, umm … hit men?" I asked.

"No, those are the handles we're known for," he said. "Riff for drums, Chill for vocals, Shredder as in top guitarist, and the all-important bass Axe. I'll be crushed if you didn't look us up."

"You're the rock band," I said. "Force Eject."

"There we go," Axe said. "Now say it with a smile."

"This is the real us," Chill added. "Regular guys."

Squinting, I asked, "Were you passing by, or …?"

"Here's the history lesson," Axe said. "They say never look a mad dog in the eyes. It's the same with Gavin, whom you will have met. We tossed him some bucks, hoping to stop the noise about inspiring today's youth. The opposite happened. Emails, voicemails, doughy handshakes." With a shrug, the handsome guitarist added, "So, we staged a concert at a friend's house, and the wrong sort crashed the party. Naturally, we are appalled to know that a hot chick is stuck with the aftermath."

"I'm not averse to cleaning up a mess," I said.

"We heard the whole deal, you're on the skids from an asshole cheating on you back home in Maine," Axe said. "If we're on tour in his area, we'll stop by and trash his house as a goodwill gesture for your team spirit, but you're wincing like it would be a bad idea. He's tough and can handle himself? The opposite of Gavin?"

"He's an elite state trooper," I said. "A cop."

"Time to go," Chill murmured to one side.

"Calm down," Axe said. "Sonny's ex-boyfriend trooper guy is a zillion miles away, with no authority to write us up for disturbing the peace over a misunderstanding that wasn't our fault. Moving on to option B, we'll buy your groceries. What do you need?"

"I only stopped in for yogurt," I said, donning a smile as I slipped past the quartet. "It was nice meeting you, Mr. …?"

"Why bother with names when we're ships passing in the night?" Axe said. "Wait, it's daylight here. I'm experiencing jet lag."

"From …?" I prompted.

"Australia and Japan," Axe said. "I'm bound and determined to make up for the awful impression our fans made with the party mess. Guys, deploy across the store. Sizing her up, I think Sonny lives on chipmunk food. Fruits, those toast things, and veggies."

"I don't need a handout," I said. "If you want to make amends, contact the owner of the house. Barry … somethingorother."

"You didn't ask his last name?" Axe said.

"That's the opposite of smart," Chill said.

No disagreement there. The man had a point. Shredder, on the other hand, contented himself with standing silently with his head tilted and his hands in his pockets, staring at me as if calculating my exact measurements in the back of his head. For a coffin, for instance.

"Gosh," I said. "It's getting late."

"According to rumor," Chill said, "You're an exotic dancer of the pole arts variety. Are you looking for work?"

"I'm a photographer," I said carefully. "While I'm in the Kona area, I am brushing up on my ballroom dancing skills—"

"Wait, wait, *waaaaaiiiiiiiittt,*" Riff said, pointing at his phone to show that he'd just caught up with the local gossip. "You're living in Barry's house with a cab driver who owns a Learjet?"

"Which answer will end this discussion the fastest?" I asked, then remembered the gist of Antoine's game plan. "Yes, my boyfriend … man friend … person of interest …" I closed my eyes. "Indeed, my enigmatic houseguest from the north owns a private jet."

Chill said quietly, "So, you're, like, his …?"

"*Friend,*" I said. "As far as I know, Antoine is discussing the jet with Harve and others at Barry's rental house."

"Guys," Axe said. "Sonny might be writing an article for an East Coast magazine. We need to leave on a positive note."

"Would cash suffice?" Chill asked.

Handed loose bills, I said, "There's a certain stigma around a stranger giving cash to a woman, but perhaps not for you."

"Good luck with the yogurt," Axe said.

No longer in the dark about how Barry's house was trashed, I watched the group high-five each other as they departed, and then I pulled out my phone to give Antoine ten minutes of advance notice.

The rock band is headed your way, I texted.

Dots appeared, then Antoine replied, *All is well?*

Yes, I'm at the store, I texted.

SFSGBMNAH. TFTU.

"Not again," I moaned, forced to make sense of the letters.

So far, so good, but maybe need another hour, Antoine texted. *Thanks for the update.*

I smiled. "Of course. Got it."

* * *

Stirring sugar into my glass of iced tea, I sat on the deck with my copy of *The Hawaiian Archipelago* open as if I was going to read. Instead, I watched the spectacle of ten men, over half of them middle-aged, sitting around the freshly scrubbed teak patio table, laughing over jokes and sending their deep male voices through the papaya trees and down the hillside toward the shimmering coast. It made sense for the local pilots to be interested in hearing about Antoine's jet, but along with Harve and Barry, Gavin, Moritz, Raja, Axe, Riff, Shredder, and Chill were in varying degrees of relaxed poses in folding chairs they'd dragged out of the garage. Sitting apart, and spending most of his time looking at his phone, Axe's son, Sam, seemed to have been roped in against his will.

In the center of everyone, with his sneakers crossed on the table and a cigar in hand, Antoine was teaching the men how to curse in Russian. Leaning forward with eager gazes, the successful older men were captivated by Antoine's cool demeanor and just about everything he said, with bursts of the all-important element of ribbing.

"Your name isn't online, dude," Riff said. "At *all.*"

"Perhaps you are spelling it wrong," Antoine said.

"If you're a bullshitter, it's in the upper register," Chill said. "But for all we know, you're speaking gibberish instead of Russian."

"Vasha nesposobnost' doveryat' pechal'na," Antoine said.

"Holy shit, it's for real," Chill said, staring at his phone. "According to my translator app, he said, 'Your inability to trust is sad.'"

"Knowing a language is one thing," Riff said. "Owning high-end gear is another. Barry, help us out. Is he a legit pilot?"

"*Excellent* idea," Chill said. "Fire up the jet and taxi down the runway. Barry will expose your ignorance in two seconds."

"I don't feel compelled to prove myself," Antoine said.

"That's a waffle," Chill said. "There's no way a Canadian cabbie would own a jet. Barry has gone quiet. He's outed you."

Smiling faintly, Antoine let a silence play out.

"The fact that you're enjoying the dare isn't helping matters," Barry said, studying Antoine with folded arms. "So, let's put it this way. You're living under my roof. I don't want to host a hustler."

"If I fail your tests?" Antoine asked.

"It's up to Sonny," Barry said. "She's up there watching us. By all accounts, she doesn't have patience for cheats and liars."

"What's in it for me?" Antoine asked.

"Pony up, guys," Axe said. "What's it worth?"

"I don't need cash," Antoine said. "As I've mentioned two times since she returned from her class, spending time with Sonny is my idea of a win. If I prove myself, you depart without further question."

Nods and smiles made the verdict unanimous.

Antoine spread his hands. "I am a cabbie. Last year, I inherited a jet from a man whose family made my sister and me orphans at an early age. As for the wherewithal to pilot an aircraft, a former cop seems on par with a cabbie. Harve has made a success of it."

"Well spoken, my friend," Harve said, enjoying his position of knowing Antoine's true identity and some of the background. "It sounds like the former jet owner was trying to right his past wrongs."

"What did he do for a living?" Barry asked.

"Banking and pharmaceuticals," Antoine said.

"All right, he's giving a smooth answer to anything we ask," Chill said. "Fire up the jet. Barry, be the control tower."

Signaling Gavin to take his cigar, Antoine appeared to be visualizing an instrument panel as he communicated with a mechanic or related personnel to verify that the ground power unit was hooked up.

"Batteries look good, above 24 volts," Antoine said, touching knobs and levers as he narrated a pre-flight checklist that I somewhat overheard. "Left and right avionics masters are on, brake set, throttle is idle. Landing gear lever, down. Flaps, up. Spoiler, retracted."

"What the hell is all that?" Riff asked.

"He's in the pre-start checklist," Barry said. "It's not like a car. Before starting the engines and introducing fuel, you need sufficient airflow. Not to mention, if the controls are incorrectly engaged—"

"How many annoying items until we're in the air?" Riff asked.

"There are six lists, with further check-offs for climb-out and cruise," Barry said. "Next time you're bumming a ride—"

"Yeah, it's complex," Chill said. "Skip to the takeoff."

With a tired sigh, Barry said, "November-alpha-three-three-whiskey, taxi to runway two-eight-bravo, hold short of runway two-eight-left."

"Taxi to runway two-eight-bravo, hold short of runway two-eight-left, November-alpha-three-three-whiskey," Antoine said.

"We're seriously taking off?" Riff asked.

"In every sense," Barry said, motioning for the group to stand up with him. "I was tempted to pitch a poker game, but something tells me it's a good thing our cabbie friend won't be inclined."

"Perhaps on a future visit," Antoine said.

By then, I needed a checklist for lifting my lower jaw back into place, while Axe was smiling from the gambling rush.

"Sam, that could be you," he said. "Antoine has upgraded himself at an early age. Imagine flying us from here to there."

"Buy his jet, I'll start taking lessons," Sam said.

"Stop being a smartass," Axe said.

"By your own assessment, the band was out of synch in Japan," Sam said. "You stressed the need for practice time."

"Is there a problem?" Antoine asked.

"No, we're good," Axe said. "Father-son stuff."

Keeping pace with Sam, Antoine said, "Becoming a pilot is a reachable goal. Is your mother a part of the band?"

"She took off when I was born," Sam said. "My father can be a pain in the butt sometimes, but he raised me on his own."

"That says a lot," Antoine said.

As the group climbed into their cars, Moritz said, "Back to it, I guess. The downstairs sanding is nearly finished."

"Sonny and I worked all morning," Antoine said. "We have errands to run, so this is goodbye until tomorrow."

"You've turned out to be pretty cool," Raja said. "How did you manage to drink ten beers without getting a hangover?"

"I grew up on Canadian beer," Antoine said.

As he joined me, I let my eyebrows do the talking.

"Clearly, the rockers are stuck in their teens," he said. "Barry has an almost paternal air with the group. He's jaded, but tolerant. From his job, I guess. Mostly, I didn't see obvious red flags."

"You've flown the inherited jet?" I asked.

"Harve told me that you piloted his aircraft like an ace," Antoine said. "Let's focus on experiencing what you talked about the other day. How the schools of butterflyfish and tangs come to rest at dusk above the reef, suspended in the darkening water like ornaments."

"It's unnerving to snorkel as the light fades," I warned.

"'Man cannot discover new oceans unless he has the courage to lose sight of the shore,'" Antoine said, then he repeated the sentiment, far more beautifully in French, "'L'homme ne peut découvrir de nouveaux océans s'il n'a pas le courage de perdre de vue le rivage.'"

"You're quoting André Gide," I said. "A famous French author."

With a serene expression, I let him believe I was intellectual and bookish, when in truth, I'd heard him quoting the line to his son.

"Berrichon, you surprise me," Antoine said.

Equally serene, his gaze conveyed that I wasn't fooling anyone.

* * *

Side by side on softly cushioned recliners that Antoine had tucked together on the deck, we enjoyed the warm night air after a delicious dinner and a long soak in the hot tub. Beyond the balcony, the fringed leaves of the coconut palms cast shadows across the garden from the moonlight, and as always, the Pacific shimmered with mesmerizing light.

"I was skeptical of the plan," I said. "But it's good to see you looking reassured. Nobody asked you to buy their shares of the *Kukuna Mahina,* or pitched a shady deal where you could double your fortune."

"You saw the gist of the back-and-forth," Antoine said. "Digs, dares, and jabs mixed with legitimate skepticism. Annoying, but within the normal range. All that's left is getting a better sense of Reginald. Thanks to Jasmine, we have a reason to visit him tomorrow."

"Sweet." Swirling my glass, enjoying the way the frozen strawberry margarita sloshed, I said, "This is a powerful drink."

"Mine as well," Antoine said. "You're the one who blended them, thankfully without any Hawaiian moonshine."

"Did you try some?" I asked.

"A sniff nearly put me on my butt," Antoine said. "You mentioned making blueberry cordial. I'm sensing a theme."

"I know how to tap the brake," I assured him.

For a moment, I pictured my farm in the distance, then I realized I was looking toward Hong Kong. Based on the photos from my trail camera, heading home to icy winds could be postponed for another week, or perhaps longer, since I deserved a break after my volunteer effort. Without a written contract, what rights did I have if I wanted to extend my stay in the rental house until the spring thaw? Sipping the mixture of orange liqueur, tequila, and frozen berries, I opened my phone to check the legal consequences of becoming a property squatter in Hawaii.

"Look," I said, indicating the screen. "The question of whether it's legal to dumpster dive still has top billing in the search results. Same with marrying a cousin or owning a tank. Apparently, people also want to make sure it's legal to drive barefoot and own a fox."

"A few hours ago, we were swimming among fish along a reef at dusk," Antoine said, stretched out in a T-shirt and silky leisure slacks. "I'm not sure I can be convinced to live in Canada anymore."

"Nonsense, you love the change of seasons," I said.

"The signs of enabling nag at me," Antoine murmured. "Mixed in with friction among longtime friends, but even families can reflect that kind of dysfunction." With a frown, Antoine emerged from distraction and looked at me. "What were you saying about tanks?"

Handed my phone, Antoine cracked up over the search results, spilling his drink all over his shirt, then his gaze turned warm and serious as he tugged me closer, kissing me with tequila and orange liqueur on his lips. We dissolved together, hungry for contact, tipsy from booze, smiling as we reached under each other's shirts in search of warm, bare skin. With breathy moans and our legs entwined, we rolled into different positions on the recliners, dangerously close to tumbling onto the deck.

Still laughing in bursts, Antoine pulled me to my feet, tossed our shirts aside, and steered us past the rice paper doors in a slow, revolving orbit into the bedroom, where he'd left flowers on the nightstands and released the sheer fabric around the bed. Awash in golden candlelight, his hands slid down to remove my pajama bottoms, then skimmed upward over my thighs and hips. A quick tug of his drawstring dropped his pants to the floor, then I melted into his embrace, savoring the warmth of his bare skin against mine. With his arms encircling me, holding me close, he explored my face with kisses, sensual and tender, whispering soft murmurs in my ear, a rippling, captivating verse in Hawaiian. I shivered, spellbound by the cadence, a transfer of his feelings without the clutter of known words.

"Aloha wau iā 'oe," I whispered.

With a smile and a kiss, he scooped me up and carried me to the bed. Joining me among the tropical quilts and fluffed pillows, he unraveled me with caresses, alternating between looking into my eyes and delivering soft kisses and ear nibbles with candlelight playing over the sheer fabric around the bed. Slipping his arm under my knee, he drew us together.

With fluttering eyes, caressing his back to tighten our closeness all the more, I arched from a bolt of pleasure, pressed into the pillows with his fast breathing and soft moans in my ear. From misty dreams of him in that same bed, Antoine was there *with* me, stirring pleasure so fast that it took my breath away. Moaning and gripping his chest, I cried out from the beauty of it, lost in the shimmering madness of ecstasy.

Euphoric, like a drifting spark of light, I felt my body being gathered up and gently settled amid the pillows with his back against the headboard and my knees folded on either side of his hips.

His fingers brushed through my hair as he made eye contact, then his hands drifted down my back and tucked me closer, sparking new rockets of pleasure. Awakened and aware, we surrendered to the new delights to be explored, slowly moving, closing our eyes, then embracing and kissing each other, until Antoine's lips found my ear, delivering rumbles of sound that shivered through me, sweetly, serenely stirring ecstasy.

With a choked-off sound he embraced me all the more tightly, softly moaning, flexed and lost in time and space. Lips brushing, hands roaming, we held each other for a long moment, cherishing our warmth and closeness with our eyes closed and our foreheads touching.

Leaning away, I ran my fingers over his chest, memorizing how he looked in the soft candlelight with the leaves of palm trees rustling beyond the rice paper doors. With a blissful gaze, Antoine watched his hands trace my curves down to my thighs, and then upward.

"I have discovered a new delight," he murmured. "My fingertips can feel even the tiniest freckle on the way up to your shoulders, like here and here. If I turn my palms outward to let the opposite side of my fingers take a turn on the way back, all I feel is softness."

"How are you so sweet?" I whispered.

"Tequila and orange liqueur," Antoine said.

Awash in endorphins, we stretched out among the pillows, holding each other in the flickering candlelight. With smiles and murmurs barely heard, we fell asleep at the ridiculous hour of eight p.m.

16

In pressed slacks and my no-iron travel blouse, I used the toaster oven as a mirror to tame my hair with a clip, inspired by Katrina's look, thinking it might have a subliminal effect in winning Reginald's trust. Splashing sounds in the bathroom told me Antoine was still cleaning up after our morning of work. While I waited for him, I put our lunch dishes into the washer and brought the filled trash bag to the garage.

With the sun in my eyes, I almost ducked for cover when I saw a stranger combing his hair in the doorway. Two seconds later, I realized it was Antoine wearing a skin-tight lavender shirt tucked into creased black slacks secured with a narrow belt, none of which were from his luggage. His damp, sun-streaked waves were smoothed down, and he had swapped his battered sneakers for stylish, polished shoes.

"Umm, are you sure?" I asked, pointing to his visible socks.

"The slacks are an unfortunate length," Antoine admitted. "To blend in as a tourist and allow for possible tangents that might unfold, I'm borrowing clothes I found in a box in the garage. Judging from your reaction, I've nailed my goal of not looking like a highly trained cop."

"Possibly a *teensy* bit too much," I said.

"According to Jasmine, Reginald is mostly homebound," Antoine said. "By all accounts, he's volatile at times, but I want to bring up the ex-cons to test out any hint of shady business deals. If he's showing signs of illness, we'll fetch Jasmine's clothes and leave him in peace."

Antoine's dark sedan reminded me of the vehicle he drove in Maine, including a pack of mint gum in the cup holder. Wearing sunglasses, he chewed at a steady pace during our drive, navigating the twists and turns of a hilly, poorly paved road on the outskirts of Kona. We enjoyed the feel of tropical air blustering around our faces, but as the tires kicked up dust on the rough road, we had to roll up the windows.

"We are on Moanalualani Road," Antoine said.

I pointed to my phone. "I'm letting the app call the shots."

"What if we careen down the hillside?" Antoine asked. "You stagger out and need to call 911. What is the street name?"

"Moana … lua … lani," I said. "I can recall it because I heard you listening to the street names on an app before we left."

"My sister, Chloé, taught me to how learn through repetition and immersion," Antoine said. "You know we were foster kids of sorts, scooped up by a crime family. Chloé made a game of sharing secrets with a revolving door of languages to keep my mind engaged. The family scoffed at it as gibberish. It's thanks to Chloé that I learned how to be resilient under extreme pressure. I'm torn about telling Zach about her."

"The way she died, you mean," I said. "From an overdose."

"Exactly," Antoine said. "It would involve showing Zach a photo of Chloé. Their eyes are similar. I'm concerned that her story will stick in his head and I won't be on hand to help." Frowning, Antoine glanced at me. "Similar to how things spun off track when I left Maine. I'm worried that we're not leaving time for a heart-to-heart talk."

"Tell me more about where you are with Zach," I said.

"Essentially, I'm three months into a reality reboot," he said. "Not the basics. It's a dangerous world. It's imperative that I win Zach's trust, but all he's ever known is a colorless, one-sided version of me. My unusual history is to blame. His mother's perception of me."

"Was it a straightforward breakup?" I asked.

"Not according to her, but be aware, Dan might twist things around over the long haul," Antoine said. "To balance the sharing, what happens when you get back and Dan knocks on your door?"

"I doubt he will," I said.

"I'm asking because you appeared to split up with him the night of the sting," Antoine said. "Then you reversed."

"I know it looked that way from the outside," I said. "Apart from our problems, Dan is a decent guy. We have to live in the same small town, so I favored the high road. For now, I prefer not dwelling on it."

"It feels important, but all right," Antoine said. "In Maine, given the volatile unknowns, I was forced to operate as a lone wolf. A careless move would have endangered your life. That same rule applied to Zach. When I try to explain, I flounder for the right tone."

"It's natural to tap the brake," I said. "Keep showing up to dispel any wrong notions. When it feels right to share more of your story, lean on how you handled the turmoil. How you coped."

"Am I allowed to respond with, 'ditto?'" Antoine asked.

"Maybe just this once," I said.

"For the upcoming visit, I'm trying to listen to his mother's hints of past faults instead of arguing," he said. "It's uncanny to see both of us in Zach. It's probably the case in all kids, but new to me. Her husband plugs away at the role of stepfather, but he's an introvert, a bit of a chore in some regards. It's his work that's enabling us to meet in California. An academic conference on the doorstep of an amusement park."

"You don't sound sold on the location," I said.

"Unchecked screaming that might be thanks to a guardrail breaking loose?" Antoine asked. "What could go wrong?"

As we neared our destination, Antoine eased to a stop as an ancient Cadillac blocked both lanes of the narrow road, with glints along the grille and front hood that added to its air of belligerence.

"Listen to him gunning the engine," I said.

"It's startling," Antoine agreed.

"I think that's Reginald's car," I said. "If people are right that he's got early dementia, I'm alarmed to see him driving."

"See if he'll tell you where he's going," Antoine said. "I'll stay here so he doesn't blaze away. We can offer him a ride."

I stepped out to the noise of Reginald gunning the gas with the brake on, causing his old Cadillac to rock with menace.

"Please stop that," I said as I reached his window.

"Who's this bastard in my way?" Reginald growled. "I bet it's one of the hooligans trying to stop me from checking my rental property. I installed cameras to make sure they respect my no-fly zone, but they're like vermin. They keep cutting the feed."

"I'm Sonny," I said. "Do you remember me?"

Squinting against the sun's rays, Reginald peered at me through dusty glasses that framed his tanned skin and unfocused eyes. I had a feeling he'd grabbed reading glasses on his way out, preferring to see the dashboard rather than the road ahead.

"You're Jason's new woman," Reginald said.

"I am *not* Jason's woman," I said. "Your voicemail is full, so I wasn't able to leave a message about stopping by to say hello and pick up Jasmine's clothes. She's aware that she's not in your favor."

"The key is under the mat," Reginald said. "Don't tell anyone."

"Can I ask where you're heading?" I asked.

In fits and starts, Reginald conveyed that he was on his own in tackling the logistics of the short-term rentals for a cottage he owned, located a mile down a connecting road. A pair of past tenants had been "a pain in the ass" from the start after he'd agreed to drop the price if the able-bodied men promised to make repairs that went hand-in-hand with rentals, like iffy plumbing fixtures, lawn care, and jammed locks.

"All they did was make messes," he added. "Men like them don't have any grit. Two seconds of hammering, and they're done."

"You shouldn't face them alone," I said. "If you'd like, my friend and I can come with you to ensure everything is okay."

"What's in it for you?" Reginald demanded.

"I believe it would put Katrina's mind at ease," I said.

"In that case, hop in and ride shotgun," Reginald said. "You're in good hands. I've brought my cane in case there's trouble."

A quick signal to Antoine conveyed the plan. He backed up to the nearest driveway and pulled in behind us once I was seated in the Cadillac, where wrappers littered the floor, and the upholstery was flaking from years of baking in the tropical sun. Every inch of the interior was coated with dust, and given that Reginald's fierce attention was trained on the dirt lane up ahead, he didn't notice me opening the glove box, or my look of worry upon finding the paperwork was a year out of date.

"Out of the way, you crazy mutt!" Reginald hollered as a loose dog darted across the road in front of us. "That animal has been a menace all day, running in and out of the yard. It's your boyfriend's doing, like I have control over my granddaughter dumping him."

I paused. "Are you talking about Jason?"

"It's his uncle's mutt," Reginald said. "I saw it at the garage a few weeks ago, jumping on my ass like I was a chew toy."

"Stray animals often look alike," I said. "Given that the motorcycle shop is down in Hilo, miles and miles away—"

I gulped, jerked forward as Reginald slammed the brake, and then he gunned backward to idle next to a one-story cottage.

"Just like I figured," he growled as his loose aim caused him to miss the driveway and cut a swath of tire marks across the browning lawn. "The front door is open, and I think that's the hooligan's car down the old coffee grove's dirt lane. It's hard to get my ass out of bed these days, so I was late in noticing the camera feed cut out in the wee hours. The outside light was busted, but there was activity in the yard. I bet they're the ones who brought the dog, and it took off. A ransom situation. Mark my words, they'll be tapping Jason's uncle for a big payday."

"My friend and I will get to the bottom of it," I said.

"Take my cane, just in case," Reginald said.

"Keep it with you," I said. "Stay in the car, all right?"

Antoine joined me on the lawn for a few minutes, gazing toward the car that Reginald had pointed out and turning his head to assess bursts of guys calling to each other in an overgrown area behind the cottage that Reginald described as an old coffee grove. From the sound of it, someone in the neighborhood was struggling to catch the dog.

"Nobody is living in the house right now?" Antoine asked.

I summed up Reginald's account of seeing camera footage indicating a forced entry, and his dim opinion of previous renters.

"Hang back while I check inside," Antoine said. "Diffusing tension is our best bet for an uncomplicated day. If trouble unfolds, I'll dive in and improvise. Roll with it. Follow my lead."

I nodded. "I'll keep an eye out."

Concerned to see the male part of his backup force disappear into the house, Reginald climbed out with a groan and swung his cane back and forth with a few practice swings. Looking spent, he joined me in the shade of a eucalyptus tree and leaned heavily on his cane. From his pocket, he pulled out a flask, first offering me a sip, then tilting it back to gulp down whatever liquid was inside—whiskey, judging by the smell.

"It's a tonic for the nervous system," he wheezed.

Nodding, I said, "Its effects are well known."

While his attention was on the cottage, I crossed to his Cadillac and grabbed the keys to prevent him from mowing down the neighborhood, then I pretended to have stepped away to stretch my legs.

"Blame my granddaughter for this moment," Reginald said. "It's been a while since she came home. I'm worried sick."

"Listen, Mr. White—"

"A fine-looking woman like you can call me either Reginald or Pop-Pop," he said, suddenly merry. "A year ago, you would have been winking and crooking your finger at me. I'm serious. I'm a catch."

"I've heard stories along those lines, but my dance card is full," I said. "If you have your phone, let's call Katrina now."

"She never picks up," Reginald said. "It's fishy as hell."

"Have you always been close?" I asked.

"Always," Reginald said. "I raised her after her mother died."

I nodded. "What about her father?"

"Dead and buried," Reginald said with sudden emotion. "Losing a link in the chain of life is the worst. It dims the world."

"Sit over here," I said, guiding Reginald to a lava boulder. "The dog is heading toward us. I don't want it to knock you down."

Suddenly, the car parked in the nearby dirt lane reversed toward us and slammed on its brakes, kicking up a cloud of dust. I watched in shock as the two thugs who'd cornered me on my way to Hilo lurched out in pursuit of the dog. The third man, dismayed to see me staring at him as he climbed out of the back seat, hesitated for a second, then ran away down the road, denying me a chance to identify him, other than a glimpse of his rough beard and long hair under a green *Kukuna Mahina* hat.

"Shit, get back here!" one of the thugs hollered.

"Never mind him," the other said. "Focus on the mutt."

Motioning for Antoine to give me a chance to handle the situation, I was surprised to realize that Reginald was right about the wild-eyed dog: it was the same animal that had nearly knocked me flat at the motorcycle garage. Amidst a cloud of dust, the thugs gave up chasing the dog, veered toward me across the yard, and arrived out of breath.

"Who the hell are you?" the bigger man asked.

"First things first," I said. "Who owns that dog?"

"Us, of course," he said. "We've got it covered."

"I'm an experienced animal trainer," I said, aiming to set the stage for pressing them with questions. "I'm happy to help."

"Knock yourself out," he said, handing me a bacon treat.

"Darned ruffians," Reginald hollered, swinging his cane. "I'll teach you to renege on a bet or whatever the hell is going on."

"The first priority is containing the darting animal," I said. "Yelling and waving a cane isn't helping. Give me some space."

As the dog paused, panting and wagging his tail, so spent from his dash through the neighborhood that he looked ready to collapse, I crossed to the spigot on the side of the house, uncoiled the hose, and dragged it to a large, upturned ceramic planter that I could sit on to spare my pants from getting dirty. As water trickled out and formed a puddle, I cooed and pretended to eat the bacon treat. Unsurprisingly, the dog bounded toward me and dropped the prized object he'd apparently dug out of the ground. In a flash, while the dog gobbled down the bacon treat and slurped water, I identified his favorite toy as a human lower jawbone.

Quickly, I dragged the ceramic planter into position over the bone, sat down to secure the evidence, and used American Sign Language to relay the shocking news to Antoine. His return signals conveyed that he was alerting 911, and if possible, I should stall the thugs.

"That's some bad twitching in your hands," the fiftyish thug said, as he used the bottom of his T-shirt to wipe his sweaty face. "Medication can cause that, and sometimes, it's permanent."

"I'll show you permanent," Reginald said, menacing the man with his cane. "You're a lawless ingrate. The worst of the worst."

"Pipe down, or we'll snap you like a twig," the other thug said.

"With that kind of talk," I said. "It's no wonder the third guy took off. Your son, maybe? Do you live in the neighborhood?"

"Cut the chitchat," he said. "That was a neat trick, covering the bone with the planter. Keep the dog away so we can get it."

"No, I feel dizzy," I said. "I need to stay put."

As their annoyance turned into action, I tightly straddled the heavy planter like a jockey while the men tried to pry me off.

"Lady, get off your ass," the big guy said. "I'm counting to three, and then you're going to need to wear eye makeup for a while."

Suddenly, the cottage door swung open.

"Darling?" Antoine said, squinting through a pair of thick glasses as he stepped out with his hair in disarray and his shoulders hunched to look harmless. "What the devil happened to my glasses?"

"They're on your face, dude," the closest thug said.

"You must be the plumber," Antoine said. "My wife wasn't here for five minutes before she clogged the toilet."

"I did *no* such thing," I said hotly.

Antoine squinted. "What are the police doing down there?"

As the thugs turned to look, he delivered a jab to the nearest man's windpipe, making him choke and clutch his neck.

"Dear God, a coconut wasp flew into his mouth," Antoine said. "We need to get it out, or the stinger will embed itself in his larynx."

Gripping the man from behind as if to perform the Heimlich maneuver, Antoine linked his fists together and delivered a succession of tight abdominal blows until the thug dropped to the grass, knocked senseless except for lengthy, wheezing groans.

"How could this happen?" the second guy demanded.

"He'll recover," Antoine said. "On to fixing the toilet?"

"I'm not the plumber," the man said darkly.

"Of course, you're here for the cash deposit," Antoine said. "Darling, keep an eye on the stung man. We'll be back in a minute."

"On your feet," Reginald growled, poking the fallen man with his cane, then flailing his backside. "This will teach you to target the elderly."

"That's enough," I said. "He's already down."

I looked up as the second man staggered out of the cottage, gagging and clutching his throat. In his lavender shirt, polished shoes, and mid-ankle pants, Antoine made a show of helping him to the walkway, then he abruptly let go, causing the man to hit the pavers hard.

Staring, Reginald asked, "*He* got stung too?"

"I'm afraid it's an entire nest," Antoine said, flexing his hand after two instances of targeted, sudden use. "I have called 911."

"That's my cue to go," Reginald said, creating divots in the lawn with his cane as he crossed to his Cadillac. "Shit, I dropped my keys."

Having watched me secure the keys, Antoine knelt by the planter and tried to build a clear picture before the police arrived. Often, pig and other animal mandibles were mistaken for human remains.

"Do pigs have fillings in their molars?" I asked.

Antoine closed his eyes. "No, I expect not."

"This is perfect," I whispered. "If I'd reported the thugs for banging on the bathroom door, the police would have accused me of overreacting. Now that I've reencountered them in a dire context, the police will accuse me of withholding evidence. Say hello to the bite-me-on-the-ass element of law enforcement. No matter what, I can't win."

"It's going to be chaotic," Antoine said, clasping my hand. "Amid the inevitable claims and counterclaims, you'll be asked if you know the men. To my understanding, you don't *know* them, correct?"

"No, I don't *know* them," I said.

"Be concise," Antoine said. "A typical problem officers face is having witnesses react to stress by sharing their life history."

"That would be wrong," I said. "A total bother."

"Exactly," Antoine said, instilling calm by leading the way with deep, slow breaths. "Tell the basics. I will handle the rest."

* * *

As Antoine predicted, chaos unfolded as the thugs claimed to be good Samaritans and Reginald hollered that he was a victim of harassment and blackmail plots. When the short thug wanted an antidote for coconut wasp venom, an EMT reassured him not to worry, then used a circling motion to signal to the officers that the thug was insane.

Antoine watched with intense focus until the ranting and hollering died down, and one of the thugs pointed at us.

"They're trying to rent the cottage from the crazy old bastard," he said. "Somebody should warn them. He's a crook."

Prompted forward, Antoine donned a smile. With his chest proudly open and his black socks painfully in view from mid-ankle pants that made him seem the opposite of an elite, highly-trained cop, he extended his arm, straight out, to shake hands with the officer.

"Antoine Chamailard, at your service," he said, presenting his badge with an elaborate flourish. "As you can see, I work in law enforcement for King and country in neighboring Canada."

"Good for you," the officer said, waving away the badge. "Stick to the basics. You're here with your wife looking for a rental?"

"I confess that we are not married," Antoine said quietly. "I claimed that because these men were casting gazes at her."

"Nutshell version," the cop said. "What happened?"

Antoine nodded. "Bon. Nous roulions pour rencontrer—"

"Hang on," the cop said. *"What …?"*

"Apologies, I switch to my native language when I feel shocked and out of my depth," Antoine said, mopping his brow. "The object under the planter is to blame. A human jawbone."

"I *knew* it," Reginald hollered. "When they rented my cottage last year, their luggage consisted of bags and shovels, and they crept about all hours of the night. They buried a body in the coffee grove!"

A scuffle broke out as the thugs cut loose and ran toward their vehicle in a desperate attempt to escape from the pursuing officers. Once they were handcuffed, the planter was lifted, revealing the gruesome jawbone and igniting a fresh burst of anger in Reginald.

"We've got cops, and we've got crooks, the same formula that was in play when I was set up as a teen," he hollered, spent and sweaty, but determined to be heard. "It's happening again. I've felt it for a year. I've got money this time, and friends in high places."

Pulling us aside, the officer said quietly, "He's rich from the wrongful conviction settlement. A success story, but this past year, he's been losing his marbles. Given the bad history and indications that he's legit and law-abiding, we're urged to avoid tangling with him."

"In Canada, we follow a certain protocol," Antoine said. "Au début de la phase … pardon me, there I go again."

"We've got your information," the cop said. "If you want to lend a hand, bring Reginald home. He's on the road illegally."

"As you wish," Antoine said. "I am happy to help."

Once Antoine loaded Reginald into the front seat of his sedan, he pulled me aside and responded to my raised eyebrows.

"My colleagues and I have encountered a certain mindset among our counterparts in the United States," he said. "There's a tendency for them to assume that police work in Canada ranges from tranquilizing bears to pulling vehicles out of snowbanks. Stereotypes can be useful when it benefits me to walk away and play a minimal role."

"You all but begged them to dismiss you," I said.

"You've used a similar ploy, portraying an airhead woman from time to time, non?" Antoine asked. "Your heated glare says otherwise. Have I expressed my admiration for how you preserved the evidence? Well done, Berrichon. I am impressed beyond words."

"Nice save," I said, smiling faintly.

17

A mile or two down the road, I steered Reginald's Cadillac into the gravel driveway of a one-story house with faded siding, partially hidden by a sprawling pink bougainvillea bush. Antoine pulled into the adjacent space, helped Reginald climb out, and leaned into the back seat to retrieve our six-pack of spring water and a handful of granola bars.

"He's paranoid about being poisoned," Antoine said. "I've assured him that these are sealed. Apparently, he hasn't eaten all day."

"You saw the gist of what I'm up against," Reginald said. "It's nonstop agony, but I'm weathering the storm for Chip's sake."

I hesitated. "Chip Henderson?"

"Let's talk where Reginald can sit down," Antoine said.

Working in tandem to steady Reginald on our way to the front door, we saw telltale signs of neglect, like wobbly walkway pavers, bills spilling out of the mailbox, and a key that had slipped out from under the welcome mat. Inside the house, dust on furniture and dishes piled in the sink added substance to the story of Katrina not visiting.

As Antoine eased Reginald onto the couch, I noticed balled-up tissues beside a pile of scribbled notes that looked like frustrated attempts to update a will. Katrina's dance trophies were arranged around the table as if

Reginald conversed with them during lonely moments. Through a bedroom doorway, I glimpsed a jumble of dresses on the floor that promised to make finding Jasmine's jackets more difficult.

"Maybe Katrina left a message," I said, pointing to the blinking light on the landline answering machine on an end table.

"Yeah, let's check," Reginald said, pressing the button.

Amid furious breathing, a man's voice growled, "You're nuts if you think you can turn the tables. Sleep tight, old man."

After a beep, another message played.

"Apparently, you're too daft to take a hint," the man said. "It's time to explain your crazy texts. Step up, or shut up."

"It sounds like one of the thugs from today," I said.

"Bastards showed up at my door full of woe," Reginald said. "You saw the result of my handouts. They're worse than ever."

"Reginald," Antoine said softly. "To ensure they're not a threat to you if they make bail, you should report these messages."

"You're an outsider, so maybe you haven't heard why I lost faith in the system," Reginald said. "It's why I stayed tolerant, even when their stories stopped adding up. I won't wreck lives needlessly."

Nodding, I said, "After today, I assume you've freed yourself of feeling obligated. Are they contacts from your prison experience?"

"Not even close," Reginald said. "It's thanks to my attorney that I set aside my dire opinion of them. He didn't always get it right, but when he asked me to pitch in, I couldn't say no. I owe him everything."

"Does your attorney live in Hawaii?" I asked.

"No, his death was another blow this past year," Reginald said. "His brakes went out on a mountain road in a snowstorm in the Midwest. Smart guy. Why the *hell* was he on the road?"

As my attention snagged on a "Petrel Martineau Dance Studio" folder among the magazines on the coffee table, my change of focus didn't escape Reginald's notice. Signaling for me to hand him the folder, he peered at the red cross-outs and notes in the margins of a loan agreement, then he nodded as if it matched his fuzzy recollections.

"Be a peach and toss this in the trash," Reginald said, handing it back. "Tell Petrel and everyone else their ambitions and dreams are on permanent lockdown. From here on out, the gumball machine will only respond to a show of support and concrete answers."

"Can you offer any specifics?" I asked.

"I'm particularly disappointed in Barry," Reginald said. "He shepherds total strangers across the Pacific every other day. Keeps 'em safe. I helped him buy his dream house, the one you're living in."

"Perhaps he doesn't know how you feel," I said.

"Trust me, calls will fly hither and yon until it's understood," Reginald said. "Good luck finding Jasmine's jackets. Last time Katrina was here, she tore through the place like a tornado."

"You remember why we're here?" Antoine asked.

"I'm dying on my couch, and you're pestering me with obvious shit," Reginald growled. "Just get the damned clothes."

While Antoine stepped away, I placed the six-pack of water within Reginald's reach and encouraged him to eat a granola bar. Sitting beside him and admiring the rattan décor, with Hawaiian cushions and thick area rugs, I assessed Katrina's grandfather as he closed his eyes and chewed the snack with dogged determination. According to Jason, far from being in his late seventies, as I'd thought at the dance studio, Reginald was in his early sixties. It shocked me to see that through illness, dementia, or both, Reginald's handsome features were shadowed by scowls and paranoid glances, with signs of haggard wariness and exhaustion.

"You mentioned knowing Chip Henderson," I said.

"'Knowing others is intelligence,'" Reginald said. "'Knowing yourself is true wisdom.' Lao Tzu. A favorite line of Chip's."

As I searched the shadows for signs of illegal street drugs, Reginald drew my gaze back to him with his trembling hand.

"Tell Katrina I'm sorry," he said tearfully. "Whatever happened out there, it's because I didn't catch on soon enough. She's smart to stay away. If your friend is the good kind of wise guy, one who knows to count his blessings and all that, ask him to intervene for me."

"I'd need to know the specifics," I said.

"If he's connected, he'll know what I mean," Reginald said. "Some big-time boss is acting like I'm dealing from under the table, but I didn't cheat anybody or gamble the silver away. If I did and forgot about it somehow, I didn't mean any harm. I'm spent and losing track."

"When was Katrina's last visit?" I asked.

"I think it was after the shitstorm happened," Reginald said. "Ask the neighbor on your way out. She's like a hawk."

"Let's call Katrina," I said. "What's her number?"

"It's a path to nowhere," Reginald said. "She told me she won't set foot in the house until I'm dead. Tell her I'm sorry."

"For what?" I persisted.

"Nothing," Reginald murmured. "I'm losing track."

I turned, hearing a car door slam outside.

"Whoever is in there, come on out," a woman hollered.

"That's my neighbor, Carol," Reginald murmured. "Now that our boy is gone, she's willing to stop in for visits."

I hesitated. "What's Carol's last name?"

"Henderson," Reginald said.

"Reginald," I said softly. "Chip was your *son?*"

"Keeping it secret was supposed to ensure a long, happy life," Reginald said, rubbing his eyes with a look of despair. "If I wasn't a stubborn cuss, I would row out to sea and join my boy, but once you get a thirst for putting things right, it's a hard habit to break. Instead of looking wide-eyed and worried about things slipping in and out of view, ask Carol, and give her a hug. She's torn in two, however she sounds."

"Get some rest," I said softly.

With Jasmine's clothes folded over one arm, Antoine signaled for me to follow him through the front door into the sunshine.

Days ago, on a different island, I'd tried to smooth at least some of the awful edges of the worst day of Carol Henderson's life. Attractive, with signs of a lifetime of sun exposure, Chip's mother greeted us on the walkway with a fierce gaze and folded arms. Despite redness around her eyes indicating prolonged weeping, she had the strength and courage to park behind Antoine's sedan to block any escape attempt.

"You look like decent folks," Carol said. "But there's talk of dirtbags scuffling with the police at Reginald's cottage."

"It's an involved story, but we were asked to bring Reginald home," I said. "I'm not sure if you'll remember me—"

"Of *course* I do, it's hitting me in a rush," Carol said. "You helped me at the marina. I've wanted to thank you for days."

"I tried to help, at least," I said.

Suddenly tearful, Carol hugged me, hanging on as if desperate to soak up my impressions of her son's last day. With Antoine standing nearby, bowing his head, Carol tried to gather herself.

"I'm prone to moments like that," she said, pulling a tissue from her pocket to wipe her eyes. "I just went through another round of arguing with the police about their claim that Chip took drugs. The fact that they were called away to an incident on *my* lane was a further blow. I pulled up ready to rip apart anyone trying to cause trouble."

"Do you live nearby?" I asked.

"My place is the next house over," Carol said.

Briefly, we recounted the incident at Reginald's cottage.

"Let's hope they're gone for good," Carol said. "My money is on them being behind the rift between Reginald and Katrina, but it's confusing. Don't be fooled by the run-down state of his house. Land equals money in Hawaii. It crossed my mind that he used it as collateral on a debt, but there's been no sign of realtors assessing the property."

"He mentioned that Chip is his son," I said.

"It's true," Carol said. "When my husband served overseas, I found out that he was having an affair. I cried on Reginald's shoulder. Chip was the result. With a job in marine biology, I didn't need support so I fast-tracked getting a divorce. We kept our affair private, especially given the prison element of Reginald's past, but when Chip and Katrina started hanging out as teens, we decided it was time to tell them."

"How did it go?" I asked.

"Reginald gathered us around the kitchen table to make it official," Carol said. "Katrina and Chip started giggling and asked what took us so long to confess. Apparently, Reginald and I weren't careful enough in our whispering after Katrina's parents died. If you haven't caught on, our extended family is living under a curse."

Antonine said softly, "Chip's death must be very tough."

"Katrina was on Oahu thanks to her job but she called straight away," Carol said. "We sobbed for an hour."

"I'm really sorry," I said.

"I can tell, honey," Carol said, smiling tearfully. "It's especially hard to have Reginald's mind failing when I need his strength."

"He's convinced that he's being poisoned," Antoine said. "He hasn't eaten all day, so we left unopened water and granola bars."

"I've been out of touch more than usual," Carol said, frowning toward the house. "Out at sea on a UH research vessel."

"Reach out for any reason," I said, texting her my information. "When you're ready, I can share photos of Chip."

"Maybe in a day or two," Carol said. "I'm still too raw."

"Is a memorial service arranged?" I asked.

"That's another reason I'm in a foul mood," Carol said bitterly. "I'm getting the cold shoulder from Ellika Arts Academy, where Chip was celebrated as a success story until the drug angle."

"I hope that gets resolved," I said.

With a parting hug, Carol backed her car out of our path, then she eased into the open space to check on Reginald.

"On to the next challenge," I said. "It's interesting that we arrived at the cottage in the same timeframe as Reginald, the ex-cons, *and* the hound dog from Hilo. I have some questions for Jasmine."

"My thoughts exactly," Antoine said, wincing as he checked his phone messages. "Agent Telford has some questions as well."

* * *

In the living room, I preferred working by lamplight, with the sliding deck doors open to let in the breeze as I wiped spackle dust off the new sections of drywall before I started painting. Along with getting some work done, I was killing time until the next complexity hit the fan.

It took less than ten minutes.

Sheltered by tree ferns, with a teak door connecting to the bedroom, a narrow back deck offered a secluded spot for showering outdoors, and for gaining entrance into the house with a note of stealth. In that moment, the bedroom floor creaked underfoot and wafts of air carried the floral scent of the visitor's straight, glossy hair.

"The front door is the standard entrance," I said.

"I wasn't sure if your new boyfriend is trustworthy," Jasmine said, climbing onto one of the countertop stools. "He's been described as keen-eyed, with a police officer vibe. Where is he?"

"Antoine is meeting with a colleague," I said.

"You read the wrong passage the other day," Jasmine said, plucking *The Hawaiian Archipelago* from the countertop. "Imagine arriving in a drab, tight outfit and clapping eyes on Hawaiians with garlands of flowers around their necks in all colors of the rainbow. You know I'm obsessed with fabric. I want to research the old styles."

"It's a good angle to study in college," I said.

"No worries, I'll buckle down soon," Jasmine said, setting the book aside. "I heard there was an incident at Pop-Pop's cottage. The thugs who threatened you, the Korkers, were arrested?"

"I'm leery of giving credence to their marketing name," I said. "They didn't learn their lesson, so I'm calling them ex-cons."

"If I'm not mistaken, it's a long-overdue major arrest," Jasmine said. "It's surprising to see you looking blasé about it."

"They're claiming Reginald baited them with texts, but it's a fabricated story," I said. "Dirtbags are good at concocting lies."

With a burst of exasperation, Jasmine slipped off the stool, snatched the cloth from my hand, and tossed it aside.

"News flash, the takedown was the result of months of hard work," Jasmine said. "At the Maui event, I secured a plastic bag with drug residue inside and used it to train a stray mutt. Knowing the dirtbags rented Pop-Pop's cottage early on, I spent some scary nights combing the yard with the dog, trying to locate a stash, but to my frustration, he kept running into the old coffee grove. One night, he found a bone."

"Dear God, Jasmine," I said.

"Before I could get a close look at it, he dropped the bone during one of his dashes through the woods," she said. "But it sent me down a different path. Stop scowling at me and look at the messages I created to rattle the dirtbags into a damage-control response."

Jasmine's early texts ranged from "with the shit I found out, I can ruin you" to "you'll learn not to cross me!" No surprise her final text, dated that morning, read, "My dog unearthed your secret!"

"Jasmine," I said, "You don't seem to realize these targeted threats put Antoine and me in danger from a couple of ex-convicts linked to at least one homicide. You also put Reginald at risk."

"Focus on the win," Jasmine said. "I was hiding nearby, so I know that my dog unearthed the remains of a murder victim."

"Who was the third guy who ran away?" I asked.

"I never saw him before today," Jasmine said. "Crooks like to cultivate minions, and there's always hard luck homeless cases. That's my impression of him, a youth with five o'clock shadow. He ran before I could get a close look. Maybe he's related to the dirtbags."

"How did you know their phone number?" I asked.

"They gave it to a guy in Maui," Jasmine said. "I have a right to feel elated, and so do you. We need to plan some next steps."

"Actually," I said. "I've got it covered."

Having listened through the screen doors and waited for my signal, Antione and Ted stepped in with grave expressions.

"I'm sorry to shock you," I said in response to Jasmine's accusing glare. "Your devotion to Katrina is admirable, but you let it get out of hand. I'm here as your advocate. You're not alone."

While Jasmine sat on the slashed, yet-to-be-replaced couch cushions with folded arms and a defiant scowl, Ted swung a chair into position and leaned closer, reflecting patience and calm as he cited the dire outcomes that might have unfolded if her plan had gone awry.

"I never saw them carrying a weapon," Jasmine said. "Sonny dove into dicey situations. I bet she never got grilled afterward."

"Trust me, Sonny got seared over an open flame each and every time," Ted said. "No matter what she went through, she respected fellow victims, and never goaded criminals with threatening texts. Instead of hiking and exploring, she's devoted time and energy to counseling you."

"I'm sorrier than I sound," Jasmine said tearfully. "When things started spiraling, I called 911. It's why the police responded so fast, but even with the dirtbags in jail, Katrina might still be in danger."

"Let's cover that base," Ted said.

In response to his signal, Katrina stepped into the room of mostly-completed repairs, looking pale and furious in a dark skirt and jacket. With her curls tamed by a clip and her neckline embellished by a strand of pearls, she stood in front of Jasmine and flipped her hands.

"Satisfied?" Katrina asked. "I was in Honolulu when I got the news that I needed to head home and deal with a nightmare."

"You're the one who started the nightmare," Jasmine protested. "You scared me when you sent that dire-situation text."

"Yes, I sent a certain emoji when you refused to grasp that I don't have time for picnics anymore," Katrina growled. "You supported me taking the new job, even though it came with burdens."

"It feels like the burdens have turned into problems," Jasmine said. "You dumped Jason and became withdrawn. Sonny got a taste of the dirtbags conveying a threat for you to take to Reginald."

"If I'm not mistaken," Katrina said, "That happened because you were goading them with threatening texts. Jasmine, I ghosted you thinking it was the kind approach, but let's get it done the hard way. I'm working my ass off to build a solid future. You're conning people and playing games. That means you're not a friend anymore. You're a problem."

"We agreed on the t-text emoji," Jasmine said tearfully. "Why would you use it to g-ghost me? It's awful and wrong."

"You're still defending your actions?" Katrina asked.

"I'll s-stop, if that's what you w-want," Jasmine managed. "But I won't apologize for t-trying to save a friend I love."

Wavering as Jasmine sobbed from the scolding, Katrina drew herself up with an air of resolve and turned to Agent Telford.

"Does that cover it?" she asked.

"If you feel this is the way to go," Ted said softly.

"Before I step away," Katrina said. "Allow me to express my disgust over the way the police are handling Chip's death. Apparently, the lessons of the past have not been learned. Should I tell my grandfather's new attorney that the FBI needs a warning memo?"

"Human remains were found on Reginald's property," Ted said. "At this juncture, I believe he's free of involvement—"

"And, *cut*." Tight and furious, Katrina showed that she'd recorded the entirety of her visit on her phone. "I've been dealing with the arrested men for years, but if you want my cooperation in providing background elements, change the narrative about Chip. *Period*."

With that, Katrina walked away into the night without casting the slightest glance at her sobbing former friend.

"You will survive this," I said, sitting next to Jasmine and pulling her into a hug. "Your approach needs some adjustments, but your loyalty and determination to seek justice are commendable. We want you to come out of this experience with your self-worth intact."

"I'm ready to give a complete statement," Jasmine said, wiping her eyes. "Maybe not straight away. I feel trashed."

"It's been a long day for all of us," Ted said, motioning for Nicole to step in from the doorway and introduce herself. "We've arranged for you to spend the night with Mary. She's staying nearby. We'll tackle the statement phase tomorrow after you've rested."

"Sonny," Jasmine whispered, "Katrina wasn't herself just now. Maybe you can help her the way you've helped me."

"I can try," I said. "But I'm not sure she'll let me."

Vibrating from the long day, I started to walk Jasmine out, but Ted motioned for me to join him in waiting on the footpath.

"Katrina is taking her time in pulling away," Ted said. "Let's see if it's about ending on a better note with Jasmine."

"She wavered for a split second," I said. "I was hoping she would soften and acknowledge that Jasmine was acting out of love. Not to mention, it should be a relief that the ex-cons are locked up."

"Instead, we've got a mystery to sort out," Ted said, pointing toward Katrina's departing car. "You can see tears on her cheeks. It would be good to put the questions around her troubles to rest."

"I'll see what I can find out," I said. "Where is Antoine?"

"I asked if I could have a moment alone with you," Ted said. "In case you have anything to add off the record."

"Other than today, it's been a quiet week," I said.

As we headed down the footpath past the office, I followed the sound of Antoine's voice to the patio, where he was reclining in a chair with his sneakers on the table and his phone in hand, smiling at whatever he was hearing, and then he delivered a captivating, inscrutable reply in French. I vowed to return to my language app, though every mistake was broadcast with a grating buzz. It required a thick skin.

"From the sound of it," Ted said, "He's getting on the right page about his impending visit. I'm sure it's a comfort to know the ex-cons won't be an issue for you. By all accounts, the third perp is a low-level recruit who's bound to be running scared. We've got his fingerprints."

"Has the crime lab identified the jawbone?" I asked.

"Through dental records," Ted agreed, opening his phone to show the bio page of a smiling, spectacled IRS agent. "Thanks to a bogus paper trail, he was thought to have absconded with payoff money to start a new life in Asia. As you can imagine, his wife and kids will be grateful to know that he didn't skip out on them. We'll test out common elements with the ex-cons and iron out the motive. One step at a time."

Pausing under the garage light, Ted shook my hand.

"I'll keep you informed as the picture clarifies," Ted said. "Your parting sentiments with Jasmine were spot on. We want her to come out of the experience with her self-worth intact. Well done."

Instead of departing, Ted winced and rubbed his brow.

"I'm sorry for butting in," he said. "But are your friends concerned that you're getting involved in another situationship?"

I hesitated. "A *what?*"

"You saved Antoine, and he saved you," Ted said, rolling one hand. "The unique bond that spirals out of high-stakes work, a mindless fling without a future context. It's a known phenomenon, and has the same doomed outlook as your misguided arc with Dan."

Gaping and blinking as his analysis went from bad to worse, I found it necessary to take a deep breath before I responded.

"Not that it's any of your business," I said. "It's possible that Dan was a 'situationship.' I'm still sorting it out, but my bond with Antoine is a world apart. How dare you weigh in on my personal life?"

"I'm sorry if I got it wrong," Ted said. "I'm somewhere between a boss and a friend, so I want the best for you. I had a work-related fling before I met the right woman. It's not a slam."

"We'll leave it at that," I said, striving for calm as Antoine arrived from the shadows. "Any last questions for Ted?"

"Not until now," Antoine said, frowning with concern. "You wanted a minute alone with Sonny to grill her about today?"

"No, I'm prone to over-theorizing when I'm tired," Ted said, reaching out to shake Antoine's hand. "Enjoy the night."

In a white shirt that set off his tan, Antoine frowned as he watched Ted climb into his car, and then he turned to me.

"I heard your sharp tone, but not the context," Antoine said. "Was he hassling you about the way I handled the scene?"

"It's not important," I said. "But if he shows up before I cool off, he'll end up with a paintball masterpiece on his front grille."

"I'll deal with him later," Antoine said. "For now …"

With an air of mystery, he opened the side door of the garage, flipped on the light, and crossed to a workbench where a spray of sawdust showed indications of activity. First, he clipped a tool belt around his hips, then he presented a stack of boards in his arms.

"Lovely," I said. "Shall I put them in a vase?"

"I mentioned wanting to build you a secret drawer," Antoine said, motioning for me to follow him to the house. "An extra option for securing your laptop and valuables. Ted has his faults, but he supplied dinner so we can eat with minimal clean-up and fuss."

In the kitchen, Antoine opened the refrigerator to the glorious sight of an antipasto plate brimming with salami, prosciutto, provolone, pepperoncini, olives, artichoke hearts, and roasted peppers glistening under an oil-and-vinegar dressing. Alongside was a lasagna that had been browned to perfection, with thick layers of ricotta and sausage.

Perched on the stools next to the countertop, we heaped food onto our plates and devolved into the happy moans and ecstatic eye rolls that were typical of people who'd prioritized work over the need to refuel. We tried different ingredient combinations, offering tastes to each other now and then, with the warming effects of merlot.

However sharply I'd rebuked Ted, his take on Antoine's visit had cut through me. Even with my gaze fixed on my fork as I selected olives, I was aware of how Antoine filled the room with his aura of alpha energy and keen intelligence, in a white shirt so thin that I could see his tanned skin underneath. In what world would I sustain Antoine's interest when my life was the opposite of stabilized and calm?

My despair was like a signal from the beyond to him, drawing his gaze and sparking a concerned frown as he reached for my hand.

"Berrichon?" he prompted.

"I'm afraid to tell you how much I—" Blinking tearfully, I pretended to have inhaled an olive, and managed, "I'm afraid to speak French with you. I'll botch the accent and get it wrong."

"Ce n'est pas un problème," Antoine said softly. "I'm saying it's not a problem. Ce n'est pas … un problème. Give it a try."

"I'm not up to it right now," I said, waving off his concern. "Blame it on an exhausting day, and seeing the victim file. You warned me against the effects of information overload."

Pushing his plate aside, Antoine rested his elbow on the countertop and leaned closer, the opposite of helpful, since it amplified his muscles, ready for action but not exaggerated. It was a matter of the package fitting the inner man, down to the warmth of his steady gaze.

"We have a lot of interactions to process," he said, "Reginald. Katrina. The ex-cons. Even Ted, since he knew about the IRS agent, but kept the connection point locked down. Sticking with the language theme, you're familiar with the line, 'Revenge is a dish best served cold.' The trouble is, the original quote reads, 'Revenge is very good eaten cold,' from the novel *Mathilde* by Eugène Sue, published in 1841."

"A French author, of course," I said.

"It is what it is, Berrichon," Antoine said wryly. "Every crime boils down to a misunderstanding, a want, a grudge, or similar issue that began with emotions and justifications swirling in someone's head. Often, there's a trail of tells and admissions that can be traced back in time. Where is the distortion point? How do we get to the truth?"

"I tend to grope in the dark," I said.

"Actually, you're highly analytical," Antoine said. "There I am, shifting sentences into other sentences to create a cross comparison. I've seen you get bogged down in the details. There's no denying it, but from time to time, you step on a sentence and catapult into the ozone. Instant awareness. I saw it in November on multiple occasions."

"Unfortunately," I said. "It's a trick that requires a punch in the face or a quick tasing of my neck. I would prefer the sentence approach."

"With a relaxed mindset and visualization techniques, it's an ability that can be strengthened and honed," Antoine said, guiding me to the shelving unit. "Lend a hand while I install the drawer, and enlighten me on a topic. A favorite quote, a song, whatever."

"Theorizing does lead to epiphanies," I said. "We're processing the week, so I'll start with my renewed passion for dance. Did you know the general concept of the paso doble is for the woman to be the matador's cape? I love the style, but think about it. The man gets to be a heroic figure in the story, while the woman is an object."

"It came to mind because Jason was off with you?" Antoine asked.

"No, he's very careful," I said. "This is the problem with free associating. I'm cross-connecting different elements."

"Might you be thinking of Reginald?" Antoine asked.

"Sure, let's go with that," I said.

Without further prompting, Antoine admitted that Reginald's erratic behavior had motivated him to use the task of fetching Jasmine's clothes as a cover to search for illegal drugs. I'd had the same thought in Reginald's living room. No matter which person Antoine scrutinized, I agreed with his sense that some elements seemed puzzling, but nothing more unusual than what we might see in the general population.

"Bear in mind, we only see the surface facets," Antoine said, lifting my chin to invite eye contact. "Like now. During our week in Maine, you had no trouble trying to speak French. It's bringing to mind Sue telling me that you came out of the holidays looking haunted and shattered. What happened on your trip to Florida with Dan?"

"It's not important," I said. "It's in the past."

"The trip was about talking in a neutral setting?" Antoine persisted. "A gift from Dan? He was following through on a promise?"

Rubbing my brow, I said, "You're right about the need to look at hints that weren't obvious in the moment. My smiles were forced. Dan's turmoil was wrapped up with things I didn't know about."

At some point, I would tell Antoine that Dan's mother had hidden my father's last journal, preferably during a calmer moment.

"If the details are off limits for now, I get it," Antoine said gently. "I'm worried that our theorizing has triggered a buried issue. Is it the sting in November? You're having nightmares from it?"

"What about you?" I asked.

"It's less apt to happen now that I've seen you alive and well," Antoine said, searching my face with a concerned frown. "Mostly well, at any rate. Instead of tackling issues that might trip us up, we've spent our time ducking down rabbit holes. I've got less than twenty-four hours to assure myself, so it would be nice to hear at least one clear answer."

"I have dreams about ghosts coming after me," I said. "But most of my nightmares are about the killers getting away. It's never the same scenario two times in a row. I'm frozen in place, and they're mocking me from the trees, or a speeding car, or the next room."

"Sonny," Antoine said, cupping my face. "Please be honest. If you need me to delay leaving for a few days—"

"I'm distracted, not buckling into a heap." Cementing my assurance with a smile and a warm hug, I handed Antoine a screwdriver. "I believe you were looking for this. Let's finish the secret drawer."

18

Lying on my stomach, I framed the smoky rush of the swirling torches of the fire dancers with my 17-40mm lens, striving for a mix of sharp background elements and blurred effects as I photographed Jason and his fellow Hawaiian dancers performing against the backdrop of night with braided wreaths on their heads and leis draped around their brown chests. Without the portable lights and reflectors that I would typically use for a nighttime shoot, I relied on a handheld flash and other makeshift options as I endeavored to capture the feel of the show, with Hawaiian drums adding a cadence that I felt through the ground.

By my side, adept at rolling away if I needed elbow room, Antoine joined me in watching the dance from the unique vantage point. Now and then, he tensed as police codes squawked in his earpiece. The fact that he was able to participate in the sting was thanks to a storm system in the San Francisco area. As he leaned close to watch me scroll through my captured shots, I savored the feel of his shaved face against my cheek.

"Forget about shovels," I said. "From now on, I'm going to use Polynesian fire torches to clear the snow. I especially like the ones that swirl on chains, but the two-sided batons might be handy when my cousins pull up the driveway."

"As always, you are a trendsetter," Antoine said.

"It sounds like the target took the bait," I said.

"Oui," Antoine said. "I will need to act fast."

"It's been spelled out," I said. "I'll stay put."

With a distracted nod, Antoine resumed directing his frown toward the rock band's table, where festive candles and occasional toasts told us it was Shredder's birthday, though the guitarist seemed quiet and miserable, looking at his phone instead of celebrating.

"Je connais ce sentiment," Antoine murmured.

"You're saying you can relate?" I asked.

"From this distance, I can't see details," Antoine said. "But Shredder appears to be looking at photos. He's in anguish."

"If I'm allowed to be pushy on your behalf," I said. "I've noticed you holding back instead of asserting your rights as a father. Far from being neglectful, you kept Zach's entire household out of harm's way. I met your foe, so I know the extent of your sacrifice."

With a wry look, Antoine smoothed my cheek. "Stop worrying about me, Berrichon," he said. "Here come the hula dancers."

As a fresh round of drums vibrated my grassy location, I returned my eye to my camera's viewfinder and adjusted the depth of field as the dancers' movements mirrored the stories they told, casting an ageless spell that felt like jumping back in time. In short bursts, I switched to video mode to capture the combined effects of music and motion, including the soft rustling of the dancers' bare feet as they shifted position.

When an alert chirped on my phone, I looked toward Antoine.

"It's game time," he confirmed.

In an instant, Antoine rolled away, climbed to his feet, and set off at a relaxed pace past the dinner tables, smiling at luau guests as he crossed toward the outdoor bar, where tiki torches cast dramatic, fiery light over the dining and performance area. Beyond Antoine's shoulders, Moritz and Raja were serving as bartenders, and by all appearances, they weren't eager to give prompt, cheerful service to Axe's son.

"Sorry," Raja said, sounding anything but sorry as he returned a credit card to Sam's hand. "The reader is iffy, but cash always works."

"Why are you being an ass?" Sam asked.

"At the summer event," Raja said. "The band stiffed us."

"Then add what you think is fair to the tab," Sam said.

"And let Riff contest the charge?" Moritz cut in. "No thanks."

"Come on, man," Sam said. "It's Shredder's birthday."

"It would be unethical to serve a birthday celebrant who's three sheets to the wind," Moritz said, resting his elbows on the bar to lean in and add, "Bartenders hear shit on a nightly basis, if you catch my drift. Hence, the wheel-greasing tip system. Quid pro quo."

"You wonder why people think you're a turd," Sam said.

"Ditto," Moritz said. "Bye, now. Step away."

With a roll of his eyes, Sam returned to his table, too distracted to notice Antoine pretending to check his phone while focusing on a figure that was reduced to a silhouette by the torches. Slowly, the target stepped from the shadows into the light, looking nervous as he approached the bar. Based on the fingerprints found in the ex-con's car near Reginald's cottage, he was twenty-four years old, and his name was Derek.

As I looked from his five o'clock shadow to his stringy hair under a green *Kukuna Mahina* hat, I was fairly certain I was seeing the man who'd ditched the dog-catching endeavor and fled down the lane, but I fell into confusion when I remembered the man on the 1871 Trail, who appeared heavyset with a thicker beard and frizzier hair. Perpetrators who were on the run often took steps to change their appearance.

"Then why wear the same hat?" I murmured.

Eyeing Derek, Raja asked, "Can I help you?"

"It's cool, I'm meeting someone," Derek said.

"It's not cool if you plan to loiter without buying a drink," Raja said, shoving a menu forward. "How about a Luau Lullaby?"

"No, a beer," Derek said. "The canned kind."

"The canned kind," Raja said. "All right, let's see your ID."

With smooth efficiency, Antoine stepped close to Derek and rested a hand on his shoulder, speaking softly and calmly while a plainclothes FBI agent in a Hawaiian shirt acted as a barrier on Derek's right. To divert Moritz and Raja from realizing that a person of interest was being steered away for questioning in a quiet location, the agent showed interest in hearing about the strength of the Luau Lullaby drink.

Having been lured out of hiding by a text from the ex-con's phone number, Derek fell into a sad level of relief as he followed Antoine to a gazebo that had been quietly sealed off as a private place for the arrest process. Surrounded by twinkling lights, Derek fell into a predictable pattern of spouting denials as agents delivered the bad news.

After Antoine's all-clear text, I packed away my camera, and took a deep, calming breath. Instead of saying goodbye privately, I would be hugging Antoine in front of FBI agents at a public event.

As I approached the gazebo, I was struck by how the subtle takedown left a lingering numbness on the twenty-something suspect. In his position, with my hands cuffed behind my back, I would be struggling to break free with every ounce of my being, but Derek's reaction was to listen with a confused frown while Ted explained the reasons for his arrest.

"Talk to me," Ted said. "Tell me your side."

"You've got it wrong," Derek said. "The guys approached me about a loose dog. I love animals. I planned to adopt it."

"What's your connection to the men?" Ted asked.

"I just told you," Derek said. "I spent the cash they gave me."

"On what?" Ted prompted. "You look a little high."

"I had a headache," Derek said. "They had a bottle from the drugstore. Coated pills, I think. I took two with soda."

"By now, those pills would be out of your system," Ted said. "You were seen with the same men in the Hilo area."

"*Hilo?*" Derek said. "No way."

"Days later, you stalked a woman on the 1871 Trail," Ted said.

"Bullshit," Derek said. "You're the one on drugs."

"To your credit," Ted said. "You showed some sense yesterday, running away when you saw tourists at the rental cottage."

"Seeing Pop-Pop is the reason I ran away," Derek said. "He's a former wise guy who's connected to the—" Abruptly self-aware, Derek shook his head. "I am pleading the Fifth Commandment."

Ted winced. "I'm not in charge of commandments."

"The Fifth Amendment," Derek said. "I just remembered."

"You're smart to want legal counsel," Ted said. "You're connected with ex-convicts who might blame you for their crimes."

"I—want—a—lawyer," Derek said forcefully.

Standing in the shadows near the gazebo, Antoine cursed in English and then more colorfully in French, and then he saw me.

"I'd hoped to keep your name out of the picture as much as possible," he said. "Naturally, here comes Ted, wanting you to make his life easier with a positive identification. Don't feel pressured."

Having anticipated that likelihood, I wasted no time in dashing Ted's hopes when he asked whether I needed a closer look.

"As I stated earlier," I said, "My glimpse of the third man at Reginald's cottage was from a distance through a cloud of dust. Derek is roughly the same height and has a similar five o'clock shadow."

"What about your previous two sightings?" Ted asked.

"At the gas station, the third man was a blur in the extended cab," I said. "The stalker on the trail looked heavier."

"Perhaps from an overlarge shirt," Ted said. "Derek is wearing a green *Kukuna Mahina* hat, and he's adept at claiming innocence."

"Let's steer clear of pressure tactics that could be overheard," Antoine said quietly. "If you were paying attention, Moritz and Raja hinted at using inside knowledge as leverage. It's a concern."

With a look of contrition, Ted managed a smile.

"As always, your instincts are second to none," he said, warmly shaking Antoine's hand. "You got your wish to be a part of the win. I appreciate your assistance. It's time to clock out."

With an added supportive shoulder clap, Ted stepped away to oversee Derek's departure, leaving Antoine to cast a frustrated glare toward Moritz and Raja and the increasingly inebriated band.

"Ted is right," I said. "Assuming your briefcase will demand special handling, you're in danger of missing your flight."

"No need to remind me," Antoine said.

Gathered into an embrace, I smoothed my hands over the pink shirt I'd bought for him to wear during his trip, since the color complemented his ruggedly handsome face, touches of sunburn, and his air of secretly being a poet rather than a seasoned cop. Following my suggestion, he left most of his sun-streaked waves and curls on top, with his temples neatly trimmed in line with a modern trend I had come to admire. Freshly shaved and smelling of tropical paradise, in cargo pants that enhanced his action-ready vibe, he was a perfect version of himself.

"I'm picturing us escaping to the forested hills," Antoine said, tucking a stray curl behind my ear. "Free from complexities and tedious others. Puzzle pieces locked into the here and now."

"That's the old you talking," I said. "Family ties are hard work. A mix of baffling setbacks and joy. I desperately want that for you, Antoine. That came out wrong. *Not* the setbacks. Just the joy."

"The trouble is, I'm new to waffling," Antoine said, faintly smiling in the torchlight, so close I could see every detail of his face. "It began three months ago when I asked myself, who is this spark of light? Can she be real? To borrow an English phrase, blah blah, indicating twists, turns, and epiphanies, ending with open air where there used to be doors. It's too late to realize I should have made this a special night."

"We both made the decision," I said.

With time running out, Antoine pulled me into one last overwhelming embrace. I held him tightly, closing my eyes to savor the feel of his arms and the warmth of his chest against my face.

"I hate amusement parks," he murmured.

"Only in theory, since you've never visited one," I said. "Zach will want to try the ride with a cage that spins on a vertical path."

"It sounds awful," Antoine said.

"It is awful," I said. "Good luck saying no."

"Don't drop your guard with Moritz," Antoine said. "And Axe, Chill, Shredder, Gavin, etcetera. I've heard Kauai is tranquil."

"This is why I'm imposing emergency-only outreach for however long you're with Zach this week," I said. "If I can't respond right away, you'll assume the worst and project a weird vibe."

"You'll stay vigilant?" Antoine asked.

"Yes, of course," I said. "Rather, oui, bien sûr."

Antoine's sighs and frustrated growls tickled my ear and his embrace tightened all the more. Drawing away, he kissed my cheek, and then after a final moment of warm eye contact, he joined the luau attendees who were leaving early to avoid getting stuck in traffic.

Having waited in the wings during our goodbye, my ride back to the rental house joined me with a look of understanding and empathy.

"Work beckons?" RG asked.

"No, he's off to spend time with his son," I said.

"Every time I give Mary a lift, I feel the tug when she walks away," RG mused. "I've held a secret candle for her for years."

Studying RG's likable face, I saw the possibilities of a viable matchup, and kicked myself for not noticing it sooner.

"Given the closure element regarding the murder of the IRS agent," RG said, "I expected to be giving Agent Telford a ride to the airport, but according to Mary, he's all the more intense after talking to Jasmine, like the arrests are an opening element of a larger matter."

"Did Mary catch onto specifics?" I asked.

"You know Ted," RG said. "Dry and guarded."

In the background during Antoine's stay, I'd understood the risks involved with opening my heart to a man who outshone all others in every regard on my scale of what mattered most. As his pink shirt disappeared into the night shadows, it was like watching a campfire snuff out. The trick of surviving my anxieties and all other tests was to rebuild my own fire to its original state, so as far as I was concerned, the more I nailed down the remaining puzzles on the local front, the better.

"Ready?" RG asked.

"Yes," I said. "I'm ready."

19

Built in the late 1800s, The Painted Church, with its wooden pews, peaked windows, and colorful hand-painted artwork on the walls and ceiling, was the perfect place to sit and let my thoughts drift like the tiny particles of dust that added sparks of light to the mid-morning rays. I chose a spot midway down the aisle in one of the pews, estimating that no more than six or seven adults would fit on the wooden seat during a service. Now and then, cars pulled into the parking lot, footfalls crunched on the pathway, and tourists stepped in with an exchange of murmurs. Phones were aimed at the wooden posts painted with festive red stripes, and then the ancient floor creaked underfoot as the visitors crossed to the front and admired the vases of tropical flowers that brightened the altar. Then, the group turned back up the aisle and told me to have a nice day.

"You too," I said.

Once I was alone beneath the arched ceiling, I admired how painted fronds topped the colorful columns, making them look like coconut palms in keeping with the Hawaiian setting, with stars scattered across the sapphire strokes that depicted the equatorial sky.

I'd sat on that same pew as a teenager when Arlene's family invited me to join them for a spring break vacation. The church was especially appealing to Arlene's father, Dr. Byron March, whose Southern roots inspired his dedication to history, with a particular focus on black and brown communities similar to his own family. During our visit to the church, he'd sent his baritone voice reverberating from wall to wall, filling the space with his favorite hymns. Sitting there years later, I still felt goosebumps from the deeper meaning he attached to that memory.

Seeing simple white grave markers beyond the windows, I remembered that Reginald's kitchen notepad had looked like a scribbled attempt at writing a new last will and testament. With my eyes closed and hand on my forehead, I tried to recall the phrasing I had seen.

I hereby revoke any wills made before this date ... I bequeath all of my personal property and proceeds ... my belongings shall be divided among ...

I didn't remember seeing any names, but creating a new document seemed like a logical step for a father to take after his son's death. Was I right in thinking that Katrina was set to inherit a fortune in property and other assets when Reginald died? As always, I warned myself not to jump to conclusions, but Katrina's display of emotion appeared to reflect genuine shock and grief over Chip's sudden death. From the beginning, I'd had my own doubts about the difference between my view of Chip's character and the official reports, but I'd also seen people whose drug abuse was so well hidden that family and friends didn't know.

Too restless to sit still for long, I stepped out of the church, crossed through the shade of the attached porch, and strolled past the walkway to the cemetery, where most of the graves were marked with rectangles of lava boulders and white crosses.

"At last, we meet again," a man said behind me.

Turning to see Axe standing there in a vintage Hawaiian shirt emblazoned with hula dancers, I realized his shadow ought to have alerted me in advance. Tanned and smiling, a mid-fifties version of fitness and good looks, Axe seemed unaware that my eyes were smarting from his cologne, which seemed to be modeled after bug repellent.

"The other day," I said, "You claimed to be a ship in the night, unwilling to reveal your name. Now here you are again."

"A-l-a-n Richardson," Axe said. "In case you want to look me up."

"Moritz and Raja told you where to find me?" I asked.

"They updated us on your latest bad news, so we're here to cheer you up with ideas on how to move forward." With a flourish, Axe indicated the shy, mid-twenties version of his good looks standing to one side in pressed chinos, a button-down shirt, wire-rim glasses, and closely cropped hair. "I believe you met my son, Samuel."

"I kept him at bay while you were inside," Sam confided. "You looked peaceful. I'm sorry if we're interrupting a spiritual visit."

"Thank you, that was thoughtful," I said. "Dare I ask for specifics regarding some mention of 'the latest bad news'?"

"The trouble at the luau," Axe said, rolling one hand. "Antoine talked to a guy with a history of drug problems, and was lucky not to end up in handcuffs himself from some sort of nab-up that unfolded. Sam went to school with the kid who was arrested. He and a few other guys tried to create a band. Mellow, folksy tracks that didn't catch on."

"The music wasn't the problem," Sam said. "My bandmates favored the party angle. I preferred going to college. About last night, I think Raja and Moritz got it wrong. To me, it looked like Antoine was helping a detective who's been looking into Pop-Pop's affairs."

"You're right," I said. "Antoine and I got mixed up in it after visiting Reginald and Carol to express our condolences."

"No surprise, Moritz is spreading a bogus version," Axe said. "He's a devotee of the 'misery loves company' camp."

"I'm aware of his special mindset," I said.

Broiling in the sunshine, and far from feeling spiritually centered, I signaled that I was leaving, but Axe held me back.

"You're described as lost and a little clueless," Axe said, sparking a pained wince and look of apology in his son. "Don't take offense. Sam and I are in a similar place, feeling stalled. For some time now, he's been aligning his Master's thesis with updating the band's sound. What's going on with the current music scene is nuts. Trap, cowpunk, dreampunk, outlaw country. We're overwhelmed with too many options."

"Actually," Sam said. "I chose styles that would blend well with your old—rather, your early work. If we're strategic about it—"

"We've shaved a year off our lives trying to figure it out," Axe said, waving away his son's analysis. "Sonny, you're young and current, with a kickass multimedia website. The drama around your move from Boston to Maine is enviable. Do you have marketing people?"

I said dryly, "They dream up weirdness all day, every day."

"For real?" Axe asked. "It's a dog and pony show?"

Relying on the basic truth that people believed what they wanted to believe, I said, "If you follow the logic, how could one person get into end-to-end awful jams? It doesn't make sense."

"I knew it was overblown," Axe said. "You're the opposite of a badass."

"Darn it," I said, "I felt I was making progress in that realm."

"Back to the band," Sam said, "I've pointed out that a campaign is a follow-up step. The new sound needs to come first."

"That's the standard pattern," I said.

"Sonny, I'm still sensing that you're here for spiritual reasons," Sam said, turning to his father. "Time to head out?"

"It's time when I say it's time," Axe said, pulling Sam to one side, but not far enough away to keep his conversation private. "Instead of bugging me about missing studio time, take a look at the options I tossed your way to solve the acne issue. It's like you're thirteen again."

"Online experts say outbreaks are normal, especially if a person has to stand around in the sun instead of escaping the heat," Sam whispered, touching the minor blemishes on his chin. "But heck, thanks for showing concern and choosing now to bring it up."

"You're one to talk," Axe said. "Calling my style 'old.'"

Adept at feigning ignorance, I studied my photo library for a moment, and then I apologized for succumbing to distraction.

"Is your music still online?" I asked Sam.

"Acoustic and slack-key guitar," he said. "Nothing with vocals any-more. It was nice seeing you, Sonny."

"You as well," I said.

Watching his son cross through the shade toward the parking lot, Axe said, "It's lost on Sam that rock isn't about careful steps. I'm driven by the power of a muse, and *you*," Axe added, eyeing me with an inviting smile, "are a ray of sunshine in a dark, confusing world. Ditch your car and come to the studio. Let's see where it leads."

"I'm not interested," I said. "Please don't ask again."

"I take it Barry or Pauline outflanked me," Axe said. "They're not over the party at the house? Told you I'm bad news?"

"The house itself told me that," I said.

"You're too young to adopt Pauline's mindset of all work and no play," Axe said. "Think what it would be like to be a guiding muse. I've already got ideas for a new song title. 'Sonny-side-up.'"

With a tired sigh, I stepped around him.

"I'm a sought-after guy," Axe said, undeterred as I kept walking. "Next time, I'll bring chocolate. I heard you like it."

"You'll still get nowhere," I said, heading toward my car.

So much for my plan to enjoy a half-hour of solitude while Pauline and Gavin finished bringing an assortment of staff to the house to discuss the possibility of selling the paintball masterpiece on the garage doors. Earlier, shortly after dawn, Moritz and Raja had conducted a jarring hour of hammering in my vicinity where hammering wasn't needed, leaving me all the more determined to understand their ulterior motives.

For sanity's sake, I was floating the idea of returning to Volcano Village to photograph Kilauea's fiery summit at night. Using different shutter speeds, creative angles, and depth-of-field settings, I could add my own unique perspective to the natural phenomenon.

First, I needed to focus on the sedan that had lurked suspiciously in the church parking lot and was now tailing me at a guarded distance. The driver's ability to hang back and draw closer with practiced efficiency had me wondering if Agent Telford was monitoring my activities. If so, it was time to convey the consequences of testing my limits.

Slowing with my signal indicating a right turn, I waited through the yellow light, then surged through the intersection against the red. Ignoring the speed limit, I weaved through connecting streets, waited until I saw the sedan speed down the main road, then I surged in the opposite direction and pulled into the shopping plaza where Force Eject had joined me in deliberating over the expiration dates of yogurt.

Near the shopping carts out front, I pretended to check my phone, confident that the driver would circle back to inspect the parking lot. Sure enough, the sedan pulled in, slowed to a crawl as it passed my car, and then backed into a space among the other vehicles.

Pretending to be on the phone with a friend, I said loudly, "I agreed to meet the contact in a public place. Stay tuned."

Inside, using window signs for cover, I looped around a pineapple display and paused behind a carousel of sunglasses, unsurprised to see Nicole emerge from the sedan in tight slacks and a revealing blouse.

"I'm checking it out," she said into her phone as the doors whooshed open. "I think Sonny was heading inside to meet an acquaintance. No, it didn't sound like an emergency, but—"

As Nicole saw me, I made a phone gesture with my thumb and pinkie, then pushed downward while mouthing, "Hang *up*."

"Ted, I need to focus," Nicole said. "I'll call you back."

"Explain yourself," I said. "No stalling."

"Listen to you, trying to sound tough," Nicole said, adding with a wry twist of her perfect eyebrows, "Is it true that you spruced up Antoine, all nice and pretty, and aimed him at his ex? Perhaps you're unaware that she's a fellow cop, a martial arts expert, and smoking hot?"

"I aimed Antoine at his son," I said quietly. "And urged him not to let anyone with a controlling nature call the shots."

"I guess that's the gist of what I heard," Nicole said, softening a little. "I'm forced to give you points for looking out for his son."

"Is this the first time you've followed me?" I asked.

"Don't worry, your visit with Antoine was given a veil of privacy," Nicole said. "We heard that you're Axe's notion of a smoking hot package. That's why Ted asked me to keep an eye out."

I hesitated. "Axe is a person of interest?"

"You'll have heard about the paper trail that led investigators to believe the IRS agent was living it up in Asia," Nicole said. "To make sure we're not overlooking a bigger picture, we're following up on tips, like a pattern of Axe stepping out of line with women and covering it up with an NDA. I could tell he was pitching you at the church."

"The nature of NDAs is that their contents rarely see the light of day," I said. "But maybe the IRS agent unearthed one?"

"With major cases, it's important to cast a broad net," Nicole said. "I overheard Axe's sad notion of fatherly support."

"He's clueless in many regards," I said. "And shameless about being on the prowl. I don't think there's a pause button."

"There's a certain type who relishes the chase," Nicole said. "Guys who thrive on turning a woman into a scared little girl."

While we spoke, I noticed how Nicole kept track of shoppers coming and going, anyone on the move. Standing with her hands on her hips, she looked action-ready at all times, as if she was poised to shove an armed criminal down a flight of stairs or dive in to shampoo a muddy dog—whatever fate threw at her in a split second.

"You've encountered Axe types in your work?" I asked.

"More times than I can count," Nicole said.

"If a guy that you're dating gets a little jealous, it means he cares about you," I said. "In the future, it might be a good idea to—"

"What are you doing?" Nicole demanded.

I shrugged. "Endeavoring to have a real moment."

"If I want your advice, I'll ask for it," Nicole said. "Focus on Gavin trying to hide behind a loaf of bread. Pretend we're friends."

"We're exchanging vacation tips," I called out to dispel Gavin's look of curiosity. "This is Arabella. She was on my flight."

"Small world, huh?" Gavin said.

I nodded. "Yes, it truly is."

"Arabella?" Nicole hissed. "Thanks a lot."

"It's a great name," I said. "Similar to Isabella."

"Nicole is my field identity," she explained. "If Antoine's enemy hadn't taken away his ability to use an alias, you would know him as Aldéric or François. But this isn't Maine, and you're not a cop. Instead of asking questions, focus on vacation-related activities. If Axe or anyone else is a problem, call us immediately. Pinkie-swear on it."

"You're not seriously holding out your pinkie," I said.

"Among cops, it's highly respected," Nicole said.

"As long as it works both ways," I said. "No more following me, and— *hey*, that hurts," I added, struggling to free my pinkie.

"You're an ace in some ways," Nicole said. "But you're too trusting for your own good. Call us if anything seems off."

"Yes, all right," I grumbled.

Instructed to wait while Nicole returned to her car, I purchased cheese, crackers, and a six-pack of coconut yogurt, despite the unreadable expiration dates. With my bag in hand, I was surprised to step outside and see Chip's mother covertly signaling for me to join her in the shade of a coconut palm planted on a patch of grass inside the parking lot.

"I saw an intense woman follow you in," Carol said, looking stylish in a watersport hoodie. "Is she one of the cops on Chip's case?"

"She's an acquaintance," I said. "Is everything all right?"

"After you left the other day, I checked on Reginald," Carol said. "It seemed natural for him to be groggy after the incident at the cottage, so I decided to let him rest. When I stopped in later, he was feverish and delirious, so I called an ambulance. The water and granola bars that you left were a game changer. I think you saved his life."

"Slow down," I urged. "Help me understand."

"Reginald doesn't have Parkinson's disease, so his bloodwork should not include related medications," Carol said. "Now that he's hydrated and his system is clearing out, he's lucid and alert. His claim of being poisoned was true. In essence, he's going through withdrawal."

"Does he know who was behind it?" I asked.

"It's almost certain the ex-cons were involved," Carol said. "Reginald is tight-lipped with his suspicions, but he's effusive about having guardian angels. You and Antoine, of course, but he talked about a pain in the butt who deserves a medal instead of a scolding."

"A very tenacious person was pursuing the ex-cons," I said, shaking my head at Jasmine's risky, but successful tactics. "Those efforts must have disrupted the poisoning plan enough for Reginald to realize what might be happening. Thank God it's been uncovered."

"I don't think the thugs were smart enough to come up with a multi-month, sophisticated plan," Carol said. "The side effects of the drugs include gambling issues and sexual urges. It fit with Reginald being a poker-playing flirt, so it looked like a slow decline."

"Is he expected to make a full recovery?" I asked.

"He's already back to his old self enough to play the sympathy card for all its worth," Carol said. "I'm even more convinced my son was a victim of foul play. I'm stripped of trust. I've heard you're in Hawaii from similar trauma, so I'm taking a leap of faith. I kept Chip's laptop away from the police to make sure his findings weren't compromised. I think he was helping Katrina with a problem, and it went sideways."

"Do you have his laptop now?" I asked.

"I brought it hoping you would offer to help," Carol said. "I'm too emotional to assess his files. If you're into whales, he's got underwater videos and sound recordings. A man possessed."

"I could tell that about him," I said.

"It came across when you dove in to help me in Maui," Carol said. "I was tempted to lend you the computer sooner, but given the precious nature of it, I wanted to ask around to see if my sense of you was on the money. People I don't like describe you as suspicious. People I trust with my life are giving you a five-star rating."

"That's heartening," I said. "In case anyone is watching, we shouldn't let on that you're giving me a laptop. We can cover the transfer with the truth. I have photos of Chip from the whale rescue."

Carol nodded and said loudly, "I brought the picture frame we talked about. Thank you for donating a photo of Chip."

"I'll print the image and put it in your frame," I said.

Having been told I was using Harve's car during my stay on the Big Island, Carol had parked in the adjacent spot. Once the device was safely transferred to my car, and the password was entrusted to a piece of paper I tucked into my pocket, we hugged in parting.

"Thank you, Sonny," Carol said.

"I'm happy to help," I said, giving her an assuring, determined look. "You're not alone, Carol. Stay strong. I'll be in touch."

20

"Is anyone here?" I called out as I stepped into the living room.

Hearing silence, even from the downstairs rooms, I crossed to my new security camera that was disguised as a kitchen timer, connected it to my laptop, and checked the footage it had recorded while I was out. The first clip showed Barry stopping by to look at the printed photos I'd left as potential replacements for artwork torn down during the party. Other clips showed Moritz and Raja opening cabinets and lifting area rugs, arguing about not finding an item they'd apparently lost.

In case they showed up and I needed to hide Chip's laptop, I opened the secret drawer Antoine had built into the shelving unit: secured with a hidden latch, and roomy enough to hold a range of items. As I sat at the dining room table, ready to explore Chip's private life, sounds took on extra resonance, like the breeze whispering through the screens facing the Pacific and the rustle of a gecko skittering across the deck.

Jotting notes as I began my search, I found a folder of videos that opened with a close-up of Reginald's face as he adjusted the view before stepping away or descending a ladder. Every clip featured five to ten people, mostly men, with Reginald always in the frame, drinking, laughing, and talking while they played poker in various locations. In one clip, dated three years earlier, I saw *Kukuna Mahina* coasters on a table and a view of the ocean beyond the windows, and realized it might be a poker game unfolding in the captain's suite during a cruise.

I leaned in, curious to see how Reginald interacted with Gavin, Barry, Pauline, Chill, Axe, Riff, Shredder, and Harve.

"Pauline, it's nice of you to join us for once," Reginald said, patting her crossed leg. "Though you're letting me glimpse your cards when you shift position. Maybe a padded chair might help?"

"In fact, I'm sitting still and holding my cards close," Pauline said. "Would you pull that stunt with any of the men?"

"Apologies," Reginald said. "I was striving to be a gentleman."

"Next time, you'll get a drink in your face," Pauline said.

"Look, everyone," Barry said. "My wife is giving us a lesson on the cautionary phrase, 'Don't play into his hands.'"

"He *groped* my leg," Pauline said. "How do I cash out?"

"Cashing out happens when you win," Barry said. "Paying up is what happens when you lose your cool and storm out."

"Speaking of phrases," Pauline said, "'Let's make it interesting,' comes to mind. How do I add Barry's boat to the pot?"

"Toss the keys on the table," Gavin said.

"What about the keys in your pocket?" Barry asked, fixing him with a piercing stare. "You use the boat more than I do."

As Axe and others cracked up, Gavin said, "Stop grinning like a bunch of randy apes, you know Barry is talking about parent and alumni outings. This happens during every game when Reginald adds pricey booze to the mix. Reason drains in proportion to the bottle."

"I've barely touched my drink," Barry said.

"Perhaps I've imbibed too much," Axe said. "Because Gavin is making sense. Next, bunnies will hop across the floor."

"Hopefully, the kind in fishnets and high heels," Chill said.

"You need new material," Shredder murmured.

"Ditto," Chill said. "You've been a buzzkill lately."

"You're stalling," Harve said. "Play, or fold."

"I'm getting there," Chill said. "Give me a minute."

After sparking the back-and-forth, Reginald fell silent as he watched the other players through his cigar smoke. If he saw poker games as a way to gain intel and best people in other kinds of games, it would lead to a list of possible enemies. Again and again, Barry came across as an irritated malcontent, the opposite of watchful, but after a half-hour of barbs and betting, he threw down the winning hand with a sly grin.

In another clip, Reginald said, "This one inmate created his own deck of cards. Every card had secret clues you could catch onto over time. As you can imagine, anything dicey was of interest to rise out of the horror of feeling trapped, so along came a guard who couldn't tolerate us having fun. He took us by surprise and grabbed the deck, all except for a two of diamonds. It came to me when the maker of all things took the maker of the cards. Heart attack. To keep the card as a good luck charm, I had to be fast and careful." With a flick of his wrist, Reginald was suddenly holding a two of diamonds, and then, lightning quick, the card vanished from his hand. "You can frisk me, but you won't find it."

Having listened with smiles that hinted at previous tricks, the players watched as Reginald removed his button-up shirt, revealing no sign of the card. After carefully searching Reginald's chair, the players assessed the table, looking for hidden slots, but came up empty. It was only when I reversed the video and studied the action frame by frame that I saw a white triangle when Reginald peeled off his shirt. A flick of his wrist planted the card in a trash bin edge-up, making it tough to see.

With a dance session in the wings, I tucked Chip's laptop into the secret drawer, changed into my leotard, and gathered my wits as I saw Moritz and Raja returning from their lunch break. After Antoine's departure, they had resumed their unfriendly vibe, ascribing to the attitude that, as the men on the scene, they were in charge of the work.

In the driveway, Moritz signaled for me to stop.

"I see you're in your dance attire," he said. "It's unprofessional to come and go without notice. Good communication is key."

"Here's the chain of command," I said, lowering my hand by degrees. "Barry. Pauline. Mary. Me. You're at the *very* bottom."

"Dang, who pissed you off?" Moritz asked.

"Unfortunately," I said, "it's an increasingly long list, with you at the top for spreading falsehoods. Antoine was helping local law enforcement. It was a need-to-know action, no gossips allowed."

"Hey, we're thrilled to have the real story," Moritz said. "Your version matches how we see Antoine. He's a good guy."

"Back to the chain of command," Raja said pointedly. "We're not on vacation. As neighbors, we have skin in the game."

"In my experience, all that matters is who *owns* the game." With an Antoine-style micro flare of eyes, I added, "I'm looking forward to a quiet evening. Make sure you're finished by sundown."

"Umm, sure," Moritz said. "Got it."

Motioning them away, I climbed into my car, no idea how many calories I'd burned trying to stay straightforward and calm during conversations. From now on, I would mirror the exaggerated attitude of the men who kept landing in front of me. Inappropriate, inscrutable, unpredictable, ill-tempered, ominous, lurking, aggressive.

It was a long list that kept me entertained during the ten-minute drive to the studio, and then I hit the brake as Jason appeared from behind a car in the parking lot. Looking handsome, as always, in his black trousers and a loose button-up shirt that draped around his shoulders, he wrenched open the passenger door and plunged into the seat.

"Park out back," Jason said, pointing the way. "Check the license plate of the utility vehicle we're passing. That's Axe's set of wheels. Long story short, during concerts, the band is known for plucking dance partners from the audience. Usually, they pick a novice who falls into giggling fits, but sometimes, they mix it up with a trained dancer who 'miraculously' blossoms in their expert hands. The current candidate is named Nicole."

I hit the brake, jerking us in our seats. "*What?*"

"Do you know a Nicole?" Jason asked.

"Maybe it's not the same woman," I said.

"Regardless," Jason said. "You need to see it."

Once I was parked behind the building, Jason led the way through the back door and up a flight of stairs to an office where electronics were stacked next to a computer on a cluttered desk. Rolling two chairs into position in front of the screen, Jason sat down and opened the live feed from the dance studio captured by a ceiling camera.

Leaning in closer, I watched as Axe guided Nicole into a dip, while Chill and Riff appeared to be admiring her curves and sexy vibe.

"Did they talk at some point?" I asked.

"Earlier," Jason said, rewinding the feed to show Nicole following Axe, Chill, and Riff into the studio with a look of wonder.

"You own this place?" Nicole asked.

"No, it belongs to a friend," Axe said, securing her knee and tucking it across his hips. "You've never taken lessons?"

"If you're asking why I'm limber, four years of college cheerleading is a hint," Nicole said, smiling as she spun out of his grasp. "Do split-lifts and thigh-stands bring any thoughts to mind?"

"Easy, now," Chill said. "We're in a public setting."

"Let her talk, I'm halfway to the store to get pom-poms," Axe said, smiling as he pulled out his phone to show a photo. "This is the cruise ship we're talking about. Small and fast, with a limit of two hundred passengers. As shareholders, we're free to hire who we want."

"For the short term, we're in a holding pattern," Chill said. "With Reginald's health in a bad state, we're not sure if we should buy birthday candles or the votives they use for a wake."

"Yuck, a funeral?" Nicole asked.

"He's joking, Reginald will rally," Axe said. "Picture sitting at a table in a hot dress. Midway through our first set, I'll put my guitar aside and rescue you from whatever boring guy asked you to dinner. With special events, we can bring in high-rollers and contacts from across Hawaii and around the world. Maybe you'll find Mr. Right."

"I thought I was your new muse," Nicole pouted.

"Of course you are, a ray of sunshine in a dark world," Axe said, taking Nicole's hand to spin her and dip her with a flourish. "You've risen to the top in minutes. Let's see where it leads."

"And so on," Jason said, cutting the feed.

"I didn't see Shredder down there," I said.

"That's the pattern," Jason said. "Lately, he's got a short fuse. I'm not sure if it's a sign of personal growth, or the opposite."

"If you had to guess at the reason?" I asked.

"Guesses won't get us anywhere," Jason said. "Human remains were found on Reginald's land. The ex-cons are finally in jail from guilt to whatever degree, but who knows if it'll stick. According to Jasmine, all the turmoil and weirdness can be traced to an arts academy event that took place on the *Kukuna Mahina*. If we double down on regaining your Latin and ballroom skills, we can participate in the shipboard dance show."

"Hang on a second—"

"It's totally doable," Jason insisted. "We would be on board for two or three days with minimal commitment in terms of work hours, leaving us plenty of time to talk to the crew and see if there are holes in the investigation into Sally's death, for example. If the ex-cons were involved, we can cement up the charges so they stay locked up. You're here for a dance session. We'll practice some possible routines."

"Notice I'm nodding," I said. "I have a weakness for intrigue, so it's on you not to take advantage. I need to think it through."

"I wouldn't imagine it any other way," Jason said, earnestly crossing his half-exposed chest. "No pressure. Scout's honor."

"Which kind of scout, exactly?" I said dubiously.

With a grin, Jason confirmed that Axe, Nicole, and the others were leaving and led the way downstairs to the dance studio. As I was buckling my shoes, I looked up when Petrel and Pauline arrived.

"Hold your head high," Petrel soothed as he ushered Pauline through the doorway. "There we are, an escape from the heat."

"Stop fussing and get the loan agreement," Pauline said.

I hesitated before stepping closer, catching onto her flushed cheeks and irritation as she reached into her bag for a compact and checked her perfect makeup. Despite the afternoon heat, she wore a business suit and a silk blouse, with an arts academy pin on her lapel.

"Sonny and I are about to practice," Jason said.

"We'll only be a minute," Petrel said, looking at me with a hopeful smile. "With Reginald in the hospital, you're my only hope of fetching the loan agreement. Hopefully, you found the folder?"

"I'm sorry," I said. "It slipped my mind."

"Petrel," Pauline said sharply. "You assured me that you had a green light. I canceled a meeting to accompany you to the bank."

"It's a bother rather than a setback," Petrel said, fluttering to her side. "My dear, let's round the bend with a nice lunch. Chat with Jason and Sonny while I make sure the coast is clear."

"Clear of what?" Jason asked. "What's going on?"

Glaring at him so intensely it seemed to affect the studio's air conditioning, Pauline wavered, and then she burst into tears.

"Jason, look what you've done," Petrel said.

"It seemed like a simple question," Jason protested.

While Petrel and I guided Pauline to a chair, Jason grabbed a box of tissues and began plucking them out for her to use.

"I'm still fuming over the party damage," Pauline managed. "If it's uptight to criticize out-of-control behavior, so be it."

"I agree," Jason said. "But I'm still unclear on the context."

"Axe parked out front in his usual way, occupying three spaces," Petrel said. "When Pauline expressed her annoyance, the young tart on Axe's arm responded in an uncouth manner."

"It's more about my exchange with Carol," Pauline said. "There isn't a right way to explain why the academy can't host a memorial service. In the end, I just stood there and weathered her fury."

"The trustees abhor bad publicity," Petrel said, patting her hand. "But let's be honest, this isn't just about work. We've all felt the sting of your husband's sharp wit. Over time, it takes a toll."

"It's a daily thing," Pauline murmured. "When I was rinsing my hands in the bathroom sink this morning, my wedding ring caught the light, and I fixated on the splashing water. I know it's hard to picture me on a hike, but I was carefree early on, the opposite of uptight. There were bugs in the air and my hair was a mess, but that's where my adoring prince proposed, next to a stream of churning bright water. I'll never forget the feel of it, and I'll never forget how he described me as his rock."

"You're more than that," I said softly.

"No, it's me in a nutshell," Pauline said. "Anchored in place while the water splashes and tumbles and does whatever he wants."

"I know why you hang in," Petrel said. "Your parents divorced when you were a child. It's disheartening when history repeats itself."

"Except my mother was the one who gave into temptation and broke up the family," Pauline said. "Dear God, I am blurting private business in a public setting. It's time to regain control."

"Your outburst is safe with us," Petrel said.

"Let's call it a moment of sharing," I said.

Smiling, Pauline said, "Done. I'll be right back."

As she headed to the restroom, I turned to Petrel.

"It's none of my business, but I'm surprised that you're talking about getting a loan," I said. "The studio is beautiful."

"My dream is to build a wellness hub upstairs," he said. "Beyond my office, the space is a dusty lost cause. I've got a lineup of massage therapists and yoga instructors who are eager to rent space."

"To help with costs over the long term," Jason explained.

"And by the way," Petrel said. "I tried to get the loan agreement myself and found Carol with a locksmith, changing the deadbolt on Reginald's front door. Pauline isn't the only one who ended up standing in silence during a lecture about people not being supportive. Sonny, you're the last one to see Reginald. Is his mind on the mend or not?"

"Petrel, you're not being fair," Jason said. "Sonny is here to revive her skills. Our session has been booked for days."

"Of course, you're right," Petrel said, clasping my hands. "The idea of standing in the way of dance is unthinkable."

"Sonny," Pauline said, looking polished as she returned from the bathroom. "Every time I turn around, I'm called upon to thank you for a show of kindness. At some point, we should have lunch."

"That would be nice," I said, though my only options for dressing with style were the "slutty numbers" in Mary's bag.

"We'll talk soon," Pauline said. "Petrel, onward."

Once they stepped out and the sign indicated a lesson was in progress, Jason focused on his new mission of creating at least one freestyle routine with spicy elements of Latin and ballroom steps.

"Let's test your tango skills," Jason said.

With our shoulders offset and my right hand draped over Jason's left hand, I checked my reflection to correct my posture, with my left thumb hooked under his bicep to enhance our stylized embrace.

Drawn into motion, I fell into rhythm with Jason's steps, keeping pace with his "slow, slow, slow, quick-quick, slow" prompts. Unlike the partners from my youth, Jason propelled our movements with his chest and core, creating a sensation of being supported and guided through each sequence, with our knees softly flexed as we glided across the floor.

"Get ready for a promenade," Jason said.

Following the path of his outstretched arm, with our shoulders nearly parallel, Jason added spicy interest to the promenade with twist-turn steps, impressing me with the steadiness of his shoulders.

Despite how quickly Jason was reviving my dance skills, the idea of committing myself to a performance and joint investigation on the *Kukuna Mahina* amounted to asking for trouble. As always, a simple approach was best. If Reginald's friends and acquaintances could be convinced to open up, the last of the mysteries could be understood and solved.

"Sonny," Jason said as I missed a step. "For the sake of our shins, you need to focus if we start practicing flicks and hooks."

"I let distraction drift in," I said. "I'll do better."

"Let's try some ochos," he said.

As we resumed our rounded, closed embrace, with his shoulder rotations guiding my movements, I enjoyed the spicy feel of stepping onto my right toe, pivoting in place, and then stepping onto my left toe with my hips rolling in the sinuous, back-and-forth cadence. Asking for a repeat ocho, Jason sharply reversed, sending my lower leg into a boleo backward swing that amounted to gracefully kicking my butt.

Eager to test the limits of my abilities, Jason eased me along with narration, like, "Quick-quick, *and* quick-quick slow."

Breathless but focused, aware of his sharp footwork in my lower vision, I responded to his call for a dip, arching into his supporting arm and the sensation of being drawn to my left, as if I was a vessel he was filling with water. Guiding me upward and calling for another ocho sequence, Jason's thigh signaled a parada, with his right foot sliding into place below me. Smoothly rotating my shoulders and then following with my hips, I performed the slinky steps around his extended leg.

"*Perfect*," Jason said. "Well done!"

With a triumphant smile, he scooped me up for a victory twirl, and then he planted me on my feet and planted his cushy lips on mine, tasting of a sports drink that he'd had earlier in the day.

Abruptly, Jason let go with a look of dismay.

"My bad, Sonny," he said. "I got carried away."

"It was platonic, I hope," I said.

"Sure, let's call it platonic," Jason said. "But honestly, it started to feel like dancing with Katrina. If she's done with me, I'll need to create a future where I'm able to move on. I glimpsed that just now."

"Have you slipped up with other dancers?" I asked.

"No, this was an exception to my strict rule," Jason said, looking torn and confused. "The reason I started dancing was to impress Katrina. She's always been my motivation for never cheating."

"First loves have staying power," I said.

"Now there's an empty space all day every day, so I'm veering," Jason said. "You've become a friend, Sonny. I'll maintain the brake, but to be honest, I figured it wouldn't feel too off, given Antoine's abrupt exit at the luau. It looked like you argued, and then he left."

"It's hard to encapsulate what went on at the luau," I said. "Far from arguing, we had a harmonious, fast-paced visit."

With my hands on my hips, I reflected on the amazing wins of the past few days: all the sanding and repairing, perpetrator nabbing, living on snacks to accomplish as much as possible, and our special moment of finding human remains in a derelict coffee grove.

"Then again," I murmured. "It's possible I need a do-over."

21

At a glance, the newly installed drywall in the kitchen, living room, and hallway looked promising, but patchy after the first coat of paint. To enjoy a few days of living in paradise, I decided to hold off on all the finishing touches. Free work should translate to a few free nights.

At dusk, hurrying to the hot tub to escape the mosquitoes, I kicked off my flip-flops, swung my legs over the edge, and sank into the hot water up to my chin with a sigh of pleasure. Mist curling up from the surface added to the primordial feel of the coconut palms and the surrounding garden. With my head on a pillow, I watched the orange glow of the sunset spreading across the Pacific while one of Chip's underwater recordings drifted toward me from the house speakers. I'd found videos that showed Chip uncoiling a hydrophone from the side of a bobbing boat until the cable stretched to its full length. Then, he snugged headphones over his ears and smiled as he listened to the calls of humpback whales.

According to his notes, the soundtrack was made in a stretch of water near the newest volcano along the Hawaiian Island chain. Twenty-two miles off the coast of the Big Island and 3,200 feet below sea level, the Kama'ehuakanaloa Seamount was a seething epicenter of muffled detonations, explosive thuds, simmering, sudden cracks, and shuddering rumbles that vibrated the speakers on the deck wall. Faintly at first, the buoyant, resonant song of a humpback whale subtly accompanied the volcanic noises, slowly increasing in volume as if in defiance of the crushing under-water pressure that other creatures couldn't withstand.

Deep beneath the ocean's surface, beyond the reach of sunlight, the 40-ton whale would appear only as a silhouette drifting above the churning fires of planet Earth. After a restful interval, and without apparent need for an extra intake of breath, the whale emitted another haunting, echoing call that couldn't be translated into words. Was it a male calling to his mate? A mother singing to her calf? A weather report on surface conditions? Each song's ending faded into subsonic waves that, according to Chip's notes, could travel up to 10,000 miles across the ocean—double the distance from the Kona house to my farm in Maine.

From Chip's photo library, it was clear that nearly everyone I'd met had joined him for a day of whale watching at some point. Several photos showed Katrina and Jason exchanging smiles or training binoculars on the spouts of distant whale pods, with Barry at the helm of his boat. With a zoom lens, Chip photographed the underside of a humpback tail just be-fore the whale's deep dive, with notes describing the markings that helped him track each animal over a span of years. In a separate folder, there were records of DNA analyses with cryptic notes, which I assumed reflected additional efforts to monitor whale pods.

In recent months, Chip had gathered a collection of documents bear-ing Reginald's signature, including property deeds and loan applications. I looked everywhere for memos and calendar alerts that might show Chip's direct involvement in Reginald's business dealings. It bothered me that he might have been searching for signs of deals involving the ex-cons, but for all I knew, Chip wanted to celebrate Reginald's rise from his dark early years by striving to be a kind-hearted philanthropist.

Half a day into my investigation, I was no closer to finding evidence of foul play in Chip's death. The only suspicious detail was Chip's focus on documenting the rock band's party, though I hadn't found any proof of serious misconduct like drug use or inappropriate sexual activities. The party must have been deafening, with a level of chaos that allowed Axe, Chill, Riff, and Shredder to walk away unscathed and post bad-boy clips on their social media platforms. Gavin was poised to make money for Ellika Arts by selling the paintball garage door "masterpiece." Even Moritz and Raja were profiting in the aftermath of the riotous party, despite taking part in the chaos and causing some of the damage.

Suddenly alert, certain that I'd seen a shot of Moritz throwing a lamp against a wall in the downstairs apartment, I climbed out of the tub with a burst of splashing, tossed the lid over the water, and lurched up the stairs in my flip flops on rubbery legs from the relaxing soak.

Once I toweled off, I crossed to the table where I'd left Chip's laptop and clicked through the dozens of photos documenting the rock band's party. Frame after frame showed strangers grinning as they tossed cans onto the lawn or leaped up to kick a wall. From time to time, either Moritz or Raja or both could be seen in the background in a frenzy of "going along with the crowd." Scrolling back through the timeline, I stared at a shot of a blurry forearm captured in front of the lens. Zooming in, I decided I wasn't looking at Chip's tanned, youthful arm.

"It looks like Gavin's plump arm," I murmured.

Thinking it through, I imagined Gavin waving his hands and calling for people to show sense. Unable to stop the chaos, he might have felt compelled to document the damage, though as far as I knew, the evidence hadn't been used to hold any of the culprits accountable.

Scrolling back to earlier shots, I clicked through a series of photos showing Moritz and Raja being stopped at the door and frisked by Axe, Chill, and Riff. Grinning in the last photo, Axe held a tiny object in his hand. A game of catch ensued, and then a spark of light told me the object had been dropped and kicked into the crowd. In later shots, I saw Moritz and Raja nearly getting trampled as they crawled through the thicket of drunken revelers, but they apparently didn't find the object.

Recalling the clip of them looking under rugs that very morning, I put on my work clothes and wasted a half-hour checking the shop vacuum they'd been using since the repair project began. Pausing in frustration, I remembered seeing a broken vacuum in the garage.

Outside the kitchen door, I hesitated, hearing Moritz and Raja commenting on the whale recording. Once a wash of departing headlights confirmed they were heading to their shift at a local bar, I continued into the garage, hauled the broken vacuum to an open spot on the floor, and pulled out the bag, which was filled to the exploding point.

Cutting an X across the top, I peeled the sides down to reveal a compacted wad of dust, dried grass, eucalyptus leaves, and desiccated flies. Prodding with my fingertips, I found a post-style earring with an opal stone that might explain the spark of light in the photo. As I searched further, I gathered torn pieces of a note and matched the edges. Based on the documents on Chip's computer, I recognized the "R" and "W" as part of an exercise to practice Reginald White's signature ten or more times. It wasn't necessarily a red flag. In the past, I'd spent time perfecting a stylized signature for my artwork, and given Reginald's apparent dementia, Katrina might have needed to sign documents on his behalf.

One after another, I brushed dust off objects that turned out to be a twig or a bottle cap, and then, just like Axe had done, I held up a silver USB stick, though for all I knew it was legitimate trash, and not the object that Axe had taken from Moritz's pocket at the party.

I didn't find a companion for the earring, but in case it was helpful, I set aside two receipts from a jewelry store on Oahu.

After tucking the finds into a sandwich bag for later examination, I shed my dusty clothes, put on my T-shirt and floral pajamas, and opted for a quick dinner of an avocado and cheese sandwich.

To end the day on a positive note, I opened my phone and smiled at the selfie Antoine had sent, showing his comical apprehension as he draped his arm around Zach inside the mesh cage of a ride just seconds before they shot into a spinning vertical track. It wasn't until I saw the photo that I fully understood his sense of feeling ready to connect after decades of caution and vigilance. From a man who'd been so hounded by an enemy that he'd scoured all traces of himself from the internet, he'd taken a selfie with Zach, a sign that he'd entered a new chapter. During his stay, I'd followed the old rule of respecting the need for concealment, except for my photo at the snorkeling site that captured our alien-like shadows on the reef floor with a turtle in the foreground.

Thanks to Ted's thoughtless take on Antoine's visit, I pictured Zach's smile turning into a frown as he looked at me, the classic response to a potential rival for a parent's affection. I vowed to be fascinating, trouble-free, and bulletproof by the time we met.

"Not the right word," I said. "Even though it fits."

Outside, the muffled detonations of the Kama'ehuakanaloa Seamount promised to spark the wrong kind of dreams. Using the remote control, I turned off the soundtrack and increased my chances of falling asleep with a snack of calcium-rich cheese and a tumbler of whiskey.

Gulping down a burning slug, I blinked away the shimmering effect in my eyes, then sipped the rest in a ladylike fashion, nestled into the couch cushions with *The Hawaiian Archipelago* in hand. Specifically, I wanted to reread an amusing passage describing Isabella's night among congenial Native Hawaiians in a "dilapidated frame-house, altogether forlorn, standing unsheltered on a slope of the mountain" in Waipio Valley. Among the hardships were sizeable voids instead of proper windows.

"Presently," Isabella wrote, "a large cat jumped through the hole and down upon me, followed by another and another, till five wild cats had effected an entrance, making me a stepping-stone to ulterior proceedings. Had there been a sixth I think I could not have borne the infliction quietly. Strips of jerked beef were hanging from the rafters, and by the light which was still burning I watched the cats climb up stealthily, seize on some of these, descend, and disappear through the window, making me a stepping-stone as before …"

As I set the book aside and drifted off to sleep, the image of wild cats leaping through a hole morphed into people emerging from the darkness and using me as a stepping stone. First came Agent Telford, then Barry, Gavin, and Pauline, then Axe, Chill, Riff, and Shredder, who frowned as he stared at his phone. My sly-eyed neighbors tossed peanuts in my face, sending me tumbling down a hill into a shadowy world where ghosts clawed at my ankles and killers yelled in my face.

You know what'll happen if you fight me.

What will you remember? What will you forget?

Stop—asking—questions!

"Hey," a woman said. "Wake up."

"N'd sleep," I murmured.

"Perfect," she said. "You've been drinking."

Sluggish and half-awake, I felt relieved as the dream menace walked away past tools and other signs indicating I was in the Kona house. Hearing approaching footsteps, I squinted as a woman's silhouette stepped close with a sloshing container that reminded me of an ice bucket. In a smooth arc, she hurled its glistening contents into my face.

Shocked by a blast of ice water, I rolled and hit the floor, choking, coughing, and aware of the woman standing over me. Lurching upward too fast, I dropped into blackness and stars, clutching the couch at the last second to avoid another hard landing. As the fog cleared, I hoisted myself upward, sat on the wet cushions, and tried to figure out whether I was experiencing another nightmare or a real attack.

"Sober up," the woman said. "I don't have time for theatrics."

Droplets glistened on my eyelashes as I focused on Katrina standing amid the shadows with her hands planted on her hips.

"Are you insane?" I managed.

"I'll be the one doing the grilling," Katrina said. "You've inserted your-self into my inner circle, including Chip, who died mysteriously after you took part in the whale rescue. You impersonated me on your ride to Hilo on *my* bike, flashed your heels around in my old dance shoes, and wormed your way into Jason's heart. Identity theft is against the law. The only good thing is that you're too dumb to act in secret."

Across the kitchen, the neon numbers on the microwave told me it was 8 p.m., a few hours after I'd emerged from the hot tub to check the party photos. Beyond the screened deck door, the coconut palms swayed gently in a light breeze, and frogs peeped from hidden corners across the yard and garden. Stiff and sore from a long day of hard work, I crossed to the kitchen, ripped a handful of paper towels from the dispenser, and used them to dry my face, neck, and ears as I stepped outside to the deck, pre-ferring to be in the open when facing a possible threat.

My dripping T-shirt clung to my shoulders and torso, chilled by the breeze coming from the coastline every night, as if from the volcano's breath on the other side of the island. I turned toward a rustling sound and saw the peacock settling his tail feathers near the garden, shimmering in the dim light like a gasoline puddle come to life.

"Well?" Katrina demanded.

"Well, what?" I said tiredly.

"Don't act like you haven't butted into my life," Katrina said. "You visited my grandfather's house. What were you hoping to find?"

"Jasmine's clothes," I said.

"That's another thing—"

"You're all set?" I asked. "Free of trouble?"

Katrina's hands swept up and down, indicating her ponytail, light layer of mascara, and her dark pants with a matching top.

"Am I not standing here in one piece?" she asked.

"You absolutely are," I said, stepping through the doorway into the living room to grab my bag from the coffee table and toss Isabella's book inside. "I'll call Mary and let her know that ninety-five percent done will have to suffice. My work here is finished."

"Wait a minute—"

As Katrina gripped my arm, I used her momentum to spin her to her knees and then onto her stomach. Gently, to prevent injury, I secured her right wrist and held it against the small of her back.

"I'm not seeing a knife," I said, checking her pockets. "That's the good news. If you escalate any more, I will call 911."

"Who the hell are you?" Katrina managed.

"My name is Sonny Littlefield," I said, shaking from fury and tears. "I've been held at gunpoint, tased, drugged, kidnapped, and told that I'm a reckless idiot by my friends. That last part is the kicker. I haven't learned that some people don't want to be helped."

"Let me *up*," Katrina snarled.

"Don't come at me again," I warned.

Once I released her, I paused long enough to confirm that Katrina's aggression had faded as she climbed to her feet.

Leaving the lights off, I stalked to the bedroom and flung open the zippered lid of my suitcase, neatening the contents enough to make room for my clothes from the day's work, my sandals and sneakers, and my damp bathing suit. In the bathroom, I swept my toiletries into a bag to sort out later and pushed past Katrina. The fact that she was popping a ginger chew into her mouth caught my attention, and then I understood: fate thought it would be amusing for me to catch a cold.

"Stay and talk to me," Katrina said. "I need answers."

"I've got a feeling you watched my dance session with Jason through the camera feed and saw him kiss me," I said, stuffing granola bars into my suitcase. "Maybe he predicted that and wanted you to be jealous. If you're smart, you'll appreciate that you've won your man."

"I haven't won *anything*," Katrina said.

"You've won this match," I said. "I'm leaving."

"Sonny, wait," Katrina said, with tears welling in her eyes as she tried to block my exit. "Give me ten seconds."

"Ten, nine, eight—"

"Stop being stubborn and take it," Katrina said, holding out the half-eaten ginger chew. "I'm sorry if it's gross."

I stared at the glistening wad in her palm. "What …?"

"*Please*," Katrina insisted.

When I grimaced, revolted by the wet, sticky candy, Katrina gripped my fingers so I couldn't escape the feel of it.

"That's how I felt when I woke up," she said. "On the *Kukuna Mahina*, I woke up in bed, no idea how I got there, stripped down to my panties, and covered with oil like I was this candy. My head was pounding. Somebody had spiked my drink."

"Oh no," I whispered. "Dear God."

"Yeah, you're quoting me," Katrina said. "I haven't won Jason, or the golden ticket, or anything else in my crazy life. I'm sorry for taking it out on you. I'm the opposite of mean and aggressive. It's from grief over losing Chip, and feeling out of control."

"I get it," I said softly. "Were you …?"

"No, fate intervened," Katrina said. "I escaped the worst-case scenario, at any rate. Months have gone by, but it's still a jarring, all-consuming wedge in my mind. That night changed *everything*."

"Of course it did," I said. "I understand."

Abruptly spent, I crossed to the kitchen, awash with goosebumps as I cleaned my hands of the stickiness that had left lasting, invisible scars, then I poured us both a glass of water. Katrina gratefully accepted the drink. A dry mouth was a universal response to extreme stress.

"You'll stay and talk?" Katrina asked.

"Yes, of course," I said.

"Feel free to start," she said. "All that stuff really happened?"

"And more," I admitted.

To finish my self-summary as we sat on the kitchen stools, I grabbed a crushed soda can from the trash and held it up.

"This past year, my world imploded too many times to stick the landing," I said. "This can is akin to what's left behind. My heart doesn't look the same or feel the same or believe in love the way it used to. I've got a list of positive mantras. They're starting to work."

"I can relate," Katrina said, turning the empty can in the lamplight to look at its crushed folds. "Welcome to adulthood, I guess."

After a moment of silence, I tried to ease her into a conversation by showing her the opal earring I'd found in the vacuum bag.

"No, it's not mine," Katrina said.

"Do you want some tea?" I asked.

"Yes, I'm chilled to the bone," Katrina said. "If you don't mind, I need a minute to catch my breath and get my head straight."

While I filled the kettle, I worried that she might be tempted to flee into the night, but after splashing water on her face, she opened a closet, reminding me that she and Jason had rented the house a few times. With a rustle of fabric, Katrina rejoined me in the kitchen, with a flowered quilt wrapped around her shoulders for warmth.

"You look like a Hawaiian princess," I said, indicating her shining dark hair. "My mind is wired to think in pictures."

"I'm part native Hawaiian," Katrina said as she resumed her seat in the kitchen. "Thanks to my grandfather's fooling around, my family tree is amounting to a forest, including the kid next door."

"You're talking about Chip?" I asked.

Nodding, Katrina said, "Between dancing and the freedom of riding a motorcycle, I've found ways to ease the fear I had early on in life. That strangers would burst in and take Pop-Pop."

"Maybe you also feared the ex-cons?" I asked.

"If anything, they were wary of me," Katrina said. "I know you were at Pop-Pop's cottage when they were arrested. Did I hear correctly that they delivered a threat that was meant for my ears?"

Reaching for my phone, I pulled up the video from the gas station and wasn't surprised to see Katrina scowling as the footage played.

"Good-for-nothing scumbags," Katrina growled. "It crossed my mind that they were disgusting enough to drug me and take advantage, but they weren't on the vessel that night. What jolted me awake was the door slamming. I was confused and dizzy, then I heard shouting and running in the corridor. A woman had fallen overboard."

"In that same moment?" I asked.

"No, the crew was short-staffed, so Sally's absence went unnoticed for a while," Katrina said. "Jason joined the cruise thinking I was cheating. It's not true. As an event coordinator, I have to be polite when guys flirt. We quarreled. It's why I was on my own. I took a shower, aware that I was erasing evidence, but I was desperate to scrub myself clean. Imagine how I felt when I discovered that the security cameras in the cabin area weren't operational. It felt like a conspiracy. A setup."

"It's definitely fishy," I said. "Last year, in the wake of being attacked, I was afraid my friends would land in harm's way."

"It's one of the reasons I kept quiet," Katrina said, pale and trembling as she stared into space. "It might have been a stranger. That would be preferable to picturing someone I've known all my life. All the local guys attended the event, as usual, except for my grandfather. In hindsight, Pop-Pop's excuse for not going, that he already felt seasick, makes sense. You'll have heard that he's in the hospital."

"Reginald mentioned that you've shut him out," I said.

"I wondered if the attack was a form of payback or blackmail," Katrina said. "Instead of telling him what happened I grilled him. He was irritated and dismissive. I'm appalled to know why he wasn't himself, but in the heat of the moment, I was convinced that I'd suffered the consequences of an iffy business deal. With criminals, it's all about delivering warnings and sending messages. Your video seems like proof."

"Do you recall if your drink tasted funny?" I asked.

"When it comes to work events, I drink iced tea with lemon," Katrina said. "Bitterness might mask a drug taste. I remember feeling dizzy. Axe and Chill were chatting up hookers in the bar. It was like an echo chamber of posturing and phony laughing, all aimed at—"

Suddenly, Katrina reached for the opal earring, looking rapt and focused, as if she was recalling a remembered scene.

"Where did you find this?" she asked.

"In the vacuum bag," I said. "Why?"

"Amid the echo chamber, I'm certain I heard a woman talking about opals," Katrina said. "Because it's her birthstone."

"Do you know who it was?" I asked.

"All I remember is hearing some mention of opals," Katrina said. "The drug messed me up. It demolished my sense of time."

"It sounds similar to what I went through," I said. "The doctors called it Swiss cheese amnesia. Even after I pieced together every second of the attack, I feared being doubted or harshly judged. There's a long history of female victims being slammed for speaking up."

Nodding, Katrina said, "I felt like I was in a hurricane that nobody else could see. Instead of rain and debris flying every which way, I wrestled with the fear of a loathsome rich jerk sneering in my face and insisting it was consensual. Chip was bound to notice my misery." With a choked-off sob, Katrina covered her face and tearfully added, "I felt alone, so I confided in him. What if his death is my fault?"

"It's not uncommon for victims to turn inward and blame themselves," I said softly. "If I'm allowed to speak my mind, withdrawing from a knowing, supportive friend like Jasmine is not the answer. The way forward involves mega doses of compassion and love."

"I came in thinking that," Katrina said. "I'll consider sharing my story with Agent Telford. He was surprisingly kind."

"I'm happy to serve as an intermediary," I said.

"I'll think about it," Katrina said, signaling that she needed to leave. "Aside from painting, the repairs look finished."

"I'll be here for a few more days," I said.

Lost in our own thoughts as we headed outside and down the walkway past the massage room and office, Katrina confided that she'd parked in a hidden spot on one of the roads that connected to the lane, more to avoid running into Moritz and Raja than to catch me off guard.

"Were they on the ship that night?" I asked.

"Yes, they were there," Katrina said, "They'll move heaven and Earth to tend bar when high rollers are in the mix. Trust me, I got in front of every man in town to check for signs of guilt. Chip did the same, also to hear opinions on the lapse in protocol that led to a death. With Moritz and Raja, pushing for details is pointless unless there's a profit angle for them. Through footage from the security cameras that worked, Chip confirmed they didn't leave the bar during the critical time."

"I can picture them tumbling over each other to profit from an awful experience," I said. "Are they a couple, or …?"

"They're known to have an unhealthy knowledge of must-see straight-guy porn," Katrina said. "As far as I know, they're not gay, but they're two peas in a pod when it comes to get-rich-quick schemes and related habits. I can picture them growing old together."

"Did you hear any mention of someone losing an item at the party?" I asked. "I've found bits and pieces along with the earring."

Katrina shrugged. "Create a lost and found."

"Are you okay to drive home?" I asked.

"Says the woman who drank herself to sleep," Katrina said, adding with a wince, "I did watch your dance session. Especially with spicy styles, it's easy for the line to blur. My fears proved out."

"The kiss was platonic, but it's a sign that Jason is struggling to hang in," I said. "Ask Jasmine what she thinks."

Katrina nodded. "Thank you for listening."

"Any time," I said.

As Katrina walked up the lane and turned left onto a trail, the flashlight feature on her phone helped me track her progress through the shrubs and trees. Once I heard her car heading away, I checked for lurking shadows, retreated into the house, and fetched Chip's laptop with a renewed focus on anything related to the *Kukuna Mahina*.

22

"Sonny?" Mary said.

Cracking an eye open, I looked past the Antoine-scented pillow I was clutching and regarded the dustcloth in Mary's hand. My brow scrunched as my gaze lifted past her stretch pants and flowered blouse, all the way up to her bright smile.

"Rise and shine, sleepyhead," Mary said. "With the project nearing completion, I figured it was time to stop in and ensure everything is ship-shape. Plus, I wanted to be on hand for any *surprises* that might unfold. Chop-chop. Up we go."

I paused for a moment. "Huh …?"

"Leave it to you to get tuckered out at the wrong moment," Mary said, bustling through motes of sunshine to eliminate dust with a frenzy of wip-ing and swatting with the cloth. "Get your buns in gear so I can neaten up the bedding and pillows. With a little elbow grease, we'll turn this careen-ing cart around. You'll thank me for it."

"What time is it?" I managed.

"It's eight o'clock, honey," Mary said. "Just about twelve hours after your latest miracle. Imagine my shock when Katrina showed up at my family's house on the north end of town, in tears to apologize to Jasmine for causing months of anguish. We talked into the night. That is, Katrina and Jasmine talked while I conked out. Anyway, Moritz and Raja are clearing eucalyptus leaves from the walkway to eliminate tripping hazards and curtail the scent, which I absolutely love, but it's not for everyone. We aim to put our best foot forward around here."

Clicking her tongue at the clothes I'd ditched at 2:30 a.m., Mary fetched a laundry bag and set about gathering shirts, pants, towels, and the spare bathing suit that I'd hung out to dry. Working quickly, she wiped down the sink, added a crisp point to the toilet paper roll, and sighed over the hotel shampoo bottles littering the shower stall.

I pushed upright, bleary-eyed after a long night of watching videos from the arts academy event on the *Kukuna Mahina*.

"Mary," I said. "While you're here, I'm trying to get a sense of Sally, the waitress who died. Was she dating anyone?"

"As a waitress myself, I expect she was too exhausted to do any fooling around," Mary said. "Maybe that's why she resorted to drugs. Waitressing can be a marathon, especially with high rollers in the mix."

"Do you know any specifics?" I asked.

"With event voyages, the passenger list is limited to people who want to mingle with their own kind, if you get my drift," Mary said. "Fellow rich folk. From what I heard, the locals were there as well. Barry, Pauline, Gavin, Axe, Riff, and the rest of the band. Harve helped with security. I heard Moritz was behind the bar, and Raja was waiting tables, or the other way around. Often, it's all hands to the pump."

"Did Moritz and Raja mention a missing item?" I asked. "Sorry, not from the cruise. From their work here in the house."

"Now that you mention it, they asked me to keep an eye out for a USB stick," Mary said. "I'll give you fair warning that they're claiming to have heard volcanic activity echoing from the house."

"It's part of Chip's research," I said, playing a clip that I'd saved to my phone. "From the Kama'ehuakanaloa Seamount."

Mary stopped cleaning and listened, captivated by the volcanic thuds combined with haunting humpback whale calls.

"Chip made this recording?" Mary asked.

"According to his notes," I agreed. "He planned to clean it up and put it online. I hope to finish the editing for him."

"His mother will love that," Mary said.

"This kind of project is my go-to lane," I said. "Putting meaning to lives that were cut short. In the process, I end up discovering secrets that *might* have led to a person's untimely demise …"

"It's a part of your special nature," Mary said. "Now, for the last time, get your buns in gear. I'll have breakfast ready in a minute."

Staring after her departing back, I understood that she might have felt cut off from contributing to the house repairs. If she wanted to boss around Moritz and Raja for the rest of the day, I was all for it.

While Mary busied herself in the kitchen, I pulled Chip's laptop from the dresser to review the videos that documented Sally's activities on the *Kukuna Mahina*, starting with a segment that showed her spiking Jason's drink. At first, I was frustrated to find that the clip ended before the drug took effect. Now I knew to follow Chip's lead through the timeline of videos, realizing that later clips would fill in the gaps.

I finished the first video and clicked on the next one.

From a corridor ceiling's vantage point, I watched Sally enter a restroom and knew ten minutes would pass before she stepped out. The following clip showed Sally returning to the bar, where Moritz and Raja were smirking at Jason's confusion and inebriated staggering.

In the next clip, Sally looked glassy-eyed as she paused in a corridor to sway to the beat of the music coming through her earpieces. She laughed, giddy and doubled over, and then she hauled herself upright and collided into Shredder, who was heading in the opposite direction with a distracted frown, and zero interest in helping her. After watching the ten-minute clip to the end, I rewound to a moment when Sally paused before heading up the stairs to the upper deck. Having been drugged by an attacker five months earlier, I could relate to her confusion and disorientation.

With a significant difference.

During my ordeal, I'd floundered my way through every sound, every awkward lurch, every effort to orient myself in a spinning, distorted world. When Sally reached the staircase, it seemed to me as if she was being strategically coached. I replayed the footage from the start, with imagined narration that matched her pauses, smiles, dancing, and the nods that seemed to signal enthusiastic agreement, as if someone had created a voiceover to softly encourage Sally onward through her earpieces:

"Stop and look down. Lift your right foot first. That's it, you're doing great. I love your smile. Use the railing for support. Lift your left foot next. Be careful! Pause if you're feeling dizzy. Just a few more minutes and we'll be together forever. Keep going. Almost there."

Awash in a rush of goosebumps, I understood that my theory involved a killer watching Sally through the corridor cameras.

In the coming days, I would find a way to check security footage of Chip's behavior for a similar pattern the night he died. If my theory proved out, and both he and Sally were led to their deaths, the earpieces and the devices would have been dislodged during their sudden plunge into the turbulent waters of the Pacific, never to be found again.

"If so, the evidence is gone for good," I murmured.

With the footage replaying in my mind, I stored Chip's laptop in a drawer and tidied up the bed, per Mary's wishes, while I thought about my next move. First, I needed to press Jason for his sense of the doomed cruise. Was he aware that he had been drugged? If he was, who did he blame, and had he figured out a possible motive?

Dimly, I was aware of Mary's restless activity in the kitchen and living room, dusting, sweeping the floor, and opening the door to look out into the sunshine. Over and over, she heaved impatient sighs, and then, as a car approached up the lane past the trees, filling the rooms with a wash of reflected light, Mary rejoiced and clapped her hands.

Fluffing the pillows, I froze as Harve's voice boomed, followed by a windstorm of familiar sounds: a crisp cadence of high heels on the walkway, complaints delivered with a Boston accent, and the hiss of a tailored dress protesting against the heat and humidity of the region as it struggled to keep up with the call for swift action.

"Where is she?" my mother demanded.

"Resting," Mary said. "She had a long night."

"When Alison ditched her promising career in Boston and moved to Maine, I predicted a quick decline that would end in a halfway house," my mother said. "Are the police on their way?"

"Goodness, no," Mary said. "The clutter is part of an upgrade effort. Moritz and Raja, stop gawking and get back to work."

"I'm honored to meet you," Moritz said.

"My hand hasn't been kissed in years," my mother said. "You could be an ambassador. The tropical shirt is a confusing element."

"It's standard attire at our country club," Moritz said. "If you need an *escort* during your stay, I can provide glowing testimonials."

"Moritz, enough," Mary chided.

"One hopes that admonition will suffice," my mother said tartly, and then she abruptly stiffened. "I'm either hallucinating from the heat, or a peacock is peering at me through the window."

"He's a local pet," Mary said. "Sonny is motioning us onward. There's nothing like a mother's love to help turn a corner."

To my surprise, my eyes brimmed with happy tears as I waited for my mother to come in, carrying her huge designer purse suspended in the crook of her arm. I didn't mind the look of exasperation that went hand in hand with circumstances that pitched us together. It wasn't every day that Evelyn Littlefield of Newton, Massachusetts, could be coaxed onto a plane unless shopping and museums were guaranteed perks at the other end of the flight. She'd crossed the Pacific to comfort me.

"Mom," I said. "Your back doesn't handle travel well."

"Nonsense, I'm here for you," she said, lightly hugging me with a waft of perfume. "I'm not one to say I told you so, but Dan took on a tone with me the first time we spoke in the wake of whatever awful crime. You remember that moment. I've never forgotten it."

Failing to find a suitably dignified chair to sit in, my mother dropped the weight of her purse to the floor, smoothed her chignon, though every auburn hair was already in place, and folded her arms.

"I can't believe you're here," I said.

"Stop making it sound as if I haven't been supportive," my mother said with a subtle nod toward Mary, lest we devolve into our usual squabbling in front of others. "I've done the best I can as a single mother. What do you need, darling?"

"I wouldn't mind some tea," I said.

"Of course," she said. "How do I reach room service?"

"This is a private house, not a hotel," I pointed out.

Abruptly closing her eyes, my mother murmured, "Breathe in, breathe out. Quell the negative, and look to the horizon. A new normal is ours to build, one step at a time. The future is bright."

I frowned. "What are you reciting?"

"A mantra my therapist prescribed," she confided.

"Mom, what's going on?" I asked, searching her face. "Something is wrong. Have you come to deliver bad news?"

"Alison, calm yourself," she said.

"A stock collapse?" I asked. "Foreclosure? A tax evasion charge?"

"I'm here to discuss Neckles," my mother said.

I paused. "Good God, you're getting married?"

"*Alison.*"

My mother's skill in delivering silent messages was second to none. On top of a micro flare of eyes, which now seemed ordinary and simplistic, my mother was able convey complete sentences, including punctuation, through subtle shifts of eyebrows, pursed lips, earring tugs, Morse code finger taps, and other means, holding a person spellbound through the work of deciphering the entirety of her thoughts. In short order, the complete translation was conveyed and understood.

I am here for personal reasons that cannot be discussed in front of strangers and a peacock. Period, Alison. Say something that fits.

"Mary, with the project almost finished," I said, "Can you discuss the checklist with Moritz and Raja out in the yard?"

Mary looked crestfallen, but when she saw Moritz and Raja hovering behind her, she followed through on shooing them out.

At last, my mother sat next to me with a confiding air.

"Neckles is a temporary handle for the Newton Clues and Evidence Society," she said. "We're working on the right acronym. To my surprise, my bridge club wasn't appalled by your plunge into crime and chaos. They started cancelling our games to discuss the specifics of each case. Dan was in for some serious questioning. Our group was poised to summon him, so he would be well-advised to part with you on good terms. We've got high-level officials in our group."

"Yes, I know the company you keep," I said.

"By all accounts, you've landed in another arc of trouble," my mother said. "I've come to speed things up. To lend a hand."

I paused. "Regarding …?"

"Solving the crime," she said.

Deeply touched and incredulous in equal measure, I fell into a facial workout that left room for future wrinkles to take hold, followed by a surrender posture as my mother's glare intensified.

"You've never supported my curious streak," I said. "As recently as last week, you accused me of being an adrenaline junkie."

"Stop fussing, we have a busy day ahead," my mother said. "In order to operate with clout in Hawaii, my colleagues advised me to network with an array of connected individuals with a loose cover story around investments that might take a wrong turn. The fee structuring of certain ventures needs to be scrutinized, etcetera, etcetera."

I raised my eyebrows. "All of which means …?"

"Stop dawdling and get dressed."

* * *

Informed that my mother needed privacy in conducting business with her "associates" and "local contacts," I sat in the passenger seat of the luxury car that Harve had secured at my mother's direction. Tinted windows shielded us from the Hawaiian sun as Harve and I watched the bank's glass front doors for the better part of half an hour.

"What's she doing in there?" Harve asked, mopping his brow from sweating out his confinement in a dark chauffeur suit.

"She's formed some sort of crime-solving club," I said. "On the belief that it will improve our bond, so I'll need to be supportive if she gets a cold shoulder from whoever she's meeting in the bank. If she comes out looking shocked and despondent, help me sell it as a win."

"Keeping an eye on you suits my side hustle with Ted," Harve said. "With that in mind, what's with the laptop you snuck into the car, thinking I wouldn't see you tuck it under your seat?"

"It's Chip's computer," I said. "With Moritz and Raja lurking and hovering when we left, I didn't get a chance to hide it."

"You've caught on that they're keen on parlaying information into a golden ticket," Harve said. "Moritz had one growing up, but according to his version of events, he got a cheat for a stepdad."

"Gavin mentioned a rocky history," I said.

"I'll start with the world according to Moritz," Harve said. "In his eyes, Gavin is behind the implosion of the family fortune, his mother's drinking, and her untimely death. If you sit down with Gavin with a whiskey in hand, be prepared to hear the opposite story."

"Care to share your sense of it?" I asked.

"Gavin is an ambitious hustler, and Moritz is a lazy, no-account ding-a-ling," Harve said. "My sympathies lie with the naïve woman who let the men in her life handle the financial wrangling until it was dust in the wind. Apparently, your mother is made of sterner stuff. She went into the bank empty-handed and is coming out with a shiny briefcase."

"Yes, I see it," I said. "What do you think it contains?"

With a shrug, Harve put on the cap that added to his sweat but protected his balding head from the heat, then stepped out to open the back door for my mother. Once her bare legs and high-heeled shoes were tidily tucked in, Harve gently closed the door, just as my mother had dictated—so that the act wouldn't sound like a cannon blast.

Wearing dark glasses, she tapped on the partition between the front and back seats. Once it was opened, letting her perfume fill the cool interior, she handed me a list of additional stops she planned to make, then the glass partition purred shut against my questions.

"Where to next?" Harve asked.

"Thankfully, a Japanese restaurant," I said. "A relaxing brunch will give us a chance to discuss the contents of the briefcase."

"You're truly in the dark?" Harve asked.

"Stick with answering my questions," I said. "How do you explain the fact that some of the security cameras on the *Kukuna Mahina* were working the night Sally died, while others were offline?"

"I've been carrying the weight of that night for months," Harve said. "According to rumor, I was in charge of security, but for the record, I urged the shareholders not to proceed with the arts academy event. All they saw was the potential for grumbling and lost income, so I pitched in despite questionable electronic coverage and a lack of trained staff."

"I heard you own some shares of the vessel," I said.

"A crumb, rather than a slice of the pie," Harve said. "It was arrogance at work, thinking I was capable of filling three slots. If Reginald had been his old self, he would have canceled the voyage, regardless of the loss of profit. He's a stickler for details, but he was under the weather, so he asked me to take his place. I figured lawsuits might hit the fan, but Sally didn't have anyone to stand up for her or cry foul."

"You've heard the latest on Reginald's illness?" I asked.

"Someone tried to upend his careful approach," Harve said. "Clearly, you're not just patching drywall up at the house. Agent Telford will be steamed to find out that you've got Chip's laptop."

"I will hand it over eventually," I said. "Though technically, it's Carol's call. She entrusted the search for answers to me."

In the restaurant's parking lot, my encounter with the morning air was brief; my mother signaled that brunch was not on the agenda. When I climbed back into the car, Harve looked incredulous.

"Your PI training didn't impart the basics?" he asked. "Wait until she's inside, then sneak in and hide behind some greenery."

"Maybe she needs to powder her nose," I said.

"Then that'll be your excuse too," Harve said.

"Right," I said. "Good idea."

Unlike my mother, who steamed past the hostess without a word, I gratefully took a large, leatherbound menu to hold up while I strained to hear my mother's conversation with the bartender.

"I have a *yen* for karaage and yakitori," she said.

The bartender hesitated. "You're here for the …?"

In response, my mother gave a sharp reply in what sounded like fluent Japanese, triggering a rushing sound in my head.

"Alison," she said, looking exasperated to see me there as she stepped away from the bar with a thick envelope in her hand. "I told you we're not here to eat. If you need to use the restroom, make it quick. We have one more stop before my meeting at two o'clock."

"What's in the envelope?" I asked.

"How can you have solved crimes without knowing the basics?" my mother said. "Nothing happens without bargaining chips."

"Only with people you know and trust," I said.

"Exactly," my mother said. "Off you go."

With a sigh, I grabbed a takeout menu on my way out and rejoined Harve in the front seat with a renewed commitment to stay supportive in the face of my mother's departure from forty-nine years of being a pillar of restraint and decorum. It took her bridge club to inspire her burst of 'help,' but never mind. It was a heartening change.

"The next stop is my favorite thrift store," I said. "It's touching that my mother remembered me talking about it after past visits, but I bet she'll ask you to park blocks away to avoid an imaginary musty smell. She's allergic to second-hand items, including frayed cash."

"Which begs the question," Harve said. "How did your mother hook up with a rugged outdoorsman like Raymond French?"

"I think her rigid side was from being married to Donald Littlefield," I said. "I'm glad she loosened up when she was younger."

"Especially if you're the result," Harve said, then he paused expectantly as if waiting to hear an updated version of my origins.

I frowned. "Why do you look doubtful?"

"I don't know," Harve said. "Why *do* I look doubtful?"

"If you're coming unhinged, can it wait until tomorrow?" I asked.

Harve held up his hands. "Whatever you say."

As always, vehicles were vying for a space on the busy street lined with one-story businesses, including a dive store, a coffee bar, and Hawaii-style shops. Once Harve squeezed the car into an open spot, I grabbed my bag, climbed out, and signaled that I wouldn't be long.

My mother's window slid down.

"Why isn't Harve opening my door?" she asked.

"I told him you planned this stop for my benefit," I said. "Though, instead of nodding and smiling, you look irritated."

"Harve?" my mother said. "Come and assist me."

"No, hang on," I said. "This is a thrift store, full of used clothing, bedding, jewelry, books, spoons, and used *everything*."

"I'm able to read the sign," my mother said.

Motioning for Harve to stay behind as he tried to follow us, I stood to one side while my mother swept into the lamplit interior, where the scent of potpourri greeted me. Instead of declaring that patchouli should be a controlled substance, my mother secured a handbasket and forged onward. Racks of carefully laundered vintage bags, jackets, shirts, pants, and dresses formed narrow tunnels through the carpeted interior, with a central island of jewelry cases surrounding a cheerful woman writing prices on tiny labels near the cash register. Having left my treasured vintage bag finds in Maine, I crossed to the bin and inspected an assortment of sizes and styles. One bag had a mysterious yellow stain on the bottom.

"Look," I said, holding the stain in front of my mother. "I love the gaudy flowers. Do you think it's a *diaper* bag?"

"One imagines it might have been," my mother said, examining a wall of photographs through her reading glasses.

"Should I *buy* it?" I asked.

"Alison, I'm concerned to see how indecisive and clingy you've become," she said. "I can't focus with you hovering."

Setting the bag aside, I felt a jolt of alarm as my mother removed an 8" x 10" framed photo of strangers from the wall and dropped it into her basket. Far from casually browsing, she appeared to be crossing off a specific list of items. The last time I'd seen a woman with a look of following orders that weren't readily apparent from the outside, she'd plunged from the *Kukuna Mahina's* upper deck into the bay.

Intensely alert, I watched my mother check the inside cover of a book of poems and tuck it into her basket. Moving onward, she crossed to the central jewelry cases, surveyed the array of used silver and gold merchandise, and decisively rested a manicured fingernail on the glass above a necklace with an engraved heart.

"I'll take the gold locket," she said. "Plus, the hoop earrings with the misguided glass bead, the man's garnet ring, and the awful watch with an expandable silver band that can't be comfortable to wear."

The clerk hesitated. "If other watches are more to your liking …"

"It was specifically requested, along with a certain blue necklace box that was left in your safekeeping," my mother said, extracting a signed, official-looking sheet and holding it out for the woman's inspection. "If you skim past the legalese and focus on the closing paragraph that outlines the parameters of your loan agreement, along with the signature of my local associate, you will see that this is your only option."

"Hang on," the woman said, putting on her glasses. "I'll need to see your identification, and … oh dear. Yes, I understand."

Once my mother directed the flustered clerk to tuck her purchases into a *new* shopping bag, I rushed to hold the door shut.

"It's time to explain what you were doing in the bank," I whispered. "Which 'associate' you're talking about, how you can speak Japanese, and why you appear to be carrying out an agenda."

"I've been assured that everything will be explained at my two o'clock meeting," my mother said. "Now, please open the door before I explode from the scent of potpourri and the proximity of men's boxers on that rack. Who would buy second-hand underwear?"

"I agree," I said. "But you will explain in the car."

"Open the door," my mother prompted.

To end the stalemate, I pushed the door open, waited for my mother to sail past me, and then I collided with Agent Telford.

"There's our busy bee," Ted said dryly.

Words escaped me, other than "Uh-oh."

23

Less than five seconds into Ted's attempt to stop my mother from leaving and redirect her future plans, she summoned the full extent of her imperious nature and sharply motioned for him to stop.

"I am a private citizen on my way to an important meeting," she said. "If you make us late, you will be clipped in half by my high-level associates and an agent from the Federal Bureau of Investigation."

"Gosh, that's surprising," Ted said.

"This is a serious circumstance, unsuitable for a dry tone," my mother warned. "Step aside, or I will unleash the floodgates."

"As luck would have it," Ted said, flashing his badge, "I am Edward Dry-as-the-Sahara Telford, Special Agent of the Federal Bureau of Investigation, and while I did not arrange to meet with you today, you will, in fact, be meeting with me, starting with a ride in an official vehicle. Already, we're making friends and coming to an understanding."

"Harve, it's time for you to step in," my mother said.

"With all due apologies, Mrs. Littlefield," Harve said. "My freelance engagement with the bureau entails alerting Ted to fishy undertakings that I come across, and your various stops had a ripe aroma the moment you exited the bank with a briefcase. Hence, I made the call."

"You're fired," my mother said.

"Accepted and understood," Harve said, loosening his tie and tossing his hat through the open window of his luxury rental. "If I am allowed to weigh in with my professional and personal opinion, you truly are acting out of love for your daughter. It's heartwarming."

"I've always acted out of love," my mother said.

"It's why I always try to avoid arguments," I said, leading us from the hot sunshine into the shade of an awning. "But we have a backdrop of serious circumstances. Who is pulling the strings?"

"I don't have the time or patience to deliver a civics lesson," my mother said. "On what grounds am I being questioned?"

"If I'm not mistaken," Agent Telford said, "one of the items you have secured for a third party is a blue necklace box that has come to our attention as a red flag. Often, when a model citizen like yourself takes actions that seem out of the norm, it's in response to a concern or threat that's out of the norm. Were your finances compromised?"

"Certainly not," my mother said. "Technically, my Hawaii contact is a new acquaintance, but he framed my involvement as assisting my daughter with her new focus on victim advocacy. She'll know who I'm talking about, given his knowledge of a sensitive personal matter."

I shook my head. "I'm in the dark."

"It's about the *historical* record," she specified.

I sighed. "Recent history? Past history?"

"A bit of both," my mother said.

Sensing a moment of gridlock, Ted gave us some room.

"My contact knows about your father's private journals," my mother whispered. "Apparently, Dan's mother hid the last volume during the investigation into Raymond's death. Even if it was an absent-minded slip, her behavior could be seen as obstruction of justice."

"How could anyone in Hawaii know about it?" I whispered. "If not for my video chat with Dan, even I wouldn't have a clue—"

Suddenly, I looked at Harve, who'd made note of my kind approach to the breakup after listening in from the doorway of an airport conference room. In response to my glare, demanding to know with whom he'd shared my private business, Harve scratched a spot over his ear with his forefinger upraised, as if aiming a sidearm at the sky.

Reginald White, a.k.a. Pop-Pop, was my mother's secret contact?

"Mom," I whispered. "Did your so-called 'associate' use the story as a blackmail element? Did he threaten to expose Dan?"

"No, he stressed his admiration for your compassion," my mother said. "Others in your shoes would relish tanking an ex."

Not for the first time, I kicked myself for dating a state trooper with a troubled history. Back in May, my inner pessimist had known it would loop back like an escaped animal and bite me on the ass.

"Alison," my mother said. "I see you kicking yourself for being careless, reckless, short-sighted, overly curious—"

"We have a federal agent waiting," I hissed.

"And prone to picking the wrong men," she continued. "We've come full circle because it was my local associate who pointed out that whatever his flaws, Dan is a decent man with a noble calling. It doesn't seem fair to throw him under the bus over a technicality."

"None of Raymond's journals were secured as evidence," I said. "Most likely, your impulse to help me will suffice as a reason for taking action. Tell the truth. Be specific. Running errands for an 'associate' isn't against the law. Neither is shopping, etcetera."

"You're good at this after all," my mother said.

"I'm just getting started," I said.

Securing her shopping bag with my back to Agent Telford, I aimed my phone into the interior to photograph the items she'd purchased. Flipping through the book, I saw a handwritten sentiment next to a love poem, *This is me and you, babe, from Axe.* I nearly dropped the necklace box when I opened it and saw forty or more loose diamonds.

"Well, well," my mother murmured. "Those stones look to be 3 carats, well-cut, eye-clean, and in the G, H, I color range."

"Obtained through back channels?" I whispered.

"Overseas, based on the box," she said. "Be aware, gems of this quality will be marked with micro tags. I picture someone hiding them in a safe spot while they're lining up a shady jeweler."

"What's behind your appointed errands?" I asked.

"Apparently, my contact is seeking to regain the upper hand," my mother said, smiling as she reflected on her conversation with Reginald.

"Using the Beaufort scale for wind levels, he likened his intentions to a 19-24 miles per hour fresh breeze, just enough of a gust to create whitecaps on the sea. I must say, he was quite charming."

Given Reginald's speed in launching a targeted plan to get answers, I found it unlikely that anyone with an interest in the confiscated diamonds would describe him as charming in the days ahead.

"Notice I'm being patient," Ted said with a look that signaled the opposite. "Have we cleared up the history element?"

"First, it's confusing that you prioritized tracking us down," I said. "Maybe there's a concern that *you're* not sharing?"

"I'm concerned that you're stalling," Ted said. "But I prioritized catching up with you because Katrina reached out this morning and gave you all due credit for her impulse to step forward. Her account has given me leverage in challenging the view that Chip's death was a self-inflicted overdose. I'm treating it as a murder case."

"Well," I said, "In exchange for letting my mother off the hook, I can deliver evidence that will knock your socks off."

"Luckily, the store sells socks," Harve pointed out.

With Ted's guarded agreement on the terms, I explained my theory of Sally's death, with some of the narration that I'd imagined had led her to the upper deck. While describing the videos I'd found on Chip's laptop, I pointed out that it might be possible to identify the model of the device in Sally's hand. Had she bought it herself, or was it a gift? Next, I pulled out the sandwich bag with the vacuum bag finds, and pointed to the USB drive as an item that Moritz and Raja might be seeking.

"It's not often that I get goosebumps," Ted said. "But I did just now, hearing your theoretical take on Sally's last moments."

"Alison," my mother said. "How much is the FBI paying you?"

"We'll talk about it later," I said.

"Salary?" she prompted. "Overtime? Benefits?"

"*Mom.*"

With closed eyes, she murmured, "Breathe in, breathe out, and look to the horizon. A new normal is ours to build …"

To my surprise, Nicole had been watching from Ted's car while the interactions took place. Using the front hood as a work surface, she and

Ted labeled an evidence bag for Chip's laptop, and catalogued each of the items I'd found in the vacuum, including the opal earring and the torn-up sheet that looked like a concerted effort to practice writing Reginald's signature. With a grudging look of wonder, Nicole gave me a thumbs-up before joining Harve in the rented limo.

"I'm sure you understand a full statement is necessary," Agent Telford said, pointing to a dark sedan pulling up to the curb. "Mrs. Littlefield will meet with my team while Sonny and I address a related matter. By all means, Evelyn, call your attorney on the way."

"It will take more than one call," my mother said.

"Given the underlying matter," Ted said. "The details of your visit should be restricted to trusted, high-level contacts."

"Neckles will insist on being involved," my mother said, already on the phone as she accepted an agent's hand into the sedan.

Frowning, Ted said, "She heard me, right?"

"She heard you," I agreed. "When setting ground rules for my mother, be ready for her to take your exact words to the wall."

"Meaning?" Ted asked.

"You'll find out when your phone starts ringing," I said. "Unless your errand involves me, I have my own agenda to carry out."

Smiling, Ted opened his car door. "You're in luck."

* * *

Relegated to the back seat of Agent Telford's vehicle, I found it easy to keep track of the dark sedan that was taking my mother to a secure location for a debriefing. Through traffic and along major roads, Ted occasionally rubbed his brow as he answered calls from the Neckles group. During a break in the traffic, he gave me an exasperated look in the rearview mirror. I shrugged in response: "Welcome to my life."

A mile later, the sedan carrying my mother slipped into the garage of an office building, and Ted swung into the lot of the local hospital. Once we were parked, he climbed out with his briefcase in hand and revealed that Reginald White had arranged for us to meet.

"Naturally," Ted said. "We're surprised by your mother's trust in him. Did she mention meeting Reginald at any point?"

"Of course not, she would have told me," I said.

With an air of skepticism, Ted retrieved a tablet from his briefcase to show me a photo of my mother standing arm in arm with Reginald, along with respected members of the hospital staff.

"When was this supposedly taken?" I asked.

"Shortly before dawn," Ted said. "Per Reginald's request, Evelyn went straight to the hospital and met with him in his room."

"This isn't real," I said. "It's a fake."

"My team had fun asking if it might be 'doctored'," Ted said, smiling. "There are doctors in the shot, but it's not doctored."

"My mother might be experiencing a midlife crisis," I said. "This past year has brought chaos to both of our lives."

"If so, it's hidden behind an extremely strong front," Ted said, indicating the catering van pulling up next door. "Evelyn's Neckles group has secured authorization to attend her debriefing via a video link, and they've taken the liberty of ordering lunch for the occasion. My team is in for a rough ride, but they'll be well fed."

"Then that's the meeting I want to attend," I said.

"Reginald's doctors think a visit from you would speed his recovery," Ted said. "For all we know, enlisting your mother's help might have been a drug-induced moment. If he's muddled or forgetful, we'll keep it short so he's at least able to thank you for your help."

"In that case, it makes sense," I said.

For once, I felt immune to the panic that stepping into a hospital often triggered. As we emerged from the elevator and walked past patient rooms, a doctor met us outside Reginald's door.

"Having played a role in saving his life, you're on the approved visitor list, Miss Littlefield," the doctor said. "But there are lingering effects from the poisoning. Let's make sure he's not overtaxed."

"We understand," Ted said. "Ready?"

When I nodded, Ted swung the door open.

My first surprise was seeing Reginald dressed in dark slacks and a blue shirt, rather than a hospital gown. With his reading glasses on and a pen ready to take notes as he studied a folder of documents, he sat at a round table near the window, smiling and rising to his feet as we entered. He looked a world apart from the confused man Antoine and I had brought home. Reginald's gray eyes sparkled with vitality as he warmly shook my hand, and he smelled of a woodsy cologne that banished the hospital scents. About five-foot-ten, with graying hair at his temples, he had the charisma and good looks I'd seen in the videos of his card games. Now that he was clear-eyed, I saw his resemblance to his son.

"My dear, how wonderful to see you with the cobwebs cleared away," Reginald said, kissing my hand, and then holding out a chair for me to sit beside him. "Agent Telford, thank you for coming."

"It seems I owe you an apology," Ted said, assessing Reginald carefully as they shook hands. "For not suspecting the hidden circumstance behind your behavior last time we met."

"Hopefully, I didn't land a punch?" Reginald said.

"How much do you remember?" Ted asked.

"Enough to be pleased that you brought your briefcase, with all its enlightening exhibits," Reginald said. "But first things first. I would be grateful if Sonny can walk me through what happened. My memory is adrift with imagined elements like coconut wasps."

While Reginald listened attentively, I summarized the path that led to the capture of the ex-cons and explained the wasp reference. For clarity, I included direct quotes, such as Reginald saying to one of the ex-cons, "You're a lawless ingrate. The worst of the worst." In response to Reginald motioning me to continue, I focused on his forearms above his shirt cuffs. Specifically, he wasn't wearing a hospital ID wristband, which reinforced my initial impression that he'd emerged from illness, but had ironed out an extended stay beyond the norm. As my gaze lifted to his face, Reginald offered a faint smile, as if he'd hoped to confirm my ability to pick up on subtle clues that, for example, Ted hadn't noticed.

"Thank you, Sonny, let's pause there," Reginald said. "It's important to put the culprits into context. We never served time together, so they weren't friends, or even friends of friends."

"Their attorney is suggesting otherwise," Ted said. "To gain leverage, can you provide specifics on when the drugging began?"

"I've been able to recall signs of illness as far back as ten months ago," Reginald said. "Possibly earlier. Headaches, confusion, and lassitude that I chalked up to a lack of sleep. Stomach ailments that I blamed on over-the-counter painkillers. As for a motive that might warrant putting me out to pasture, one matter stands out as contentious."

"The argument over the future of the *Kukuna Mahina?*" I asked, and then, as Reginald's eyebrows encouraged me to continue, I added, "I heard that some people are seeking to scrap the vessel for a modest short-term gain, but you want to see if the profit margin improves?"

"Ted, why are you the one with the badge?" Reginald asked.

"Sonny is here thanks to my belief in her abilities," Ted said. "Which shareholders have complained the loudest?"

"I'm sure you understand my hesitation to land anyone in the crosshairs of the legal system," Reginald said. "At this juncture, the fastest way forward is for Sonny to see the presentation you prepared for my edification. Stand up and growl a little during the show-and-tell, just like you did with me. I'll remember it forever."

"Today's visit is limited in scope," Ted said. "Without any context, I don't see any reason to broaden the discussion."

"That's sent me in a new direction," Reginald said, turning to me with a look of interest. "I'm told that you own a horse."

"A Belgian draft horse," I said.

"I envy that knowledge and experience," Reginald said wistfully. "I've been fascinated to read Isabella Bird's descriptions of the different horses she rode during her travels across Hawaii. Most were surefooted and courageous, but Kahélé was obstinate and contrary, putting his head down and twirling in circles instead of pressing forward."

"All right, Mr. White," Ted said tiredly.

"Gentlemen," I said. "Either shake hands and agree to work with each other, or I'm out the door. You have five seconds."

"Well done, Sonny," Reginald said. "To bring you up to speed and address my memory issues at the same time, a reenactment might be useful. For the surest effect, I'll play my opponent, Agent Telford, to the best of my recollection. Are you willing to play my role?"

"Yes, go ahead," I said.

With a look of irritation and crossed arms, Agent Telford watched as Reginald cleared his throat and opened the folder he'd apparently planned to use all along. Unsmiling and stern, he signaled for me to sit back so he could place items on the stretch of table in front of me.

"For people associated with the Ellika Arts Academy, the *Kukuna Mahina*, and assorted other areas in my sphere of interests," Reginald said, "the risk of a sudden death from a freak accident or an overdose is statistically higher than the national average."

"By how much?" I asked.

With the folder open, Reginald delivered a crisp summary in time with slapping photos of male and female victims in front of me. "Dead. Dead. Dead. Dead. Dead. Dead. Dead. Dead. Dead. Dead. These last two are clinging to life on ventilators. Near death and too thready for hope. Near death and in danger of having the plug pulled."

A silence elapsed as I stared at the pile.

"Agent Telford?" Reginald prompted.

"It's a different experience seeing it from the outside," Ted admitted. "Police tactics can seem insensitive. It's possible… highly likely… it's *clear* that my approach was harsh and unwarranted."

"I appreciate that rare acknowledgment," Reginald said. "Thanks to Jasmine, Sonny, and Antoine, I woke up feeling like myself. It's tempting to blame the captured culprits and move on, but I can't afford to be naïve. Prison changed me from an easygoing kid into a penny-pinching grouch, but it's not possible to keep that mindset in Hawaii. Amid the hiking and relaxing, I met more than one captivating woman."

"What about her?" Ted asked, sliding Sally's photo toward Reginald. "Young and pretty. A waitress on the vessel."

"I draw a firm line if a woman looks wounded and gullible," Reginald said. "Her face is familiar, but once I started feeling off-kilter, I didn't want make my illness worse by sailing in rough seas."

"If you recall, you told me that you're a catch," I said. "According to Katrina, your family tree is more of a forest."

"You've spoken to Katrina?" Reginald asked.

I paused. "Yes, umm …"

"I won't pressure you into spilling her private business," Reginald said. "But it would be good to know what kind of fallout I'm facing. My worst fear is that she was targeted by the ex-cons."

"Katrina has reported certain concerns," Ted said. "Now that your illness is in perspective, I imagine she'll reach out."

"No, she needs to keep her distance until I understand the threat level," Reginald said, lining up a few victim photos. "Katrina's parents died from an overdose. I believed it of him, but not of my daughter. This teenage boy who died on Maui was the son of a woman I dated, but our DNA has yet to be compared. Chip was looking into it."

"Chip looked into his death?" Ted prompted.

"Chip's focus had to do with building our family," Reginald explained. "A thriving, connected pod, similar to what he saw in whales. I adored my son's boundless exuberance, but when my mind was in gear, I locked down my estate to protect my heirs from fortune hunters, and frankly, from each other. Upon my death, they get what they get. Period."

"Including Katrina?" Ted asked.

"It's set in stone," Reginald said. "The rest of my estate is devoted to the greater good. A modest scholarship fund for Ellika Arts. Again, locked down. To be honest, I left some of the choices to my attorney, but he's among the deceased in Ted's folder. I'm getting muddled," Reginald added, rubbing his brow with a look of fatigue. "I was drugged over a span of months. If an unknown aggressor is in league with the arrested men, it was useful for them to tank me, but keep me alive."

"To get away with hiding diamonds, for instance," I said.

"I can't abide corner cutting," Reginald agreed. "Don't bother asking for specifics on the apparent white-collar crimes. It's like trying to make sense of a mirage. You're right to see the cruise ship's fate as a tipping point. It's not a slot machine. I made that clear when I invited people to invest within their comfort levels. If someone I've known for years has turned to the dark side, I will be devastated."

"We'll need a full list of names," Ted said.

"I won't offer cheat sheets and shortcuts that might reinforce narrow police thinking," Reginald said. "I've devised a better approach."

As Reginald opened his hand to reveal a fishing hook designed to look like a delicate caddisfly, I took it from his palm and examined the feathers, smiling to see art similar to the flies my father had made.

Opening his other hand, Reginald held a unicorn key fob that stirred restlessness in Ted, and then a heated glare.

"An ordinary item has special meaning if it belonged to someone who passed away," Reginald said. "Sonny's gaze is filled with wonder. Ted's scowl shows that a victim's death remains unsolved."

"The items from the store belonged to the victims," I said. "You're planning to test people to see how they react."

"Exactly," Reginald said.

"You're coming out of illness," Ted said. "The arc you're talking about would require a top field agent, trained to pivot on the fly."

"I've got a family member in mind," Reginald said.

"Your inner circle can't be trusted," Ted said tiredly. "It's time to explain why you dragged Mrs. Littlefield into action. The way things stand, people are starting to imagine all kinds of—"

As I leaned toward him and listened closely, eager to find a solution, Agent Telford paused for a moment, and then he looked at me the way my dog, Luke, would come to attention if someone was poised to toss his lobster toy across the yard on a long throw.

"There *is* somebody that we can trust?" I asked.

"This is the magical element right here," Reginald said, patting my hand with a paternal air. "Wide-eyed fluff that makes you want to snuggle close and bare your soul, then you say the wrong thing, and suddenly, knives start coming out of nowhere."

"You might have forewarned me of your intentions," Ted said.

"Cue the complaints of limited resources," Reginald said, struggling to stand. "Is it me, or is the room starting to spin?"

"Mr. White … *hey,*" Ted said, diving out of his chair to catch Reginald as he collapsed to the floor. "Get some help."

Already on my way to the door, I saw the doctor stepping from a room, and reported Reginald's fainting episode.

"In our experience, Mr. White's sudden spells end with the introduction of special privileges," the doctor said dryly. "But I am alerting the nursing staff, and here they are, rushing to his aid."

"Until that point," I said. "We had a good visit."

"Look who's here," the doctor said, smiling as my mother approached. "Mrs. Littlefield, count me among your fans here in the hospital. I play golf with your 'associate' from time to time."

"If you're seeking a donation, reach out to my attorney," my mother said, waving him off. "Alison, we're finished. It's time to go."

"It's the opposite of finished," I said.

"Darling, you know how I wilt in the tropics," my mother said. "The Neckles group is beseeching me to head home for a debriefing and a quiet cocktail party, but I was hoping to at least have coffee before I'm delivered to my flight."

"I'm sorry, it'll have to wait," I insisted.

"Very well," she said. "I'll make some calls."

Down the corridor, Ted was conducting an animated phone conversation. Once he caught sight of me, he put the call on hold.

"I assume Reginald is fine?" I asked.

"He wanted a private word," Ted said, smiling and shaking his head. "I'm spreading the news that my never-say-never citizen agent has risen to the top of the pyramid of Reginald's secret heirs."

"Best of luck with whoever it is," I said. "My mother has deigned to have coffee with me. Are we free to leave?"

"I'll admit, this is an iffy start," Reginald said, having been wheeled to his room's doorway. "Give Sonny a minute. She'll get there."

24

"Sonny," Ted said. "Between your mother's involvement, and the rumors Reginald is spreading among the hospital staff, the story that you're his secret heir is not a proposal anymore. It's a reality."

"As Antoine would say, au contraire," I said.

In a conference room where we could speak privately, Ted paced away and stretched his neck like a boxer between rounds, then he came back to petition me with what he hoped was a winning gaze.

"You went after the thugs who poisoned Reginald," Ted said. "People are seeing it as seeking revenge on his behalf. You stepped up for Carol Henderson at the marina, and Katrina as well. With a little spin, a little magic, we could play the idea to the hilt."

"I'm intrigued by the possibilities," I admitted. "But given that rumors are already flying around, we need to alert Antoine so he doesn't get blindsided. It's important that he stay focused on his son."

"Sonny, you're putting a lot of faith in a guy that you barely know," Ted said. "You had some brief encounters with Antoine in November, with a handful of days here in Hawaii. What if he doesn't react the way you expect? He's the opposite of supportive?"

"That's certainly how you're coming across," I said. "If this is how you plan to address my priorities, you can count me out."

Eyeing me as if I was an escaped zebra that he needed to contain, Agent Telford realized his options were reduced to one.

"Bureaucracy demands that I do the initial outreach," Ted said. "I'll use speaker mode, so you're assured that I'm handling it with your wishes in mind. I agree that family should come first."

"Thank you," I said.

Pacing away a few steps, Ted adopted an upbeat tone.

"Antoine, I'm flattered," he said. "You picked up right away."

"You caught me at a convenient time," Antoine said. "And I've been hoping to hear how the interrogations are going."

"The kid from the luau hasn't budged," Ted said. "He claims his only involvement was the dog-catching exercise."

"If it's true, the guy from the earlier events is still at large," Antoine said. "Has the extended-cab truck been found?"

"No, it's probably under a tarp in somebody's yard, but we're pressing forward on all cylinders," Ted said. "I assume you would tell me if any of the players put in a bid for your Learjet."

"No, it was a five-minute wonder," Antoine said. "We've reached the other reason I picked up fast. Instead of trusting that I would alert you to any follow-up trouble, you put a tail in place."

"Our intention was to ensure your safety," Ted said. "You sent the tail packing, so let's not turn it into a cross-agency battle."

"You're aware that I'm taking personal time off," Antoine said. "That's why I'm furious. Your clumsy agent scared my son."

As I stepped forward, ablaze with anger, Ted sharply signaled that he was handling the complexities to the best of his ability.

"The fact that you're visiting family is the reason I took extra precautions," Ted said. "I'm sorry for any fallout. Rest assured, I buried the private stuff, like your son's stepfather bailing and heading home. The signs that you and Zach's mother are rekindling the flame."

"Agent Telford—"

"Antoine, I'm up to my eyeballs in a complex case, so pardon me for pressing onward," Ted said. "To avoid any further mix-ups and confusion, let's consider this call an official parting of ways. Best of luck with your personal endeavors. A happy ending is long overdue."

As he ended the call, Ted's wince told me I was better off knowing the truth. Gaping, with a range of protests and arguments whirling in and out of focus, I wanted to insist that his agent got it wrong, but the gear that was supposed to complete the work was a crushed can.

"Did that really just happen?" I managed.

"Zachary's mother is a career cop, a few years older," Ted said softly. "The roadblock of Antoine's lifelong enemy is suddenly gone. I have zero doubt that his feelings for you are strong, Sonny, just like Dan's feelings are strong. Love is often a tangled web."

"Notice I'm not arguing," I said.

"You've formed an unhealthy attraction to rescuers who need rescuing themselves. If that's him calling," Ted added as my phone rang, "bear in mind that he feels beholden to you for helping him end the threat that kept him in chains for years. He's a good guy, fair and honest, so my guess is he's seeing the need to share the news."

I stared at Antoine's name on my phone screen.

"It's not fair to tell him how I feel," I managed. "I don't want to be a roadblock or a charity case. What do I say?"

"Tell him your mother is visiting," Ted said. "Promise to call back later. That way, you're assured that he'll stay focused on his son, and you can gain some perspective before you respond."

"You've got it all figured out," I said.

"Yeah, I do," Ted said. "Answer the call."

"Umm, hi," I said, unable to keep my voice steady.

"Have you been in touch with Agent Telford?" Antoine asked.

"That's an odd opener," I said. "Did an emergency come up?"

"No, I'm calling on a personal note," Antoine said. "You know I'm not a fan of sharing feelings over the phone, but we've spent some days apart, and it's important to be honest. We skipped this part. Being clear about the future and what we need."

"Please don't," I whispered.

"Please don't what, Sonny?" he asked.

"My mother is visiting."

Antoine paused. "That's a surprise."

"Mary is from a world where—" I faltered, then pressed on, "She's from a world where mothers are comforting, so she thought it would be a good idea. There's a new venture called Neckles," I added. "The Newton Clues and Evidence Society. Be aware, they're delving into the various cases, so you might want to block unknown callers."

"Sonny, you sound really shaken," Antoine said.

"It's from—awareness of how I've botched my healing journey," I said. "So, I'm wrapping things up. I'm launching a new plan."

"When and where?" Antoine asked.

"I'm shooting for tomorrow," I said, reading a scribbled note Ted was holding up. "Late at night? Yes, late at night because I've got stuff to do during the day. Snorkeling, and … futzing around."

"Call me back when you have a free minute," Antoine said.

"That's a tall order," I said. "I'm sorry to be in a rush."

"I get it," Antoine said. "We'll catch up later."

Once I hung up, Agent Telford blew out a breath.

"It's not a surprise that your distress came across," Ted said. "In his shoes, I would call your friends to rule out hidden threats. In the meantime, I want to convey a possible plan to consider. Tomorrow night, you would check in for a flight, head down the ramp, and exchange outerwear with an agent who can pass for you. Your phone, your cameras, the whole works would depart from the Big Island."

I hesitated. "*Without* me?"

"Staging a fake departure is a way to gauge reactions among the local players," Ted said. "Especially Barry, a commercial pilot who has contacts at airports. To be clear, I'm not asking you to actively portray Reginald's secret heir. It's a misdirection element you can use or discard as you go along. Given the fast build-up to this moment, you've already developed an instinctive awareness as a starting framework. I've heard how you coped in November, using hypnosis to jog your memory."

"It didn't work," I said. "I didn't peg my father's murderer."

"Maybe it'll be sharper this time," Ted said. "You'll narrow the field until we've built a solid case with concrete evidence."

I looked down as my phone rang in my hand.

"Answer the call," Ted said.

Seeing that it was Sue Black, I tried to keep an upbeat tone.

"This is a surprise," I managed. "Hopefully, you're not about to say my farm has been engulfed by fifty feet of snow."

"Antoine reached out," Sue said. "It's unclear why, but he's concerned about your welfare. Is it true that your mother is visiting?"

"Yeah, umm …"

As Ted led me forward and opened the door, my mother's voice in the corridor went from a muffled drone to audible complaints about the tropical heat, the faulty air conditioning system that wasn't removing humidity properly, and the fact that she'd worn the wrong shoes for standing around while her daughter took her sweet time. Further, she had a plane to catch. Could anyone fast-track getting a cab?

"Oh my God," Sue said. "Your mother *is* there."

"We did a little shopping," I said. "The usual fun stuff, banking, and skirting past lunch. It's news to me that thrift stores aren't a problem anymore, and she can deliver sharp retorts in Japanese. People, right? There's always a hidden side."

"What's that sound I'm hearing in the background?" Sue asked. "Like someone snapping their fingers."

Focusing on Ted's thumb and middle digit, ready to deliver another prompt, if needed, I finished formulating my explanation.

"Mom has never been a fan of my curiosity," I said. "All of a sudden, now that she's involved with the Newton Clues and Evidence Society, she's on board with me being kidnapped, tased, and held at gunpoint. Her friends are impressed."

"No wonder you're upset," Sue said. "I know it's hard to see, but she's there out of love, despite any underlying motives."

"I'm sorry to be in a rush, but people are out of patience," I said. "I'm getting a slide-to-second-base signal, a death-by-neck-injury signal …"

"Call me back soon, okay?" Sue asked.

"I will," I promised. "Give my love to everyone. Not Antoine. Rather, make sure he stays focused on family. On his son."

As I hung up, Agent Telford looked spent.

"I won't ask for a final answer until you've caught your breath," he said. "But in the meantime, know that I singled you out from the crowd for a reason. First of all, the results speak for themselves. Talk about moving the ball down the field. You can't abide injustice, and you're inflamed to be told to stay in your own lane. In my mind, the solution is simple. Take the lead. Prove yourself beyond any doubt."

I focused on Agent Telford's determined gaze.

"If people are posing theories about my identity, it's important to get up to speed before I return to the house," I said. "I'll need a summary of the bank transactions, the thrift store items, and assistance in fast-tracking the search for clues on Chip's computer."

"Absolutely," Ted said. "In fact—"

"I'm not done," I said. "If the thugs were tasked with carrying out dirty work, their unavailability will enhance my chances of looking useful, so it's imperative that they stay in jail. Also, to spare me another round of strange search results, is it illegal to make copies of the Japanese cash?"

"Maybe I should fetch a pad and pen," Ted said.

I frowned. "You didn't come prepared?"

"I'll use my phone's voice recorder," Ted said.

"It would be helpful to have a better sense of Jasmine's opinion of the players," I said, "Is it okay for me to talk to her?"

"Given Jasmine's local knowledge and skillset," Ted said, "she's already vetted and ready for action. First, we've factored in escorting you and your mother to an upscale restaurant for coffee and hugs."

"You've derailed Jasmine's plan to attend college?" I asked.

"We're arranging for her to get class credits for her contributions to the project," Ted said. "In the fall, she'll hit the ground running."

"That's impressive," I said. "I'm tempted to call it smart."

Ted spread his hands. "Thank you for noticing."

* * *

In a two-story, Hawaii-style strip mall, flanked by swaying palm trees, a short flight of stairs led to an office with window film that let in outside light but blocked anyone from seeing the interior. Electronics were stacked on every shelf, and three FBI agents, including Nicole, looked up from computers as I stepped in with Agent Telford.

"Welcome to the inner sanctum," Ted said with a flourish. "Restricted access. This is an achievement, Sonny. A rare pinnacle of—"

"Whatever," I said. "Where is Jasmine?"

"Hang on, first up is a debriefing to guide you through the items that were collected, with a playbook of actions moving forward," Ted said, pointing to a printed, multi-page document. "As you can see, we've set it up in three stages, each with a title that reflects the goal. This is how we roll in the bureau. Careful, strategic steps."

"I see the thrift store items on the table," I said.

"Reginald raised some valid points," Ted said. "Any details he provides could skew our thinking, so we're building an understanding of each item from ground zero. I'll walk you through what we've unearthed thus far. Once you're out and about, you'll contrive an excuse to hold items in front of people to see how they react."

"That'll make for a lot of awkward moments," Nicole said.

"No worries," I said. "I can swing it."

As Ted led me around the table, I confirmed that the ripped-up note, showing "Reginald White" written ten times with unique flourishes, was an attempt to perfect his signature. Beside the reconstructed practice sheet was a document with the same flourishes evident throughout confirming that Reginald was the *Kukuna Mahina's* main shareholder, with co-owners scattered across the Big Island. To avoid oversteering me, Ted didn't disclose his best guess about who might have taken pains to mimic Reginald's handwriting. Perhaps Katrina had needed to sign paperwork on Reginald's behalf in recent months. In case anyone mentioned the PIN code linked to a related account, I committed it to memory.

Next, I studied the items from the thrift store. The garnet ring and a pair of hoop earrings had belonged to a man who'd lived in San Francisco, with no clear local ties. As I examined the framed photograph of six men holding a bowling trophy, Ted hinted that he knew the context, but wanted me to research it independently. Beside the necklace box, a small evidence bag contained the fifty high-end diamonds sparkling with icy light. I would be given five fake diamonds to show around.

"Hang on," I said. "Whoever was hiding the diamonds will panic. It's not right to endanger the thrift store owner."

"She closes the shop regularly," Ted said. "One of our agents is helping her pack for an exciting trip to visit her grandchildren. As with your departure tomorrow, it will be helpful to see if anyone calls the owner non-stop, demanding to know when she'll be back."

I picked up the book of poems, flipped to the note, *This is me and you, babe, from Axe*, and asked if the recipient was known.

"For all we know," Ted said, "Axe had ten copies in the wings to hand to attractive women. See what you can find out."

Next, I picked up and studied the silver watch. Seeing tiny diamonds and other hallmarks of a luxury item, I examined the inscription on the back: *You're an ace, kiddo. With love, from your old man.*

"Reginald bought it for Chip a few years ago," Ted explained. "As you can see, it's a business-style watch, classy and high-end. Mrs. Henderson chided Reginald for not grasping that Chip yearned to own a diving watch built to withstand deep water, so this silver model was replaced with the one Chip was wearing the day he died."

"Did Chip ever wear this silver watch?" I asked.

"Apparently, he wore it as a show of appreciation," Ted said. "To end the guilt element, Reginald brought it to the store."

For a moment, I wrestled with the knowledge that I was holding a personal item once owned by the whale rescuer I'd briefly met on Maui. Now, the watch was another form of ghost gear.

"Do you need a break?" Ted said softly.

"No, let's push on," I said, returning the watch to the table.

A stack of Japanese yen sat next to an envelope with more numbers that I strived to memorize. The deed for the rental house listed Reginald as a former co-owner brought in to swing the steep price, and I recognized the loan agreement for "capital improvements" for the dance studio. Next, Chip's laptop displayed security footage of Jason and Katrina arguing on the cruise ship, followed by a clip showing a blur of activity that turned out to be Sally kissing Jason in the wake of drugging him.

"If you look closely," Ted said, "Jason was glassy-eyed and he pushed her away. In the background, Moritz is smiling. The clip was tucked away on Chip's computer, so it's important to question Jason because if our team is cleared to conduct a sting on the *Kukuna Mahina*, he would be there as a dance show participant, and hopefully as an ally."

"I understand," I said. "I'll prioritize it."

Soon, I was standing in front of the playbook again.

"As you can see, we've created a targeted approach in a short matter of hours," Ted said. "Impressive, isn't it?"

With a pointed look, I secured a pen from the tabletop, clicked the release button, and with firm cross-outs, I simplified the FBI's strategic playbook from "*Sonny Continues Playing Dumb; Sonny Sparks Panic and Chaos; and Sonny Confronts Culprits with Targeted Threats*" to read, "*Test Phase; Listening Phase; Action Phase.*"

"Crisp and succinct," Ted said. "Duly noted."

"What's on the USB stick?" I asked.

"Mostly, bank account numbers," Ted said, handing me an identical device. "This replicates the information enough to look the same, but with coding that will ensnare anyone who tries to make use of the files. We're not sure if it's an account of money laundering, or if it's evidence that was gathered to report the illegal activity."

"In other words," one of the agents said, "Don't just hand the USB stick to whoever takes interest. Test people to gauge what they know."

"Ultimately, you want the stick to be handed along?" I asked.

"Yes, to whoever barks the loudest," the agent said.

I nodded. "Let's get to it."

"You'll need to not blink in the face of pressure tactics," the agent said. "If you blurt knowledge of the items that we've gathered—"

"That my *mother* gathered," I said.

"We should rehearse some scenarios," the agent persisted.

"Actually," Nicole said. "If you were paying attention, Sonny memorized the account numbers and has her own plan in mind. Our approach will mess her up. If she's ready, we're ready."

Ted studied me. "If she's right, we can skip further discussion. I didn't want you to feel swamped and unsupported."

"Swamped is my go-to lane," I said. "But it looks like I won't feel unsupported. Do I hear a sewing machine next door?"

Ted smiled. "Indeed, you do."

"I'll show you the way," Nicole said, guiding me into the hallway and then signaling for me to pause. "Thanks to some bad boy moves that were silenced with NDAs, Reginald is gearing up to clip Axe hard. Basically, the ride is over. At times, I feel for Axe. He was a genius at his craft back in the day. If there's anyone who might be coaxed into disclosing secrets, it's Axe's son, Sam, but snitching on his father would ruin his life."

"How do you do this for a living?" I asked.

"Same as you," Nicole said. "One sad moment at a time."

Despite the need for haste, Nicole arched an eyebrow as if awaiting thanks for her support, and then, with a wry dimple, she held up a well-conditioned bullwhip like the one I owned in Maine.

"This is a surprise," I said.

"I heard how you used a bullwhip to hold off a suspect," Nicole said. "A sidearm isn't possible, but this is a hobby item."

"It's good for releasing stress," I admitted.

"Show me how to use it sometime?" Nicole said.

I cracked a smile. "When I'm finished playing dumb."

In the doorway of her studio, Jasmine was a blur of black, chin-length hair with pink highlights as she engulfed me in a hug.

"Thank you for pitching in, Sonny," she said, adding an extra squeeze before releasing me. "Thank you for caring."

"I'd prefer helping from a safe distance, but that's apparently not in the cards," I said. "You're not back to bailing on college?"

"Far from it," Jasmine said. "I'm aiming for a degree in criminal justice, so I'll start in the fall with class credits. Like you, I don't need lessons on how to be an artist. That part of me is hardwired." With a look of worry, Jasmine added, "Regarding the news about Antoine—"

"Forgive me for sounding sharp," I said. "But I'm wrestling with the fact that I brought it on myself. Look at my hands. They're shaking at the mention of his name. If I am to be effective—"

"I get it, Sonny," Jasmine said. "I'm banking on Ted's agent getting it wrong, but it's still raw. We'll leave it for now."

Snagging my arm, Jasmine gave me a quick tour of the bright room of sewing machines, tables for laying out fabric, and shelves stocked with an array of shimmering fabric in a rainbow of colors.

"I'm sure you've heard that Katrina and I are back in gear," Jasmine said, unzipping a garment bag to reveal a shimmering dance costume made of sequins, fluff, and little else. "It took a while to convince her that Jason's kiss was platonic. You're not tempted, I assume."

"I'm tempted to say no to wearing this," I said, holding up the flimsy micro dress. "I thought you were designing upscale business attire with special pockets for hidden listening devices."

"Dance costumes will take more time to create," Jasmine explained. "Ted is asking for a layer of ballistic fabric."

"Jasmine, I'm hoping to resolve the case without a sting," I said. "To wrap it up fast, I need your best guess on who hired the thugs. Don't tell Ted that talking to you is the extent of my plan."

Jasmine engulfed me in another hug, expressing effusive thanks for my faith in her opinion, intelligence, and abilities.

"*Shh*," I cautioned. "We're in stealth mode."

"On more than one occasion," Jasmine said, "Barry, Axe, and Chill got tipsy and pitched sugar daddy arrangements with Katrina. Testing the waters through joking. Bob, also known as Shredder, casts piercing gazes at Katrina from time to time, as if he's sizing her up for a coffin."

"That's how I felt about his vibe," I said.

"Petrel gives the band free rein in the studio," Jasmine continued. "I've wondered if he uses the footage for leverage. Thankfully, Katrina had the sense never to tell Jason about a time when Barry stopped in unexpectedly when she was stepping out of the shower at the rental house. Barry's excuse about needing to fetch paperwork never sat well with her, especially after the awful incident on the *Kukuna Mahina*."

"This is the opposite of narrowing the field," I said.

"Ted is hoping our efforts will spark fast results, but I think that's a stretch," Jasmine said. "The culprit, if there is just one, knows how to pull the strings from the shadows. They're smart and wary."

"I agree," I said. "I hope you're balancing your win against a hard dose of reality. You could easily have become a casualty."

"Katrina is the one to worry about," Jasmine said. "She's cool and cagey when I press her for details. It's all but a given that she's planning a secret sting of her own. That means we've got two days to get a plan in place, with certainty around who we're trying to catch."

"Gosh, is that all?" I asked.

"Stop stalling and put on the dress," Jasmine said. "It's a means of gauging your dimensions for every kind of clothing."

"Given that my neck and my femoral arteries will be exposed, I think you can skip the ballistic layer," I said dryly.

"Come on," Jasmine prompted. "Hop in."

With Agent Telford and his team in the next room, I locked the door and stripped off my clothes down to my bikini undies.

"Uh-oh, full stop," Jasmine said. "The dress is along the lines of a bathing suit, especially down below. If you end up in some dance routines, a *lot* of real estate will be exposed during splits, flips, lifts, and any related swirling and twirling of your bare legs."

"I get it," I said. "So?"

As Jasmine glanced down a few times, I grasped what she meant.

"I haven't shaved for a couple of days," I said.

Patiently, Jasmine said, "Wearing a costume comes with the burden of adhering to societal norms. It's a salon-level situation."

"Along with possibly getting axed by Shredder and Axe, I'll need a Brazilian wax?" I asked. "Let the good times begin."

Ted knocked on the door. "Is everything okay in there?"

"There's a high-end salon down the road," Jasmine called out. "Book an emergency appointment for a client who needs southern border management, and don't ask a bunch of dumb questions."

"Yeah, go ahead and take charge," Ted muttered.

Jasmine beamed. "I'll be his boss one day."

25

If my hunch about Moritz and Raja was right—that they'd been on a multi-month quest to retrieve the silver USB stick—it made sense to question them about it last of all. To spare me a trip to the house, Jasmine gave me a new dance leotard and a sheer blouse she'd made using fabric with eyes peering through winter branches. In the studio's parking lot, I waited for the ballroom basics class to finish and head to their cars, then I stepped in with the bag of thrift store finds, my heart madly racing while I swapped my sneakers for my dance shoes. I'd fallen into a cocky attitude when discussing my loose plan. Now, I had to make it work.

"There you are," Petrel said, crossing toward me in dark trousers and matching shirt. "While you're waiting for Jason, let's take each other for a spin. It's important to practice with different partners."

"Maybe another time," I said. "I'm having a slow day."

"It's no wonder, the way you've been working all hours," Petrel said. "Hopefully, your mother will encourage you to rest."

"No, her visit had to do with business affairs that needed sorting out," I said, offering a breezy account of my mother's hectic lifestyle as I reached into my bag. "During my visit with Reginald, he asked me to bring this envelope to you, and I've been trying to find the owner of a USB stick that I found the other day. It's not yours, by any chance?"

"It's not the kind I've ever used," Petrel said. "You're a darling for reminding Reginald about the loan agreement."

"Actually, he didn't need reminding," I said. "A show of support might be a good idea, if you're one of his close friends."

"I will make a point to stop by once he's home," Petrel said. "If you're sore and strained, make sure to do a proper stretch."

"I will," I assured him.

Facing my reflection in the mirror along the front wall, I started with a star pose, planting my feet wide and stretching my arms to enjoy the full-body benefit. As I leaned to the left to loosen my ribcage, I heard Petrel opening the envelope in the hallway as he headed toward his office, and then his footsteps signaled his quick return.

"Sonny," Petrel said. "Did Reginald mention specifics?"

"Not about the envelope," I said. "Is anything wrong?"

"No, it's—I need to make some calls."

Wilting at the thought of causing anxiety in a man who might be innocent, I told myself to stay strong through the tests.

"What's up with him?" Jason asked, crossing the dance floor in a loose shirt and dark trousers that showed off his toned physique, then he quickly added, "Let me start with an apology. You've become a friend, Sonny. I'm sorry for crossing the line during our last session."

"Unfortunately," I whispered. "Chip's photo library includes a video of you kissing Sally, the waitress who died."

"Crap, that means Moritz was telling the truth," Jason said, rubbing his brow with a confused look. "I thought he was lying to hide the fact that someone spiked my drink while he was behind the bar. It felt like a setup, especially with the claims that the cameras weren't working. If I'd been awake and alert, I might have realized that Sally was acting out of character and having a tough time. How did Chip find the footage?"

"I wish I knew," I said. "There's confusion about why you were on the vessel that night. Explain why you were there."

"After Katrina started her new job, she stopped putting guys like Axe in their place," Jason said. "It crossed my mind that she was cheating, so I filled a slot in the dance show to keep an eye out. I've come to understand that Katrina was striving to take her job seriously. Even with assholes and skirt-chasers, it's necessary to be professional and polite."

"You truly get it now?" I asked.

"I do, Sonny," Jason said. "I haven't touched alcohol since that cruise. If the latest rumor is true, that someone drugged Reginald to sideline him for selfish and awful reasons, I know how he feels."

Under my hard, scrutinizing gaze, Jason looked forlorn but braced to weather a scolding for his lapse of judgement. With Ted's reassurance that Jason's patterns had been examined and that he was considered a potential ally in my work, I took yet another leap of faith.

Scarcely moving my lips, I whispered, "You're right that Reginald was poisoned. I'm here to carry out his hush-hush plan."

"You can trust me," Jason covertly whispered.

"I've brought a bag that contains mementos, keepsakes, Japanese yen, and so on," I whispered. "Reginald knows the backstory behind every item, but I'm mostly in the dark to make sure I nail looking clueless. The idea is to test people, and … just go with it, all right?"

"Take the lead," Jason whispered. "I'll follow."

With a nod, I said loudly, "As I mentioned, Reginald has come up with a fun way to tackle his memory loss. Bring the card table to the center of the floor where the light is the brightest."

More importantly, I wanted to operate under the camera to attract Petrel's curiosity and allow Ted's team to observe reactions.

"I will be glad to assist you," Jason said, taking care not to mar the dance floor as he positioned the table. "I am intrigued."

For the benefit of the camera, I gave a breathless account of my mother dragging me across town to carry out errands for Reginald, whom she'd met through puzzling, yet-to-be-explained circumstances in the distant past. As a local with many contacts, perhaps Jason could help me deepen my understanding of the items from the thrift store.

"For instance, who did this belong to?" I asked, pulling the garnet ring from the bag and holding it up. "Is it familiar?"

"I have seen many," Jason said. "In my day."

"And so on and so forth," I said, setting the rest of items around the outer edges of the table. "Earrings, a locket, an expensive watch with an inscription that says, 'You're an ace, kiddo. With love from your old man.' Might it have belonged to Chip Henderson?"

"I do not know," Jason said. "Might it?"

With a wince, he signaled that he was doing his best.

"There's a book of poems with a sweet sentiment written by Axe," I said. "It's sad if a romantic gift ended up at the thrift store. Same with this heart locket with a woman's photo. Reginald can't recall who she is, but feels there is a hidden significance to uncover."

"Sonny," Jason whispered, frowning at the photo of a group of men holding a bowling trophy. "This guy in the middle looks like the IRS agent who flagged some deductions on the dance studio's tax return. I think it was a minor thing, but Petrel had to pay a fine."

Kicking myself for not studying it closer, I rubbed away a smudge on the glass and confirmed that the bowler in the middle was the IRS agent who'd disappeared, plunging his wife and children into confusion and anguish. Through what specific means had the smiling father of two been cut down in the prime of his life? The FBI file hadn't disclosed a cause of death. All I knew for certain was that I'd glimpsed his jawbone.

"This is sparking another thought," Jason whispered of the USB stick. "There's a story about Axe taking a travel drive from Moritz. It had to do with some sort of feud over the family's money."

"*Very* helpful," I whispered, tucking the stick down my bra. "Don't mention it to anyone. My approach needs to be strategic."

"I'm afraid I've stepped in it," Petrel said, heading toward us across the dance floor and arriving flustered. "I was on the phone with friends and began describing what I was seeing down here. It's important for us all to understand Reginald's mindset, so they're coming to help."

"I'm grateful," I said. "Are any of the items familiar?"

"It looks like a yard sale," Petrel said, nearly spilling fake diamonds as he opened the necklace box. "Let's tape the lid."

"Why?" I asked.

"If they get stuck on someone's shoe, they'll damage the floor," Petrel said, crossing to the door. "I hear vehicles arriving."

That quickly, my contained approach veered as Pauline and Gavin stepped in, followed by Axe, Sam, Shredder, Riff, and Chill. As the group gathered around the table, murmuring to themselves and reaching in front of each other to grab items, it was impossible to overhear specifics or tell the difference between a puzzled frown and a guilt-riddled scowl. At one point, Sam asked about the book of poems.

"Dad," he said. "Who was the recipient?"

"My cleaning lady, for all I know," Axe said, holding the book in front of me. "Explain what the hell this is about."

"My thoughts exactly," Chill said, reaching past Axe to dangle the gold locket in front of me. "Is this your idea of a joke?"

While I motioned for calm, Riff shoved in to fan the fake Japanese yen in my face, Shredder motioned him away with the garnet ring in hand, Petrel asked Gavin to be careful with the necklace box, lest the gems get stuck on someone's shoe, then Pauline clapped her hands, stepped in front of the men, and motioned for them to calm down.

"Instead of peppering Sonny with questions," Pauline said. "Let's give her a chance to explain the full picture."

"Thank you," I said. "As you may have heard, the two men who provided security at certain events were arrested. The extent of their crimes is unclear, but their wrongdoing appears to have included slipping drugs into Reginald's food to knock him out of action. There are hints that the two men, a.k.a. the 'Korkers,' were not acting alone. If anyone saw signs of trouble along these lines, it's time to step forward."

"Reginald gave the ex-cons a helping hand when their probation or whatever came to an end," Riff said. "If they turned on him, it's his own fault. None of us knew about their prison history."

"Harve exposed all that after an event in Maui," Pauline said. "They quit without replacements lined up, but stick with this moment. Is there a common thread among the items? They seem random."

"Reginald is trying to reclaim his memories through items that nag at him as important," I said. "Chill, perhaps you can open the discussion by telling us why you're upset to see the heart locket."

"I reacted before I opened it and realized it's not the necklace I bought however long ago," Chill said, pointing to the photo inside the heart. "This is Gavin's ex-wife, not my old girlfriend."

"Then allow me to express outrage," Gavin said, dangling the heart in front of me. "You can't imagine it might be painful?"

"Frankly, no," I said. "Given that it ended up in a thrift store."

"Surely not," Pauline said, shaking her head at Gavin. "You parted on bad terms, but she was Moritz's mother."

"Moritz is the one who dumped her belongings," Gavin said.

"Sorry I'm late," Harve said, ruining a key moment by arriving in a Hawaiian shirt and a cheerful mood. "What's the fuss about?"

"Reginald is trying to recover his memories with this array of items," Petrel said. "He's enlisted Sonny's help."

"That's a good point," Chill said, eyeing me suspiciously. "A week ago, you were a stranger. Now you're close with Reginald?"

"It's not hard to understand at all," Sam said. "It's all over town that Sonny played a role in nabbing the ex-cons who've been a pain point for Pop-Pop. There was a third arrest at the luau."

"That's right," I said. "There were three perpetrators."

"Whatever," Axe said. "Let's focus on this moment."

"Sonny, can I speak with the group alone?" Harve asked.

With a flip of my hands, I gave up imagining that Ted had been serious when he described my undercover role as a source of satisfaction and personal fulfillment. As I stepped away and fumed next to Jason, who gave my shoulders a cheering rub, I realized that the PI meant to speak loudly enough for me to overhear his message to the group.

"Listen," Harve said. "We need to respect Sonny's privacy regarding the *other* rumor floating around. Evelyn Littlefield is a known force among bigwigs and bankers on the East Coast. Perhaps she and Reginald crossed paths during a business trip. Aside from that, we've all experienced Sonny's warmth and sincerity. Reginald is fond of her."

"After one or two meetings?" Chill asked.

"It's a measure of how much others let him down," Harve said. "He's not shifting gears to punish anyone. In the wake of not remembering details, he's striving to know who he can trust."

"This is sad news," Pauline said. "In not paying attention, we assumed the worst of his behavior. We did let him down."

"Now that we know, we'll fix it," Gavin said.

As a car alarm blared outside, it took two seconds for Harve to alert on the sound, jog to the door, and confirm his hunch.

"That's Sonny's ride, a.k.a. my ride," he said, signaling for me to join him. "Keep at it, everyone. We'll be back in a jiffy."

On our way out, I said, "I'd barely gotten started."

"Nonsense, you hit it out of the park," Harve said. "Reginald favored letting people stew after seeing the items, and he wanted me to be on hand in case complexities hit the fan. Like right now."

Clasping the top of my head, Harve manually directed my gaze to Shredder, who'd put his utility vehicle into gear and reversed into my car to deliver an attention-getting, bumper-to-bumper tap.

"I need to speak to Sonny alone," Shredder growled.

"This happens to be my ride," Harve said, reaching into the car to shut off the alarm and restore quiet across the lot. "Plus, I saw you take the garnet ring. You seem to forget that I flew you and your special guy from island to island. I'm sorry that he died."

"Why is Reginald rubbing it in my face?" Shredder asked.

With a sigh, I said, "If pressed to hazard a guess, maybe he's concerned that you're scowling at people and slamming into cars instead of dealing with your grief. Secrets have a corrosive effect."

"It's caused an ulcer," Shredder admitted.

"You were relaxed in Petes's presence," Harve said softly. "Smiling and pointing out the plane window to show off your favorite places. You were your real self, answering to your real name, Bob."

Pacing, the amped-up guitarist struggled to maintain the tight lid he'd kept in place for however long, then suddenly, he gave up.

"Pete liked my band nickname," Shredder said. "When we met, he was married with kids, but we clicked. It's thanks to me that Pete came out, but it's thanks to the band that I'm a success. Axe was obsessed with maintaining the status quo for one more year, then another. I think it got to Pete, all the delays. He filled the void with drugs."

"Did you question his death?" I asked.

"Of course I did," Shredder said. "We have a place in San Francisco. Privacy, except for like-minded friends. His kids are in college."

"So, the timing felt off," I said.

Studying the ring, he said, "In daylight, I can tell this is too small to be Pete's. Seeing it on the table was triggering."

"That's understandable," I said.

"Let's talk about you for a second," Shredder said. "If the rumors are true, that you're Reginald's long-lost daughter, you'll need to answer for the fact that one of his heirs died when you arrived."

"Who's barking up that tree?" Harve asked.

"Not me, except for normal outrage if a good guy met his maker for selfish reasons," Shredder said, eyeing me curiously. "I'm not buying that angle. You walked away from Littlefield money. Even as a friend, Pop-Pop will open doors, but he's a stickler for rules."

"Let me worry about me," I said. "The other night, I saw you trying to drink your sorrows away. Next time you're facing a lonely moment, pick up your guitar instead of a bottle. If there's such a thing as ghosts, they're based on us. Nobody likes dealing with a drunk."

"You're giving me chills, sounding like Pete," Shredder said, signaling an end to his moment of opening up. "Harve, send me the bill for fixing your piece of junk. You can see it was only a tap."

With a tight nod as a goodbye, Shredder slipped into his sports utility vehicle and swung out of the parking lot with a whir of oversized tires and engine power. In the following quiet, my shadow provided shade for Harve as he knelt to examine the front bumper.

"I've got more news," Harve said. "FBI agents are secretly completing the painting and repairs at the house, so you're not bogged down with that element. Moritz and Raja called in sick for their shift at the bar. We're taking it to mean they heard about the USB stick through the grapevine. After a rough day, you're in for a rough night."

"Actually," I said, "I think you might be more suited to the secret heir gambit. My approach caused property damage."

"Check it out," Harve said, signaling for me to kneel next to him near the bumper. "How much should I charge Shredder?"

Touching the fender, I couldn't find the slightest scratch.

"Shredder is among the people who never returned the key after borrowing this piece of junk," Harve said. "While we were inside discussing the thrift store items, he backed up his vehicle, nice and neat, and used the key fob to set off the alarm instead of causing damage. Still trying to play the tough guy, but in the process of confessing what his misery is about, he's a changed man. This is a beautiful moment."

"I don't suppose you have tissues," I said, suddenly tearful from the stresses of the day. "I was about to throw in the towel."

"I texted Jason to bring your belongings and the thrift store items," Harve said, indicating my coach exiting the dance studio. "Since we're in the testing phase, it's important to give people plenty to talk about, and nothing shows a woman's power better than alpha males kneeling at her beck and call on the pavement. Jason, get to it."

With a towel in hand, Jason made a folded cushion on the asphalt and settled his left knee into place, with his right thigh providing a horizontal perch for me to use when swapping my shoes.

"I'm not sitting on your knee," I said. "Stand up."

"It's too late to worry about my pants getting dirty," Jason said. "I've done this for Katrina a zillion times during shows."

"Think how she would see it," I insisted.

"I've apologized and tried to make amends," Jason said. "At this point, Katrina needs to do the same, but after watching events unfold in there, I'm even more convinced that Jasmine is right about a hidden element that hit the fan. Chip is in the grave, and Reginald is in the hospital. I'm done being complacent. It's time to take action."

"You heard the man," Harve said. "Sit down and change your shoes so we can proceed to dinner. Ted's treat, so let's aim high."

"I'm craving Mexican food," I said.

"Done," Harve said. "Lace up. Let's roll."

* * *

Judging by Barry's slightly rumpled pilot's uniform, he'd responded to his group's call for action the moment he'd landed. I'd responded to a call for action as well, parking in the connecting lane to pull in directly after him, preventing any chance of him gaining the upper hand.

As Barry squinted against the glare of my headlights, I shut them off as a gesture of civility. It still irritated me that he'd bought into Moritz's efforts to undermine my worth, but all of that could be overlooked if Barry showed genuine concern for Reginald. It would amount to digging himself out of a hole. In his fevered state the other day, Reginald had told me that Barry was the person who'd let him down the most.

"This is odd," Barry said, frowning at the bumper as I climbed out with a bag of snack food. "With an impact that set off the alarm, I would expect a mess, but it's not dented or scratched."

"Shredder wasn't the only one who reacted badly to the mementos that caught Reginald's interest," I said. "You've come at night, against the rules, so I assume you're here to apologize for the group."

"Actually, it's the opposite," Barry said. "Instead of focusing on the work here at the house, you're involving yourself in private matters, not to mention snorkeling and dancing the hours away."

Upon reflection, his attitude was unsurprising.

"From the sound of it, you're still buying into Moritz's false narrative," I said, pulling a stapled document from my bag. "Fortunately, I have tallied my work hours and Antoine's as well. If you would like, I can prepare a cost estimate to illuminate the value of our free labor. As for Moritz and Raja, they haven't shown up for work in two days."

"Out of frustration," Barry said. "They've paused their efforts to emphasize that you're not pulling your weight. From here on out, you'll need to submit a targeted agenda at the start of each day."

With raised eyebrows, I said, "You want me to ask *permission* to come and go in between my free, grueling, hard work?"

"Sonny, I'm exhausted," Barry said. "Let's get this done."

"By all means," I said, proceeding past the garage.

Leading the way into the house, I tossed the shopping bag onto the table and set the lights ablaze to offer a spectacular view of the interior for Moritz and Raja, who were lurking in the garden. It suited me for them to listen in, so I opened the doors to let in the breeze.

At the threshold, Barry stopped in his tracks.

"Holy shit," he said. "It's like the mess never happened."

"In part, it's because Moritz and Raja weren't here to undo my progress," I said. "The building inspector exposed that element."

Having not visited the house all day, I was startled as well, staring from the gleaming perfection of the walls to the new drapes and couch cushions, with the pillows neatly in place. Instead of a layer of plaster dust, the floor was freshly polished, free of extension cords and tools. Past the living room and kitchen, the bed looked like an oasis, with plumped pillows, a quilted coverlet folded at the bottom, and a small teak tray set with a pink hibiscus flower, and, if I wasn't mistaken, a chocolate treat.

With my eyes threatening to brim over, I crossed to the kitchen with dogged determination, silently chiding the well-intentioned helper agents for throwing me off my game with touches of kindness. Back on track once I reached the countertop, I used a throwing knife to slice a lemon on the cutting board and poured two glasses of sparkling water.

"I'm not thirsty," Barry said. "From what I understand, you weren't here all day. How did you finish the work and clean up?"

"Not to belabor a point, but Moritz and Raja have been disruptive, so I've been sneaking in and out through the back lane," I said, holding out the USB stick. "Is this yours, by any chance?"

"No, it's not familiar," Barry said, pausing to frown at Chip's watch on my wrist before unsticking the knife from the cutting board and putting it in the drawer. "This is not a kitchen knife."

"It does have a look of overkill," I said.

"The sunset photo is a perfect touch," Barry said, pointing to the metal print on the far wall. "You didn't mention a price."

"It's another freebee," I said. "Rather, let's see it as a trade for a slightly extended stay, unless you're keen to kick me out."

"That wouldn't feel fair," Barry said. "Fixing the hot tub alone saved me ten grand. As for your tally of hours, it's hard to tease out who did what in the repairs. It's not to be seen as a revolving door for your family and friends. One expects the place suits your mother?"

"It's too rustic for her taste," I said. "She's on her way home."

Barry paused. "She flew eleven hours for lunch?"

"It's a breeze in first class," I said.

"I guess I've heard that opinion a time or two," Barry admitted. "To spare you another intrusion, let's have a look around."

With his attention directed elsewhere, my inner pessimist noted that, in the past, I had outed precisely *zero* murderers in advance of a near-death showdown moment. Hopefully, Katrina's grief over Chip's death was genuine, Ted was on the side of good, and his team had enough sense to vet Harve before trusting him with sensitive information. If Jason, Mary, or RG were responsible for any of the awful wrongdoing, my crime-fighting days would be over. I would throw in the towel.

As Barry prowled from one repaired element to the next, I reminded myself that, in general, checklists were comforting and necessary, a sign that important steps were done properly. With that high-minded thought out of the way, I decided the skill would be an asset in carrying out a wide spectrum of unlawful activities, especially as Barry conducted his silent inspection of the shining success story with a frown, testing the straightness of shelves, tugging at the teak molding, and poking the freshly painted surfaces, as if expecting the drywall to crumble. In his shoes I would show at least some semblance of appreciation, but he seemed bent on uncovering a sour version of how I'd succeeded, against all odds.

With Ted's stipulated ten-minute visitation window adding pressure, it was time to hit the gas, and by then, Barry deserved it.

"While you're here, I've got ideas for other artwork to compliment the sunset print," I said, crossing to the shelving unit to open the secret drawer. "How about a shot of the resident gecko?"

Unsurprisingly, Barry looked confused as I unlocked the back latch and slid the thin drawer open, revealing two laptops and the paperwork Ted's team had planted during their clandestine visit.

"What the hell?" Barry murmured.

"I didn't touch the paperwork," I said.

"I'm reacting to the drawer," Barry said, studying how the front panel blended in with the shelves. "This is nuts."

"You didn't know it was there?" I asked. "That *is* nuts."

"To be honest, the sensation isn't new to me," Barry said. "At one point, I had a route that kept me away for long stretches. Every time I got home, it felt weird and disorienting. I get it. People move things around, but this … who the hell put it here?"

"The builder, maybe?" I asked. "Or a previous owner?"

Like a man recovering from a hangover, Barry rubbed his brow and muttered to himself as he studied a loan agreement listing Reginald White as a previous co-owner of the house, with scribbled notes hinting at Reginald's desire to contest elements of the contract.

"Is that your father's name?" I asked.

Barry paused for a second, then he closed the drawer and checked the latch to see how it worked. In the sudden silence, my folded arms released automatically, and my heightened senses, fueled by adrenaline, assessed possible escape routes through the kitchen and living room, although to a scary degree, I *wanted* Barry to make a move.

"Why would you ask that?" he said, still studying the drawer.

"You seem confused," I said. "I'm trying to help."

"Easygoing Sonny, always quick to lend a hand," Barry said, coming to rest with his arms folded. "I'm sorry I missed your show-and-tell performance at the dance studio, though apparently, it's still going on. If I'm not mistaken, you're wearing Chip's watch. You're turning your head like I'm supposed to notice the hoop earrings, too."

"I'm making sure there's a clear path to the door," I said. "Reginald was poisoned, and he believes the culprit was a friend."

"His former cronies have been arrested," Barry said, calmly reaching for the shopping bag. "The group wants me to take a crack at assessing the thrift store finds. It's not your burden to shoulder."

"Cashing out happens when you win," I said. "Paying up is the right phrase for tossing down your cards and storming out."

Barry hesitated. "Where did you hear that?"

"I'm quoting one of your dry comments during a card game," I said. "From a video I found on Chip's laptop. I think with enough time, he would have been the one to upend the poisoning effort, but he was distracted by a pattern of *other* concerning events."

Barry frowned. "Such as …?"

"Today's heightened interest in ordinary items has put me all the more on edge," I went on. "If there's an explanation for the huge reaction at the dance studio, not to mention this moment, I'm all ears."

Measuredly, Barry said, "The items strike people as calculated rather than ordinary. Reginald is upending business matters—"

"Illegal matters?" I asked. "Is that what's at stake?"

"Where is your change of focus coming from?" Barry asked. "Chip's woolgathering? Reginald's drug haze? It's time to explain."

"Dear God," I murmured. "You didn't say no."

"I don't fly well in the stratosphere unless I'm in a plane," Barry said. "You approached Reginald's friends for our input—"

"Actually, the group barged in uninvited," I said. "Instead of a gentle discussion, it turned into a hollering match that ended with Harve's car getting front-ended. If you want to participate, come back with a better story than, 'We're used to getting our own way.'"

"Given that the bag is in my hand," Barry said, "the practical solution is for me to take over the project and leave you in peace."

"Be careful of your salt intake," I said.

Barry squinted. *"What…?"*

In the same second that he opened the bag and realized he'd secured a pound of peanuts, his phone rang with an alert, prompting him to pull the device from his pocket and frown at the screen.

"Problem?" I asked.

"There's a prowler at my house," he said, eyeing me warily. "If we were playing cards, I would see this moment as off."

"That's a fun story to share with your insurance company," I said. "By all means, dash away. Make sure to call first next time."

"You've changed your tune," Barry said softly.

"It's time to go," I said. "Leave the snacks."

Following along as Barry left, I saw him fumble with his keys, back out of the driveway, and speed down the lane.

"Moritz," I hollered. "Do you want the USB stick, or not?"

Amid the rustling of two shadows emerging from the ferns, I fetched a glass of water and set it on the dining room table.

"Nice work, getting rid of Barry," Moritz said, breathless as he arrived. "We nearly shit ourselves when you asked if he recognized the USB stick. We've been searching for it for months."

"Yes, I know," I said, holding the stick an inch above the water inside the glass. "Tell me why, or it's going into the drink."

"Careful, it's our only copy," Moritz said, stepping closer with calming motions. "I'd be stunned if you haven't heard that Gavin robbed the family coffers. *My* family coffers. Once I gathered enough evidence, I warned him to restock my trust fund, or face the consequences."

"We agreed to the party as an exchange point," Raja added. "Figuring Gavin would behave with witnesses around, but he got Axe and the band to frisk us at the door. They made a game of kicking the stick all over the place until it got stuck in a crack or something."

"Putting aside the wrongness of venting your anger on the house," I said, "did Chip help secure the evidence against Gavin?"

"Well," Moritz said guardedly. "We caught onto his interest in certain events that took place on the *Kukuna Mahina*. With our focus in mind, we endeavored to stoke Chip's suspicion of Gavin."

"You met him," Raja said. "Chip, that is, too straightlaced to hack into somebody's laptop, but he got Gavin's password."

"Chip passed it along to you?" I asked.

"In exchange for his silence with regard to our clandestine mission, we gave him the photos that Gavin took at the party," Moritz said. "He never mentioned whether the shots helped with his quest."

"Enough small talk," Raja said. "We've retrieved the evidence, and *this* time, we'll meet with Gavin with nobody around."

"The smarter move is to tell the authorities," I said. "But I'm guessing you won't. Your priorities are totally off."

"It's none of your business," Moritz said, motioning for me to hand over the stick. "Keep your mouth shut, understand?"

I nodded. "Yes, I understand."

With high-fives and grins, they sauntered away, planning to get drunk and celebrate what they thought was a stroke of luck.

In the ensuing quiet, the room seemed to shimmer with vibrations as I faced my last night in the house, just as its transformation into a paradise destination was complete. I'd helped heal the house, but in doing so, I was all the more conscious of the difference between things and living things. No power on Earth would restore a lost life.

With a tired sigh, I flipped off the lights and headed into the bedroom, eager to take a hot shower and collapse into oblivion.

“And that’s how it’s done,” Nicole said from the shadows.

“Actually, I’m belatedly remembering that Barry is a commercial pilot with a great deal of responsibility,” I said. “What if I’ve distracted him to the point where he flubs his next flight?”

“The steps are computerized,” Nicole said, shaking her head over my annoying moral compass. “With checks and balances.”

“Aren’t you supposed to be outside?” I asked.

“I’m allergic to mosquitoes,” she said, bouncing on the bed a few times. “If only Dan was here. We could have a threesome.”

“I need sleep, Nicole.”

“I’ve heard he’s finally in counseling,” she said, holding the bathroom door open when I tried to close it. “Come on, don’t be shy. I’m curious to see if you’ve got a rash from the Brazilian wax.”

“I’m fine,” I said. “There’s a bottle of dark tequila on the shelf. I won’t tell anyone if you have a shot while on duty.”

A minute later, I paused to savor the sound of her uncorking the bottle, the gurgle of liquid pouring out, and Nicole expelling Hawaiian moonshine across the room, her eyes ablaze with heat.

“Nicely played,” she wheezed.

“Are you done being an ass?” I called out.

“Yeah,” Nicole said, gasping. “For now.”

26

Shortly after dawn, I sat on my favorite lava ledge, adjusted my mask over my eyes, and surged forward, using the momentum of a rebounding wave to carry me into deeper water, where Antoine's shadow had merged with mine over a span of idyllic days. I'd allotted myself that one sunrise to fume and grieve and smolder with regrets. It was within my power to be happy for Antoine, but for now, I released myself into the wild.

With strong flipper kicks, I burned off energy with a 20-minute swim. On my way back, I slowed my pace as I reached the canyon between two long coral outcrops, where golden sunlight carved slanted rays through the saltwater and added vivid dimension to the bubbles churning across the coral formations. I set my camera for underwater light and photographed a bird wrasse poking its nose into a crevice, then I steadied myself against the waves to capture a video of an octopus undergoing subtle shifts in camouflage coloring, either in response to my presence or, for all I knew, reacting to a dream as it slept away the morning hours.

Up ahead, a barracuda swiftly turned away, sparking goosebumps with its black eyes, extended lower jaw, and razor teeth. With minimal flipper kicks, I filmed it near the surface, following along as its sleek body shone against the coral amid wave-patterned light, with a school of butterflyfish in the frame. I was lucky to see any details when ocean water seeped into my mask and stung my eyes. Amid the laborious task of rinsing the glass and snugging the mask into a tight fit, I saw Ted walking along the lava shoreline in his dress pants and street shoes, sleeves rolled up, holding an umbrella to shield himself from the sun's glare while he sat down near my towel and opened his copy of *The Hawaiian Archipelago*.

The danger of getting a serious sunburn was increasing by the minute, so I followed an inward-bound wave to the lava ledge and climbed out, dripping as I crossed to Ted and toweled off my hair.

"This is an enlightening read," Ted said. "Ms. Bird uses the Hawaiian word 'pali' to describe the thousand-foot cliffs in the Waipio Valley. In the early days, they climbed up and down with ropes. After Western ships arrived, the Hawaiians tackled the cliffs on *horseback*."

"Animal instinct outstrips the human mind," I said.

"'Most of the tracks,'" Ted read, "'are worn by water and animals' feet, broken, rugged, jagged, with steps of rock sometimes three feet high, produced by breakage here and there. Up and down these animals slip, jump, and scramble.'" With a snort, Ted added, "Isabella writes, kind of calmly, 'On a few of these tracks a false step means death.'"

"You're making me want to visit the Waipio Valley," I said.

As I sat down, Ted updated me with a minute-by-minute account of Gavin, Axe, Chill, and Riff spiriting away the entire contents of the secret drawer, including a decoy laptop labeled as Chip's computer and a USB stick identical to the one Moritz had taken.

"The pilfering gives us a reason to change the locks," Ted said. "Let's see how Barry handles that. From here, you can clean up at the hotel room we've secured for your use, then during your dance session, propose a get-together at the house for 8:00. We'll have things set up for you to leave amid a puff of smoke, including a bag the players will *assume* contains the thrift store items. It'll be out of their reach, at least at first. Along with it will be an invitation for Reginald's birthday party on the *Kukuna Mahina*. The team has outdone themselves with the planning."

"Umm, *hello*," I said. "I'm supposed to get to the airport by ten o'clock. Not to mention, you're expecting me to pull sideways hints out of my ying-yang without the slightest sense of where to start."

"I will endeavor to unhear your unique phrasing," Ted said. "We've got another day of stirring the pot. Out at sea in the *Kukuna Mahina*, we can control who arrives and who leaves. I've got agents learning how to carry out the services of stewards and related personnel."

"Is a multi-day sting really the only option?" I asked.

"Sonny, you've aced every step, with major wins along the way," Ted said. "Why is there a wall instead of a sense of achievement?"

"Gosh, I can't imagine," I said.

With a persevering look, Ted opened *The Hawaiian Archipelago* to a flagged page and landed his finger on the text halfway down.

"During the ride to Waipio," Ted said, "Isabella wrote thusly about one of the death-defying, vertical climbs: 'My horse went up wisely and nobly, but slipping, jumping, scrambling, and sending stones over the ledge, now and then hanging for a second by his fore feet … the girth was loose, so as not to impede the horse's respiration … it was once or twice necessary to run the risk of losing my balance by taking my left foot out of the stirrup to press it against the horse's neck to prevent it from being crushed, while my right hung over the precipice …'"

"I read that part," I said. "Isabella stuck with it, blah blah."

"I'm a straightlaced guy trying to understand a woman who blazes her own unique trail," Ted said, tucking the book to one side. "Like Isabella loosening the girth so her talented horse could breathe, I'm doing my best to keep you safe and whole, Sonny."

"Safe, maybe," I said. "I'm far from whole."

"Reginald is tempted to draw up adoption papers," Ted said. "Carol Henderson is amazed by your slideshow celebrating Chip's life, and most telling of all, Nicole is confronting me about how I'm pushing you too hard. That, my friend, is an achievement."

"Thanks for the update," I grumbled. "Don't forget your book."

"Don't forget you're part of a team," Ted said.

With a shoulder bump, Ted climbed to his feet and made poor footing choices all the way across the lava to his car. At some point, I would look into the unicorn key fob he'd reacted to during our meeting with Reginald. Which victim was driving Ted to keep the case on track?

* * *

"Sonny," Petrel said, arriving from his office in a flustered state. "Shredder has *quit* the band without warning and left for San Francisco. It happened overnight. You're the last one to talk to him."

"Apparently, he's wanted to leave the band for years," I said. "You saw his reaction to the garnet ring. It sparked an epiphany."

"Indeed, I did see that," Petrel said. "Everyone reacted to one item or another. Except me. I spent my time putting out the fires."

"That's surprising," I said. "As a choreographer, you're wired to explore hidden pain. You believe in truth and self-expression."

"Be still, my heart," Petrel said, clutching his chest.

Having hung back after our dance session, Jason tossed aside his face towel and stepped closer, unable to contain himself.

"There's been a development?" he asked.

"Are you having dreams about Sonny?" Petrel prompted.

Jason gaped. "Why would you ask me that in front of her?"

"There's no need for blushing," Petrel said. "Young men are bound to have naughty dreams. In my more composed experience, Sonny is a shining figure emerging from the mist with gems and odd elements. It has me asking myself, where is the choreographer who relishes obscure routines? Paying bills has pushed pathos to the sidelines."

Nodding, I said, "You're the opposite of Barry. Last night, he tried to bully me into giving him the bag of keepsakes. If not for an urgent matter at his house, who knows what might have happened."

Petrel hesitated. "Barry rattled you that much?"

"He's got a drawerful of razor-sharp throwing knives," I said. "When I used one to cut a lemon, he got *very* upset."

"If anything, I'm glad to know that he's found an outlet for the steam that boils over from his stressful job," Petrel said. "Did I hear correctly that you're polishing dance routines for the *Kukuna Mahina*?"

"Jason and I are leaning toward somber themes," I said. "People wrestling with inner demons and hiding the awful secrets of others. *Knowing* about a transgression, yet staying silent."

"Keep talking," Petrel said, walking forward in a trancelike state with his hands expressing a vista of possibilities. "We can create an ad teaser for pharmaceutical companies that treat forms of psychosis. My rival on Oahu is making a fortune from that kind of gambit."

Warmly clasping Petrel's hands, I tried to embody the shining, helpful being from his dreams, smiling encouragingly to inspire him to share his thoughts about anything but creating an advertising teaser. With a slight paunch reflecting his love of island cuisine, Petrel refused to show anything but joy over the friendship we had quickly forged.

"What is it, my dear?" Petrel asked.

"You've created a wonderful space for dancers," I said. "I've come to cherish my lessons, so I'm pausing to thank you."

"Oh, darling, this is too much," Petrel said, dabbing his eyes. "From a blank gaze, you've become a beacon of positivity."

"With that in mind," I said. "I'm thinking of hosting a gathering at the house to discuss how we can help Reginald."

"It's a marvelous idea," Petrel said. "Say, eight o'clock?"

"You read my mind," I said.

While Petrel made calls alerting the group, Jason joined me along the back wall as I swapped my dance shoes for my sneakers.

"Before you ask," I whispered. "You can't come to the meeting tonight. The point is to test and pressure people."

We'd already discussed the fact that if Jason wanted to join the cruise, his focus would need to be limited to dancing. Ted didn't feel it was a gamble to let the dance pro in on the secret; if Jason shared it with others, he would land in the crosshairs as a suspect.

"This is a moment of trust," I stressed. "You can't tell *anyone*."

"I get it," Jason said. "You can count on me."

With my sunglasses on as I crossed to my car, I paused to examine an auto detailer's coupon flyer tucked under the wiper blade. Never mind the low price. What caught my attention was the promise of leaving surfaces and windows fingerprint-free. Having dealt with the fallout from police officers chasing false leads that landed me in trouble, I decided it wasn't a bad idea to wipe away all traces of my use of Harve's car.

I hesitated, surprised to see Katrina climbing out of a dark sedan with her bodyguard. Staying a few steps ahead of her escort, she conveyed with a pointed gaze that she had a clandestine agenda in mind.

"I'm sure you can guess why I'm here," Katrina said. "Instead of staying away from Jason, you had another dance lesson."

"Two minutes," the agent said, tapping her watch.

As her escort stepped away, Katrina blew out a breath.

"Forget all that," she said. "It's only today that I took a close look at a photo I snagged of the stalker on the 1871 Trail. You know I'm mistrustful of the police, but I need to share it with somebody."

"Text it to me," I prompted.

Once the shot downloaded to my phone, I zoomed in on the bearded man, confirming from the timestamp that Katrina had snagged the image five or ten minutes before I'd seen her group.

"It's blurry," she said. "It's hard to know if his posture is stooped from age or the guilt of trying to eavesdrop. The blur worsens if you zoom in. What do you make of the white flecks in his beard?"

"It might be glints of sunlight," I said. "His face is in shadow, but his extra pounds are clear. The third arrestee is skinny."

"Skinny people can wear loose clothes to fly under the radar," Katrina said. "A fake beard, too, though I can't imagine it in the heat. If the stalker truly was heavy, Petrel doesn't fit my sense of a covert type, but Harve came to mind. Why would he follow us?"

"Aside from him being a PI?" I said dryly. "It didn't sound like Harve, but I suppose trickery is a part of his trade."

"He's always got a side hustle going on," Katrina agreed, switching gears as her bodyguard returned. "Sonny, *please* tell the truth."

"Jason and I are just friends," I said.

"The rumors spun my head around," Katrina said with fake drama. "I will try to stay calm and patient, but it's really hard."

"Hopefully, the assurance will stick this time," the frazzled bodyguard said. "Is there anything I should bring to Ted?"

"I need a vacation from my vacation," I said.

She smiled. "I'll pass it along."

Plunged into a robotic state, I drove to the hotel room Ted had secured for me. Showered and dressed in my travel clothes, I conducted a quick analysis of the photograph to confirm that it hadn't been altered. Leaving a trail of granola bar crumbs in my wake, I rolled my luggage to Harve's car and followed the directions on the auto detailer's flyer.

At a stoplight, where doubts surfaced, my vivid recollection of Chip's grin and high-five snapped me back into gear. In a split-second of time, he'd delivered a call to action that I still felt in my hand.

At last, able to rest for a fleeting moment, I watched the auto detailer carrying out his meticulous work with sprays and microfiber cloths in his small garage, grateful that he stuck to the promise of a ten-minute miracle makeover. When I handed him the coupon and a wad of cash, he noticed the latex gloves on my hands, and then his glance and raised eyebrows asked if he'd just cleaned the interior of a murder vehicle.

"No, umm … I've got allergies," I lied. "To cleaning solutions."

"No worries," he said, handing me an envelope.

Frowning at the script lettering, I said, "Why is my name on this?"

"It's an ancient practice intended to make sure property gets into the right hands," he said. "I'm surprised you don't know about it."

I hesitated. "So, the flyer that was left on my car …"

"Must've been carried there by a volcanic breeze." With a wink, the detailer tucked my cash into his pocket and headed back into his garage. "Tell Pop-Pop I appreciate the business."

In the parking lot, I opened the envelope and found a photo from the thrift store showing Katrina handing the necklace box of stolen diamonds to the shop's owner. Also enclosed was a note from Reginald.

Given the music in the background, I can't hear their conversation. The owner is rattled by the FBI's involvement, so I'm forced to accept her claim that she can't recall specifics. My trust in the justice system is shot, but my faith in you is deep. All other traces of the visit are erased. Go with your gut.

"Dear God, why?" I moaned.

27

For once, I was alerted in advance about an unruly mob arriving an hour early. In the gathering dusk, aware that agents were hidden in strategic locations around the property, I felt fairly calm as I scanned the undergrowth along the lane for signs of the peacock's eyes and iridescent tail feathers. Instead, my headlights reflected off the fenders of five vehicles spilling out of the driveway in front of the garage. As always, not one person in the group had given a nod toward carpooling.

I parked the car facing downhill, slipped off my gloves, left my purse behind, and collided into Axe on my way out.

"It's rude to arrive an hour early," I said.

"Well," Axe said. "It's rude to change the locks without permission from the guy who owns the house. Whatever you're up to with your power play, it's officially over. Stop playing dumb."

"That's hilarious for reasons I can't explain," I said. "But did you know the meaning of 'dumb' has to do with being speechless?"

"That's Sam's department," Axe said, indicating his son standing in the shadows. "Flex up. Show Sonny what you've got."

"Dad, this is completely wrong," Sam said. "You ranted all day about Shredder leaving the band. We need to practice."

"Nobody's stopping you," Axe said.

"Sam," I said. "If you need a ride …"

"No, it's fine," he said. "I'll call a rideshare."

Blinking back tears, Sam headed down the lane, no doubt wondering why he'd hitched his star to his father's fickle dreams.

"That was shameful," I said quietly.

"Here's the sad story," Axe said, unlocking his phone and handing it to me with his photo library open. "Thanks to Barry's contacts, we tracked Antoine to California. Check out his main squeeze. Beautiful, focused on family, minds her own business. They've got a kid."

After watching Axe use his passcode, I was able to permanently delete his photo library. Copies would still exist if he had a cloud account, but in that moment, I'd reversed his smile into a look of horror.

"You deleted my whole library?" Axe demanded.

"Oops," I said. "My bad."

"Sonny," Harve said, jogging toward us. "To the surprise of *everyone*, Reginald just emerged out of the shadows."

"The bastard walked in on the sly?" Axe asked.

"Bear in mind, Reginald is fresh out of the hospital," Harve cautioned as the guitarist stalked away. "Sonny, listen—"

"No, you listen," I said. "Apparently—" Seeing the fancy pen in his pocket, I grabbed it and spoke furiously into the button area, "Apparently, the reason Ted sent an agent to tail Antoine was because Barry, Axe, and whoever tracked Antoine to California. If it takes hacking into every cloud account on the island, I want the related photos deleted."

"Sonny," Harve said. "That's a regular pen."

"I need to take action," I said. "Can you lift Barry's phone?"

"Piece of cake," Harve said.

Pausing in the shadows, I studied the silhouettes gathered in the flickering glow of four large candles on posts around the patio. Touching his brow now and then, Reginald appeared to be feigning forgetfulness, blinking when asked even the simplest of questions, and turning to Carol, who had apparently given him a ride to the occasion.

"I worried that walking up the hill would be a strain," Carol said. "Can anyone fetch a bottle of water? It has to be tightly sealed."

"You know why," Reginald said. "I'm under threat."

"Not anymore," Petrel said. "You're among friends."

Just then, Harve bumped into Barry, slipped the phone from the pilot's pocket, and reached back to give the device to me.

Working quickly, I pried off the waterproof case, cracked open the hot tub's lid, and watched the phone slip down, trailing a stream of bubbles. For a maximum shock effect, preferably after I left, I motioned for Harve to put the empty case back into Barry's pocket.

Catching Carol's attention, I signaled for her to skirt around the group and meet me in private. We hugged when she arrived.

"Reginald is a wreck over the photo of Katrina in the thrift store," she whispered. "If she's involved with stolen gems—"

"Carol, listen," I said. "Every person that I've come to trust believes that Katrina didn't play a role in the poisoning, and was going through her own version of harassment. When I talked to her today, she promised to be patient and lie low. Reginald needs to do the same."

"I hear you," Carol whispered. "But in discussing matters just now, it came out that the group took Chip's laptop."

"They stole a decoy laptop," I assured her. "The files are pared down and encoded to keep track of activity. That way, innocent interest can be separated from an intent to bury or alter evidence."

"The waiting is agonizing," Carol whispered.

"We *will* get answers," I said. "Keep the faith."

With their gazes on Reginald, the group didn't realize that I'd arrived until I joined Carol in emerging from the shadows. After a tight hug, I pulled away with a pointed gaze to remind Reginald that he'd enlisted my help for a reason. His fierce return gaze informed me that if Carol hadn't knuckled him into submission, I wouldn't either.

"I thought you might come with Katrina," Reginald said.

"Her plan to join us got *shredded*," I said.

I hesitated, grasping that I'd just alluded to destroying evidence within eavesdropping range of FBI agents, but if Katrina was buying and selling stolen diamonds, it would take more than a grainy photo in a thrift store to build a case, and Reginald wasn't the only one who'd been slammed by narrow police thinking. I'd turned the photo into confetti.

Regrouping fast, I said, "I was present when the *doctor* urged you to rest. Bring Carol to the coast. Enjoy the sea air."

"I do enjoy a fresh breeze of 19-24 miles per hour," Reginald said. "But what's *really* needed to stir my spirit is more of a severe gale, 47-54 miles per hour. Imagine the fun of racing along."

"They're referencing the Beaufort scale of wind," Barry explained to his group. "Developed in 1805 by a British Admiral, Sir Francis Beaufort. It's promising that you remember it, Reginald."

At that point, I resorted to my mother's silent coding of pursed lips, merciless eye contact, and Morse code finger tapping on my bicep, having folded my arms as a further show of being in charge.

"Reginald," Carol said firmly. "Coming here *was* against the doctor's orders. Let's head home before we both collapse."

With a look of irritation, the alpha millionaire who abhorred delegating important matters to others softened, and hugged me.

"Along with worries about Katrina," he whispered. "I wanted to make sure you're not overwhelmed. Clearly, you're locked in."

"Get some rest," I said softly.

Silence fell as Carol and Reginald became silhouettes on their way up the steps leading to the footpath and down the lane. With an exchange of glances, Barry, Axe, Riff, and Chill revealed themselves as a united front, while Pauline, Gavin, and Petrel appeared to be a satellite tangent within the Kona group galaxy. Furthest from the center, Moritz and Raja were hanging back to see if their agenda could be sorted out by others, and two roadies who had been unlucky enough to be in Axe's vehicle when the call for action arrived had dragged beach chairs from a nook near the downstairs apartment to check the feed on their phones.

As Harve joined me by the candlelight near the table, I studied his extra pounds. "Was it you on the 1871 Trail?"

"Can you seriously picture me on a hike?" Harve asked.

"I guess not," I said. "Why is my bullwhip on the table?"

Harve smiled. "It's always good to have tools on hand."

"Sonny," Barry said. "In fetching the private paperwork and laptop this morning, Gavin left you a note. Harve has explained that it got blown to the floor. I can see where you might have suspected a burglary, but I wish you'd thought to call me before changing the locks."

"I guess that covers it," I said, pushing past Barry to address everyone. "Life won't get back to normal until Reginald understands the full extent of the poisoning plot. The ex-cons who provided security at special events have been arrested on a range of charges, but one of their cronies might still be at large. It's important to share what you know."

"We've talked it through, and barely recall the two guys," Chill said. "Security personnel are trained to be inconspicuous."

"Moving on," Barry said. "Based on what we saw tonight, Reginald is still prone to confusion, which makes him an easy target."

Gavin added, "You're *clearly* Raymond French's child, so the rumor that you're Reginald's daughter is ridiculous. One can't help but see your pattern of activities as a gold-digger scenario."

"My dear friends," Petrel said. "We're supposed to be thanking Sonny. Instead, I've landed in an Italian opera where the heroine is pitted against a bunch of greedy, petulant men with flawed priorities."

"Yes!" I blurted, then added, "To be honest, it's refreshing to see glimmers of concern in the group. Days ago, Reginald was a maligned, misunderstood pariah. He's big enough to reflect on his flaws and strong views. Whatever it takes to know why he became a target."

"It went beyond strong views," Barry said. "We get it, now. The reason is clear, but tell me, Sonny. Why make it your problem?"

"It's odd for you to ask," I said, "Amid stories of lost friendships, secret agendas, and bitter feuds. You, alone, are a poster child for bad decisions and dysfunction. I'm reminded of the old saying, 'If three people call you a jackass, it's time to buy yourself a saddle.'"

"Why do you keep singling me out?" Barry demanded.

"Careful," Petrel cautioned. "As a person who delivers barbs all day, every day, you're not in a position to complain."

"Here's a question," Axe said. "Where's the booze?"

"Yeah," Chill said. "This is supposed to be a party."

"Except, you arrived an hour early," Harve said.

Suddenly, Pauline motioned with both hands.

"In rolling my eyes in despair," she said, "I've caught sight of a large envelope, a trail of festive ribbons, and, if I'm not mistaken, the bag of keepsakes hanging from the coconut tree above us."

With a sigh, I abandoned a scholarly approach.

"It sounds like Barry didn't tell you he tried to rip the bag from my possession last night," I said. "The next thing I knew, someone had broken in and stolen the contents of the secret drawer. Now that you've explained your reasoning, neither Carol nor I will contest anyone's intention to make use of the laptop that was taken from the house."

"Our motives are entirely above board," Gavin said. "Some of Chip's work could be considered intellectual property."

"Happy digging," I said. "Knock yourself out."

"I'm heartened by your reasoned response," Barry said. "The tense start could have been avoided with better communication. I should have been told about the change of locks. This is my house."

"It's Pauline's house, too," Petrel said pointedly. "Gavin, if I may loop back to your sour remarks, Moritz has accused *you* of being a gold-digger, and judging from his scowling, he's not over it."

"Right now, I'm glaring at Sonny," Moritz said, stepping forward into the candlelight. "The USB stick froze our computer."

"I warned you not to use it," I said, turning to Barry to explain, "Their blackmail plot against Gavin went wrong when Axe and Chill played kick-ball with the damning evidence in the first moments of the party. Moritz and Raja flew into a rage and trashed your house."

Barry hesitated. "Are you shitting me?"

"They've been correcting some of the damage," I pointed out.

"Yeah, for a paycheck," Barry said.

"It's good to have this out in the open," Gavin said, glaring at Moritz. "When will you let go of the baseless notion that I'm to blame for your mother's financial downfall? Instead of making smart choices, she drank the hours away and listened to her idiot son."

"The USB stick told a different story, asshole," Raja said. "Chip helped us gather the evidence, and guess what? He ended up dead."

"What the hell are you implying now?" Gavin demanded.

Stepping into the shadows, I watched as Barry confronted Moritz about the damage in the house, Raja blamed Axe for frisking them at the party, Pauline asked Gavin why he took Chip's laptop, and Petrel blamed all of them for alienating Reginald. When Katrina's name was mentioned as the person who might have poisoned Reginald, Pauline scolded the men for being chauvinists, and Chill told her to stop being hysterical.

"Everybody needs to calm down," Barry said, motioning with both hands. "The intent behind getting together hasn't changed. As Reginald's friends, we should be the ones to help with his therapy sessions. If you fetch the bag, Sonny, we will get out of your hair."

Moritz snorted. "Here we are again, Barry delegating hands-on work to others. I hope Sonny falls and sues your ass."

"Notice that he means it," Gavin said. "Asking the fire department to fetch the bag isn't an option. It's not an emergency."

"I've got the perfect solution," Chill said, crossing to the table to grab my new bullwhip. "According to Harve, Sonny planned to use this tonight as a party trick to lighten the mood. We've got places to be, so the time has come, sweetheart. Get up on the table."

"Alison," Pauline said, "don't degrade yourself by indulging their frat boy mentality. Petrel, chime in. I'm sure you'll agree."

"Sadly, I might want to use a bullwhip in a dance routine," Petrel said with a twist of eyebrows. "Blame my creative side."

At first, I was in sync with Pauline's reaction to the proposal, then it occurred to me to take a page from Antoine's book. Lean into what people expected. Meet them where they were comfortable and carry out my own agenda. Play it my way, with an unexpected twist.

"As the saying goes, let's make it interesting," I said. "Five direct hits for five hundred bucks. Put your money where I can see it."

With a sad level of zeal, the men started pulling out their wallets, then Axe emerged from the huddle and held up the wad of cash.

"Five *consecutive* hits," Axe stipulated.

"Allow me," Petrel said.

Accepting his hand, I stepped from a chair onto the table, lifted the five-and-a-half-foot, eight-plait, single-belly bullwhip, immersed in darkness except for the candles blazing with golden light on four bamboo posts, smelling of citronella to banish mosquitoes and close enough to feel their warmth. Gauging that the end of the braided lash was too short to harm the backed-up onlookers, I squinted at the bag above me.

"It's too far away," Barry said.

"You're trying to make her fail," Pauline accused.

"I'm pointing out a fact," Barry said.

Faintly, I flashed a satisfying, pre-trick smile.

Above my head, the whip whirled, purring with an attention-grabbing whistle, and then my mind was lasered in on executing the measured strokes of the cattleman's crack to snuff out the candle on my right, followed by the "scoop vacuum" sidearm crack, repeating the actions until all four candles were extinguished. With a final whirl of the whip, I sent a downward lash toward the remote control on the table's edge, plunging the house and yard into darkness, except for the moon and the plumes of smoke curling upward from the extinguished candles.

"Holy *shit*," Axe breathed.

"It's like you've never placed a bet before," I said.

"You got us," Barry admitted. "You didn't specify hitting the bag."

"Alison, I will cherish this moment forever," Pauline said. "Where can I buy a proper bullwhip, and when can I take a lesson?"

"The creative angles of it are endless," Petrel said, reaching up to offer a hand down. "Easy does it, don't twist your ankle."

"Thank you, Petrel," I said.

"Of course." He kissed my hand. "Gentlemen, I think it's only right for you to prove your worth by fetching the bag yourselves."

"Pour me a whiskey," Pauline said. "I'll pull up a chair."

"So much for your wide-eyed innocent vibe," Chill said with a mix of respect and wariness. "What's your follow-up act?"

"Cleaning up after a long day," I said.

With raised eyebrows, I motioned for Axe to pay me.

"Yeah, here's your winnings," he said, smiling to convey his unsavory notion that we might be a match after all. "Your place, or mine?"

Plucking the cash from his hand, I shifted through the bills, verifying the total, and then I extracted a twenty and returned it to Axe.

"Buy yourself something pretty," I said.

To my surprise, Barry stifled a snicker.

Per the plan, Harve's lively chatter distracted the group as I unlocked the kitchen door and looked around the lamplit interior to seal the memory of my hard work in my mind's eye. While Chill yelped after snapping his left testicle with the bullwhip, I reached for the remote control and played a sound recording of someone taking a shower.

With my nitrile gloves on, I slid into Harve's car, released the parking brake, and eased down the lane with the engine off and the door open to avoid a telltale slamming sound. After disappearing into the night, I would emerge from the borrowed ride without a trace, and then, if I didn't balk at the last second, I would vanish from the radar.

* * *

In the airport parking lot, Ted answered my call immediately.

"How are you holding up?" he asked.

"Please tell me you're ready to make an arrest," I said.

"It's hard to disrupt a tightknit group," Ted said. "We'll keep adding pressure until someone cracks. I know you need a moment to reassure your friends. Keep it simple. I'll see you on the other side."

"I think that's a death reference," I said.

Silence unfolded. Ted had hung up.

At an arranged time, I held a conference call with Arlene, Joan, Sue, and Kate to share my news, strictly on a need-to-know basis.

"You've got the protection of a contract?" Kate asked.

"Mom's attorney made it ironclad," I said.

"Let me get this straight," Arlene said. "You've got a signed agreement with the FBI, and they're recognizing your abilities?"

"The team is following an official playbook I spelled out," I said. "This time around, there's a world where the culprits line up in a row and declare their hopes and dreams. As in, 'Sonny, I want your help with tax evasion, gem smuggling, and money laundering,' or 'Sonny, I hate to be a jerk, but I'm not leaving until you're dead.'"

"That's *not* funny," Joan said.

"Joking is a sign of how confident I feel," I said, watching the winking lights of a plane thundering overhead. "I need to sign off. I'm with a team, safe and sound. Mum's the word, capiche?"

The hubbub of their attempts to express questions and concerns was cut off as my index finger pressed the disconnect button.

Still hoping for a sting-nixing miracle, I stacked my camera bag on my suitcase, walked into the echoing terminal, and approached the agent at the counter rather than checking in at a kiosk. A pretty thirtyish woman with a friendly smile, she noted my name and apologized for having to step away. When she returned after calling a man whose phone was submerged in a hot tub, I slid a sheet across the counter.

"Can you verify this information?" I asked.

"I'll give it a shot," she said.

Smiling at first, then turning pale, the agent read the printout outlining the airline's policy against sharing passenger information or offering inappropriate favors to friends, family, or airline employees.

"As a strawberry farmer," I said. "I don't have the time or patience to pin my hopes on a married man. I'm a fan of simple principles like nipping problems in the bud and learning from mistakes."

Realizing she was being given *one* chance, after which she could say goodbye to her dependable job, she nodded tightly.

"Thank you, Miss Littlefield," she said. "Enjoy your flight."

"And best of luck to you," I said.

Mercifully, the TSA line was short.

With Ted's note in hand and the terminal diagram in mind, I passed the cookie vendor and the magazine shop on my way to an announcement speaker blaring information about outgoing flights at different gates. A TV monitor on the wall added to the noise, and passengers were talking to their companions or chatting on their phones. I paused, unable to stop my hands from trembling as I faced hearing Antoine's voice for the first time in days, and possibly for the last time in my life. My hope of leaving a breezy voicemail was crushed within five seconds.

"I can barely hear you," Antoine said. "You're at the airport?"

"I'm late, so I'll keep this quick," I said. "I'll be hopping from island to island in search of whales as part of a magazine article."

"Why did you delay calling me?" Antoine said, suddenly loud and clear as the announcement ended. "This doesn't feel right."

"I favored giving you space," I said. "I know you're rekindling the flame with Zach's mother. I've come to terms with it, so all that remains is wishing each other well and going our separate ways."

"Je le savais, this is Ted's doing," Antoine said. "The agent he sent as a follow-up move was a rookie who got it wrong, Sonny. Cross to a spot where we can talk without background noise."

"I'm sorry, but my circuits in this realm are shot," I said. "You gave a wind-up with a certain tone. I didn't imagine it."

"Sonny, listen to me—"

Pressing my finger against my right ear, I strived to hear him over the blare of an announcement, but his words were garbled.

"What—is—your—flight—number?" Antoine hollered.

With closed eyes, I crumpled Ted's instructions. "I'm glad we got a chance to see each other, but the timing isn't ideal," I said. "Especially for you, but luckily, we forged an agreement. I focus on me. You focus on Zach. And *whoever*. I handled inheriting a farm and all the surprises that came with it. I'm strong, and I'm fine on my own."

Jarred by a shoulder clip, I nearly dropped my phone.

"Sorry," the man said, moving on with a pointed look that told me he was an agent endeavoring to get me to the departure gate.

"What was that?" Antoine asked.

"A distracted guy," I said. "I need to go."

"Sonny, for the love of God—"

"It's a dangerous world, Antoine," I said. "Prepare your son to face it. That's the plan. That's the goal. *Stop* trying to rescue me. It's misguided and unwanted. I'm fine on my own."

A thousand feelings needed to be expressed, but I hung up and fell into power breathing as I neared the gate, gulping air as if I was in a dash for my life, but gripped by the sensation of moving in slow motion. As I showed my boarding pass, the agent had to steady my hand.

"Nervous flyer?" she asked.

"I'm strong," I said. "I'll be fine."

Steadying my luggage as I navigated the junction between the terminal and the enclosed ramp, I felt the embrace of tropical air. Up ahead, two FBI agents in plainclothes confirmed that the flow of passengers had ended. Whirled in place, I protested as my jacket was peeled away and put on by the woman, and then I gulped as a straight-hair wig was jammed onto my head and fluffed to look natural. My hands clutched at my bag for a second, and then I watched the agent tuck it under her arm and glance at my phone. With a toss of curls, she continued down the ramp as if nothing out of the ordinary had happened.

"All clear," the man said into his radio.

The Sonny doppelganger apologized for her late arrival, then the plane's heavy door slammed shut, with the coils of the ramp advancing toward us, as if we'd been swallowed up by a giant snake.

"I'm not strong and I'm not fine," I said tearfully. "I need to check my trail camera. I want to be *her*. I want to go home."

"Take a breath," the agent said. "You look the way I must have done when I was standing at the altar, ready to sign my freedom away. That's how it felt for a second, but then my future wife was walking toward me, like a beam of light on her father's arm, and—"

"Cut the chatter," Ted ordered sharply over the radio.

"Sorry, got it," the agent said.

Together, we stood amid the rush of hot wind thundering from a departing jet, and watched as my intended ride was towed away, past luggage carts and fuel tankers in the darkness, with its interior visible through the rounded windows. Near the wing, a woman with unruly curls smiled at a passenger who took the next seat, and asked if he could tuck her precious camera pack into the overhead compartment. Eager and efficient, ready for the next chapter of her carefully planned life.

"Why can't that be me?" I whispered.

"It is you," the agent whispered back. "Or, near enough."

28

The scent of ocean air and the growl of outboard boat engines were ever-present from the upper deck of the *Kukuna Mahina,* docked at Kahului Harbor on Maui. As I sat at a round table and opened an agency-issued laptop, the wake of a passing yacht splashed against the waterline and flashed in the noon light, intensifying the subtle sensation of being disconnected from land. Now and then, the FBI data specialist in charge of the laptop adjusted the table's large umbrella until my bare ankles and slutty high heels were protected from the fierce tropical sun.

"Is that better?" the agent asked.

"It's perfect," I said. "I've been surprised not to see Harve fulfilling a security role. He's familiar with the vessel."

"Harve is looking into possible associates of the current arrestees," the agent said. "To close the lid during our 'project.'"

"A closed lid feels like a stretch," I said. "Aside from knowns like Mary and RG, ninety tourists have booked passage for the cruise."

"All parties are being vetted," the agent assured me. "Some are repeat passengers suspected of using the networking events to identify who might have cash they're looking to triple in the short term. Behind the scenes, our team is calling the voyage a white-collar crime roundup. Making it a reality has taken months of planning and a lot of hard work."

"*Months* of planning?" I asked. "Interesting."

Turning back to the laptop, I launched Chip's underwater recording of whale calls to sell my claim that I needed to edit his memorial slideshow. In no time, I found Ted's folder of victim files by searching for recently opened items. Eight of the twelve victims were women under thirty. One in particular caught my eye: a twenty-two-year-old female who'd been found clutching a unicorn key fob like the one Reginald had held in front of Ted in the hospital room. Skimming through the personal details, I felt a bolt of shock when I saw that, at one point, Agent Telford had been the victim's foster parent. With her death officially deemed a self-inflicted overdose, he'd quietly absorbed it into his larger case.

After prying into FBI files, I wasn't in a strong position to complain, so I returned the laptop to the agent with a grateful smile.

"Remind me where that whale call was recorded," he said.

"Near the Kama'ehuakanaloa Seamount," I said. "The youngest volcano off the Big Island. It's 3,200 feet below sea level."

"It's funny to hear you sound smart," the agent said, then, awkwardly, he added, "Because of the miniskirt and, you know, the skimpy upper coverage. You're brave to participate in the roundup of johns."

"It's not fair to saddle others with it," I said.

"Now that Reginald is back in gear," the agent said, "he wasted no time in firing the security crew for the lapse of protocol, thereby allowing FBI agents to fill the slots during the cruise. You heard about the kerfuffle when your doppelganger stepped off the plane on Kauai and vanished into the night. Ted had to hold his phone a foot away to prevent hearing loss when Reginald panicked, thinking you'd been kidnapped."

"I figured Ted would have told him the plan," I said.

"Reginald isn't even allowed to attend his own party," the agent said. "All is well that ends well. The pot is stirred to the nth degree."

Ted had scolded me for taking it upon myself to rebuke Barry's contact at the ticket counter, but I had zero regrets about protecting Antoine's privacy. Disrupting Barry's influence made it a win-win.

As Nicole approached along the deck, snapping gum and swinging her hips in a seriously wrong microskirt, the agent lasered his attention on his laptop. Catching on, Nicole reached past him in a way that landed her cleavage within kissing range of his face, and then she settled her sunglasses on her nose and motioned for me to get moving.

"You're up, Littlefield," she said. "Not that we're keeping score, but my technique outstrips your sad efforts by a wide margin. The more randy sons of bitches we eliminate from the passenger list, the easier the final phase of the operation will be."

"I'm told that some of the johns are 'regulars?'" I asked.

"In every sense," Nicole said. "I heard you're still finalizing the memorial service. No wonder you're cast in gloom."

"I like keeping busy," I said.

Nicole grinned. "Use that line on the next guy."

For the third time that day, I tugged down my micro skirt, steadied myself in the high heels that flapped with every step, and left the Hawaiian sunshine behind as I entered the room where a female agent adhered clear patches onto my thighs to capture the fingerprints of aggressive johns. It was a humbling experience, sparking thoughts of the drug addicts and desperate single mothers who were forced to walk the streets and frequent bars, risking their health and lives for a pittance.

Dressed for battle, I stepped into the carpeted bar, where the clatter of plates grew louder whenever kitchen staff stepped through the galley's double doors. With a nod, the FBI agent bartender handed me an unopened bottle of mineral water and a glass filled with ice.

It took just sixty seconds for a sixty-something man to straddle the adjacent barstool as if he'd done it a thousand times.

"Hey, beautiful," he said.

My warning glare was intended to slice him in half, though I had a feeling the effect was diminished by the false eyelashes that instilled a sense of peering through a hedge. No matter. I was determined to rescue the man from his depraved, lesser self.

"Ouch, you remind me of my neighbor's cat," he said.

"I'm waiting for a friend," I said. "Step away."

"Next, you'll tell me your friend is not a man to be trifled with," he said. "But I know it's a part of the game to jack up your price."

"To be clear," I said. "I don't trade sex for money."

"Everything about you proclaims the opposite," he said.

"If a guy walks in here wearing a football jersey," I said. "Would it be appropriate for me to demand that he crouch and hike a ball?"

"Is that a fantasy of yours?" he asked.

Doggedly, I pressed on, "Your ring says you're married."

"Thirty-two years and counting," the john said. "This kind of moment is why we've lasted. Playtime is a critical element."

Unable to endure his creepy gaze for more than a few seconds, I looked across the bar and saw the chef watching me from the galley doorway. As his cigarette flared, adding to his wreath of smoke, all I could see of his face was a dark beard, the short cap typical of his trade, and his silver watch winking at me as if in amusement.

Thanks for the support, I conveyed with a glare.

Abruptly, the john's doughy hand squeezed my thigh so quickly that I flinched, despite two similar experiences earlier in the day.

"What have we here?" he said, encountering the clear tape.

"Fingerprints don't show up well on bare flesh," I said. "Carefully, lift your hand, or you will be dropped with a taser shot."

"Perhaps you've heard that I love the chase," he said. "I have five hundred in cash. If all goes well, we can talk about a trip to Japan."

I hesitated, bound by instructions not to compromise the viability of the bar arrests by delving into specifics of the larger case.

"Why Japan, particularly?" I ventured.

"I've cultivated a side hustle that brings in tax-free money to play with," he said, holding out a hundred-dollar bill. "Here's a down payment. Let's finish getting to know each other in private."

Pulling the microphone on my top a little closer, I said, "I've got an ancient mariner here who needs special assistance."

"You're arranging a threesome?" he said excitedly.

"I'm with an entire team," I said, sliding down from the bar stool. "In the words of Sir Francis Bacon, 'The better information one has, the more one will be able to control events.'"

He frowned. "In what context?"

"Just keep it in mind," I said.

As agents stepped in to introduce themselves, I returned to the fingerprint technician, surprised to find Agent Telford waiting for me with a concerned frown and folded arms. Once the tape evidence was secured, he signaled for the technician to step out for a minute.

"Sonny," Ted said, sitting in the opposite chair with his elbows on his knees. "Instead of taking downtime, you're working on Chip's memorial service and involving yourself in matters that can be handled by agents. It's not surprising that you're withdrawn and sullen."

"I'm not *sullen*," I said.

"Morose," Ted persisted. "Ill-humored, somber—"

"This is what you get when you recruit a citizen volunteer," I said. "I can't wave a magic wand and drop into cryogenic fuel mode."

"I've gotten clearance to offer you a stipend," Ted said.

"I told you what I want," I said. "A fast exit with minimal follow-up. To walk through a door and vanish so I can finish the healing work."

"Where to this time?" Ted asked.

"Provide the ride to shore," I said. "I'll handle the rest."

With a patient look, Ted said, "I'm told that you're grumbling about not having access to your laptop and phone. You're not being singled out. Thanks to the tight lid and targeted messaging, the shell company's major shareholders will be present during the voyage to socialize and strategize before the board meeting that Reginald has scheduled for the morning after his party. He won't be joining the cruise, so—"

"Tell me about Harve's assignment," I said. "Why is he chasing leads when it might have been him on the 1871 Trail?"

"Harve was elsewhere that day," Ted assured me. "As an outside hire, his activities have been carefully scrutinized."

"We're a day away from the official launch for the cruise," I said. "I assume you've vetted the crew from past voyages?"

"Of course," Ted said. "What's got you on edge, Sonny?"

"In the bar just now, the chef was staring at me with an intense vibe," I said. "He was smoking, so I couldn't see his face."

Ted frowned. "You truly felt that he was off?"

"Not off, exactly," I said. "When he took a drag on his cigarette, his watch was winking at me like—" I froze, gripped by a bolt of recognition. "Chip's watch is still in our possession, but the one the chef was wearing was similar. It feels like he wanted me to notice it."

"We'll check it out calmly," Ted said, speaking into a radio to order agents to stay alert in the galley area. "If he's there, hang back."

Leaving my high-heeled shoes behind, I padded beside Ted with a racing heart, daring to hope that I'd sped up the search for connected guilty parties. As a shell company hire, the chef would have been on board during the cruise when Katrina was drugged, stripped down to her underwear, and left to wake up feeling horrified and bewildered.

In the carpeted bar, my bare feet encountered grit and unpleasant wet spots, but I focused on the galley's double-doors, anxious to identify entrances and exits in case our questions sparked the chef's impulse to flee. Pausing to motion for calm, Ted shifted his jacket lapel to allow for quick access to his sidearm as he pushed open the doors and scanned the metal prep stations, ovens, and open stoves.

"This area is restricted," a man warned.

"I need a word with the chef," Ted said, flashing his badge.

"You've found him," the portly man said. "If you're looking for a snack, vending machines are your best bet."

"Where is the *other* chef?" I demanded.

"I'm the top man, and dear God, you can't imagine the fallout if someone of your sort is seen here," he said. "Off you go."

"Sonny, it's easier if you step out for a second," Ted said.

As the double doors closed in my face, I peered through the windows, leaning to the right and left to search every corner of the kitchen. Through the gap between the doors, I heard the chef protest that he had no knowledge of a watch-wearing smoker that day or any day. Afraid that the culprit was being protected, I opened the doors a crack.

"He has an athletic physique," I said.

Ted reached back and shut the doors.

I pushed them open. "And he has a beard."

With a frustrated sigh, Ted stood in front of the doors to prevent me from further attempts to join the discussion as cooks, dishwashers, and waitstaff were summoned by the real chef and questioned. Finally, one of the waiters admitted that he'd seen a stranger taking a cigarette break in the doorway about half an hour earlier.

Through the crack, I asked, "Why didn't you question him?"

"Where is that voice coming from?" the waiter asked.

"Focus on describing the smoker," Ted said.

"There are lots of unfamiliar faces on board," the waiter said. "I figured the crew got fired after the last outing some months ago."

"A woman fell overboard," the chef confided.

"Does the watch-wearing smoker sound familiar?" I said through the crack. "Maybe there's a second galley with different staff?"

"This is the only galley," the chef said, then added, "Why are we being grilled by one of the hookers who frequent the ship?"

"So, prostitution is a known element?" I demanded through the crack.

"Thank you, all," Ted said. "I'll leave you in peace."

Stepping through the double doors, Ted secured my elbow and led me through the bar as I cast glances over my shoulder.

"A different chef was *there*," I insisted.

"I alerted my agents," Ted said. "The security footage will tell us how the smoker got in and out of the galley."

With a grim expression, the agent in charge of surveillance opened his laptop to display a series of blank shots captured by cameras in the connecting corridors. Aside from showing himself to me for ten seconds, the smoker had the vanishing ability of a ghost.

"Ted, the stalker on the 1871 Trail had a beard," I said. "A secret heir, maybe. An unknown. Instead of vetting the crew properly, you've let a top-tier threat throw down the gauntlet in front of me."

"Sonny, we have been vetting the crew for days," Ted said. "Often, an instance like this will end with a kitchen worker admitting that a friend from belowdecks stopped by to grab a snack."

"He was wearing Chip's watch," I insisted.

"I have a silver watch at home," Ted said.

Furious and rattled, I led him to a private corner.

"I found out about your runaway foster child," I said quietly. "Dropped out of high school. Prostitute. Drug mule. Wild child until the bitter end. She overdosed in Hawaii at twenty-two, clutching a unicorn key fob. You failed her in life. Now you're looking for revenge?"

Ted hesitated, and then wilted under my glare.

"You caught on that I was harsh with Reginald a year or so ago," Ted said. "He's got an eye for the ladies. There's no doubt about that, but I've come to see that he's not a predator. He's a patriarch. That's what the lab analyses in Chip's laptop are about. He tracked down possible relatives and collected their DNA from soda cans, dinner napkins, etcetera."

I paused. "Was your foster child related to Reginald?"

"She was a possible grandchild that Chip was endeavoring to confirm," Ted said. "In his eyes, the bigger the family, the better. Reginald related it to the tight bonds that whales experience."

"What about Sally?" I asked.

"As far as I can tell, Sally wasn't on Chip's list of potential relatives," Ted said. "In other words, we're looking at a spectrum of possible motives behind the pattern of deaths. It's important for you to know that I haven't discussed the DNA angle with Reginald."

"You're worried it would inflame him into action?" I asked.

"Look how I'm handling just one close connection," Ted said, rubbing his brow with a look of misery. "It felt like kismet when my wife and I met a foster child named Liberty, who hit it off with our toddlers. It was great until puberty and neighborhood bullies hit the fan. I'll never live down how I reacted when Libby started picking fights with my …"

"With your biological kids?" I asked softly.

"Foster kids have a spooky awareness in that realm," Ted said. "She wanted to expose my flaws as a cop and a father, so she muddied her departure with false trails. I broadcast our intentions, desperate to convey our hope of adopting her officially." Blinking away tears, Ted added, "Libby wouldn't want revenge. She would want justice."

"She's the reason you're a champion of female empowerment," I said. "You want to fill the ranks and create role models."

"It's a goal," Ted said. "At times, it feels like a losing battle."

"Have you sought counseling about Libby's death?" I asked.

"Don't start," Ted said. "You're a fine one to talk."

"Check the crew list," I said urgently.

"I will," Ted promised. "No stone left unturned."

* * *

Midway through a lackluster practice session, I watched Jason step away and towel off his face in the round auditorium that people described as the heart of the *Kukuna Mahina*. With plush, star-patterned seats surrounding the stage on all sides, I felt a flutter of nerves over the prospect of performing in front of over a hundred people in a few days, but Jason's version of stage fright was uniquely connected to the sting.

"It's from seeing you in the hooker outfit this morning," Jason said, arriving in front of me with a look of distress. "I was pumped about getting answers, but not if it means turning you into a bullseye for dirtbags to pursue. What if you're taken by surprise?"

"Let's test it out," I said.

Reaching out to contain me, Jason regrouped fast as I went from being a compliant follower on the dance floor to taking the lead, using my shoulders and core to drive my actions either to evade him or execute counter-moves, including a carefully applied, injury-avoiding armlock, until at last, I was holding Jason face-down on the floor.

"Okay, uncle," Jason managed.

"Satisfied?" I said, helping him to his feet.

With my hands on my hips, I watched Jason pace away, worried that I'd dented his male ego, then I saw that he was smiling.

"I'm having an epiphany," he said. "Dumb guy that I am, I didn't think to look beyond your skill as a follower. Now I've experienced the real you. I'm honored that you trust me to lead, Sonny."

"I had my own scare this morning," I said. "A reminder of how surprises can hit the fan. If the sting is too much—"

"Not a chance," Jason said, cupping my cheek the way a brother might do, gently and without any hint of flirting. "You've sidelined your vacation to right the wrongs, so I'm not about to bail. I know you wanted time to practice on your own. We'll resume in a few hours."

With a parting fist bump, Jason walked away with his tablet in hand, narrating his ideas about our new freestyle routines.

"Perfect timing," Jasmine said, arriving with a burly agent twice my size. "Let's make sure you survive your solo session."

Side by side, we stood out of the way as the agent shimmied up two lengths of sheer fabric hanging from the center ceiling. After testing its strength by swaying side to side across the stage in a graceful sweeping motion, he slid down, dropped to the floor, and deemed the fabric was strong enough to support my weight. To keep the extra piece out of the way, I tied it to a loop along the back wall, where movie screens were poised to provide digital backdrops for performances.

"The auditorium has a cozy feel," I said. "I've lost touch with the sense of being on a ship. It's from the soundproofing, I guess."

"Do you need help with your session?" Jasmine asked.

"I'm making it up as I go along," I said. "Several times, my friend, Sue Black used hypnosis to help me remember details and traumatic events. We're in the lull before the storm, so it's a good time for a deep dive. Don't tell Ted that I'm swinging from the rafters."

"Oops, better luck next time," Ted said behind me.

"I'm looping Jason in on our next fitting session," Jasmine said with a pointed look that asked me to keep her updated. "It's important to match your costumes down to tiny details."

"Got it," I said. "I'll stop in when I'm finished."

Once we were alone, Ted said, "I wanted you to be the first to know that the mystery chef does show up on the security footage after all, coming on board to oversee the delivery of specialty desserts. He paused to have a smoke, admired the way you were putting the would-be john in his place, and left two minutes later. He's not a concern."

"Are you sure?" I asked. "His vibe was very intense."

"If so, it was from admiration," Ted said. "Back to the here and now, I've heard that you're planning to dim the lights and wander around in a state of self-hypnosis. Gosh, what could go wrong?"

"As you can see," I said, tying the fabric noodle around my waist. "I'm on a tether that will keep me from falling off the stage."

"I'll stay on hand just in case," Ted said.

"I'm not in the mood to be thrown off by your sniffing, yawning, and texting," I said. "Shut the door on your way out."

As I lingered for a moment, Ted raised his eyebrows.

"Problem?" he asked.

"Now that I'm tethered, I can't reach the remote control," I admitted.

Once he handed me the device, Ted searched my face, as if weighing his hidden concerns, and then he softened into a smile.

"It seems the mystery chef delivered more than specialty desserts," he said. "Instead of cast in gloom, you're keen and focused."

"I'm back in gear," I said. "Spread the word."

Once I was alone, I adjusted the soft pads of a sleep mask over my eyes and tucked the remote control into my waistband for easy access. First, I stepped forward until my tether stopped me, and then I explored its gentle curbing influence as I moved from place to place. Revolving to wrap the fabric around me, I reversed out of its embrace, memorizing how each moment felt so I wouldn't be startled in my focused state.

Relaxed and softly breathing, I conjured the balsam scent of the forest where my last hypnosis session took place, and imagined the sun flickering over my eyelids. Watching the light, feeling a sense of peace, I pressed play to launch a song from my empowerment playlist. "Hunter," by Björk, began with a stirring beat and ethereal music, then drifted into lyrics that carried me forward, both literally and inwardly.

Reversing back in time, I walked through the airport terminal, where news reports of Chip's death flickered endlessly across television screens. Pausing to look around, I noted the passengers and personnel who crossed my path, including an FBI agent reading a magazine. I took my time to catch any details I might have overlooked, though my main intent was to sharpen my awareness for future surprises and shocks.

Seeker. Searcher. Tracker. For better or worse, I was built to not back down until the puzzling, conflicting, intersecting arrows in my mind aligned into a successful capture and pointed toward home.

29

In front of the mirror in Jasmine's shipboard studio, I admired the fit of the white pantsuit she'd created. For my blouse, she'd used "Pink Plumeria Party" fabric that added a pop of color. With pearl earrings and a plumeria blossom pinned to my lapel, I waited while Jasmine twisted my ponytail into a smooth look on one side and a swath of wild curls on the other. As a finishing touch, I slipped my feet into fuchsia flats and grabbed the clipboard of paperwork that ranged from cabin assignments to official notifications that amounted to extremely bad news.

"Hopefully, you're not still obsessing over being fair," Jasmine said. "You're the boss, bent on upending the status quo, blah, blah. People are staying quiet at the expense of decency and justice."

"I hear you," I said. "I will strive to be ruthless."

With a fist-bump, I put on sunglasses and headed for the gangway, where an FBI agent in a steward's uniform unfurled an umbrella to shield me from the sun. Below us at the end of the ramp, Harve was mixing up the luggage so people arrived in a predetermined order.

"Sonny," Mary said, beaming at me in a Jasmine-designed red hibiscus shirt. "Look at you, all dressed up and in charge."

"We meet again," RG said, puffing from carrying their luggage. "Be aware that others in our group are irritable. When we told them about our free tickets, there was an exchange of confused frowns."

"We had some last-minute cancellations," I said. "It seemed a shame for the cabins to stay empty, so I invited a few friends."

I signaled for a steward to show Mary and RG to their cabins near the berth that Jasmine, Nicole, and I were sharing.

"You there, with the umbrella," Gavin said, winded from hauling his luggage up the ramp. "Why are you standing around instead of helping us with our—" Abruptly seeing me, Gavin turned to Barry standing behind him. "Check out the welcoming committee."

In a handsome blue shirt, the pilot was in the midst of smoothing his cropped salt & pepper hair when he looked up with a start.

"It's like you read my mind," Barry said, almost knocking his luggage into the bay as he hurried to confront me. "Just when a flicker of understanding and shared goals appear out of the chaos, you boil my phone in the hot tub, slice my candles in half, con us into fetching peanuts from the coconut tree instead of the special items, vanish without a word, and then show up here?" Barry added. "It's time to explain yourself."

"Forgive me if I look startled," I said. "I was braced to receive effusive thanks for my hard work, plus fervent apologies for making me feel so raw and harassed that I fled with the clothes on my back."

Barry sighed. "Fine—"

"Never mind," I said brightly. "Due to overbooking, your group has been allotted three rooms. As a shareholder, I'm sure you're aware that it's a safety violation to linger on the gangway."

"*Actually*," Barry said, jangling a cabin key. "Pauline and I get priority access to our luxury suite. I confirmed it online."

Reaching for the key, I tossed it into a trash bin.

"Under our new management policies, your privileges are revoked," I said. "The locks were changed, and since Chip's mother is settled into your former cabin, please refrain from banging on the door."

Barry gaped. "Who gave you the authority to—?"

"Darling," Pauline said. "I imagine Carol is on board to attend Chip's memorial service tomorrow. I don't see why it wouldn't be possible for the men to bunk together. Move along with the luggage."

"I'll catch up with you," Barry said, waiting until Pauline and Gavin departed before returning his glare to me. "People are wondering about the special mementos. I assume you brought them?"

"They're collecting dust at the bottom of my luggage," I said. "To be honest, the memory project was a dumb idea."

"Might I take a crack at it?" Barry asked.

"No," I said. "By the way, Moritz and Raja will be manning the bar. I know, you're angry with them, but they stepped forward with useful information. Please don't clog traffic on the gangplank."

"It's called a gang*way*," Barry said.

Suddenly furious, I said, "How dare you come in with an attitude after having Antoine stalked across the Pacific? I talked to your special friend at the ticket counter. Prepare to be iced out."

"Riff and Chill were too cowardly to admit they used my contacts to track Antoine," Barry insisted. "Hence, *my* phone got trashed."

"Sorry, I'm with Reginald," I said. "Low on trust."

"Super," Barry said. "Welcome aboard, to me."

Watching the seething, muttering pilot depart, I celebrated the dark victory of creating fractures among the alpha males.

Next came Petrel, plucked and pre-tanned to look his best during the cruise. Dressed in white pants and a Hawaiian shirt that caught the sea breeze, Petrel indulged his new habit of kissing my hand upon arrival. I reminded myself to stay guarded. No favorites allowed.

"Forgive Barry's short fuse," Petrel said. "He nearly burst a vessel when he saw that you'd left peanuts in the coconut tree. Perhaps there's a reason you're building suspense around the special items?"

"I have a confession to make," I said.

Petrel stepped closer. "Yes …?"

"You know that Jason has been on the vessel with me for a few days," I said. "It's been eye-opening. *Very* taxing."

"Heavens," Petrel said, looking breathless as he fanned his face. "He's bound to show a certain amount of athleticism."

"Whatever I ask for, he delivers," I purred. "Impetuous and eager to please. Hopefully, you'll be kind when you come to watch."

Petrel hesitated. "Perhaps I'm misreading this thread."

"We're creating some new dance routines," I said. "I'm not a choreographer, but I hope you'll be supportive about it."

"Of course," Petrel said. "Never mind where my thoughts went. I got the message about not blocking the gangplank." Abruptly, Petrel giggled. "Gang*way*, rather. I repeated your mistake."

"We'll talk later," I said.

Sweating and hungover, with his shirt loosely buttoned to show his amped-up muscles and patches of chest hair, Axe motioned me aside, and then tottered backward as the steward stopped him.

"Shit in heaven, *no*," Axe said, squinting against the sun. "What's with the dark lipstick? Never mind. I'm here to relax."

"Sam," I called out, seeing him struggling with sound equipment. "Just bring your guitar and luggage. The speakers, microphones, and related junk will be picked up by an estate agent."

"*Estate* agent?" Axe said. "I'm not dead yet."

"Your net worth is what's dead," I said quietly. "Instead of evolving after multiple sexual harassment settlements, you're like the forever chemicals we hear about in the news. The toxicity never ends. Hence—" I winced and spread my hands. "Reginald is putting an end to your shipboard concerts. It's not good for the brand to let you blast noise and raucous taunts at passing boats and endangered wildlife. You know all this, after Chip got in your face about it. You almost came to blows."

Axe stared at me. "Who told you that?"

"Everyone," I said. "It's common knowledge."

Just then, Sam arrived with a sound system case, favoring his father's intended plans, but looking confused by what he'd overheard.

"You downplayed fighting with Chip," Sam said.

"Sonny is making up shit to cause trouble," Axe said.

"Far from it," I said. "But Sam, Reginald wants to give you a moment in the spotlight as an opener for the dance show."

"Dad?" Sam asked. "Is that all right?"

"It's on the roster, so it's time to start practicing," I said, motioning for Sam to step onward with his load. "We'll catch up later."

Axe's glare never left my face.

"You're trying to turn my son against me?" he asked.

"If a stranger can do that in a matter of days, it would be sad and tell-ing," I said. "And by the way, stop claiming that Shredder's departure is a mystery. Like Reginald, he needs to heal from a confusing void in his life. The death of a loved one. Instead of showing signs of having a better side, you're the shredder in the group, taking what you want, no matter the cost to others. It's over, Alan Richardson. No more calling the shots."

"You're in over your head," Axe said.

"I'm a world apart from the women you've cancelled out," I said softly. "Now, get your self-involved ass off my gangway."

With a wary glance toward my scowling, umbrella-holding escort, Axe summoned a smile that was devoid of warmth.

"I can't wait for Sam's performance," he said.

"That's a start," I said. "Enjoy your stay."

As I glared after the retreating guitarist, Jasmine pulled me aside to report that a complexity had quietly hit the fan.

"I've contained it," she whispered. "But we should hurry."

Leaving the agent to handle the rest of the boarding elements, I fol-lowed Jasmine down the stairs that led to the cabins we'd assigned to Mary, RG, Carol, Jason, and ourselves to form a tight line of homefront defense. We paused to ensure we were alone, then slipped into Jason's cabin, where Katrina was thinly disguised in a work hat and overalls. Far from mending the fence with Jason, she looked stubborn and furious.

"We'll deal with the current wrongness in a minute," I said. "Explain the box of diamonds you brought to the thrift store."

"So much for being on my side," Katrina said.

"I'm not here to make friends," I said, handing her a notarized letter. "In case an enemy is killing his heirs, Reginald stripped you of your inher-itance. Who gave you the box? I need specifics."

"Bear in mind," Jasmine said. "The fact that we're letting you explain yourself is a breach of the rules. Show some respect."

With a pained look, Katrina flipped her hands.

"The box was left in my mailbox with a note that was supposedly from Pop-Pop asking me to bring it to the thrift store," she said. "He professed ignorance. The store owner professed ignorance. To get to the bottom of it, I left the box to see who showed up. When increasingly threatening notes told me to fetch the merchandise, I held my ground. The box would have rotted there if your mother hadn't stepped in."

"Did you preserve the notes?" I asked.

"They're in a bank box," Katrina said. "Notice my lack of reaction to being disinherited. All I care about is getting justice."

"Prove it," I said. "What else can you add?"

"Not to turn the tables," Katrina said. "But picture my shock when Harve showed up after you and I talked and asked to see my photo from the 1871 Trail. I'm like, great, head away on your merry little sting and leave me to deal with the crime boss on my own."

"Ted vouches for Harve's whereabouts," I said.

"I don't trust anyone," Katrina said. "Including the man in the room who upended his worth by kissing another woman."

"I was drugged," Jason said. "Why won't you listen?"

"All right, enough," Jasmine said. "Ted is in a panic after you ditched your security detail. After a minor blow-up, he'll agree to let you stay, but only under strict conditions. You will remain here with Jason. An agent will step in during the times when Jason is performing."

"I'm under house arrest?" Katrina demanded.

"Tomorrow, we're hosting a memorial service for Chip," Jasmine said, holding out a laptop. "To add a personal touch to Sonny's slideshow, you will spend your time creating a voiceover. Not to end on a weird note, but given the possible threat to your life, we've left prepackaged food and beverages. Be aware and careful at all times."

"Are you done pretending to be a grownup?" Katrina asked, unable to suppress a smile. "I know it's out of love."

"Don't get me started," Jasmine said. "I have work to do."

With a roundup motion, Jasmine led the way out of the cabin. In the corridor, when she tapped on the door of the supply closet, it nudged open slightly, revealing two FBI agents squeezed into a small space with desks and various electronics.

"*Never* leave this post unmanned," Jasmine growled.

Receiving nods and salutes, she closed the door.

"I've streamed enough crime shows to know that cops need to tinkle when the killer is close," Jasmine said. "I won't stand for it on my watch."

"Is it true that Reginald isn't allowed on board?" I asked.

"Apparently, his argument with Ted about playing an active role devolved into a thunderous din," Jasmine said. "Neither one of them trusts the other to get it right. Reginald owns the venue, and Ted owns the sting. At least, Ted imagines that he owns the sting."

"I think we're giving him an ulcer," I said. "Let's have tablets ready when we drop the news that we snuck Katrina into Jason's cabin."

Jasmine smiled and initiated a high-five.

"Back to work?" she asked.

I nodded. "All day, every day until we're done."

* * *

Amid the gold light of sunset, with Maui's green hills fading into the distance, I held a fresh plumeria blossom to my nose to inhale its citrus fragrance while Mary, RG, Carol, Jasmine, Nicole and others lined up on my right and sent flowers into a tumbling trajectory into the Pacific. All too soon, like Sally's fleeting life, the blossoms were lost to sight in the ship's churning 20-knot wake. Behind us, a group of strangers had gathered for the informal memorial service near the spot where Sally had tumbled over the railing, either out of respect for the waitress who'd served them on a past voyage or to honor a loved one they'd lost.

"Sonny," Mary said, earnest and lovely in a pink sweater, with her hair stirring in the breeze. "RG and I think you should join us for meals and downtime so we can keep an eye out for trouble."

"My boss wouldn't like that," I said wryly.

"Who might that be?" RG whispered. "On our way here, I could have sworn I saw Agent Telford slip into a control room."

"I can neither confirm nor deny the man's identity," I said.

With a knowing nod, RG said, "Got it."

After we hugged and wished each other a restful evening, I lingered on the deck, savoring the salty freshness of the sea breeze, and waited for the next wrinkle to hit the fan. It took less than a minute.

"Sonny, there you are," Barry said, freshly showered and spiffed up with hair gel that told me his dinner plans were interrupted. "If you would be so kind as to follow me, your input is needed."

"You don't want to pause and pay your respects?" I asked.

"Most of our group paid our respects to Sally months ago," Barry said. "At dawn, the day after we realized all hope was lost."

"Your complaint has to wait," I said. "I'm off duty."

"The mantle of leadership is weighty," Barry said, shepherding me into the corridor and down a flight of stairs. "I'm following the example of others by providing information to curry favor."

"Did you know that 'currying favor' is from a poem about a deceitful horse?" I asked. "A French poem, of course."

"Yes, I did know that," Barry said, arriving at a cabin door where angry male voices sounded like a giant hornet's nest. "We're not playing cards, Sonny. Welcome to the reality you've forged."

With a flourish, Barry opened the door to the sight of Moritz and Raja standing on the coffee table to command attention as they auctioned off the cabin they'd secured, per their practice on every cruise.

"Bartenders are allotted space in the crew quarters," Barry said. "They booked this space for one reason. To profit from it."

"I'm told they do this on every excursion," I said.

"If I'd known, I would have stopped it," Barry said. "This is scalping. Illegal in some states, and wrong for the brand."

"Of course," I said. "Thank you for alerting me."

Stepping over unzipped suitcases with clothes spilling out, I quieted the noisy bids and counterbids and looked toward the doorway to confirm that Ted had understood the need for help and sent two steward-agents who were ready to take Moritz and Raja to the nearest marina if they refused to surrender their cabin key without further fuss.

"What about *your* private cabin?" Moritz demanded.

"I'm sharing with two other women," I said. "Why did you keep using the word 'yen' when you were bartering with Riff?"

"Not that it's any of your business," Riff quickly interjected, "but it's a common term used for all kinds of contexts."

"Let's see if our morality expert agrees," Barry said.

As Riff dove forward to keep Barry from opening the side zipper of a red suitcase, the two men devolved into a struggle that involved elbowing and cursing as they fought for control on the floor.

"Gentlemen, *please*," Petrel said, to no avail.

"Here we go," Barry said, rolling away and climbing to his feet with a wad of Japanese banknotes. "Exactly as described."

"What is wrong with you?" Riff demanded, flushed and furious. "You have no right to question my hobbies, or dig through my luggage like a—wait a minute, explain 'exactly as described.'"

"You have a snitch in your midst," Moritz said, patting Sam's shoulder as he left. "Sweet dreams, two-faced cheats."

"Sam, what the hell?" Riff said.

"How was I supposed to know it's off the list of permissible subjects?" Sam asked. "I was drinking from stage fright and lost track of Raja refilling my glass. It's new to me to perform alone."

"Drinking will make it worse," Petrel said.

"Sam, I'm sorry for not checking with you first," I said. "We'll set aside time to talk about it. For now, the group can divvy up the cabins as follows: Axe and Sam; Gavin and Petrel; Chill and Riff."

With that, I nodded in thanks to the agents, who'd brought a shipping package to spare me a trip to the control room. With the padded envelope in hand, I retreated past the luggage and stepped into the corridor, only to find Barry and Gavin following on my heels.

"I didn't wage battle with a suitcase for nothing," Barry said. "On top of trashing my house, Riff has been sneaking foreign currency through customs in his drum set. Where's your outrage?"

"I'm hungry," I said. "It's dinnertime."

"*Barry*," Pauline said from a nearby doorway. "Instead of being ready on time, as promised, you're a rumpled mess."

"He was fighting with Riff," I said.

"Dear God, you were a *part* of the din?" Pauline asked.

"Sonny, stay put," Barry said. "I'll be back in one minute."

Once the pilot entered his cabin, Gavin stepped closer.

"This gives us a chance to talk," he said quietly. "At the snorkeling site, I didn't want to shock you, but the truth of the matter is that Moritz might have played a role in his mother's death."

"Did you tell the police?" I asked.

"To no avail," Gavin said. "We'd divorced and I was living elsewhere, so I couldn't provide specifics. A careless police officer conveyed my suspicions to Moritz. You've seen the result. He's vengeful to the point where I was forced to store some of my valuables elsewhere."

"Such as?" I asked.

"The necklace box," Gavin whispered. "The thrift store has a security system and a trustworthy owner, or so I believed. I'm willing to see your mother's involvement as a misunderstanding and a mistake. All is forgiven if the diamonds are safely returned."

"I'm so glad to clear this up," I said, slipping a business card from my pocket. "If you reach out to my mother's attorney, he'll verify your records against the Gemological Institute of America serial numbers engraved on each of the diamonds. They're 3 carats, well-cut, and eye-clean, so I assume they're from a legitimate source?"

"That was my understanding, but scams and rip-offs are rampant these days," Gavin said. "Rest assured, I will sort it out."

"Gavin, regarding your wife's death—"

"I was told quite firmly to leave the theorizing to the police," he said. "Here's Barry back in one minute, as promised."

With a bright smile as he stepped away, Gavin didn't appear to hear Barry asking if their dinner plans remained unchanged.

"What's up with him?" Barry asked.

"He'll either tell you or he won't," I said, shoving the envelope into Barry's hands. "I expedited your purchase of a replacement phone with all the features that normal channels couldn't handle."

Barry paused. "My new phone is in this package?"

"I'm forced to favor your claim of innocence," I said. "But the jury is still out. Stalking fits your pattern of poor judgment."

"Let's agree that mistakes were made on both sides," Barry said. "With a surprise board meeting in the wings, we can't afford to devolve into petty squabbles. As sensible adults, we're outnumbered."

"I definitely feel outnumbered," I said.

"That's because you're not appreciating the underlying stresses people are facing," Barry said. "For instance, a clause in Axe's contract stipulates that if an original member quits, the band's stability is at risk. I can see all sides of the issue. I'll vote however Reginald wants."

"What about Riff's foreign currency venture?" I asked.

"What I pulled out was a small amount," Barry said. "From what I've gathered, it's a one-time thing Riff did on behalf of a friend, so I'm content to believe that he's learned his lesson."

"If that's the norm," I said.

"That's settled," Barry said, turning toward Sam as he arrived with his backpack and guitar case. "They kicked you out?"

"No, I'm hanging out with a few friends," Sam said.

"That's great, Sam," Barry said. "Good for you."

As the pilot stepped away, Sam flipped him the bird.

"Stupid asshole, of course they kicked me out," Sam said. "No matter. I've arranged to bunk with Moritz and Raja."

"I'll find a free cabin," I said.

"No need for that, I'm cool with it," Sam said, pulling his phone from his pocket to launch a video. "Here, check this out."

Shot from the pit during a concert, Axe looked the part of a rock star, illuminated by spotlights, dressed in tight jeans with his shirt open, his gaze rapt as he blended chords with haunting guitar licks. His innate talent was apparent, though the effect was lessened as the swirling rush of sound was made tinny by a cell phone.

"It's an impossible bar, hence my version of stage fright," Sam said. "Plus, I'm supposed to tell you that artists need to stick together. You can't let this kind of talent end in the trash heap."

"In effect, you *have* delivered the message," I pointed out.

"Yeah, that's me, pitching in even after being pitched out," Sam said, tucking his phone away. "Given your farm and close ties in Maine, I'm also supposed to ask why you're messing up our lives."

"The so-called adults are doing it all on their own," I said.

"My father is ranting that the system is rigged," Sam said. "But when that video was taken, I was alone in a hotel room at six years old. Don't look sad. I'm stating a fact that I had to deal with the same way you apparently did, living under the roof of a tyrant."

"I didn't let Donald Littlefield crush my inner spirit," I said softly. "Is anything in particular on your mind?"

"There's a reason Robin Hood is considered a hero," Sam said. "Just because Moritz is jerk doesn't mean he's wrong."

"Let's tap the brake on that concept," I said.

"Ten minutes ago, you overlooked the fact that Riff is profiting from smuggling foreign currency," Sam said. "Barry will drop it as well because he's got his own secrets. Katrina snuck onboard, and Harve is coming and going in a weird pattern, so like I said, I'm pitching my tent next to the only guy who's speaking truth to power."

"You've seen Harve on board?" I asked.

"So much for being in charge," Sam said wryly.

Feeling a whisper of air, I saw that Moritz had cracked open the stairwell door. When I saw him, he leaned into view.

"You want a key to our quarters, or not?" Moritz asked.

"I was explaining the Robin Hood concept," Sam said, grabbing his pack and guitar case. "Sonny is in the same boat."

"You're still up for a solo performance?" I asked.

"I'll be there," Sam said. "I won't let you down."

As he followed Moritz through the doorway, I blew out a breath as I looked toward the security camera through which Ted and other agents had presumably tuned in. Instead of the leisurely dinner and downtime we needed, we were in for a night of fact-checking. On the plus side, doo-doo had hit the fan in hours instead of days.

30

After a long day of watching security footage and listening to conversations through a headset, my eyes burned, and my ears felt overheated and numb. Behind me, Ted was fast-forwarding through a tracking map that showed colored dots representing the Kona group attending Chip's memorial service, drinking and playing cards together, dining together, and in general, thoroughly enjoying their cruise on the *Kukuna Mahina*.

"All right," Ted said. "Let's have a quick huddle."

"It's a waste of time," I said, tossing the headset onto the desk in our makeshift office. "Instead of rattling people into making mistakes, they've done the opposite. The culprit is laughing at us."

"On the white-collar crime front—"

"Yes, we've landed some slaps on the wrist," I said, pacing to the window to glare at the Pacific. "Money laundering, tax evasion, gem smuggling. Nobody cares about that kind of petty stuff."

"It's a mainstay of my profession," Ted pointed out.

"We're here to catch a *murderer*," I said, grabbing the folder of victim photos and slapping it in front of Ted. "Instead of honing in on guilty behavior during the memorial service, there wasn't a dry eye in the auditorium. The players supported Carol in her grief, and all of a sudden, they care about whales. Money is pouring into nonprofits, and there's a new push to rid the ocean of ghost gear. It makes my blood boil."

"It's funny how irritation can twist our minds around," Ted said.

"Maybe you didn't hear the latest from Nicole," I said. "With the hookers out of the picture, she's the only hot chick in the bar. She wowed *my* ex-boyfriend, an upstanding trooper with some semblance of a moral code. Axe walked Nicole to her cabin to ensure she was safe and kissed her hand like a gentleman. It's a bizarro world."

"I'm not sure if it's kosher to say so," Ted said, "but I miss your gloomy side. The cryogenic fuel version derails from time to time."

"It's the feeling that always hits me in the final stretch," I said, rubbing my brow. "That I've overlooked something obvious."

"The hypnosis session didn't pan out?" Ted asked. "Clearly not. For all we know, we've missed ten elements, but it's balanced by ten wins, including getting answers on Katrina's experience."

I straightened. "Tell me. I'll keep it to myself."

"Before his attorney shut him up, the bar john that you referred to as the ancient mariner blurted that on an earlier trip, he contrived to spend five minutes of—" Ted closed his eyes, then pressed on, "He's fond of breasts, and Katrina's dancing captivated him. His attorney slammed the door, but we know the mariner was suspected of hustling currency. We believe he tried to hide it by enlisting Riff's help. He's refusing to admit anything beyond his 'mistake' in talking to a prostitute."

"No doubt, he'll claim Katrina invited him to her cabin," I said with disgust. "What if he did more than apply the oil?"

"Harve visited the ancient mariner's wife and obtained permission to access their home computer," Ted said. "He found footage from the night in question, with a timeline of activity that supports Katrina's sense of a quickly abandoned plan. It's unclear if the mariner had the know-how to erase the footage from the vessel's hard drive and keep a trophy file, or if he had help. With inadequate staffing, Harve prioritized searching for Sally. The control room was unmanned for hours."

"It's nice to have answers for Katrina," I said. "Otherwise, the current moment feels like what Isabella experienced on the *Nevada* when the vessel hit the Tropic of Capricorn. Scorching, airless days with the sun beating down from above. The case has hit the doldrums."

"During that part of the voyage, a flying fox bat landed on the vessel's rigging," Ted said. "If you're looking for edgy costume ideas, Isabella described the creature as having four-foot wings, a pointed face, huge black claws, and a 'savage, remorseless expression.'"

"The *Nevada's* crew captured and tamed the bat by feeding it figs," I said. "With a goal of adding it to a zoological collection in San Francisco, so it's not a story with a happy ending. Carol left the vessel to head home after Chip's memorial service, but with Mary, RG and other innocents in the audience, shouldn't we lean on subtle messaging?"

"In a boxing match," Ted said, "it's useful to drill an opponent in the gut to make him lower his gloves away from his face."

"I hear you," I said. "I'll give it some thought."

* * *

To round out a convincing show experience, Jasmine marshalled the talents of FBI agents who sang "Rolling Down to Old Maui" and other lively sea shanties from the 1800s, filling the auditorium with a stirring mix of tenor, baritone, and bass voices. Another agent tested his wits and courage with a stand-up comedy routine that landed well.

Through the sheer curtains, I could hear whispers amongst the audience as I crossed to the center of the stage, and they could glimpse my shadow reaching up to slip my wrists into the loops that Jasmine had sewn on the ends of the two lengths of fabric attached to the ceiling.

With my bare feet planted wide, I appreciated my costume's excellent fit, with lace hand shapes covering my torso. Flaring out from my hips and softly rustling as I moved was a tutu made of stiffened fabric, cut to resemble tropical ferns, flowers, and flowing grass stems. Fake lashes gave drama to my eyes, and my lips were painted into an exaggerated pout. In creating the costume, Jasmine, Jason, and I had left my character open to interpretation: a woman, a symbol of the land, or both.

Once the sheer inner curtains parted and "Numb" by Oh Land played over the speakers, I leaned forward into an arch, then backward, in sync with the haunting music, a character absorbed, lightly dancing within her own little world. In a dark suit embellished with shimmering upside-down eyes, Jason conducted spins around my tethered character.

During an uptick in the music, Jason fell into rhythm with my dancing, sculpting me into a leg extension and then a slow-motion dip. As the song rose and fell, from a sinuous tempo to percussion beats, I followed Jason's lead, checked and guided through tango footwork until my tethers halted us. Clasping my right hand, Jason spun me until I was mummified, then unfurled me into a dip with his hand on my ankle and my toe pointed, pausing in synchrony with the music. Behind me, with his hands on my waist and my arms upraised, Jason shifted onto his right foot, then his left foot, drawing me into a swaying cadence, like a palm tree in a storm, seaweed stirring in the surf, or a woman in a swoon.

As the music led us onward, I felt our partnership so keenly that, as in rehearsal, I let emotion well up and tears flow, smearing my makeup. With a murderer at large, it might be useful to appear vulnerable.

In advance of the song's finale, I performed two solo spins and channeled my momentum into a tight cartwheel, with Jason gripping my forearms to send my legs into an upside-down half-split.

Facing the audience, I held my pose as blood rushed to my head while Jason spun me into the tethers, with my ankles flexed for a secure hold. As the song ended in echoing beats and Jason slipped into the shadows, my character blinked, more ensnared than ever.

At once, Jasmine closed the curtain and Jason returned to unfurl me and land me on my feet. Breathless, I high-fived him and tucked earpieces into place to eavesdrop on the front-row seats that had been bugged. After a tumult of applause, I could identify each voice.

"A cutting routine about a controlling dance instructor," Axe said. "I'm surprised to see you clapping and smiling, Petrel."

"If there's an intended jab, it's directed at Neanderthal behavior, *Axe*," Petrel said. "But strive to see the deeper theme of conflict and temptation. Humans exploit each other, and the land."

"I don't think Sonny's makeup was smearing from exertion," Mary said softly. "I noticed Gavin slipping away during the marvelous sea shanties. I hope it's not the beginnings of a shipboard illness."

"The sea air gives him headaches," Pauline said.

"Someone should tell him he lives on an island," Axe said.

Chill snorted. "More likely, Gavin is having a good time while we're watching dance routines about how men suck."

"If you took it that way, it's telling," Pauline said.

"While Gavin is away," RG said, "Is anyone else disturbed to hear him posing theories that Moritz murdered his mother?"

"I don't have trouble picturing it," Riff said. "Having Moritz locked up would convince me that there is a God."

"*Everyone*," Barry said sharply. "It's Reginald's birthday, and for all we know, he's in a balcony seat shaking his head over people talking about shipboard illnesses and awful past events."

"Yes, let's respect the occasion," Petrel said. "After Sam's performance, the final routine is 'Lasting Impressions.' Very tame."

As I headed offstage to change costumes, I had news for anyone who expected our last routine to fit the definition of "tame."

* * *

During the intermission, Jasmine, Jason, Katrina, and I formed a half-circle around Nicole as she previewed a video that would fade in and out across the stage's curved back wall, showing locations where the victims were found, with tumbling photos of the thrift store items as graphic elements. As a last touch, Nicole had added a video showing Sally smiling and waiting tables in the background during a past cruise.

Looking furious as he arrived, Ted said, "We're five minutes out from the final routine. Why is Katrina in plain sight?"

"Gavin tried to get into her cabin," I said. "When agent-stewards dove in, Gavin claimed a headache had mixed him up. It's possible he thought it was my cabin. People think I brought the thrift store items, so he used the distraction of the show to look for the diamonds."

"You didn't think to alert me?" Ted demanded.

"You're busy finalizing the party coverage," Nicole said. "With no time to pivot, I decided it was best to bring Katrina here."

"I will escort Katrina back to her cabin," Ted said tersely. "Sonny, after your routine, Nicole will bring you to the control room. No more surprises.

We'll stage interactions with the players in strategic locations with eyes and ears in place. Until then, you will stay put."

With a sigh, I said, "The only way to know if the dance routine strikes a nerve is to question people directly afterward."

"Do—you—hear—me?" Ted growled.

"Yes, I hear you," I murmured.

With a defiant look, Katrina evaded Ted's grasp to hug me.

"Jasmine told me about the ancient mariner," she said. "I know there's more awfulness to uncover, but I wanted to tell you that I'm in your corner, and on my way back to the old me. The real me. And don't underestimate the boy's club. They operate as a pack."

"Focus on keeping yourself safe," I said.

Once she and Ted stepped away, I removed my stage robe and waited as Jasmine made last-minute tweaks to my costume.

"Okay, we're good," she said. "Let's see it in motion."

Smoothly, I performed a few practice steps and hip gyrations in my mid-heel dance shoes, with my hair tamed by faux stiletto knives, my torso wrapped in a sheath of feather symbols, my legs bare all the way up to my Brazilian wax, my backside more exposed than decorum allowed, half-hidden by a silky skirt of hip plumage that would flare out dramatically during spins, and my right calf wrapped in a hawk's tether.

With his robe removed, Jason was revealed as a dark bird of prey with a crimson neckline Jasmine had created to hint at a "pirate of the sky" frigate bird. With shoulder pads and silver feather shapes extending beyond his silhouette, the costume highlighted Jason's larger size and power compared to my comparatively bare female character.

"After the routine," Nicole said, "I'll give you five minutes to visit the group, then you will comply with Ted's wishes."

Nodding, I said, "I'm ready."

Painted with hawk features, Jason embraced me in an offset position and gave the nod for Jasmine to open the curtains and launch "Waiting for the End" by Linkin Park, a song that offered build-ups, crescendos, and a storytelling framework for our freestyle routine.

In sync with the song's extended lead-in, with my right hand in Jason's clasp and upraised, I gradually eased downward from Jason's forward lean, a first demonstration of his character's power over me, with my left foot sliding slowly backward along the floor, then as drums echoed above us, he drew me into swift turns and tandem footwork, followed by a sensual dip with my body draped and his hawk face looming over me.

Up close, we could feel each other's focus and fast breathing, with his hips and shoulder rotations sending me outward into a side-by-side open fan, and then pulling me inward through a spin. Smoothly, like a magician showing both sides of an object, Jason clasped my hands and revolved his arms over me to pivot me in front of him, blurring the lights but keeping me on a tight vertical axis in his spread-foot stance.

Spun outward, I fell into a cadence of pushing Jason's chest away as he advanced, with his hawk-like character appearing to run in place in slow motion, and his shoulder feathers flaring like an animal's hackles. With his hand on my back and the room blurring, I arched into the force of his in-place revolutions, then Jason gradually slid his extended leg between my feet to invite me into a cadence of saucy steps.

As the music intensified, we joined in our offset embrace for a series of flicks beneath each other's knees in a swift tango cadence. Breathless and focused, I relished the sensation of a sudden shoulder check that drew me against Jason with my right leg snagged over his hip.

Ever persistent, the hawk loomed close behind me, sculpting me into a body roll. Released into a spin, intensely focused, I gripped Jason's hands and felt his use of strength and momentum to launch me into a handstand split, with his hawk gaze below me. His grip tightened as I swung down and landed on my feet, and then he spiraled me to the floor like a man cutting a hole in ice with an auger, relentless until I was stretched out on my back. With my arms tucked in, I was aware of the auditorium blurring and Jason's character approaching in a dramatic knee walk.

Abruptly still, I closed my eyes as Jason lifted my limp back from the floor in the same second that the song ended, as if his character was saying to himself, *She's not responding. What have I done?*

The curtain closed amid applause that I only half-heard, then Nicole darted in to hand me a palm-sized recorder identical to the one Sally had used during the last moments of her life. Forcing a smile and a false front of calm, I joined hands with Jason and bowed when the curtains opened, then as the spotlight went out, I tucked earbuds into place and listened in on the front row as I descended the stage steps.

"The underlying theme is clear," Pauline said. "Surviving the heartache of a cheating ex takes more than five minutes."

"Indeed," Petrel said. "In the end, the ex refuses to let her go, and we're left hanging. Has she learned, or will she go back?"

"How is that possible?" Barry asked. "Her character was dead."

"Nonsense," Petrel said. "She was portraying a swoon."

"Imagine how my head feels now," Gavin said. "The video background should have come with a warning about flashing lights."

"Photos of the keepsakes were included in the video," Chill said. "Why would Sonny do that if they're not relevant?"

"Apparently," Sam said, "I'm the only one who thinks the first routine was about feeling out of control. Everyone is upset from Pop-Pop pulling the strings. By all accounts he's not on board, but I saw a guy coming out of a closet with a file box near the captain's suite."

"Says the dumbass who's bunking with Moritz and Raja," Riff said. "What's the going rate for selling your soul?"

"It's *your* fault that I got kicked out," Sam said.

"Enough," Barry said. "Head for the exit."

With a rustle of hip feathers, I emerged from the shadows. Partly from exertion, but mostly from my resolve to get answers, my hand shook a little as I held out the recorder for the group to see.

"During the intermission," I said, "This was found on the floor near your seats. One of you must have dropped it."

Frowning as he studied the device, Axe exploded.

"No more polite approach," he growled, nearly tearing my costume as he gripped my arm. "Why do you have it in for me?"

"I've warned you about your temper," Barry said, shoving the guitarist away. "And I told you not to hit the booze."

"Let him talk," I said. "Why is he blowing up?"

Motioning for his group to take over calming Axe, Barry pulled me aside, raised his eyebrows, and spread his hands.

"What the hell, Sonny?" he demanded.

"Ditto," I said. "Why are you defending him?"

"Sonny, you boiled my phone in front of witnesses," Barry said. "I have latitude in how I handle that and other red flags."

Snagging his collar, I whispered, "Imagine a man so eager to get a sale agreement signed that he resorted to forgery, not realizing his practice signatures would be found months later and pieced together. Even worse, a leaky pen left some unfortunate fingerprints."

Released from my grasp, Barry glanced toward his wife to make sure she was focused on helping Riff and Chill calm Axe.

"How is that relevant to me?" Barry managed.

"It explains why you took a quiet approach to repairing the house," I said. "Reginald, who co-owned the property, was fractious and very loud, spouting conspiracy theories about people sneaking behind his back and ripping him off. Who's covered in red flags now?"

I paused, letting a tense silence play out.

"Did you drug Reginald to get what you wanted?" I asked.

"*Shh*, keep your voice down," Barry whispered. "Reginald's erratic behavior is the reason I acted out of desperation. There were times when he looked high. I assumed it was his own doing."

"Friends are supposed to help friends," I said.

"Focus on now," Barry said. "How much does Reginald know?"

"Careful," I said. "Here comes your inquisitive wife."

"Barry," Pauline said, studying him closely. "I thought you were trying to smooth things. You look like you're having a stroke."

"Nonsense," Barry said, casting me a look that urged restraint until we could talk later. "I was congratulating Sonny."

"Look at this fun plumage," Petrel said, smiling as he fluffed my hip feathers. "With the makeup, there's an edge to it."

As Mary and RG stepped closer to deliver hugs, looking sunburned and radiant from their relaxing cruise, I let go of my urge to chase after Barry, especially as Nicole arrived with a pointed gaze.

"One quick thing," RG whispered. "Axe and Sally were more on-and-off than we knew, even after she signed an NDA about what Axe describes as a bogus story. At one point, Sally complained that the cash was running out too soon and wished Axe had seen the light."

I paused. "Sally wanted him back?"

"You know how it goes," RG said.

As they stepped away, I looked past them toward a flare of light from an exit door. A bearded figure dressed in black was briefly in view, no more than a silhouette, before he slipped out.

"Nicole," I said. "That was the bearded chef."

"Stop being paranoid, it was a bearded agent Ted assigned to keep your bare butt safe," she said. "Lest I get *my* butt handed to me, you will come quietly, as promised, for your rest period."

"Nicole, the group reacted to the videos," I said. "Axe reacted to the recorder, and I provoked Barry to the point where Pauline asked if he was having a stroke. Cooling my heels is a mistake."

"Here's the trouble," Nicole said. "Even a tough nut like Ted ends up terrified that you don't come with safety features."

"It's my decision to make," I insisted.

"The party won't be in full swing for a few hours," Nicole said. "In the meantime, I'll bring you a diet cola and celery sticks."

"A diet cola?" I asked. "And *celery* sticks?"

Nicole cracked up. "You're gullible beyond words."

"It suits me for you to think that," I said.

Ted as well. I had definitely seen the chef.

31

"I'm sorry to limit you to a general look-see at our security footage operation," the technical expert said, turning toward me from his side-by-side computer screens to repeat his apology. "Ted wants to be present when you review any of the security camera feed. That way, if you identify something concerning, he can respond alongside you."

"I understand completely," I said.

Long ago, I'd learned that people who'd risen to the top of a specialized field enjoyed having an appreciative, semi-informed audience. With nods when my remarks were on target, and gentle corrections if I misunderstood his intentions with certain keystrokes, the agent in charge of monitoring security camera footage across the vessel kept most of his attention trained on the wide screens showing different angles of the stewards and waitstaff preparing tables for Reginald's birthday party, along with the feed coming in from stairwells and corridors.

"I heard you've been feeling downcast about the lack of progress," the agent said. "Slow and steady is the nature of the game."

"We've outed some white-collar crime activity," I said.

"Don't discount the importance of the small wins," he said, taking a swig of soda from his jumbo-sized cup, and then he paused with a confused frown. "I swear this was empty a minute ago."

"I've been keeping it topped off for you," I said.

"I've downed three cans?" the agent asked, staring at the empties lined up on the desk amid a clutter of cables and wires. "Let's put a pause on the beverage front. I'm stuck here for five more hours."

"That's a *long* time," I said. "Do you mind if I meditate?"

"Sure, whatever," the agent said.

Rolling my chair away from his workstation, I reached for a glass of water I'd set aside and slowly poured it into an empty cup, filling the room of winking lights with a resonant trickling, dribbling sound, like an unchecked faucet, and then I reversed direction.

"The tinkling of water helps me relax," I explained.

"It's having an effect on me as well," the agent said tightly.

"To be honest, I'm feeling so tense that I'm *bursting* at the seams," I said. "Events keep gushing at me nonstop. The pressure is unbearable, like a giant, painful dam that's about to burst. Until we get answers, we will flow onward. We'll go, and go, and go …"

"Listen, umm, I'm losing my focus a bit," the agent said. "The timing isn't ideal, but can you man the room for a minute?"

"Absolutely," I said.

"You're scheduled to join the party at 8 p.m.," he said. "Forty-five minutes from now to get agents in place, etcetera."

I frowned. "Has a specific threat surfaced?"

"I'm only told the basics," the agent said.

"Me as well," I said. "I'll roll with it."

"Thank you, Sonny," he said. "You're an ace."

As his footsteps faded down the corridor, I rolled my chair to the desk, typed in his password, and with a few keystrokes opened a folder labeled "Activity; Captain's Suite" to see if anything could be gleaned from the footage. The first video showed a man emerging from a storage closet with a file box of paperwork, a curious detail Sam had mentioned to his group. Zooming in, I saw Harve's thick torso and "private eye" cap. Through the following clips, I tracked his journey down a flight of stairs to a door on the lower deck marked with a danger symbol.

"What's being destroyed in the incinerator room?" I murmured.

Checking a folder deemed "Not Relevant," I stared in shock to see more than one clip of the bearded chef slipping in and out of view in dark clothing and a baseball cap. In every instance, he appeared and disappeared at the far end of the frame, as if he knew where the cameras were positioned and took pains not to be filmed. In the most recent clip, the faux chef slipped in and out of view with Agent Telford beside him, and it wasn't a pursuit scenario; they were calmly talking.

"Ted, *what* are you up to?" I fumed.

Casting about for a USB stick, I downloaded both folders and scribbled a note for the agent to buy myself some time:

Following your lead with a bathroom break, and I need a sweater so I can stick to the schedule. No worries, I'll be back in a flash!

In the doorway, I checked to be sure the corridor was empty, then I slipped out and headed for the cabin I was sharing with Jasmine and Nicole in keeping with my note, but once inside, I tucked my curls under a baseball cap and disguised myself in the hoodie Nicole used for jogging. Leaving the cabin, I stretched from side to side just like Nicole always did, and trotted to the nearest stairwell with several goals in mind.

First, I wanted to know if Reginald had slipped aboard to attend his birthday party. Racing up the stairwell, I paused on the landing as I heard Chill talking with Axe and Riff near the captain's suite.

"What does it mean that my bank account number flashed by in the video during the dance routine?" Chill asked. "An offshore fund the tax man doesn't know about. Reginald is messing with us."

"Axe," Riff said. "Why are you suddenly calm?"

"Because I've got a card of my own to play," Axe said. "Reginald isn't immune to having secrets. There's an art to quid pro quo. If he's motivated enough, he'll change his tune about our contract."

"Here's an idea," Sam said. "Instead of threatening your backer, seek treatment for the issues that buried you in NDAs."

The sound of a scuffle and a yelp told me Axe might be shoving Sam against a wall, then amid Axe's apologies, furious footsteps were heading toward me. Sliding down the railing like a wayward child, I lurched across the landing, yanked open the door, and ducked into a restroom.

"Is anyone there?" Sam called out.

Hearing silence, he muttered and stepped away.

Once the coast was clear, I descended to the lower level, hoping to find the file box that Harve had carried out of the closet near the captain's suite. Depending on the nature of Sally's non-disclosure agreement, someone might be trying to erase an ugly moment in history.

I paused as I reached the lower deck, aware of the engines thrumming and a chilly dampness that I attributed to deep ocean water surging past the hull. Picturing schools of fish stirring in the darkness, I closed my eyes against the nightmarish image of Sally kicking and flailing and expelling bubbles as she screamed her last breath of air.

"Sonny?" Sam said.

"*Jesus.*"

Clutching my chest, I managed, "I'm supposed to check an engine gauge. For the … cross-head … piston … cylinder."

"Sonny, I caught sight of you fleeing down the stairs," Sam said with a twist of eyebrows. "Maybe you're visiting the incinerator room to make sure that certain documents went up in flames?"

"It's the opposite," I said. "It's thanks to you that I know about the file box being taken out of storage. It struck me as odd."

"To me, it feels like par for the course," Sam said. "As young adults, we can't afford a place of our own and we can't win a seat at the table and we can't buck the system because the system is rigged."

"The box truly put your hackles up?" I asked.

"The guy I saw looked like Harve," Sam said. "It seemed all the fishier when you claimed not to know that he's on board."

"I'll check it out," I said. "Head to the party."

"Out of the question," Sam said, experimentally opening the door with the danger symbol. "Rule number one with searches of spooky rooms is to stick together. I see the box. It's right over there."

"With papers spilling out," I agreed.

"Okay, you stay here," Sam said. "I'll dash in and grab a handful of documents. If I get jumped, scream and save yourself."

"I'm usually the one to go in first," I said.

"I've got skin in the game," Sam insisted.

Like a youth revving up to jump into a cold lake, Sam rocked in place for a second, and then he darted into the room, skidded to the box on his knees, and wrenched out a handful of papers. Lurching upward, he dashed toward me and arrived with a look of triumph.

"*Bam*, I got it done," Sam said.

"Never celebrate prematurely," I cautioned.

Crossing to the nearest light in the corridor, I saw stapled passenger lists from years before the vessel was sold. Shifting that batch aside, I fell into confusion as I studied the next page, then the next.

"What the hell?" I managed.

With a sheet in hand, Sam said, "It's in a foreign language."

"It's gibberish," I said, reading the familiar lines aloud, "consequatur laborum porro est quia delectus explicabo. It's called Lorem Ipsum, a form of dummy text used by the printing industry."

On my way into the incinerator room, I scanned the interior for shadows or whispers of sound, furious enough to *want* someone to step into view with a sly look. Instead, I saw bags neatly stacked. For all I knew, the FBI had removed the room's attendant from the roster due to a past indiscretion that posed a problem during the sting.

Kneeling in front of the box, I found receipts for supply deliveries and passenger lists mixed in with Lorem Ipsum text while Sam, undaunted by the gibberish, massaged his chin as he studied each sheet, sparking unhelpful memories of Dan falling into the same habit.

"It's odd, but explainable," I said. "Amid creating new designs for the brand, a printer malfunctioned. It happens."

"Or, they're hiding stuff with a secret code," Sam said.

I hesitated. "Who's coming to mind?"

"Pop-Pop, for one," Sam said. "His rules set the standard for most of my life. Lately, it's Barry setting the ground rules. He's the only one who could ever beat Pop-Pop at cards. I've always wondered if Sally's nondisclosure agreement was Barry's form of revenge."

Gently snagging Sam's arm, I took the sheets from his hands to remove the distraction, and urged him to take a breath.

"Explain your theory," I said. "Take your time."

"We don't *have* time, Sonny," Sam said. "If I'm not mistaken, your first dance routine was about feeling like a puppet. If you didn't catch on, the recorder you found is the kind my father uses when he's out and about so he can keep track of lyrics when he's writing a song."

"Why did Axe react when I held it out?" I asked.

"He's not at his best after hitting the booze," Sam said. "But mostly it was because the recorder he used for a long while was stolen. All the lyrics he spoke into it on the fly were gone for good."

"Might some of the lyrics have been about Sally?" I asked.

"Absolutely," Sam said. "After dating my father, Barry and Sally were an item for a while. It's why I'm fixating on these pages because a non-disclosure contract might be in code, right? To protect parties who don't want to be named? Maybe Barry hired Harve to get rid of some kind of evidence. There's got to be a reason the box is here."

"Did Sally wear opal earrings?" I asked.

"Guess who bought them for her?" Sam said. "Your favorite landlord. Upstairs, you saw my father lose it and shove me, but it didn't hurt, Sonny. I know, for a woman, it's worse. It's wrong and scary."

"Was your father rough with Sally?" I asked.

"*Mildly*," Sam stipulated. "Think how a rival might handle that kind of knowledge. Barry used it to tank my father."

"This is a lot of information, and I'm supposed to be elsewhere," I said. "There's a detective that I've come to trust—"

"No way," Sam said firmly. "The only reason I'm telling you is that you're ensnared by Pop-Pop, the master puppeteer. I know he's claiming that he was drugged. What if it's a ruse?"

"It's been confirmed by doctors," I said carefully. "I appreciate hearing your theories, Sam. It's good to be asking questions, but there's a tendency for people, even the police, to focus on evidence that supports their narrow premise. It's how people get wrongly accused."

"The police get it right fifty percent of the time," Sam said, shrugging the problem away. "I won't let my father get tanked."

"To be clear," I said. "You think Barry convinced Sally to accuse your father of abuse, and it ended with an NDA?"

"And a payout," Sam said. "It didn't break the bank or anything, but my father was upset. He truly cared about Sally."

Rubbing my brow, I understood that Sam's devotion to his father was deeply entrenched and prone to biased assumptions. Instead of breaking it down, I looped back to Chill's worrisome comment.

"In working through the band's contract issue," I said. "It's a good idea to assess the circumstances of each member. Chill, for instance. In terms of solvency, etcetera, was he flagged by the IRS …?"

"You can't imagine Uncle Chill had anything to do with the guy who got buried in the coffee grove?" Sam said, suddenly wary of my intentions. "You're either an ally, or a problem. Which is it?"

"I'm committed to keeping an open mind, no matter where it leads," I said gently. "I'm striving not to make a mistake."

Under pressure to return to base, but not wanting miss a hidden element, I joined Sam in sorting the paperwork page by page, familiar enough with Lorem Ipsum text to rule out a secret code. Some of the old paperwork was mixed in with new, but for all I knew, the box was a decoy Ted had set up as part of the sting. It needed to stay put.

"Tuck the box aside so we can check it later," I said as Sam glared at the Lorum Ipsum pages. "The party has started."

"Go ahead without me," he said. "If my father asks, I'm practicing my guitar to put his sorry efforts to shame. Actually, the band sees you as an enemy at this point, so you'd best steer clear."

"I'm sorry people see me that way," I said.

"Go on," Sam prompted. "You're ruining my focus."

Heading across the corridor, I raced up the stairs Nicole-style, then I slowed down to catch my breath. Nearing the surveillance room, I took off the borrowed hat and shook out my hair.

"I'm back," I cooed, and then, seeing the agent and Nicole waiting for me with matching glares, I murmured, "Safe and sound."

"Imagine my shock when Nicole popped in a minute ago," the agent said furiously. "I thought she'd been cloned."

I reversed direction and waited for Nicole in the corridor.

"I heard some concerning details from a person who doesn't want to step forward," I said. "That leaves me in a bind because I found a video of Ted talking to the mystery chef. He lied to me."

"You can't imagine the FBI would let you in on every covert angle taking place," Nicole hissed. "Bear in mind, every minute that I'm arguing with you amounts to a hole in the safety net."

Fully aware of the high stakes, I followed Nicole down the corridor to the upper deck, where railings, tables, and potted palms were draped with twinkling lights, and Hawaiian music drifted from speakers mounted on the bulkhead. In dark clothing, I was happy to blend into the shadows. Every other woman, including Nicole, wore a tropical-print dress with flowers in their hair, and the men wore festive, untucked shirts, per the islands' tradition. A place setting for Reginald, the guest of honor, was set at the central table, but he was nowhere in sight.

"There's Harve," I said. "I need to talk to him."

"That's a great idea," Nicole said, signaling for the PI to put down a tray of appetizers. "Keep an eye on her, would you?"

Looking content to tackle any role asked of him, Harve plucked one of the treats from the tray and wolfed it down.

"What did you step in now, Littlefield?" he asked.

"You've got two seconds to explain how long you've been on board," I said furiously. "Clearly, you've been here long enough to bring a box of Lorem Ipsum gibberish to the incinerator room."

"You lost me after the words, 'two seconds,'" Harve said. "You're holding a USB stick under my nose, so one imagines there's a damning video. What made you think it was me?"

"Your 'private eye' hat and your overall build," I said.

"Apparently, it's lost on you that private eyes don't wear private eye hats," Harve said. "I was on the Big Island chasing leads until an hour ago. Came in on an inflatable boat, very quietly after the sun went down. Ted wanted to have extra eyes and ears at the party."

"Then who was in the hat?" I asked.

"No idea," Harve said. "*But* I can report that Derek, the arrestee from the luau, grew a brain and disclosed that he was given a hat and fake hair. A beard, too, but amid running after the dog, he tossed it aside. The ex-cons sold it as traveling incognito, but we think it had to do with protecting the identity of whoever you saw on the 1871 Trail."

"The stalker seemed the opposite of a strategic boss," I said.

"I'm with you, but you've got a more immediate problem," Harve said, indicating Ted crossing toward us with a baleful glare.

As Agent Telford arrived, I lifted my chin. "I was trying to figure out why Ted lied to me about the bearded chef."

"And, boss," Harve said. "I'm sorry to add another chaos element, but apparently somebody on board has been impersonating me."

"Chaos elements are a given," Ted said. "Hence, the tight plan we put in place, not imagining Sonny would tank an agent with soda."

Harve paused. "Huh …?"

"Put your waiter role aside and help us eliminate any other holes," Ted said. "In the meantime, Sonny, your disappearance, however brief, gave my ticker a shock test. Show some mercy."

"I hear you," I grumbled. "I'm sorry."

Seeing Axe, Barry, and the others chatting with drinks in hand, I slipped away from the problematic locals and stood near the railing overlooking the Pacific, keeping an eye on the bulkhead to catch Sam's attention when he arrived. Having glimpsed the man with the box, Sam might recall a detail that would reveal the Harve impersonator. If only he'd followed the person, exposed the false identity, and reported it.

I rubbed my brow, seized by a delayed sense of danger after following a vague lead to a deserted part of the ship. Sam wasn't threatening, but aspects of our encounter bothered me, from major concerns, like his blind loyalty to his father, to the trivial annoyance of seeing him rub his chin the way Dan had done many times when he was puzzled.

"When he had a beard," I whispered.

32

Some mental leaps fizzled on impact. My leap after seeing Sam rubbing his chin stuck. Unlike the thugs, he had a foothold in a normal life. A fake beard would allow him to bend the rules in secret. If my hunch was right, I had to act fast. Sam could be reached. He could be swayed.

"Sonny," a man said softly.

Amid the twinkling lights, I weathered another shock as I stared from the man's trimmed beard to his worried eyes. The chef who'd signaled his presence in the galley wasn't a threat. It was Antoine.

"Does everyone have a fake beard?" I managed.

"No, my stubble is real," Antoine said, resting his hand on my cheek to ground me in that moment. "I've done my best to honor your independence without letting you fall into harm's way. We need to clear the air, but I just saw you zero in on a detail. What did you figure out?"

"I'm sorry," I said.

Antoine paused. "For what?"

"For *this*."

Desperate to avoid being delayed, I shoved Antoine with both hands and dashed away through the crowd, dodging and weaving until I dove into the empty corridor. Determination fueled my legs as I flung open the stairwell door and committed myself to a wild ride down the railing on my backside. Staggering and nearly colliding into the wall at the bottom of the landing, I repeated the maneuver on the next railing.

"How the hell is she moving so fast?" Ted was hollering.

On the lower deck, I was shocked to see Moritz swinging a knife at Reginald. I kicked the bartender's hand, sending his weapon clattering to the floor, then Reginald gripped Moritz by the shirt and drove him against the wall with his forearm across his windpipe.

"Vicious, immoral coward," Reginald growled.

"Enough," Antoine said, pulling Reginald away and securing Moritz with an armlock. "Relax. It's over. You're done."

An alarming sight in the corridor, with a swath of blood on his shirt, Reginald pushed past me and crossed to the incinerator room, where Sam lay on his back. Dropping to his knees, and choking in anguish, Reginald gently smoothed the guitarist's motionless brow.

"It's too late," Reginald said. "We're too late."

Numb and disbelieving, I knelt next to Sam's sprawled body and stared from his blank gaze to the bloody rips on his shirt.

"I don't understand," I said, desperate to see signs of life in Sam's face. "It can't be too late. I'm here to talk sense into him."

Reaching for my hand, Antoine said, "Sonny, it's heartbreaking to see Sam like this, but he's beyond anyone's help."

"We need a reset," I said. "It *can't* be too late."

Gently, Antoine looped his arm around my waist and lifted me to my feet, providing support as he guided me out of the room. Amid the furor of Ted, Reginald, and Moritz all trying to outshout each other, Antoine guided me to a life preserver trunk, sat me down, and tightly wrapped his arms around me for a long moment. As always, I felt the instant, radiant energy of our direct contact, and his whispered assurances had a grounding effect, warming me and clearing some of the fog.

"Sonny," Ted said. "Whenever you're ready—"

"Focus on Reginald," Antoine said. "He's injured."

"This is Sam's blood," Reginald said. "When I saw him lying on the floor, I tried to help him. Moritz took me off guard."

"I'm not going to get railroaded for this," Moritz said, handcuffed and in the grip of two agents. "Raja and I found out a thing or two from Sam bunking with us. I came down here following up on a hunch. A gut feeling. Sam ranted about a box of bogus paperwork and started making demands. It was a blur. A frenzy. I had to defend myself."

"Did you hear and understand your Miranda rights?" Ted asked.

"I heard the spiel, but I'm telling you, Sam went nuts on me," Moritz said. "He's known to pop a pill now and then to relieve the stress of dealing with Axe. Fast-track checking his bloodwork."

"How long have you been partners?" Ted asked.

"It's not fair to even call us friends," Moritz said. "You know my story. I'm a victim ten times over. I acted in self-defense."

"Best guess," Ted said. "Who's calling the shots?"

"By my count, you've got a half-dozen two-faced candidates partying on the deck," Moritz said. "Make note of the fact that I've been upfront, but that's over with. No more until I get a lawyer."

As they stepped away, I found that listening to the back-and-forth had dredged me out of numbness to a workable degree, but with clarity came my confusion over Antoine's believability and intentions. As my doubts took hold, his gaze intensified, and he cupped my face.

"Sonny, my feelings for you are deep," Antoine said. "It's not a work-related fling. Before you worry that my visit with Zach was cut short, it's the opposite. I'd planned to come back to you."

"It crushed me to hear that you'd moved on," I said. "But when it was explained to me, your ex seemed like a better fit."

"Berrichon, picture me on a carpeted hotel room floor with an ice pack on my head between bouts of vomiting," Antoine said. "Same with Zach's mother. How the misery of two people could be seen as rekindling the flame, I can't imagine. Zach made a short film about the irony of being scolded for not eating a proper breakfast of scrambled eggs."

Seeing Reginald nearby, wanting to talk, Antoine stood and motioned for him to take his seat by my side on the trunk.

"As you know, I'm not supposed to be here," Reginald said. "I've been holed up on this level for days, seeing it as the least likely place to be found out. Sonny, I've kept track of you through the security cameras. Your interaction with Sam didn't feel off. You were on the same page, seeking answers. I kept track of your return to the control room, then sounds of a fight startled me. The rest was a disastrous blur."

"Reginald," Ted said, looking gutted as he joined us. "At some point, I'll need to know how and when you snuck on board. Antoine warned me that enlisting Sonny's help would be like chasing a comet. I should have listened, especially with another comet in the picture."

"Focus on a recap," Antoine said.

"Right." Rubbing his brow, Ted said, "In striving to distance himself from Moritz, Raja admitted that having Sam bunk with them was about searching his gear. Upon finding a fake beard and a larger man's clothing, it didn't occur to them to report that they might have outed the stalker on the 1871 Trail. Instead, they came up with the idea of luring Sonny with a box of fake paperwork, adding a private eye hat to implicate Harve. Raja claims it was a harmless payback prank after Sonny gave them a USB stick that froze their computer, but given that Moritz and Raja profit from spilled dirt, I bet it was about stirring up conflict."

Nodding, Antoine said, "The wrinkle they didn't see coming was that Sam would take the bait along with Sonny."

"That's how it's looking," Ted said. "I think Sam switched gears after being seen on the 1871 Trail. Alone and desperate for a way out. Tonight, Moritz came in, said the wrong thing, and was shocked by Sam's response. He's facing a snag, since it was his knife."

Maddened to get answers when it was too late to avert tragedy, I said, "Why didn't you see the file box as a problem?"

"It was checked and dismissed as irrelevant," Ted said. "Don't forget, we're embedded in a normal crew who are carrying out routine business. The extent of Sam's guilt is unclear, but I don't believe he intended to hurt you, Sonny. In his imperfect way, he was trying to land a win and be a hero. It's a small comfort to share with his father."

"Whoever is pulling the strings is up there at the party," I said. "I dread breaking the news to Axe, but it's part of my role."

"Notice the sudden silence on the upper deck," Ted said. "Between agents rushing to the scene and Raja getting escorted away for questioning, the party came to a halt. Essentially, the sting is over."

"Not necessarily," Antoine said. "You've done a good job of staying in the shadows, so it's possible to let people believe that you've arrived in response to tonight's events. Disclose an aspect of the truth. You've had your eye on Moritz for months. Guilty parties might relax."

Nodding, Ted said, "Let's get you back to your post."

"I've been manning a sniper position at the party," Antoine explained to me. "I'm only using non-lethal rounds."

Before I could argue, Antoine enveloped me in a tight hug. I focused on savoring his warmth for a stretch of heartbeats, his muscles flexing as he offered comfort, and then, in turmoil, I pulled away.

"Any number of things could go wrong," I said. "With Zach in mind, I can't let you dive into danger. It's not right."

"Sonny, my job is what it is," Antoine said. "Neither of us wants the other to take risks, but it's going to happen. This is your sting. Your call. Trust that we can find our way through the fog."

With a final squeeze, Antoine donned his cap and crossed to a staff-only staircase. Once his "ready" signal arrived, I followed Ted up the echoing stairwell to the upper deck, where only a short while earlier, dinner was being served and people were smiling and clinking champagne flutes amid the candlelight. As Ted hung back and I stepped toward the staring crowd, my gaze was drawn to Mary and RG, who were thanking heaven to see that I hadn't fallen victim to foul play, while Barry, Axe, Chill, and the other men who'd come to perceive me as a problem exchanged glances with a pinched look, the opposite of relieved.

The closer I got to Axe, the more I saw subtleties of human instinct unfolding, with his friends shifting ever so slightly, as if to distance themselves from my grave demeanor, while Axe grew increasingly wary, until his face was pale and he was looking at me sideways.

"I've been at the party the whole time," he said. "Among witnesses, so whatever you're looking to pin on me, it won't work."

"Can we speak privately?" I said softly.

"We've caught on that an attack of some sort unfolded," Gavin said. "We've been worried that Reginald is absent."

"It's not Reginald," I said. "I'm sorry to shock you, Axe, but a short while ago, Sam engaged in a fight on a lower deck."

"Spit it out," Chill said. "What kind of fight?"

"His wounds were fatal," I said. "Sam died."

Gaping, Axe said, "Are you *insane*, saying shit like that?"

"I'm sorry to shock and distress you," I said softly. "The circumstances are unclear, but the culprit has been apprehended."

"This is nuts," Axe said. "You're playing me."

Seeing him blink and sway, I signaled Chill to steady his friend because the jolt of reality was going to hit hard.

"I'll take over from here," Ted said, looking somber as he arrived and showed his badge. "Mr. Richardson, my name is Ted Telford. I'm sorry to confirm that your son was fatally wounded."

"Sam has similar looks to other guys," Axe said. "Chill, come with me as backup. If it's a trick, we'll make them pay."

"Sam was at the table," Barry insisted. "Smiling and joking."

"Officers will be stepping in to take your statements," Ted said. "Please check your recent snapshots. It's important to build a timeline of Sam's activities in the hours leading up to the party."

Chill was too shocked to support Axe, so I looped my arm around his torso. Amid our echoing footfalls in the stairwell his breath smelled of booze and he leaned on me heavily, missing steps instead of paying attention. As we arrived on the lower deck, where FBI agents were talking outside the incinerator room, Axe nearly buckled.

"I was about to look for Sam because he wasn't answering my texts," he admitted. "It's not like him to miss a party."

"Mr. Richardson," Ted said quietly. "If you don't wish to proceed, we can make an appointment for you to spend time with your son."

"With his corpse, you mean," Axe said tearfully.

"There's no rush," I said. "Let's sit down."

"There's a body bag in plain sight," Axe said, sweating visibly. "The thought of my boy being zipped up with no air … is it possible for me to carry him out? Sonny, I'm sure you understand."

"Yes, I understand," I managed.

"An hour ago," he said. "I told Sam to stop being a—"

Closing his eyes, Axe crushed me against his chest, growling pleas for a second chance, with his biceps applying so much force that it was difficult to breathe. Every cell in his body was vibrating with self-hatred, a storm that ended as abruptly as it began.

"There has to be a way to reverse time," he said. "A day doesn't go by when I'm not … it's supposed to be *me* in that bag."

"Axe," Chill said. "You're shivering really bad."

"My veins have iced over," Axe said.

As he succumbed to shock, Ted signaled for EMTs to gently lower him onto a stretcher, then he turned once again to Chill.

"Should we reach out to Sam's mother?" Ted asked.

"There's no point in it," Chill said. "She abandoned him as a baby and never looked back. Women came and went in terms of helping, but things went to shit during practice. Sam wailed nonstop." Hearing my disgusted reaction, Chill added, "Go ahead and judge, but we cared in our own way. If you don't mind, I need to accompany my friend off this ghost ship. If you haven't heard, my retirement is at hand."

Ever an optimist about getting answers, Ted signaled for Nicole to continue the questioning on the way to the hospital.

"We'll be docking soon," Ted said. "Along with Axe, the passengers will depart, except for the Kona group, who have a board meeting in the morning. If you're ready to bail, I understand."

"I appreciate your concern," I said, wiping my eyes. "But I'm haunted by the image of Sam as a baby, screaming amid an awful din. Somebody did the opposite of guiding him to safe ground, to an inner place of refuge. I'm not leaving until that somebody is taken down."

33

In the darkness, I oversaw the departure of the last of the passengers. Every exit was smoothed with a voucher for the rides we'd arranged to destinations in the Kona area. With their headlights ablaze, taxis, minibuses and rideshare vehicles formed a crown pattern on the wharf.

"It's spooky with everyone off, isn't it?" Harve said, pausing with his minimal gear in hand. "Mary was looking for you."

"You're not leaving with her?" I asked.

"Thanks to you, she's going with RG," Harve said.

With a wry smile and a fist-bump, the PI headed down the ramp.

At 1:15 a.m., I followed the sound of Mary's voice to the deck, where she'd overseen a quick cleanup of the party mess. Tables were stored away, linens were bundled, and glasses were washed and stowed in the galley. All that remained of the festive atmosphere were the icy lights wound around the railings and draped across the bulkhead walls.

Seeing me, Mary and RG peeled away from their conversation with Barry and Gavin, who were contemplating the Pacific.

"I guess we covered the shock and bewilderment angle when we talked earlier," Mary said, looking tearful as she hugged me. "I must say, those opal earrings are a lovely compliment to your blue eyes."

"They're not mine," I said. "It's a long story."

"Your long stories have reached new heights in Hawaii," RG said wryly. "Join us for dinner before you head home."

"I'll be in touch," I assured them.

As Mary and RG took their luggage and stepped away into the darkness, Gavin arrived by my side and studied me.

"Being invited to the board meeting is an indication of Reginald's faith in you," he said. "Might we get an agenda in advance?"

"It doesn't feel right to discuss business," I said.

"Of course," Gavin said. "Apologies, I'm still addled from shock."

Barry greeted me with a grim expression and folded arms, the opposite of a man enjoying the sea air. Standing next to him, I rested my forearms on the railing, content to let a silence play out.

"You're stealing from the dead, now?" Barry asked.

"It sounds like you're recognizing the jewelry that Sally wore when she tumbled over the railing. This," I added, touching my left ear so the opal glistened, "is identical to an earring I fished from your vacuum bag, along with a receipt from a jewelry store on Oahu."

"There's no need for a cat and mouse routine," Barry said. "Yes, Sally and I had an affair. Yes, I've had nightmares from her death. Perhaps you didn't hear that she dumped me for another guy."

"Did you confess to your wife?" I asked.

"Gossips did the heavy lift," Barry said. "You're wizened enough to know it takes two to make a marriage work."

"Pauline cried when she talked about your courtship," I said. "She described her elation when you proposed. I was moved."

"Interesting," Barry said. "I proposed at a business conference."

I hesitated. "Not on a trail next to a flickering stream?"

Joining me in resting his forearms on the railing, Barry looked grim but determined, with beads of sweat on his brow.

"In your thirties, people start telling you it's time to settle down," he said. "Years down the line, your life is the opposite of settled. I'm sorry to feel sympathy for Donald Littlefield, but I know a thing or two about accepting another man's child. If I had it to do over again …"

Barry paused as the twinkling lights shut off.

"What's that about?" he asked.

I shrugged. "It's, umm … probably a normal element."

Startled by a whirring sound, I gaped as Barry fell against me with a short knife lodged in his kidney area. With a furious glare, he grappled with me as if he believed I was responsible for the attack, seeming muscular and enormous, with a chest that felt like iron as I struggled to push him away without driving the knife deeper into his back.

Suddenly, Gavin wrenched us apart and hit my hidden ballistic vest with a sizzling taser blast. Confused, but unwavering, I tossed the taser and spun Gavin onto his stomach on the deck. Reaching for the handcuffs that I'd tucked into a pocket, I stared in shock as Pauline rushed in and dropped Barry with her own taser blast to his neck. With a mad look in her eyes and her skirt hiked up, she sat on the deck and used both high heels to shove her flailing husband under the railing by degrees.

"*Stop*," I hollered, to no effect.

Pinning Gavin as he fought my hold, I snapped handcuffs onto his wrists just as Pauline kicked her husband over the edge.

Lurching forward too late, I heard Barry screaming, followed by a splash that announced his rough entry into the harbor. While Pauline leaned against the railing, gasping from exertion, I slid over the edge to a perilous degree and saw an FBI scuba diver securing Barry in a rescue hold and pulling him out of sight below the ship's prow.

"Is it over?" Pauline asked. "Is he gone?"

Sagging in relief, I realized part of Antoine's covert plan was to give Barry a protective vest. No wonder he'd felt like a sumo wrestler. He must have wondered if I'd tricked him with a false front.

"Well?" Pauline demanded.

"He's gone," I said. "Notice the absence of hollering."

"I saw red when he described our marriage as 'settling,'" Pauline said. "My knife was suddenly in motion. It was reflex."

"I urged you not to be rash," Gavin said. "Barry's body will show a stab wound, and Sonny is a witness. My taser malfunctioned."

"Actually, I knew to expect trouble," I said, pulling the victim photos out of my pocket and placing them in front of Pauline, with that night's casualty on top. "Sadly, I didn't catch on in time to save Sam."

"Easy does it," Gavin cautioned. "Sam was her son."

I hesitated, startled by Pauline's choked-off sobs.

"Dear God," I said. "You and Axe …?"

"The walk-in-the-woods story I told you in the dance studio wasn't about Barry," Pauline managed, swiping away her tears with a look of self-loathing. "I was seventeen and stupid, drawn to Axe's sex appeal and brilliance. Ask about his early songs. They're about me."

"I can imagine the allure," I said. "You ended up pregnant?"

"Months of throwing up and becoming less desirable by the minute," Pauline said. "I thought if Axe spent time with our baby, changing diapers and seeing himself in Sam's eyes, it would put him in a faithful frame of mind and cement our bond. Instead, he brought in another mother who was breastfeeding. I don't know how I survived that."

"You survived it by 'doing' Axe again," Gavin murmured.

Lurching to her feet, and wobbling in her high heels, Pauline shocked me again by crossing to Gavin and kicking him.

"Hey, take a breath," I said.

"You have a nerve finding fault with me," Pauline seethed, heedless of my presence as she glared at Gavin. "Half of your bright ideas have ended with a foul-up, and the latest takes the cake. How *dare* you not tell me that your slimy cohorts were recruiting Sam?"

"There isn't an app for securing qualified applicants," Gavin snapped. "I didn't step in because for the first time in his life, Sam showed gumption. If you'd taken him into your confidence …"

"Dear God," Pauline said, looming closer as he cowered. "Are *you* the reason Reginald started pressing me to mentor Sam?"

"You could have done it without admitting your connection," Gavin said. "As for Reginald, your temporary solution dragged on. I told you it wasn't sustainable, and now he's out for blood."

As Pauline abruptly turned toward me, I braced myself for an attack, especially as she kicked off her high heels, but when she arrived and knelt within striking range, I saw that, along with signs of an adrenaline rush, her instinct to survive had kicked in, a bright, burning look in her eyes that could shift from eagerness to aggression in an instant.

"There's a world where Gavin ends up with Barry," Pauline whispered. "Drugged and drowned in the wake of Sam's death."

"If I'm not mistaken," I said carefully. "You're in this jam because of rash decisions. It's not helpful to lose your cool."

"I almost confided in you on the 1871 Trail," Pauline said. "Not my secret. Just my worry that Sam was mixed up with the ex-cons."

"Do they know you're his mother?" I asked.

"They would have thrown it in my face," Pauline said, wide-eyed, as if not entirely sure. "At some point, I would like to know how you've built a fantasy of love around Raymond French. I hated my biological father. He's the reason my parents divorced when I was barely out of diapers. I told him to stick his money up his philandering ass, then all of a sudden, I was seventeen and pregnant. He convinced me I could have it all. A baby, a college degree, a life. You know how that turned out."

"Are you talking about Reginald?" I asked.

"When he met my mother, he was fresh out of prison," Pauline said. "A far cry from his current moral incarnation."

"It was a big deal for Reginald to keep your secret," I said. "To never acknowledge his grandson. It feels like an act of love."

"If so, it's a clueless version of love," Pauline said. "In return, I've been like a cat he was trying to wash, scratching, fighting, and hating him in anticipation of him telling the world that I abandoned my baby. Last year, the threat felt imminent. People always joked that he should take a pill. Why not three? It put an end to his blasted moralizing."

"Maybe it's upsetting that Reginald helped Axe," I said. "Given that fame fueled his flaws. You want a new path. Your own wealth."

"*Exactly*, the same way you broke ties with the Littlefields," Pauline said. "Best of all, I was able to be there for Katrina."

I hesitated. "She's important to you?"

"If there was a way to adopt her without raising suspicion, I'd do it in a heartbeat," Pauline said. "She's smart and talented, everything a mother could want. Her early life was a nightmare."

"Another problem I fixed," Gavin murmured.

Instead of fighting the handcuffs, Gavin fiddled with the connecting link, creating a pathetic rustling sound. Plotting and scheming. Planning to pin the blame on Moritz, perhaps. I pegged him as a knee-jerk operator, fretting in front of his dirtbag cohorts about people who might topple the cart, dropping hints instead of giving directives so he could pretend that he wasn't responsible. Pauline's tears over Chip's death had seemed genuine, but if she'd enlisted Gavin's help in getting rid of Katrina's parents, she'd learned to look on the bright side. As she lifted Sam's photo and gazed at it under the stars, another thought struck me.

"Axe kept your secret and rose to the occasion of being a single father," I said. "There's a psychological quirk called transference. Maybe trashing Barry's precious house was an act of frustration."

"You might be right," Pauline murmured.

"Don't add fuel to her fantasy," Gavin said. "It's because of me that Sam learned to play the guitar, and Katrina overcame her turmoil. I convinced Petrel that she had potential as a dancer."

"Katrina has potential, period," I said. "Jason as well. If they'd been alert, they might have caught onto Sally's high behavior. And by the way, Gavin, your Japan contact confessed to drugging Katrina."

Pauline's keen look wasn't a surprise, but it was concerning, since it marked an end to the possibility of a careful approach.

"It's normal to blurt nonsense after a shock," she said, setting Sam's photo aside on the deck. "Everything feels distant and misty, then clarity arrives. Riff made mention of a Japan contact."

"You're the one who hated Sally three times over," I said. "First with Axe, then with Barry, then with Axe again. What galls me is that I arrived *one* day too late for Chip to see me as an ally," I said with sudden fury. "Through receipts, hints from Moritz, and other means, he was closing in on the idea that Gavin stole Axe's recorder and created a voiceover that lured Sally to the railing, and to her death. I have a bad feeling that Chip confided his suspicions about Gavin to you, Pauline."

"Sally's death was a suicide," she insisted.

"Your lies are falling apart," I said. "While your kill squad was eliminating rival heirs, weak links, and an IRS agent who was poking into tax evasion issues, you thought, why not make it a baker's dozen? At the memorial service the other day, Barry handed you tissues, no idea you're the reason his ability to find love elsewhere was cursed."

"He's not seeking love," Pauline said. "His heart is made of stone."

"Gosh, honey," Barry said, dripping seawater from head to toe as he stepped from the shadows. "It's good to know you care."

Pauline gaped. "How are you …?"

"Alive?" Barry said. "Yeah, thanks for skewering my ballistic vest with one of your knives. Talk about making a point."

"I thought you were about to attack Sonny," she said.

"Great story," Barry said. "Except me and the FBI guys heard you over their nifty earpieces. The older our son got, the more he looked like Axe, so yeah, my heart iced over and turned to stone."

"Barry," I said. "If you love your son, he'll need you more than ever. As for you, Pauline, I'm aware of the knife in your hand."

Squinting against a piercing light, she said, "What's that?"

"It's a marksman alerting you to his presence," I said. "He'll use a bean-bag round that can cause broken ribs and other injuries. The road ahead is hard enough. Don't compound your troubles."

"You're supposed to be on *my* side," Pauline said. "We're a sisterhood, fed up with men upending our lives. Eons of abuse."

"What about Reginald?" I asked. "Instead of outing you as a possible suspect, he made us uncover the truth the hard way."

"The truth is in handcuffs," Pauline said. "Gavin is a man to be feared, manipulative and cold. He's made my life hell."

"Dear God, Pauline," Barry said.

"How dare you judge me?" she seethed. "It's thanks to me that you got your precious house that you constantly cite as a refuge you'll enjoy after we divorce. Admit it. You're a gutless enabler."

"You're right, I've worked at keeping my head in the sand," Barry said. "To win back my self-respect, I will keep raising your son as my own, and I will try to remind him of your good qualities. Agent Telford, she's more fragile than you realize. She might hurt herself."

Prompted to step from the shadows, Ted calmly motioned with both hands and softly directed Pauline to drop the knife.

"This can't be real," she whispered.

"It's real," Ted said. "Sonny is right, you don't want to end up with injuries. If I'm not mistaken, you're drained from grieving over Sam's death and worried about Axe. He's fine, by the way."

"I want to see Sam," Pauline said, choking and tearful. "It's too late, but I want his soul to know I was proud of his solo performance. He needs to know that I love him, and I'm desperately sorry."

Stepping closer, Ted said softly, "Axe expressed concern that you've lost your way after a lifetime of difficulties. He's showing compassion, Pauline. Caring and ownership for his role in the tragic arc. He's asked permission for you to stand by his side once Sam has been released for burial. I agree, Pauline. It's a goal to strive toward."

"It's years too late," she gasped.

"Pauline," I said. "On a dark night, a man's ghost embraced me when I felt terrified and alone. Follow the impulse to hug Sam and talk to him. Tell him that you love him, because—" With my throat tightening, I managed, "Do it now, before his spirit drifts away."

As the knife fell from Pauline's hand, it sank into the decking enough to block the moonlight and cast an arrow-shaped shadow pointing toward Earth's core instead of toward home. Seeing it with brimming eyes, unhealed and unable to face the empty farmhouse where my father's life had ended a year and two weeks ago, I navigated my way through a tide of incoming FBI agents and stepped into the corridor I'd dashed down in a vain attempt to reach Sam before the worst happened.

Kneeling next to my bag, I yanked out my copy of *The Hawaiian Archipelago* and secured it in my front waistband.

"Sonny," Ted said, out of breath as he caught up with me. "I know you wanted a fast exit, but it's not a healthy choice."

"After the hurricane," I said, "Isabella described the captain of the *Nevada* as 'beyond all praise' in piloting a vessel with shot engines, a dire list to port, and a propulsion wheel out of the water."

"Sonny," Ted said, reaching for my hand. "Once you shake off the awful shocks, you'll grasp that this is a major win."

"I'm like the *Nevada*," I said. "Antoine is like Captain Blethen, beyond all praise. There's a reason Zach's mother picked him."

"I was wrong about Antoine and his ex," Ted said.

"I haven't told this to anyone," I managed. "But during our last argument, Dan told me that I'm not wife material. I'm not mother material.

There's always a hidden opinion, a secret first love, an awful truth that's waiting in the wings to knock me on my ass."

"Sonny, don't put stock in words that were spoken in anger by a man who was riddled with guilt," Ted said. "You're loving, loyal, and fierce in equal measure, the perfect person to raise a child."

"I used to believe that," I said. "Now I'm listing to port with shot engines. I can't muster a flicker of faith in a man after two days apart, let alone two weeks or two months. It's from my own choices, so it's on me to handle the fallout. Mary came up with the idea of releasing a person into the wild. It helps to think in those terms."

"Antoine does *not* want to be released," Ted said.

"He'll be coming down from his marksman perch," I said, unzipping my bag to secure my prepaid cards and driver's license. "I don't need a stipend. Show your thanks by explaining how I feel and why it won't work. If you can bring my bags to Mary, I'll fetch them when I'm ready. If I'm ready. My statement will have to wait."

"You can't leave your phone behind," Ted insisted.

"It's a way for people to track me," I said.

"Sonny, for God's sake," Ted said.

"The four most uttered words of my life," I said, hugging him tightly. "I know thoughts of Libby are clouding your judgment of me. Your heart is in the right place, Ted. Libby knew it and felt it, so you need to let yourself off the hook." Pushing out of his arms, I added, "Thank you for believing in me. Stay well. Be safe."

"Call me *any* time for *any* reason," Ted said. "I mean it."

"Stop worrying," I said. "I'll be fine."

Before I reached the gangway, I remembered to unzip my ballistic vest and let it fall to the deck, like a shell symbolizing my broken former life. Embracing the idea of being a silhouette, a mere shadow, I stole through the wharf, past the yachts and pleasure boats, the buildings and docking vehicles, and headed to the parking lot, where three silhouettes similar to mine were quietly talking next to three sleek motorcycles.

"Here she is," Jasmine said, stepping forward to hug me. "Oh my God, Sonny. We heard the whole thing through earpieces."

As Jason enfolded us in a tight, four-person embrace, we cried for Sam and Chip, and the others whose lives had been taken, and then I focused on completing my fast exit. At my request, Jason had brought the same motorcycle I rode to Hilo, and Jasmine had designed a jacket that sparked tears all the more. On the back, facing anyone on the road behind me, was a digital painting of palm leaves with a subtly hidden likeness of Lakshmi, the Hindu goddess of prosperity, abundance, and love. I hugged Jasmine, seeing the design as a guiding symbol to strive toward.

"Come and stay with us," Katrina said. "Let us take care of you. Pop-Pop will be crushed if you don't let him thank you."

"I'll catch up with him later," I said.

"What's the plan?" Jason asked. "Where will you go?"

"Wild places off the beaten track," I said, fastening the helmet strap. "No more putting it on the back burner."

"Do you need cash?" Jasmine asked.

"No, but—" I closed my eyes, deciding it was too late to wonder if it was illegal to ride a motorcycle at night, and then I smiled. "I'm thrilled that you're close again. Keep it that way. Stay safe."

"Come see us before you leave town," Jason said.

I nodded. "Of course. I'll be in touch."

Mounting the seat, I balanced the bike's weight with my sneakers on the pavement, and turned the key, sending a familiar rumble through the air. In the distance, a figure stood on the deck of the *Kukuna Mahina* with my ballistic vest dangling from his hand. Torn, but determined, I revved the throttle, and sped away into the Hawaiian night.

34

Through store clerks and kindly pineapple vendors, I found lodgings that at first made me smile, having memorized Isabella Bird's description of her overnight stay in "a dilapidated frame-house, altogether forlorn, standing unsheltered on a slope." The lockless door didn't bother me because I always kept my wallet either in my pocket or in my waterproof pouch, and the yard's assortment of cats begged for my attention and treats, purring and meowing their way into my heart.

And then my second dawn in the rustic bungalow arrived.

Hearing my landlady fluffing a rug on the porch of her significantly improved house, thanks to undemanding tourists who arrived with cash in hand throughout the year, I put on the complimentary flip-flops provided by the establishment and crossed to her in my shorts.

"Well, hello," she said brightly. "How did the snorkel gear work out?"

"It's a little worse for wear, but never mind that," I said, holding out my bare ankles to show three itchy red marks. "Your many cats and kittens have fleas, which explains the bottles of witch hazel, itch reliever, and calamine lotion jammed into closets."

"*Well,*" she said, crossing to a table to fetch her copy of *The Hawaiian Archipelago*. "Right here in the section about Isabella's trek to Mauna Loa, she wrote, 'We shall not get a wink of sleep, for the place swarms with fleas. They are a great pest of the colder regions of the islands.'" Closing the book, the landlady said, "You did confess that you're fresh from a trip to Mauna Loa. On a motorcycle, no less."

"I joined a group that went up in a minibus," I said.

"Hopefully, not the minibus that spun out of control on the pahoehoe lava field the other day?" she asked. "Thank heaven a rescue helicopter was patrolling the area."

"The driver lost consciousness, but it was sorted out," I said. "The flea account in Isabella's book describes conditions in 1873, but instead of arguing, the simple solution is not to let the cats into the house while I'm out exploring. Also, it was jarring to come back to the television blaring. I unplugged the cord for a reason."

"While I'm in there cleaning—"

"I can handle the minor dusting myself," I said.

"It's hard to turn away from the news about that major crime case," she persisted, peering at me through her glasses. "The police say it's a rare example of the answers and evidence just falling into their laps. Open and shut in a matter of hours."

"If you can keep the cats out, that would be great," I said.

"Again, who knows where the fleas came from," she said. "My nephew was supposed to fumigate the place, but he's gone *missing*."

"Gosh, look at the time," I said, kicking off the flip-flops in favor of my sneakers drying on the bungalow's front stoop. "Coffee would have been nice, but I'll grab breakfast elsewhere."

"I hope his awful friends aren't to blame," she said.

"La, la, la, la," I said, plugging my ears on my way to my motorcycle. "I will see you later. If not, keep my deposit."

"You're booked for another night," she called out.

"Lock the doors after dark," I said. "Stay safe."

Thrumming the throttle, I backed the motorcycle onto the road and thanked heaven that I'd kept my meager belongings in the roomy saddlebags. Instead of showering after my morning swim, I would use the outdoor spigot to rinse off, dry my clothing in the sun, and find a phone to call Mary to check the weather conditions in Maine. For three days, storms brewed the moment I floated the idea of heading home.

At the snorkeling site I'd discovered the previous day, I parked the motorcycle in a shady spot in plain view of the section of lava where I would risk furthering the sunburn I'd gotten from swimming without the protection of a neoprene shortie wetsuit. Even at 7:45 in the morning, the combination of sun and water was a searing force. From a thrift store, I'd bought a small beach umbrella that was meant to be clipped to a chair. With my towel stretched out on the black lava, I sat down and opened my travel satchel to pull out my favorite new find: a brass pirate spyglass from the 1800s, or so the proprietor had claimed.

Scanning the round curve of the horizon, I searched for the spouts of whales and the leaps of spinner dolphins. My view swept past an older man in a dinghy bobbing alongside a sleek yacht with its sails furled on the boom. Thirty or forty yards from the shoreline, with a white hat protecting his head, the man was painting the boat's name on the bow.

Scanning onward, I mistook an ocean swell for a whale spout in the far distance, and then I swung the scope back to the man in the dinghy as the sketched letters snagged in my mind.

"B-e-r-r-i," I read aloud with confusion, "c-h-o-n."

Polishing the lens to ensure clarity, I adjusted my view to study the man, and then I lurched to my feet in a blaze of fury.

"Pop-Pop!" I hollered. "Put the brush down!"

"Ahoy, Matey!" he replied, tapping his ear. "I can't hear you!"

"Put—the—brush—down!" I hollered, cupping my hands to my mouth as I crossed to the water's edge. "I'm not okay with you making use of that nickname! It's special to me!"

"I'm glad you like it," Reginald called out.

"I—am—telling—you—to—*stop!*" I hollered.

"I would love that," he said. "We'll have breakfast."

"Where?" I demanded.

"On my yacht, of course," he said. "I'll alert my chef."

With that, Reginald adjusted his hat and rowed around to the stern, leaving me to fume as he loosely tossed a rope onto a swim platform. Wobbling as he stood and using his arms to keep his balance, he lurched toward the platform and then plopped into the water.

"Oh dear!" Reginald gasped. "Help!"

"You're mistaken if you think I will swim out to rescue you," I hollered, and then, seeing a mother staring at me with an infant in her arms, I said, "He pulled a stunt like this in the hospital, falling out of his wheelchair. He's faking it to get me to go out there."

"He's been ill recently?" she asked.

"Umm, sort of, yes," I said. "It's a long story."

"I think he's going under," the mother said.

"He'll pop up," I said. "In fact, the man's name is Pop-Pop, as in what a gun sounds like when— *crap*, he's not surfacing."

Tossing my sneakers aside, I dove into the water and started churning toward the boat at a fast clip of freestyle strokes thanks to a summer of focused practice in Maine lakes. Reaching strongly forward with my arms, I forced my legs up and down in a steady cadence, gulping breaths to my right, with Pacific saltwater burning my eyes, entering my nostrils from my crushing pace, and rinsing my mouth with each stroke.

Gasping as I reached the yacht's stern, I blinked away the salt in my eyes and saw Reginald standing above me on the swim platform, backlit by the sun, and smiling as he clicked a stopwatch.

And he wasn't alone.

"I think you beat the average pace of 100 meters in two minutes," Antoine said, reaching out to assist me. "Very impressive."

"Use both hands," I managed. "I'm cramping up."

Securing Antoine's wrists, I planted my feet on the platform and kicked with all my might, sending him over my head in a smooth arc. He straightened in flight, extending his arms to enter the water in trim form, with scarcely a splash. Wearing a white shirt, he spun underwater, then surged upward and arrived in front of me with a grin.

"Well done," Antoine said, blinking water from his eyes.

"I would be yelling if I wasn't out of breath," I said.

With an arm around my torso, Antoine swam to the platform's edge so we could float securely instead of treading water.

"It's thanks to me that the helicopter was on hand to pluck you from the frozen slopes of Mauna Loa," Antoine said, brushing wet curls from my forehead. "You can't imagine I wouldn't seek you out for some quality time. We've been married for nearly a week."

"Okay," I said. "I'm not sure what happens in Canada—"

"Your friends stressed a careful approach," Antoine said. "Receiving opposite signals, I pressed forward with declarations in Hawaiian, followed by a comprehensive sealing of the deal. The next day, I referred to you as my wife. It's a part of the official record."

"You're being ridiculous," I said, laughing despite my efforts to sound serious. "I happen to be on a healing journey."

"If you could retire that concept, I would be grateful," Antoine said. "No more careful approach. I'm going to be bold, cheeky, resourceful, and relentless until you see that we can be a team in every sense. Once the snow storms clear away, we need to head home. Together, Sonny. Your place, then mine, or vice versa. It's not only possible, it's doable. For now, let's enjoy a stretch of fun and adventure on the open sea."

"With a certain person as a deckhand?" I asked.

"Sadly, I'm booked for the foreseeable future," Reginald said, rowing his dinghy into view, and then pausing with the oars dripping. "I've got a daughter with serious problems to sort out, so listen up. Thank you. I adore you. Keep in touch."

I paused. "That's it?"

"'The breeze is freshening, and the *Costa Rica's* head lies nearly due north,'" Reginald said, squinting to recall the final words of Isabella Bird's account. "'The sun is sinking, and on the far horizon the summit peaks of Oahu gleam like amethysts on a golden sea. Farewell forever, my bright tropic dream! *Aloha nui* to Hawaii-nei!'"

"It's perfect," I managed. "Take care, Reginald."

With Chip's watch on his wrist, the smiling millionaire tipped his white hat, gripped his oars, and rowed ashore, where three motorcycles were purring to a stop. With a flourish, Katrina unleashed her mane of Hawaiian curls from her helmet and joined Jason, Jasmine, and Carol in smiling, waving, and making heart symbols with their hands.

With water cascading from his sleeve, Antoine lifted his phone and leaned close, smiling, kissing my cheek, and fiddling with the focus to take selfies with views of the yacht and the shore.

"Zach wants constant updates," he said. "On how I'm faring with my most harrowing sting of all, securing your love."

I hesitated. "You told Zach about me?"

With a wry look, Antoine angled his phone so I could see the screen as he swiped through photos of me sanding drywall, feeding grape jelly to a gecko, smiling as I texted my friends, and other special moments that put my solitary photo of our distorted shadows to shame.

"You might have told me the selfie moratorium was officially lifted," I said. "I don't suppose you brought my phone?"

"Along with your cameras, luggage, and bag with the cabbie-style flip phone in its proper place," Antoine said. "To be fair, I've had a three-month head start on knowing where I want to land."

Tanned and handsome, with a mop of sun-streaked curls, Antoine refused to look like a bad risk, as I'd originally thought.

"We're within missile range of an active volcano," I said. "I can agree to proceed carefully. That's it. End of discussion."

"Per your mistrust of a positive outlook," Antoine said. "I don't know how to sail a yacht this size, and neither do you, so we are in for some rough going, with hollered directives and people getting knocked into the water by the pole that holds the sail."

"The boom," I said.

"Indeed, the engine might explode," Antoine said.

"Not *ka*-boom, *the* boom," I said.

"See?" Antoine said. "We're already arguing. Up you go."

With a smile alluding to knowledge of sailing and an intention of teasing me nonstop, Antoine gave me a hand up into the *Berrichon*.

About the Author

Nina DeGraff's Sonny Littlefield novels are based on her own experiences as a photographer, and the years she and her husband raised sheep and horses on a small organic farm in rural Maine. During her travels to jungles, coral reefs, and other destinations, Nina is always on the lookout for ways to incorporate interesting characters and realism into her fiction. In writing the series, she draws heavily on her own brushes with disaster, moments when she pressed her luck too far, even the time she brought a tip to the police and ended up helping them solve a crime.

Nina's albums of nature audio tracks are available through Spotify, Apple Music, and other streaming services. Examples of her photos and videos are on her website, www.ninadegraff.com. Her Etsy shop is open when time allows. Her fabric designs, some of which are created with her mystery novels in mind, are available through Spoonflower.

If you enjoyed "Dead South," please consider putting your review on my Amazon book page. To stay in the loop about future books you can follow me on my Facebook page, "Nina DeGraff Books."